Circle of Saints

Harry Threapleton

ISBN: 978-1-5272-7021-3

DEDICATION

For Bubba

CONTENTS

July 2025

September 2025

July 2025

September 2025

July 2025

September 2025

July 2025

September 2025

January 2026

ACKNOWLEDGMENTS

How to begin? First of all, I'd like to thank my families. Yes, you read that right; while most are lucky enough just to have one of these, I have the incredible privilege of having two supportive, fun, kind, loving groups of people that give me sanity and help (and food) whenever I need it. So Mum, Pops, Dad, Ali, Alex, Daniel, Remy and Bailey, thank you so much for everything you've shown, done and given for me these past sixteen and a half years. I hope to make good on it.

Next up, there's my friends. You've all shown me strength and positivity whenever I needed it the most, perhaps not even realizing that you were, so thank you all for standing by my side throughout all these years. While I'm lucky enough to have too many of you to name you all, there's a select few groups I want to thank in particular (I may repeat some names but that's your fault for hanging around me too often). The other six of "The Seven" from Lanesborough - Edgar Black, James Fulcher, Finn Gosling, Edward Osborough, Will Simpson and Dan West - the other five of what we call the s*n*st*r six (parts of the name censored because I have no idea if that's something I can put in this book legally without asking permission and I'm not risking it) - Izzy Benson, Edgar Black, Anya Hunn, Martin Scruton and Will Simpson – the Scene Change drama group, my fellow choristers from Guildford Cathedral and the St John's choir group, the old year eight skype gang, and of course everyone in the West House community at St John's. You're all legends, so thank you!

To all my Beta and Theta readers outside the family circle who took the time to read and critique this book – Izzy Benson, Spike Prichard, Lucas Patel (the gun-nut) and Daniel West, with special thanks to Kayla Vicenti who read and critiqued it from start to finish, and James Fulcher who read and critiqued it TWICE! – without your support, feedback and criticism there would be no book and so I owe this one to all of you. I've got to mention Will Simpson here as well, because that feedback you gave me on the prologue ages ago actually made a lot of difference, even if it were just a chapter, so cheers mate.

To Phoebe Simpson, the phenomenally talented cover designer of this book. You're an incredible graphic designer, thank you so much for all the work you've done. On the day I write this, I've just learnt you've been accepted to do graphic design at university with awesome grades, so all the best for the future! Perhaps one day you'll even do cover designs for authors old enough to drive!

To Katherine Dienes-Williams (I do hope I spelled that right), and all the staff and fellow choristers at Guildford Cathedral. Without all your support, hard-work and kindness throughout those six years of my time at the Cathedral, I wouldn't have had the discipline, drive or perseverance needed to write something as big as this, nor would I have had the hard-working role models that you all are to remind me that there are no limits to a person's achievement if they are motivated and determined enough to pursue their goals.

Last, but certainly not least, are the people who worked tirelessly for both my enjoyment and development in all areas of my education – my teachers. All have you have had such a huge role in making me what I am today, and although you may not realise it, you have one of the most important jobs in the world, in shaping the lives of the dozens of students that come your way every year, and giving them the knowledge and passion needed to pursue what they want in life. You are all incredible, inspirational people, and I'm so lucky to have been taught by every single one of you. As this is a book, I think special thanks are in order for my English teachers. From reception (shell) to now, from early spelling to my first novel, you've helped and guided me in my reading, writing and general learning, and I think it goes without saying that this book wouldn't exist without you. So, I shall name you all: Mrs Ward, Mrs Hood, Mrs Dix, Mrs Sutton, Mr Williams, Mrs Mendoza, Miss Ball and Miss Tiller. Even more special thanks go to Mr Loubser from Lanesborough and Mrs Underwood from St John's. Mr Loubser inspired my passion for English and writing and constantly demonstrated the importance of discipline and organization to me - two skills which no author can do without – while Mrs Underwood has reminded me of the joys of the subject this year, has been thoroughly supportive of my work and has even been reading the manuscript of this book. Not to sound like a broken record, but without all of you there would be no book, so thank you so much for the non-stop persistence and enthusiasm that you brought and bring to every lesson, and for the many lives you shape for the better!

Now, I believe a story's in order. Let's take a trip to Nightdrop City, in the year 2023. There are some people over there whose lives are about to turn on their heads. I'll be waiting for you when you get there…

July
2023

LYNDA, JIM
JULY 27TH, 2023
THE NIGHT OF BROKEN PROMISES

If there was ever a place which represented the corruption and rot of the human race, it would be Nightdrop City.

Teeming with crime, pollution, and a past that the natural world wanted so desperately to forget – it wasn't any surprise how quickly it would decay people into fractured messes of their former selves.

Had anybody been able to predict how this one city's sinister history would meet its uprising technology of the future – how the maniacs and machines of this land would unite and ruin the lives of hundreds – then they would have torn it down brick by brick.

But nobody did, and on one night in the middle of July, the start of something dreadful had already begun.

***

Lynda sighed, relieved, as she collapsed onto the sofa. Getting her son to sleep had been a long battle, ten times harder tonight with his father being away, but there was nothing that a bedtime story couldn't fix. Being a detective was hard. Being a mother was worse.

She didn't mind too much. Lynda loved what she did, both at work and at home. By day she would be rescuing kidnapped kids and reuniting families, while at night she would read bedtime stories to her own child.

Of course, it would have been easier if Jim were here.

Her husband, Jim, a detective like her, was away morning and night, constantly trying to catch a killer before they took another life. It was a fix for him, a deep-rooted obsession to put a stop to the evils of this city. But the evil never ceased, nor did Jim, so he'd continue fighting, hour after hour. Lynda secretly found it incredibly heroic, but at times like these she would panic, praying her husband would just come home and be safe for the night.

'In other news,' said the woman on the television screen, 'Sebastian Brigson, lead scientist of Signision Robotics, claims he will be able to "change the world forever" with his latest breakthrough in medical robotics.'

Lynda rolled her eyes. For years Signision had been teasing their revolutionary mechanical ideas, yet they appeared to be building a reputation for cancelled projects. Whether it was employees calling a strike or the funds being cut, they hadn't launched a decent product for an aeon. She doubted this time would be any different.

'The project, Brigson claims, will fuse both medical science and top of the line programming to create a revolutionary machine capable of identifying, targeting and treating illness and injury, all in a single body scan!

'The project seems to have gained intrigue from all sorts of groups, and speculation has arisen about whether it could be militarised for the treatment of soldiers on a battle-field. It looks like we'll have to wait and see whether this-'

A startled look grew on the newswoman's face as she put her hand to her earpiece.

'Breaking news has just come in,' the newswoman continued. 'According to our sources, several detectives looking for the notorious "Phantom" have managed to track him down to a warehouse in the south side of the city. It has been said that multiple gunshots have been heard by witnesses in the surrounding area, and it's believed that a shootout may have occurred between the Phantom and Nightdrop police officers. No casualties have been recorded at this time, but we'll keep you updated throughout the night.'

Lynda put her hand over her mouth. Jim would have been with that group, and he hadn't returned for hours. Could he have been shot? Or worse…

A sound of twisting of locks suddenly echoed through the flat. Lynda jumped up in a panic but was relieved to see Jim entering through the door, his face a mixture of fatigue and hopeless dread.

Tough would have been the first word to appear in an individual's head if they took a glance at Detective Jim Griffen. Words that followed might have included synonyms such as *hard* or even *cold*, but Lynda knew none of these terms were truly correct. Of course, it was true that James, or Jim as most called him, was larger than most men in their thirties, with a thick, muscular build, and arms and legs that could have been made of rock. It was also correct to say that he tried with great exertion to hide his feelings from those around him – but Lynda knew that he was far from the emotionally resistant cop that people assumed him to be. He held his feelings within himself like they were toxic, but on rare occasions, they would leak out and become exposed to the world. As Lynda looked from his scruffy brown hair down to his weary, melancholy face, she saw that this was certainly one of those times.

She ran up to embrace him, but he barely reacted. As she

pulled back, she regarded the plain sorrow in his eyes. 'Jim, what's wrong?' she asked her husband.

Jim didn't even look at her as he spoke. 'We lost him, Lynda. He was across the damn room and we lost him.'

'Hey, slow down. Lost who?'

Jim sighed. 'Who else? The Phantom.'

The Phantom. A name conceived by the press to describe what was the epitome of evil in the human race. The term they used was serial killer, but monster seemed a better fit – one who seemed to have no motive for his killings but that of pleasure, earning his title from his first kill back in early 2023 - that of a chemical driver, whose body was found sizzling in a barrel at a warehouse, a note in his hand hanging over the edge. It appeared that the killer had used acid from his truck to dissolve the poor man, but that wasn't the only peculiar aspect of the case. What stumped the many detectives of the homicide division, even Jim, was that apart from the body and the note, there was no evidence that anybody else had been in the building to murder the man. No fingerprints, footprints or fabric hairs, nor any signs of a struggle or reports of any noise in the area. As Jim had said to the reporters, "A ghost could have done it."

'It was all a trap, Lynda,' Jim told her. 'He sent me that email himself to get me at the factory alone… It was so he could kill me.'

Lynda gripped the counter, making her knuckles a strained white. 'Jim, you could have died. Tell me you at least saw his face!'

He shook his head slowly. 'He was wearing a hood, and it was dark. All I know for sure is that he's British, male, around… five foot nine?'

'It could be him then?' Lynda asked. 'Maybe you were right all along!' Jim had owned suspicions on the Phantom's identity for a while now. He believed that the killer was an ex-psychologist named Marcus Arwick whose family had been killed in a drunk driving incident. Ever since then, all those even partially responsible for the death of Arwick's family had been victims of the Phantom's killings. It was too good a coincidence to let go.

'Well, our guy *was* British,' Jim validated. 'But it's all just circumstantial evidence, not proof. It's not like we can take him in for questioning either, not until *your* department find him, anyway.'

Lynda held her hand up in self-defence. Quite recently, Marcus Arwick had made the top of the missing persons department's search list. 'We're trying our best, Jim. You know we've been working like hell to find this guy.'

He pulled her towards him kindly and kissed her on the forehead. 'I know. You more than anyone else…'

She nodded and smiled sympathetically. 'So, what happened next?'

'With what?'

'Oh, I don't know, in your confrontation with a well-known serial killer?'

Jim chuckled, but his face straightened out as he shook his head. 'I was talking to him, trying to reason with him – pretty stupid come to think of it, you can't reason with a monster. After that, I hear sirens. Turns out the others were tracking me down.'

'You… didn't have backup?'

'It was okay Lynda, I had it-'

'Under control?' she said in a raised tone. 'No Jim, you didn't! There's a reason we have backup, it's so you can be helped if things go south!'

'Which wouldn't have happened were it not for-'

'You were having a chat with a serial killer, how the hell did you think it was going to go? Let me guess, the others came because you hadn't communicated your plan with them, and that's what started the shootout.'

He nodded silently, ashamed.

'What happened next?'

Jim looked away. 'The shootout ended, and the Phantom ran. He warned us all that any man or woman that followed him would pay in the long run.'

'And you followed him, didn't you?'

'Well…'

Lynda groaned.

'Because…' Jim attempted to clarify. 'Because I was worried about your safety. It's the only reason why I went in there alone in the first place. I need this guy caught fast, and I can't do that by following the rules all the time.'

'Jim, the rules-'

'If you'd seen those messages, you'd understand!' Jim snapped. '*You* haven't seen the threats he sent me, Lynda! As long as he's out there, we're all at risk. You. Me. Jake…' He trailed off and looked down in shame. 'And I didn't catch him… Yeah, but you're right, I've probably just made this all ten times worse.'

She put her hand on his arm to comfort him. 'Look, Jim, you did what you thought was right. Who knows whether it was the correct choice or not? But you made a call and stuck with it. And… I know you didn't get him today but-'

'What do you mean we're not safe daddy?' said a child's voice from the kitchen door.

It was Jake, their little boy. Since Jake had come into their lives half a decade ago, he had been Jim and Lynda's world, the only thing that brought peace to their busy lives. Their child brought kindness into Nightdrop like a candle would bring light into a dark cellar. He was perfect in their eyes.

Lynda watched as Jim approached their son. 'Hey mister,' he said. 'What are you doing up so late?'

Jake looked down almost guiltily. 'I was worried about you daddy. I thought you weren't coming back.' The sadness in his voice made her heart ache.

'Ah, come here Jakey,' said Jim as he crouched and pulled the boy into his arms. 'I promise that I'll always come back. *Always.* And I'll always be here to protect you from the nasty people in the city. I'm a police officer; it's what I'm good at.'

He pulled back so he could look his son in the eyes. 'You understand?'

'Yes Dad,' said the boy as he wiped his eyes.

'Now,' Jim said to his son, 'I think it's time to sleep, don't you?'

Lynda smiled as her son and husband walked away to Jake's bedroom.

The last smile she would have for months.

***

Jim settled his son into bed, making sure to put the pillows high, as Jake liked them.

'What if the Phantom comes to take me away?' asked the boy fearfully to his father as he lay in bed.

Jim studied his son anxiously. 'How do you know that name, Jakey?'

'I heard you and Mommy talking about him.'

Jim rubbed his eyes wearily. He had been too loud. 'Well,' he replied to his son, 'if he does come, which he wouldn't be able to… I'll show him who's boss.' He raised his fists in a boxing stance, which made Jake chuckle. 'Even if he cared enough to try, he wouldn't be able to get up here! The doors to this building are locked shut and we're on the fifteenth floor.'

'Yeah, I guess,' his son responded.

Jim smiled. 'You, my friend, do not need to worry about anything. Except…' he strolled towards Jake's bedroom door, 'for tiredness, which turns all of us into very scary monsters. I'll see you in the morning, all right, Jakey?'

'Okay. Night Daddy,' said Jake.

'Goodnight Jake,' said Jim with a father's smile, as he shut the door.

Jim strolled back into the main living area and saw Lynda curled up on the couch. He slumped beside her, curious as to what she was watching.

'More news has just come in about the warehouse police shooting,' said the woman on the screen. 'It has been officially confirmed that there were no officer fatalities and only one severe casualty, a large stroke of luck for our police department. Unfortunately, the notorious Phantom is still at large, with Homicide Captain Edward Murdock advising all citizens to-'

Jim grabbed the remote and switched off the television.

'Hey,' she protested, 'I was watching that.'

He hugged her. 'There's no point in getting ourselves worried about this Phantom guy, all right? He wants us to be afraid, to think we're not safe, but he's wrong. He's just a man, not a monster. And men make mistakes. One day he's going to slip up badly, and that's when we'll get him for good.'

Lynda put her head on his chest. 'I know, Jim. But you've got to admit, it's pretty frightening being in the same city as this maniac-'

A terrible wailing emerged from their son's bedroom.

'Jake?' Jim shouted, before sprinting down the hallway. As he burst through the door, his heart sank.

'Hello Jim,' said the man in front of him with a slight chuckle. His voice sounded young but deep, clearly British, and his face was hidden by the large black hood of his sweater. Both of his hands were in dark gloves, his right clenched tightly around Jake, who was writhing ferociously like a fish on land, his left holding the glinting steel of a knife.

'Please…' Jim begged. 'Take it easy all right.'

The man seemed to smile under his hood. 'Of course, Jim. Nice and easy.' He calmly brought the glinting blade to Jake's throat. 'See. That was easy enough.'

'Let my son go, you bastard!'

'Daddy help!' Jake screamed through his tears.

The Phantom shook his head. 'You're going to have to ask a bit more nicely than that, Jim.'

Jim closed his eyes and swallowed his anger. Calmly he put

out his hand in a desperate signal for him to stop and pleaded with the monster in front of him. 'Look, I don't know who you are, or what your goal is here, but please… let my son go. If you want vengeance, for whatever I did to you, then you take it out on me. My family have nothing to do with this.'

The Phantom nodded, lowering the knife with shaky hands and loosening his grip on Jake. 'Neither did mine. But that didn't stop any of this.' He sighed. 'Your request is fair enough. Let the boy go and kill you instead, right? I *have* wanted to kill you for so long Jim… and one day I will.' He brought the knife back and Jake screamed again. 'But for now, I think your son will suffice.'

Jim screamed in pleading protest – but it was done.

All the Phantom had to do was slice the knife across in one fluid movement. Then the blood began to pour. Jake fell on his knees, rasping, before completely collapsing onto the ground.

Jim was only half aware of what happened next. He heard his wife screaming as she ran up behind him. He saw her pull out the gun and shoot the Phantom three times. He heard the window smash and watched as the killer fell down fifteen floors to the street below. He heard the crunch as the Phantom's body hit the ground and the grief-struck moaning of his wife. None of that felt significant, though. Nothing felt significant anymore.

And Jim sat there until the morning, cradling his dead son in his arms.

***

July
2025

JIM
JULY 8TH, 2025
THE BODY AT THE HARBOUR

Jim arose from his nightmare alone in his bed, startled to hear brutal hammering at his door. His head was hot and drenched in sweat, and it felt as if his brain was sloshing in his skull like warm ice cream. He turned to his clock. It was almost two years after the horrific memory that kept re-emerging in his troubled sleep and, as long as this nightmare had felt, it was only 5:35 in the morning.

Thud thud thud.

He was incapable of imagining who would knock at this time - trying to think was like looking into a muddy lake. The banging came again, each hit of his front door pounding against his skull like a hammer.

He groaned and peeled the thin duvet from his sweat-drenched body.

One foot out. Second foot out.

Thud thud.

'I'm coming down!' he shouted irritably, before stomping

down the stairs. He viciously swung open the door, revealing a young, anxious-looking man on the other side.

'What do you want?' Jim said in a gruff tone.

'Is this the house of James Griffen?' asked the young man. He was a lean gentleman, slightly shorter than Jim, looking as if he was in his late twenties. He had dirty blonde hair, a sharp jaw, and one of those faces that seemed as if they were fixed in a constant state of anxiety. There was a sense of familiarity in looking at this man, one which relieved Jim yet put him on edge. However, any initial apprehension was immediately warded off by the amusing observation of the man's attire – a crudely ironed shirt, crisscrossed with sharp creases, and trousers so long that they practically touched the floor.

'James Griffen…' Jim searched about in his head. They were two words which currently felt as if they had little meaning. 'That's… me…'

'Are you all right?' the man asked. Jim couldn't help but notice all sorts of minute details about this man, such as the toothpaste stain on his tie, or the slight twang in his American accent.

'Uh… yeah. I suppose,' Jim responded. He paused to try and scan the man's face through his head. 'Are you a police officer?'

The man pulled a police badge from his pocket and displayed it to Jim. 'Detective Thomas Knightley,' he declared. 'Most people call me Tommy though.'

Jim sighed. 'What have I done wrong now?'

The detective replied with a baffled look. 'I'm not here to arrest you, Mr Griffen.'

'Well, isn't that a relief? Well, what else could a police officer at my front door possibly mean? Do you have questions for me or something?'

Tommy frowned. 'No Jim, that's not it. I was told you weren't going to like this, but… we need you back.'

Jim stared blankly at the young man for several seconds before grabbing the door. 'Well, it was nice to talk detective, but I'm afraid I rather enjoy unemployment.'

Tommy shoved his foot in the door as Jim began to swing it shut. 'Jim, please. We're a little lost with this new case, we need your help.'

Jim laughed. 'Wow, welcome to Nightdrop, where detectives beg civilians to help with their murder cases at half-past five in the morning!' He shook his head and sighed. 'Never did I think a day would come when the police would be begging me to come back to them. Sorry kid, I quit for a reason. If you're worried about going back to them empty-handed, just tell whoever's in charge I'm ill, all right?' He pushed against the door.

'Jim, wait!' Tommy pleaded. 'Please, we've been on this one since half-ten last night. It's unsolvable!'

'Unsolvable? You get stuck after one night of work and it's *unsolvable?*' Jim opened the door just a crack. 'Why's that kid?'

'Well,' said Tommy, 'it's a suicide. At least it should be according to the evidence.'

'So, what's the problem?'

'The problem,' Tommy continued, 'is the manner of this man's death. He seems to have killed himself, but the way he did it makes no sense. Some people think he was just making a point but… something feels off. We don't want to miss anything so we want a fresh set of eyes on the case, and what better eyes could we get than those of the best detective in the police force? If that really is true…'

'Ex-detective actually…' Jim corrected. 'Is that why you were sent for me? They genuinely think I'm the best?' He shrugged apathetically. 'Ah well, it's not like that's a title I intend to reclaim. I'll see ya around, kid.'

Jim kicked Tommy's foot and slammed the door. As he approached the stairs, he heard Tommy calling from outside.

'You're not even going to listen to the details?' the young man called in exasperation.

'Ain't got the time,' Jim replied. 'And I feel like a corpse. Ever had a hangover, kid? Or are you too young to drink?'

'The man was found in the harbour…' Tommy shouted.

'Exactly!' Jim replied. 'He drowned. Suicide. Story over.'

'Except he didn't drown! That's what's odd. His body wasn't found in the water, it was found in one of the harbour's riverside warehouses with numerous bruises all over him, holding a wrench in his right hand. It seems unlikely that he beat himself to death, right? And even more unlikely that a tiny wrench could make that many bruises all over his body.'

Jim froze midway up the stairwell and frowned as he felt temptation stir within him. 'Right… well, it must be murder then. It has to be. I'm sure your guys could solve that.'

'Except there was no sign of a struggle, no accounts by any of the guards of any sort of scream or cry for help, no fingerprints, hairs, or smudges on the dead guy's clothes or body and, aside from the wrench, no clue yet as to anything which could have given him those awful bruises. I suppose you could say…' he paused. *'It's like a ghost could have killed him.'*

Jim immediately ran down the stairs and unlocked the door, swinging it wide open to look this man in the eye. 'I don't understand. Why me? Nearly two years I'm gone and suddenly you need my help. What's so special about this case?'

Tommy sighed, like a parent about to tell their child something difficult. 'Okay, you want to know why I'm really here? It's not just because we're struggling, we're not that lazy. The only other case this police department has experienced that's anything remotely like this one is that of the Phantom…'

Jim closed his eyes. 'And the only officer who could get anywhere, in that case, was me.'

Tommy nodded. 'We're clueless on this one, Jim. We've been studying it for hours, looking through every bit of evidence, and it still makes no sense! Mary thought-'

Jim's eyes widened a little at this. The mention of his old captain filled him with an unusual mix of regret and intrigue. 'Mary asked for my help?'

Tommy looked bewildered. 'Well yeah. I mean it was my idea, but she backed me like hell when we asked the chief-'

'I'll get dressed.' Jim said and quickly ran up the stairs.

'So, you're coming then?' Tommy shouted.

'Give me five minutes!'

***

'Well, this is all a little cliché,' Jim remarked as he left the house in a sorry excuse for smart clothes.

Tommy frowned. 'What are you talking about?'

Jim shut the door and walked confidently to the police car in his driveway. 'Smart detective is paired with an annoying new detective to solve an uncrackable case. This used to happen far too often when I was still working, I didn't realise they'd still bother me with people like you when I retired!'

'Listen, I'm not too happy about it either, but if everything goes to plan, we'll never have to see each other again. Care to get in the car?'

Both men entered the vehicle and made their journey to St Mark's Harbour. Jim had a strong personal belief that the city's traffic was far worse than its crime, and in a way, he could have been right. At this rate, it seemed like the cars would move faster if they were parked.

'Hey kid, can't we just flick our sirens on?'

Tommy turned his head in frustration. 'Why do you keep calling me "kid," I'm older than twenty!'

'Because you look like a prepubescent kid, that's why.'

Tommy laughed. 'Yeah well, I bet you can't even run a mile without your bones creaking.'

Jim rolled his eyes and focussed on the distant traffic lights. 'When will these people move?'

'I don't know! When the light's green?' Tommy said sarcastically.

Jim turned his head angrily. 'You know what? I'm *so* glad I'm working with you. Murdock must have thought it was hilarious when he assigned you to me! Stupid piece of-'

'He's not stupid,' said Tommy, 'short-tempered, maybe, but he just knows that you need somebody to keep you in line.'

'Oh yeah, big guy? You think you're that somebody?'

'He must have thought so. Mary too, evidently.'

'Wow, you're really going up in the world, kid! First few weeks on the job and the chief's taking your suggestions.' Jim mocked. 'I don't get it, why would you choose this job? Why would anybody for that matter?'

Tommy glanced at him. 'Yeah, I see what you mean! Soon as I get here, I get thrown into what's probably the craziest murder case in years with a drunk partner who's not even a real detective. Yeah, I have no idea either.'

Jim nodded his head sideways. 'Well, you could always quit.'

After a few more minutes, the two of them had made it to the harbour. Jim spotted a rusty, moss-lined warehouse ahead of them, with yellow police tape barricading its sliding doors. At the peak of the building, Jim could just make out a metal sign of three flames covering a gear, the well-known logo of Nightdrop's most prestigious scientific corporation, "Signision Robotics." The warehouse had likely ended up disused a few years prior, but was yet to be destroyed – be it down to legal reasons or a general lack of care or motivation among the people. This warehouse was just one example of the stark truth of this city; the buildings, cars, businesses, even the people were just shells of what they used to be.

Leading up to the warehouse was a rotting wooden dock. The right side of this was lined with dozens of red and white sailing boats, save for one space in the centre of them all, where a short length of chain drooped pathetically over the edge. While Tommy walked to the harbour, Jim decided to park himself at the side, intrigued by something there.

'You coming or what?' asked Tommy impatiently.

Jim glanced nervously at the large row of sailing vessels.

'Tommy, I'm afraid you were right. This man was murdered.'

'You haven't even seen the body yet!' Tommy exclaimed.

'I know,' said Jim, 'but tell me, kid. Why would a man kill himself via blunt head trauma when he's surrounded by ropes for hanging, boat propeller blades for cutting and the whole damn ocean in which to drown himself?'

'I'm pretty sure I said all of that about half an hour ago, right before you dismissed me.' He shrugged. 'But fine, why would he do that? Maybe he was trying to make a point.'

'Maybe. But no, for one big reason which leads me to my second question; what's missing in front of me right now?'

Tommy looked out into the open ocean, made grey by the thick clouds. 'I don't know?' he said. 'The sun?'

'And you call yourself a detective.'

'I didn't.'

'Look down, Tommy,' said Jim.

Jim watched Tommy as he looked down at the space in front of him. The only space missing a boat on that side of the harbour. Suddenly the young man realised what was missing.

'A boat,' he said.

'Correct,' said Jim, 'and as you'll notice, these ten boats in front of us are all-'

'Exactly the same,' said Tommy in an unimpressed tone.

'Well, yeah. Exactly,' said Jim, a little wound up by Tommy's interruption. 'You can see that all of those sailing boats have similar names on the front, Blue Mountain, Green Forest, names like that, so odds are that they're owned by the same company and that if they were to go out, a few would go out at one time, not just one. Even if just one were to go out, why would they take the boat from the middle, instead of the boat at the end? The only occasion where I could see this happening would be if a boat needed repair, but these boats are in pristine condition, and I doubt a crash would ever occur on the Hudson without the press being all over it. My conclusion: this was not an authorized absence.'

Tommy pondered, 'And if one is missing…'

'Then who took it?' Jim asked. 'A missing boat and a dead man all in one night? Sounds like way too much of a coincidence to me for it to just be a suicide.'

There was silence for a moment. 'Incredible,' muttered Tommy. He saw that Jim had heard him. 'That somebody would do something so obvious.'

Jim rolled his eyes and walked to the warehouse.

'But what if there *was* a crash yesterday? Maybe the boat has gone off to get prepared.'

'Then I'm wrong. It's called a hypothesis Tommy, I'm not one hundred percent certain that it's correct.'

'How certain are you then?'

'Oh, about…' he scratched his head, 'ninety-five percent-ish? I feel that if there was a crash, they wouldn't have brought it back with the other boats before taking it out again, and I doubt they'd have wedged it in the middle of them all even if they did.' He pointed back to the space without a boat. 'Also, if you'd looked carefully; you would have seen the chain that once held the boat in place cut in two. Not gonna lie Tommy, I kinda thought you'd see that one yourself!' Jim smiled at him condescendingly. 'Come on kid, it's time to see the body.'

They began to walk again, and Tommy looked back stunned

at the severed chain on the floor that he'd missed before. 'What could cut through metal like that?' he asked Jim.

Jim shrugged. 'Honestly, no idea. Ninety percent of the criminals in Nightdrop couldn't even cut a rope when I was a detective. Maybe they used some kind of blowtorch to melt it, although I have no idea how hot you'd need-'

His phone began to ring. He frowned agitatedly and reached in to pull it out and check the number, to find it was a random, unrecognisable number. He cancelled the call.

'Who was that?' Tommy asked.

Jim frowned. 'Some random number's been calling me all week. Come on, let's go.'

Up close, the warehouse looked even more battered, and it seemed to have all its colour drained from it. The walls were peeling off layer by layer, some patches revealing the metal skeleton beneath, and the symbol of flames above had experienced so much painful rusting from years of foul river-side weather that there was not even a vague reminiscence of the paint that had previously coated it.

Jim winced as he sniffed the sour, sewage-smelling air. 'Man, this place needs a do-over.'

'Mr Griffen,' exclaimed a pleased voice a few metres away. 'Glad you came.'

Jim looked across to see a large woman with dark skin and curly black hair. He gave her a small smile, 'Hey Mary,' he said.

'Did you see that?' she exclaimed, turning to Tommy. 'A second longer and I would have thought he was happy to see me! Good to see you again Thomas,' she took out her hand before hesitating, 'or would you rather be called Tommy?'

'Tommy, if that's all right, ma'am. Glad to meet you again.' He shook her hand.

Mary smiled. 'I know I'm your captain, but please call me Mary. Especially considering it should've been this guy,' she pointed to Jim, 'who got my job.'

'I never wanted anything to do with it,' Jim said with an awkward smile. 'Detective work was the only job for me.'

'Yeah, well, I wish that were still true. We're in dire need of more detectives at the moment! Not that you can't cope, Tommy.' Her smile dimmed slightly. 'Anyway, I guess you two want to see the body.'

'I think so,' said Tommy, 'although this smart-ass seems to have already worked out that it was a murder.'

'No surprises there!' she joked. 'I'll show you to him.'

She led them to the centre of the room, where they saw a large lump covered in a dusty white sheet. All the surrounding CSI workers watched as Mary pulled it off, revealing a man so bruised and twisted that he was practically a mess of discoloured skin and snapped bone. Jim observed the twisted contortions of anguish on the man's face, as if it were frozen in a silent, tortured cry for help.

Jim crouched low to inspect the body further. The moment he was around a five-inch range, he started picking up minute details; the ink smudges on the body's hand, the wedding ring, the milk stains on his blazer. He felt his mind buzzing and whirring, inventing possible scenarios and eliminating each one quicker than his conscious mind could catch up with.

Then an idea emerged, a horrid, tragic thought. He froze, his face full of dread.

'Jim?' said Tommy, concerned.

'*Daddy*,' screamed the voice in Jim's head.

'Is he just concentrating or…'

'I don't know,' replied Mary. 'Jim?'

'*Help!*'

'Jim,' he said softly.

'*Please!*'

'Jim,' repeated Tommy more firmly.

The dazed ex-detective spun round to meet the worried eyes of his fellow associates.

'Sorry,' he said. 'I do that sometimes. Zone out. You'll get used to it in time.'

'What's wrong, Jim?' asked Mary.

'With me? Nothing! Really, it's nothing, I just… thought of something.' He glanced over to the deceased man's crippled body before stopping himself. *It can't be him. It can't be, Lynda shot him.* He turned back to his colleagues, 'was there anything in this man's pockets?' he asked.

'Only some keys and a return train ticket to the other end of the city from this morning. Why do you ask?'

Jim shrugged. 'I thought it might confirm a little theory of mine, and it did. Take the body to the medical examiner, get her to do a full synopsis.'

'But there's no proof of murder!' exclaimed Mary.

'There is proof Mary, I promise you, but it's up here,' he pointed to his head. 'I'll explain more later but for now, I need to just process this information, and I need that medical examination as soon as possible. Please, I need to know if I'm correct!'

She sighed, 'all right Jim, I'll take your word on it…'

'You're the best captain there is, Mary. And… friend.'

She smiled. 'I try to be. And remember,' she put a comforting hand on his shoulder, 'I said it two years ago, I'll say it now. You know who to talk to if you need help.' With that, Mary walked away.

Tommy crouched low by the body. 'Poor guy, he looks like a mess.' He frowned when he noticed Jim staring at him strangely. 'Sorry, I just haven't seen… a body before.'

Jim furrowed his brow and smiled. 'Really? Well, you're taking it a lot better than I did my first time, kid. No puke or anything.'

Tommy smiled nervously and wobbled as he began to stand up. 'Well, I haven't had breakfast, I guess that helps.' Something caught his eye, and he peered into the slightly open jacket of the man on the floor. 'What the hell?'

'What is it?' Jim asked.

Tommy squatted on the ground again and extended his arm at full length before reaching into the jacket.

'Wait, Tommy you don't have any-'

Too late. His hand had gone in.

'-gloves.' Jim followed with a sigh.

His partner fumbled in the pocket for a while, before pulling out a finger-sized, rectangular, reflective object. Following a bit of close inspection, he informed Jim of what it was.

'A memory-stick?' Jim asked to clarify. *This is new*, his brain said to him.

'Uh-huh,' Tommy followed. 'I mean it could just belong to the victim…' He didn't sound so certain.

And he shouldn't be certain, Jim thought. *This is too unusual.* 'Mary!' he called to the captain, who was talking with a group of crime scene investigators. 'What did this guy do for a living?'

'He was a lawyer,' she replied from the other side of the room, 'a pretty good one too, apparently. Works for that large firm in the centre of a city.'

Could just be his work, he thought. Still, not many high-brow companies put up with the security risk of removable media like USB drives. 'We ought to check this out,' Jim said quickly to Tommy. 'The sooner we get back to the station the better.'

They said their goodbyes to the captain and made their exit. The moment they had got into the car, Tommy slammed his foot on the pedal.

'Thoughts?' Tommy asked.

'Huh,' Jim replied. He had zoned out again.

'Any thoughts, Jim?' Tommy repeated.

Jim furrowed his brow. 'Well, if it was a suicide, I doubt it happened yesterday morning. Firstly, the man was wearing a suit. Not many people would take the time to put a suit on if they were planning on killing themselves before going to work. Equally, on the suit, you can see some milk stains. Tell me, Tommy, if you were considering suicide, why would you bother to eat breakfast?'

Tommy nodded as he processed this. 'Could have been he wanted a nice last meal. But I see what you're saying. It's likely that he didn't kill himself that morning. So why would he have the motive to do it later in the day? Maybe the wife cheated? He was fired?'

'Perhaps. We could always question his workplace, the people he's related to, but the way I see it, that's a waste of time. This man had a railcard in his top pocket. It's fair to assume that a railcard in your work suit means you take the train to and from work every day. If he ended up at the train station towards the end of the day, why not have a little leap onto the rails? There were also many buildings that he would have passed by if he was walking home from the station - which I presume to be the case given there isn't a civilian car anywhere near the crime scene – why not jump off one of those? There are even weapons stores – all potential methods of ending his life. But what does he do? He goes to a harbour on his way home and beats himself to death with a spanner. A harbour, a place surrounded by water, and he beats himself to death.'

'Okay, but I'll play devil's advocate,' said Tommy. 'The spanner was in *his* hands. There aren't any other fingerprints or hairs but his own, his hand was clenched stiffly around the spanner when the rigor-mortis kicked in, and according to Mary, marks on his palm and the age of the fingerprints compared to the time of death show clearly that this man was holding the spanner before he died. Maybe he just wanted to die that way.'

'Tommy, do you ever stop saying maybe?'

Tommy held up a hand in self-defence. 'All right Jim, I'm just doing my job. I mean come on, haven't you heard of Occam's Razor? The simplest answer is almost always the most likely?'

Jim rubbed his eyes. 'Yeah, like this case is simple at all. And here's a little anecdote for your whole "*simple explanation*" outlook. Have you ever heard of a man named Marcus Arwick?'

Tommy frowned as if trying to remember. 'No.'

'How about the Phantom?'

Tommy glanced to Jim awkwardly and then fixed his eyes to the road. 'Well, of course, who hasn't heard of him?'

'Well, just over two years ago, a drunk driver caused an accident that ended up killing Arwick's wife and daughter. There were reports that Arwick was driven insane before he subsequently went missing. A few months later, the truck driver was killed, along with the truck driver's boss who should never have hired him given his charges of alcoholism, his friend who'd been sitting with him in the truck on that night, and the judge who hadn't given him a large enough sentence half a year prior. Guess who killed them? The Phantom. Crazy coincidence, right?'

Tommy hummed in agreement; his face baffled as to where this was going.

'Well...' Jim continued. 'A few weeks into the Phantom case, the Phantom himself came to pay me a visit. He held a knife to my son's throat. I begged him for...' Jim felt his voice crack slightly. 'Anyway, that night the Phantom was shot three times by my wife, before falling out the fifteenth-floor window of a building. Nobody could survive that. So, Tommy, guess who the dead man under the hood was?'

'Marcus Arwick?' Tommy asked, a look on his face suggesting he was afraid to make Jim upset.

'Nope,' Jim replied. 'According to the police department, the man's name was Daniel Crockett. A surgeon who must have had a taste for murder. Could have been a friend of Arwick's but how am I to know? Maybe it was just a coincidence, or maybe he used Arwick's family's death as some strange justification for his killings. Anyway, the point is, Marcus Arwick wasn't the Phantom and has been missing ever since that case. As far as I'm concerned, kid, Occam can shove that razor of his up where the sun doesn't shine, because in my experience, focussing on the simplest answers can lead you down the wrong path before it's too late.'

Tommy rubbed his forehead, taken aback by what he had just heard. 'Jeez, I'm sorry, Jim. I mean we all heard stories but… blimey, none of us knew it was Lynda who got him.'

Jim scratched his head awkwardly at the mention of his wife. 'Yeah well, I'm sure you'd do the same if a man killed your son.'

'Daughter actually,' Tommy replied hastily, causing Jim's head to jolt up in surprise. 'But yeah, I think you're right, I would want to kill that man if he wasn't already dead.' When he saw the stunned look on Jim's face, he smiled not unkindly. 'Don't worry Jim, you're not the only one in this car who's lost someone.'

***

JIM
JULY 8TH, 2025
CORPSE-SHAKER

As Jim approached the doors of the grand, yet battered Nightdrop City Police Department, he almost felt a warmth inside of him, one which he could not quite explain.

Why didn't he feel angry? He had just been sucked back into the job he had grown to despise. Yet, for the first time in a long while, Jim felt slightly more lifted now than he had this morning.

But what changed?

He looked to his left at Tommy.

No, that couldn't have been it, could it? Just because the kid knew what it was like to lose somebody else. So did the rest of the police department. Why should this have been any different?

He shook away his thoughts in denial and continued following Tommy and Mary across the car park.

'What's next boss?' Tommy asked Mary.

'Well, we'll need to get the evidence properly analysed, and the body needs to be inspected by our Medical Examiner over at the morgue,' Mary replied. 'Jim, you can head to the front desk. There you'll receive some necessary equipment that you may be wanting for the case; a micro-recorder, a notebook and pen, and an authorised voluntary assist badge. May I remind you that A.V.A. badges are proof that you're working in co-operation with the police force, but certainly do not give you the right to speed, enter crime scenes or make arrests.'

'Yeah, got it,' Jim clarified.

'Do you?' she asked, stopping at the great stone stairs before the police building. 'Because I persuaded Murdock to bring you in here, Jim. The last thing any of us needs is you going off the rails!'

'I got it Mary; I'll behave myself!'

She nodded. 'I suggest you both wait in your office for a while until Tessa's finished. I'll call you when she's ready to share her findings with you both and you can go down then. You met Tessa yet, Tommy?'

'Who?' Tommy inquired.

'Our medical examiner.' She nodded over to Jim and smirked. 'Jim'll introduce you.'

Tommy gave Jim a puzzled look. Jim rubbed his face in dread and sighed. One of the many joys of leaving this place was the thought of never speaking to that madwoman again. So much for the benefits of retirement.

***

Two hours later, he and Tommy found themselves before a white door with MEDICAL EXAMINER'S OFFICE printed on its front.

Jim knocked. There was no reply. He knocked once more. Again, no response. He almost knocked a third time, but instead paused and turned to Tommy.

'Listen, Tommy... you probably deserve a little warning. Tessa… Well for one she's-'

The door immediately swung open, revealing a short lady with hair like straw sprouting randomly from her small spherical head and sparkling blue eyes like rare jewels. She wore a vibrant light green blouse, a pair of rough coffee coloured trousers and a pristine white lab coat.

'Jim!' she exclaimed; her voice so high pitched with excitement that it could have been mistaken for a scream. 'How wonderful it is to see you!'

'Hi there,' Jim replied through a fake smile. He waited a few moments for something to happen while she just stared at him with a far too pleased grin. 'This is Tommy,' he said, pushing Tommy forwards slightly in a haste to distract her gaze. 'I suppose you two haven't been formally introduced yet.'

She looked over to Tommy and instantly her smile flattened, and her eyes raised like she was looking at a zoo animal. 'Tessa. *Great* to meet you.' Her tone was a mix of apathy and annoyance.

Tommy glance over to Jim with a look as if to say, '*what did I do?'* to which Jim just shrugged in response.

'Well come in then,' she urged. 'I have a corpse you'll *love* to see!'

Tommy gave Jim another questioning glare. Jim nodded in a *welcome-to-my-world* sort of way and they both followed her into the room.

Inside was a cluttered, sickly sweet-smelling office, filled with books on biology and chemistry. In the back corner was a wooden desk, strewn about with pencils, pens and empty ink cartridges. On pegs by the door hung an assortment of strangely stained lab coats.

Tessa walked over to the computer and activated the monitor. Tommy and Jim stepped behind her to look and were instantly greeted by the image of the purple, bruised and twisted corpse.

'Well, this one's a real handsome fella,' she remarked. She tapped on the screen a couple of times, revealing several photographs of the corpse from different angles. 'I mean, a spanner? How weird is that?'

'What did you find?' Tommy asked, seemingly increasing in discomfort as each photograph flickered onto the screen.

'Not much,' she replied with a pout. 'The killer did well to cover this one up, didn't he?'

'So Jim's right?' Tommy asked. 'It is a murder?'

She nodded. 'Most likely, although you're the detectives. I have found a few features of interest. Specifically…' She navigated to a photo of the man's neck and zoomed in on two small black dots at the side. 'Small pinpricks in the side of his neck. Seems like the killer injected him with something, but I'll get back to that later. In addition, an autopsy of the brain suggests this poor man was exposed to high currents of electricity. Some burn marks at his temples and around the back of his head support this idea. Any guesses about that?'

Jim turned to Tommy, curious as to whether the detective would think of anything. 'Well, don't look at me!' Tommy exclaimed.

Tessa continued. 'Lastly, there were numerous chemical substances found in the victim's blood, presumably these being what the killer injected. They include extremely high amounts of adrenaline, high quantities of vitamins and electrolytes, some morphine and Ibuprofen. Nothing that'll give you a firm lead unless you can think of a reason why they'd all be used at once. But there is one particularly unusual molecule in all of this…' She tapped her screen several times, revealing an image of a highly complex drawing of a white molecule on a black background.

'This is cylopatonine, nowadays known as "corpse-shaker." You might remember its discovery on the news a few years back. It's a sort of molecular ball that travels through the bloodstream that breaks into two smaller molecules that trigger a heavy release of endorphins and white blood cells. It's also a huge stimulant, hence its recreational use. Sadly, people have found ways of both stealing and abusing the drug, and so it's been made illegal to purchase by anybody but hospitals.' She turned and gave a zany smile to Jim.

Jim shook his head, bewildered. 'Why would a killer inject their victim with a substance to help their injuries?' he pondered.

'Perhaps the victim was an addict?' Tommy proposed.

'Unlikely,' said Tessa. 'Long term addicts have signs of addiction – bags under the eyes, sometimes nose bleeds, low white blood cell counts when not under the influence of the drug. If he was a user, he would've been a fairly fresh one, but I don't see why he'd inject himself with all that other crap. Besides, the pinpricks haven't healed enough to be any older than since about nine o'clock last night.'

'This drug,' Jim asked. 'Would you happen to know if we have any records of any suppliers?'

'Well, I'm just the medical examiner, but from what I've seen across the past year, the number of cases of cylopatonine addicts in the city has shot up. It would seem there's a fairly fresh face in town providing the stuff. Somebody the police department can't get their hands on. You'd have to ask the relevant detectives.'

Jim nodded and began to speed out as quickly as possible. 'Well thank you, Tessa, that'll be all. We appreciate the help as always.'

'Well, I must say it's *wonderful* to have you back Jim!' she exclaimed.

The two detectives evacuated the office, and Tessa beamed in Jim's direction.

'Come back to visit soon!' she beckoned to him.

'I'll… make sure of it,' he lied.

Tessa smiled in his direction, before glaring at Tommy and slamming the door.

'What a nut job,' Tommy remarked.

'True,' said Jim. 'But that nut job just gave us our first lead. You ask around if anybody has any idea about our supplier of cylopat- cilopro-' Jim shook his head, '*corpse-shaker*. Maybe question a few users if you find any. In the meantime, I'll talk to Mary and have a look at our evidence from the case.'

'Sounds like a plan,' said Tommy. 'Don't do anything stupid while I'm gone.'

'It's all right Tommy, you can trust me.'

***

Tommy had been wrong to trust him.

When Tommy had returned to their office, he glared at his partner in shock. 'What the hell are you doing?' he shouted.

Jim was sitting at the desk, the monitor of the computer tipped over in front of him and some screws in his hand. 'Just fixing the USB support,' he replied casually. 'Can't exactly plug this thing in if there's no jack.' He held up the silver USB stick that they had found in the victim's jacket.

'How do you have that?' Tommy asked, running over to him. 'It was being investigated as evidence!'

Jim shrugged. 'It's fairly small. Easy enough to slip under Mary's nose.' He glanced at Tommy and laughed. 'Don't give me that look, you were the one who took it out *without gloves*.'

'But Jim you can't just take it while it's under investigation, and you certainly can't just plug it into an office computer when we have no idea what's on it!'

Jim looked up and shrugged. 'What more information could we possibly get from this thing than what's on the inside? It's not like there were any prints on it, not even yours apparently, despite you just yanking it out of the man's pocket *without any gloves on*.'

'All right, all right!' Tommy sighed and slumped into a chair, placing his hands on his head. 'If there were no prints then that'll probably be the victims, right? Meaning what's plugging this in going to tell us exactly?'

'But that's where you're wrong, Tommy. The USB stick didn't have any prints *at* all, not even the prints of the victim. Which means that if anything, it belonged to our careful, print-free killer. It's for that very same reason that I don't believe the spanner was the weapon that killed the man. It was riddled with his finger-prints, meaning it was probably being used by the victim as self-defence-'

'Jim!'

'Right, I'm losing focus, but the point is that this USB stick does not belong to that body, and I don't see much point in waiting until they have a "secure way" to inspect what's inside.'

'So you're just going to plug it straight into an office computer and hope it doesn't add a virus to the system?'

'It won't! Relax, I know what I'm doing!'

'No, you don't!' Tommy frowned and rose again, before anxiously pacing up and down the room. 'Do you not know what rules are exactly?'

'The rules?' he responded with a smirk.

'Yeah you know, the things that you lack any respect or knowledge for, those things that keep this place together and stop it from being a chaotic mess.'

'They're detective rules,' Jim said as he began screwing the base of the computer back in. 'I'm not a detective anymore, remember?'

Tommy looked like he was about to combust. 'Meaning you don't mess with detective computers!'

'How did your investigation go?' Jim asked in a clear attempt to change the subject. 'You took a little longer than expected.'

Tommy sighed. 'I'm not moving on from this. Put the memory stick down!'

Jim shook his head in disbelief. 'Fine.' He placed the USB stick gently onto the table. Tommy made a move as if to grab it, but Jim quickly slammed his hand on it, and his partner retreated backwards, like a snake eyeing its prey. 'How was your investigation?' Jim asked again.

Tommy folded his arms. Jim observed that there was a yellow

folder wedged underneath his left shoulder. 'All right, I suppose. The detectives gave me a list of names of most of the "corpse-shaker" users across the city but ultimately told me not to waste my time as they always refuse to mention any details about their supplier. I tried anyway, of course. Had to question about five of them until somebody got talking. I've got it all here,' he said, pulling the yellow file from under his arm. He chucked it to Jim. 'Take a look.'

Jim stared at the file in mild shock and flipped off the cover. Inside was a single sheet of paper, detailing an addict's entire confession of where she got the drugs and who she got it from. 'How did you-?' Words could barely leave his lips. 'You're telling me that those other detectives have been struggling for weeks, months even to crack where all these drugs were coming from, and you got the name of the supplier in a few hours?'

Tommy smiled smugly. 'You have your tricks, I have mine. I used to be a psychologist, know the human mind like a textbook! It was simple enough. This drug group's a big deal, not like your average supplier, the kind you'd probably throw against a wall and shout at. They change their address every week and blackmail their buyers with death threats so that they don't reveal any information about them. If anything, they're more like a gang, or some kind of messed up cult. Call themselves the "Children of the Reaper." But if this information's correct, I can ask Murdock to send a Tactical Response Team into their current location to find and question them. A drug organisation and a killer in one go, how's that?'

Jim raised his eyebrows, half irritated, half impressed. 'In which case, we don't have a moment to lose.' He flipped the computer back onto its base and commenced to switch it on.

'You're not coming, you realise. You can help at a crime scene, but this kind of thing is police officer work only.' He frowned as he saw Jim lift the memory stick again. 'What… are you doing?'

'I told you,' Jim replied. 'I'm investigating the evidence.' He lifted the memory stick and flip the cap off.

'Jim, I told you to stop! We have no idea what's on that thing! You could put a virus on the system! You could get me fired!'

Jim smiled sarcastically. 'You need to learn to relax more Tommy.' He shoved the memory stick into its slot.

Tommy was shouted in protest and lurched towards him, but it was too late. The computer began to produce a series of loud whirrs and beeps, and a red light began to glow on the keyboard. On the screen, huge chunks of white text whirred past in a blur, before the whole thing went black and the computer was silent.

Jim pressed a few keys on the keyboard, and nothing happened. The computer seemed to have been completely fried, perhaps the killer's idea of a joke.

Tommy rubbed his eyes. 'Nice one, man. Real nice. You've just wrecked our computer.' He began to walk away. 'I better tell the I.T. guys about this before-'

Suddenly the screen flashed back on again, and where there had once been darkness was now what looked like a badly scribbled white outline of a circle with a single line passing through it diagonally to the bottom right, splitting it two segments. In the top right segment of the circle was what looked to be the symbol of a falling star, while in the bottom left segment Jim noted the drawing of a skull.

Behind this image seemed to be the faint silhouette of a man, completely motionless, and after a few moments, the white circular logo in front of him disappeared completely. From the silhouette, two bright lights suddenly shone from where one would expect the eyes to be situated, their vibrant glow a sky blue.

'Hello Jim,' said a distorted voice from the computer.

Jim frowned at the screen, and he felt Tommy crouch beside him to inspect what he was viewing. 'What the hell is this?' the detective remarked.

'The fact that you're watching this video means that you or your partner found my memory stick,' continued the distorted voice. 'Well done, although I did make it impossible *not* to find.' It chuckled a little, its voice raspy as it did so. Jim noted with a feeling of dread that the accent of the distorted voice was British.

'I have two agendas, Mr Griffen. First, I shall help my colleagues save humanity, or at least help them do what they believe will save humanity. Then, I shall finish what I started two years ago. I am in greater power than I ever was before and have far more resources at my disposal. That is all the information that I will give you, for now, I will let you work out the rest. I suppose it'll be more… *fun* that way.' The voice chuckled again.

'But I warn you, Jim, there will be times where you will think you are catching up to me, times where it will seem like you have the upper hand and are so close to succeeding. You will be wrong. I have you on a hook now, and all I need to do is reel you in, so don't annoy me. Continue our little game, or… well, you must be able to remember what happened last time. We are the Circle of Saints. *Perire finite non est.'*

The video went into static and shut down. Tommy immediately pulled it out of the USB slot, leaving the two of them in stunned silence.

'What was that all about?' Tommy asked.

Jim got up and sprinted out of the room.

***

'*Jim!*' he heard Tommy shout behind him as he bolted down the front steps of the police department. '*Stop! Wait, damn it!*'

Jim crossed the road and headed for Tommy's police car. When he remembered that he was no longer a detective, and so the door would be locked, he slammed his hand against the roof.

'Yeah… nice try bud.' Tommy was running down the steps, his keys dangling from his fingers.

Jim shook his head frustratedly. 'What do you want?'

'I want to know what the hell is wrong with you?' Tommy asked him.

Jim just looked at Tommy blankly, as if he were transparent. 'We need to go now. It's him, Tommy.'

'Who, Jim?'

'The man I told you about before, the clever bastard who outsmarted me over and over and over years ago. If we do this quickly, we may be able to beat him at his own game, but we'll need to hurry, and we need to do it alone. For all we know, he could be anyone, so I've got to act fast!'

'Slow down. What are you talking about?'

'The man on that video… he was the man who killed my son, I'm sure of it. Now open the damn door!' He hit the car again.

'Watch it!' Tommy shouted. 'Jim, that man… you told me he died. Daniel Crockett, you said. Your wife shot him three times, he fell down fifteen floors, and he died. *How* can he be back?'

'I don't know…' Jim threw his head back in anger. 'I know, it's ridiculous, it's crazy, it makes no sense. Maybe Crockett didn't die at all, maybe we were wrong! Maybe it wasn't even him but… I can just feel it, Tommy. The stuff that man on the video said! The sound of his voice!' He shook his head. 'I don't know why, and I don't know how but… I think the Phantom's back.'

***

JIM
JULY 8TH, 2025
THE WAREHOUSE IN THE WOODS

'You're going to have to explain this to me a bit clearer,' Tommy urged.

Jim pressed his foot even harder on the accelerator.

'Do you even know where you're going?'

'Course I do,' Jim replied, 'you got the address, remember?'

'You memorised it?' Tommy was staring at him in concern. 'Jim, I want you to speak to me honestly. Why are you so certain he's back?'

Jim sighed. 'Didn't you hear him in the video? A male, with a British accent, just like my son's killer. A man who can murder without a trace, just like my son's killer! He even admitted it himself! "You know what happened last time." He meant when he killed Jake! How do you not get it?' He slammed his fist against the horn, causing it to blare out.

'Okay, okay, chill out! Look, if it was somehow him, why would he bother hiding his face?'

'I don't know Tommy!' he snapped. 'I… I don't have all the answers right now.'

Tommy stayed silent and glanced away from him. They were making their way to the edge of the city; the Hudson stretched out in front of them. Beyond a rusty metal bridge lay acres of green forestland. *Just over there,* Jim thought. *Somewhere in the shadows of those woods.*

'Jim, I'm not sure about this,' said an anxious Tommy.

'I ran outside, and you gave me the keys,' Jim replied. 'You let me do this!'

'I wasn't thinking, all right?' Tommy responded. 'You were freaking out and screaming! I'm currently having second thoughts…'

'Why?' Jim asked. 'What's there to be afraid of?'

'I don't know maybe the fact that we're police officers and we're driving to a drug distributor. I bet they'll be more than happy to welcome us… Maybe we should have done a little more preparation before rushing into your car and-'

'Can you relax, kid! This is just the same as when we go to any drug distributor and ask them questions. We'll just tell them that as long as they give us the information we need; we won't arrest them.'

'Oh! Oh that's great! Well I'm also sure they'll be *very* happy to cooperate with you.' Tommy stated with sarcasm. 'After all, they're only an armed gang, and you're a regular civilian without anything so much as a bulletproof vest. What could we possibly have to worry about?'

'I've got a bulletproof vest,' Jim clarified. 'Even Authorised Voluntary Assists have to wear them, the city's crime rate's bad enough!'

'Oh, well, that's a relief! You won't be killed after the first shot! Jim, we didn't even consult the chief!'

'Why would we need to ask him?'

'So we have backup to assist us, maybe?'

'Well in this job, sometimes things like backup and regulations just slow you down, especially when we have no idea who we can trust.'

'What does that mean?' Tommy asked.

'If the man who killed my son has returned, he might not even be Daniel Crockett! How am I meant to trust Murdock or any backup for that matter when-?'

'It's *not him,* Jim!'

There was a deafening silence in the car for a moment. 'Excuse me?' Jim whispered.

Tommy sighed. 'It's not him. Face it, Jim, it can't be. The man who killed your son is dead, and all this compulsive running into danger is the kind of thing that gets people like Jake killed in the first place.'

Suddenly the car braked furiously. Jim grabbed Tommy by the shirt and pulled him to eye level. 'Listen up, Knightley. Two years ago, my life was ruined by one crazy asshole with a knife! I lost my kid, my wife left me, I couldn't bear to talk to my family, my job was a constant hellish reminder of my pain and I've been alone, living a life of nightmares and drinking in a *shitty apartment* ever since. Do you think, if there was even a remote chance that madman was back, that I would hesitate to go and find him? If it is him, then we need to be quicker than him, and we can trust nobody, *nobody!* That means no preparation and no standard procedure. If you dare argue with me, I'll take your gun, throw you out the car, leave you at the roadside and finish this myself. Do you understand me?'

Tommy gasped as Jim released him from his clutches. Jim looked away to the windscreen, fuming. In his peripheral vision, Tommy was silently patting his suit down with restrained violent jolts.

'You do that to all your partners?' Tommy finally uttered.

'I haven't had a partner in a long time,' said Jim. 'I liked it that way.'

They were silent for a small while. 'Well if it helps, I don't particularly like you either,' Tommy remarked, 'but we're stuck with each other. I don't care if you're the best detective this city's ever had, you need to sort out your temper or we're going to end up killing each other.'

Jim grunted and began to accelerate the car once more. The trees in the distance were growing larger by the minute, like a monster ready to swallow the car whole. Jim felt Tommy shiver beside him and sighed. 'Frightened?' he asked.

Tommy shook his head slowly. 'Course not. Why would I be frightened of driving to the front door of a drug gang?' He turned to Jim. 'Hey, speaking of the memory stick…'

'What about it?'

Tommy cleared his throat. 'Well, I was a little curious. They mentioned the Circle of Saints.'

Jim shrugged. 'And?'

'Well, there've always been rumours, you know? "Nightdrop's secret cult." "The bogeymen." Criminals swearing that it was "the Circle" that did all those horrible things, not them! You don't suppose they're actually real, do you?'

This caused Jim to burst out in laughter. Tommy was lost for words.

'Oh dear, Tommy, you think *that's* important!' Jim exclaimed.

'Well, if the man in the video really *is* part of the Circle of Saints, then we could be talking about some kind of conspira-' Tommy must have seen Jim shaking his head in amusement. 'What?'

'People can call themselves anything kid, it doesn't make a difference what. The Circle of Saints is a myth – a legend made up just to make the city sound cooler. Nothing more. Hell, I even remember reading the old stories to my-' The smile on Jim's face had disappeared, and in its place was a disturbed frown. 'Anyway, you don't need to worry. Magic rocks aren't the scary things in this city.'

The trees had swallowed them now. They were in the stomach of the forest. Tommy rubbed his forehead nervously as they proceeded down the winding gravel road. The sun was not apparent in many areas due to the thick leaves, and they even passed a steep gorge.

After a while, Jim swung the car around a bend and slammed his foot on the brake. They were parked right before another large warehouse, not extremely dissimilar from the one seen prior at the harbour.

'Here already?' Tommy asked.

'There's only so much forest these guys could have gone into before they hit the national park,' Jim replied. 'Now, do you want to come with me, or should I let you sit in the car?'

'Oh, hilarious!' muttered Tommy as he got out of his seat.

They approached the rusty building slowly, the leaves and twigs scattered about the floor crushing and snapping under their feet as they did so.

'What is it with all the warehouses in this city?' Tommy asked nobody in particular.

Like the other warehouse, this one was dull and run down, yet it was more intact from lack of exposure to the fierce, erosive sea. It appeared that this too used to be a storage facility, though lack of a flame symbol suggested it wasn't one of Signision's.

The two arrived at the towering door, wary to knock for what was on the other side. Jim pulled out the tranquillizer gun that the police department had given him and raised it in preparation.

'Ready?' he asked.

Tommy took in a deep breath. 'I don't really have a choice in the matter.'

Jim pounded at the door three times.

No response.

Again, he hit his fist against the door, but after a minute of rustling leaves and faint birdsong there was still no reply.

He started knocking again but found himself interrupted.

'Oh, what the hell,' said Tommy as he pulled out his pistol. He pointed it so it was angled away from them and fired three ear-piercing shots into the air.

'Tommy, what the hell are you-'

The doors swung open, revealing a group of three young men and two young women, each carrying shotguns.

'Drop your weapons!' shouted a man with black hair and a bandana.

'Look,' Jim started to explain, 'we're not here for trouble, we just-'

The man fired a bullet at their feet. 'Drop them!' he shouted, cocking his shotgun. The four others quickly cocked their shotguns in response.

'All right!' exclaimed Tommy as he cast his gun to the floor.

Jim looked over to Tommy, rolled his eyes and reluctantly placed his weapon on the ground. The shooters relaxed their weapons and Jim started to walk towards the entrance. Immediately they raised their shotguns again to point at his head. Jim put his hands high in the air.

One woman placed a hand to her ear. Jim vaguely heard the echo of a voice from what looked to be an earpiece. 'We have visitors, boss,' the woman said to the voice. 'Two men, each with weapons. Look like cops to me.' There was more muffled speaking, to which the woman replied, 'Yes, Boss.'

The woman lowered her shotgun. 'Sorry fellas,' she said, 'but today ain't your lucky day.' She turned around and walked back into the warehouse, nodding to the man with the bandana. The man she nodded to pulled a pistol from his pocket and aimed it for Jim.

'Wait, no-' Jim protested.

But it was too late. The man fired the gun.

Jim felt a sharp pain in his neck. He stumbled back for a moment and then dropped hopelessly to the ground.

As the light faded, and the world turned grey, Jim saw Tommy put his hands to his forehead, an anxious look on his face. Soon he was shouting. 'You idiot. You stupid-'

And then the man shot Tommy too, and Jim instantly wished he'd never come here. Right there, he and Tommy would die, the murders would continue, and it would all be his fault.

Tommy fell, an angry look on his face, and soon both of their bodies were being dragged slowly and painfully into the black warehouse.

And just like that, James Griffen shut his eyes.

***

September
2025

SAM
SEPTEMBER 9TH, 2025
THE STING OF THE SILVER BULLET

Everybody had told Sam that his dreams would never come true. Nobody had told him that his nightmares would.

He was stuck in a fierce gridlock that seemed to move slower than the stationary buildings surrounding him. He checked his watch anxiously. It was six minutes past nine. He sighed. His first day and already he was late.

Throughout his childhood, from the moment he moved to America as a ten-year-old and witnessed a cop catch a criminal first-hand, Sam wanted only one thing; to be a detective. It was certainly an ambitious goal – one that his peers thoroughly teased and mocked (that and his unusual British-American accent). His teachers always assured him it was a ridiculous aspiration, and his mother would constantly fret about the danger. His father, however, being a police officer himself back in Britain, thought it was a fantastic idea. Sam would always remember the day he had come home from school crying after being laughed at for his dreams. He had run straight to his room, slamming the door behind him in the process before burying himself in his bedsheets.

His father had walked in a few moments later. Sam didn't want to talk to him at the time, but his father refused to leave. That was the best thing about his dad. He would always do what Sam needed, not always what he wanted.

'What did they say this time?' his dad asked.

Sam sniffed. 'The usual. Kicking me and asking if I'll arrest them. Rubbing bits of litter in my face. "Detective Sammy" this, "Officer Turner" that. "He wants to be like his dad, but his dad had to move to America because he was so bad." No accent stuff this time, at least.' He sighed. 'Why does it always have to be me?'

His father lifted the cover of the bed to see his son scrunched in a ball, teary-eyed, sniffing. 'The reason they pick on you, Sam, is because they think they have the reason to need to.'

Sam turned around, baffled. 'What the hell does that mean?'

His dad smiled. 'It means they think they need to bring you down because they're worried you're better than them. They look at you and see how determined you are, how certain you are of what you want to do in life. They see how carefree and satisfied it makes you, and it makes them jealous. I got them too when I was your age, and those types of people never stop returning to try to hurt you.'

Sam crossed his arms. 'Well that sucks.'

His father nodded. 'Yeah, but it's a double-edged sword. The very fact that they want to bully you shows that you have many advantages over them, advantages that will help you in later life. But if they really are bothering you, then I have the perfect trick. It won't only stop their teasing when they do it, but it may even stop their teasing forever. You want to hear it?'

Sam's eyes widened. 'Yes! Please!'

His father smiled. 'Do nothing.'

Sam gave his father a dumbfounded expression. 'Do nothing. How's that going to stop anything?'

'Well,' his dad pointed a finger at him 'the only weapon those idiots have against you,' he poked Sam hard in the chest, 'is their words. If you do nothing, no matter how bad it makes you feel, how will they know that they're the only weapon is still working? That doesn't mean don't tell us, of course. In fact, you must tell us every time somebody like these brats does something to upset you. But the moment you do nothing, they will think their only weapon against you is broken. Sure, they may try other things, but as long as they don't resort to violence and you use the same strategy, they'll be gone forever.'

Sam nodded as it started to make sense. 'But what if they do resort to violence?' he asked.

His father's smile became a wicked grin. 'Then you stick it to those idiots where it hurts 'em.'

Sam burst into laughter, and soon after his father joined him. He felt better from that moment onwards.

'But remember Sammy. Wit beats violence, every time. A sharp mind will cut a sharp sword in two. And as for giving up on your dreams?' his father said, rummaging inside his pocket. He pulled out a small silver bullet, about nine millimetres in diameter, what he'd later know as a .357 magnum round. Engraved on the side, Sam saw, was a symbol resembling a lion's head on a shield.

'The silver bullet was a very special award in my police department. Every year, they'd award it to the officer with the greatest determination and bravery in the force. I never got one, and never thought I would, until my final year.

'When I received the bullet, it was one of the proudest moments in my life, and I remember saying to myself that it was all worth it. All the teasing, all the work, all the pain and labour and sacrifice was worth it just for that single moment. I hope, Sammy, that one day, you will have that moment too.' He ruffled his son's hair. 'Never give up on what you love, Sam. Never.'

Sam's father had always kind to him. That was what made it even more tragic when he had been arrested four years later.

Sam snapped out of his thoughts as the traffic finally moved, and he felt a wave of anxiety flush over him as he approached the last turn on the road. Would the chief be mad? How would his partner feel? The thought of working with somebody else instantly filled him with dread every time he considered it; especially given the recent stories in the news, tales of partners shooting each other in the back

The outside of the building, despite the department's best efforts to keep it well maintained, was derelict and graffiti-covered, filling Sam with despair. Surrounding walls of chipped stone and deep blue, glass windows, some cracked and stained, were many wide pillars, which stretched far into the sky so that they scraped the passing clouds. The higher Sam looked, the better kept the building appeared, a large marble balcony resting on the pillars – decorated by an assortment of animals such as a flaming bird and a sabre-toothed tiger. All of this was topped by a pointed blue glass roof, which although untouched by human hands had fallen prey to years of dust and bird excrement. He emerged from his car and rushed for the entrance, uncertain of how this day would turn out.

Once he entered the building, however, he was blown away by the stark contrast of its interior. While outside the building was battered and destroyed, the inside was magnificent and clean, with many officers bustling about what could have been a temple rather than a police station. The atrium was the size of a cathedral, with the many glass-panelled floors twisting around the sides, putting each floor of the building with their many offices on a spectacular display. The ceiling that surrounded the dazzling azure glass roof was made of white marble, polished like a rich man's new shoes. In the centre of the room were numerous rows of computers and phones, an entire set for each person working there, and each set of equipment separated by low, thin, card walls. From Sam's view, every one of these minuscule offices was occupied; the people there presumably taking calls, guiding detectives and searching for case information. Everybody appeared to be in full focus.

Security let him through fairly promptly, knowing he was new here and so wouldn't have any identification. As soon as he passed through, Sam heard a young man's voice to his right.

'Can I help you, sir?'

Sam turned to spot the man sitting at a small wooden desk by the door. 'Oh, sorry… I'm Sam Turner,' he said, approaching the man, 'it's… my first day here.' He rummaged in his bag and fished out a small batch of signed paperwork for the receptionist.

'I see,' said the receptionist as he slid the sheets towards himself. After a few key taps and some scanning, he handed it back to Sam. 'You're all hooked up into the system now. Let me just find your stuff.'

After a few moments, the man handed Sam several pocket-sized items. One of which was a reflective bronze badge; the Nightdrop emblem (a raven flying over the moon) embezzled on its front above the letters "NCPD." Beside this were two small white circular devices, a dark blue notebook, and a reflective, jet black pen with some kind of gold writing inscribed on its side.

'I'm guessing you know what these are?' said the receptionist, pointing to the small white circles.

Sam studied them closely. 'They're micro-recorders, aren't they?'

'They are indeed. Fairly standard stuff from the academy. You should get your firearm later but for now, you're all-' The computer in front of the man made a loud pinging noise. 'Ah,' said the receptionist. 'I'm so sorry, I ought to have mentioned this as soon as you arrived. You should report to the chief's office immediately. He has a bit of a temper, especially when it comes to people being late. Just head through those double doors under the stairs over there and you'll see the lift.' The man gestured to a pair of blue doors underneath a large staircase at the back of the building.

Sam thanked the man and approached the doors, behind which was a corridor stretching down to a lift. As he walked down, he noticed the corridor was filled with portraits of officers who had lost their lives in duty; 'West, Benson, Vicente, Fulcher, Knightley, Prichard, Patel - the list went on and on. It made sense, he supposed - this *was* one of America's most crime polluted cities - but the thought didn't make Sam feel any better.

Sam pushed a square blue button on a silver panel and the lift door opened with a hissing noise. He entered the glass lift and looked around. A square panel protruded from the wall, with a camera and a black button contained within it…

Sam pressed the black button, and instantly a woman's voice erupted from the speaker. 'Where would you like to go, sir?' asked the voice.

Sam furrowed his brow. 'The… chief's office, please?'

'That's fine sir, I'll send you on your way.'

The lift shot up with a great hiss. After a few more moments it decelerated and the doors separated in front of him, revealing a small corridor, leading to a bright white door, titled CHIEF OF POLICE: EDWARD MURDOCK.

Sam observed the bold letters anxiously for a moment. This

was it, the start of a job he had worked so hard to gain. He observed a small black box with a red LED on it, which he assumed to be the buzzer. Before he even had time to press it, the door made a whirring noise, and the red light started flashing green, signalling that somebody had opened it from inside the room. The office was magnificent. The furniture - two small velvet sofas, a wooden coffee table, and an enormous oak desk - was all organised neatly around the expansive floor space. The office had a warm wood smell, and its oak floor was irradiated by the warm morning sunlight that shone through the two great glass panels in front of Sam.

Behind the desk sat the police chief - a sturdy-looking man, seemingly built solely from skin and muscle. His face bore thin, undulating lines and he had a bushy handlebar moustache which complemented his firmly straight, receding brown hair. Delicately balanced at the end of his nose was a pair of black-rimmed glasses and he refused to smile as Sam entered the room.

On Murdock's left was a curvaceous, stern-faced woman with strong brown curls in her hair, presumably Sam's captain. On Sam's side of the desk sat a short, olive-skinned gentleman with a similar uniform to Sam, who, unlike the others, managed to smile at him. This gesture of kindness seemed to put him off more than the stern looks of the other two, making him feel uncomfortable and on edge. Sam rarely trusted immediate kindness from strangers – he always felt there was some ulterior motive to it.

'Look who's finally arrived,' said the chief condescendingly. 'What took you so long?'

Sam shut his legs together and straightened his posture, 'there was a lot of traffic, sir. It shouldn't happen again.'

'Shouldn't? Or won't?'

'Won't.'

'Won't, *sir*. Now siddown.'

Sam awkwardly stumbled to the second chair placed out for him and quickly sat in its place.

The chief sighed and clasped his hands on the desk. 'All right, I'll keep things brief. If you want to survive inside or outside this station, there are some rules you need to follow. You'll have been taught many of these at the academy, but I like to add a few of my own. Beside me is our homicide captain, Mary Parker. She is also my acting deputy while I wait for somebody to fill in that role following the *incident* a couple months back. Rule one, you speak to her and me with respect and address us correctly. This applies to all officers within this station, including any who may rank below you. Understand?'

'Yes sir,' said Sam and the other man simultaneously.

'That's more like it,' Murdock replied. 'Rule two, this place doesn't exactly work like all the others. Go to Manhattan and you'll find the police tied to the system by thick strings. We at Nightdrop, on the other hand, are a bit more… flexible.' He stood up. 'For example, as I've said, I am the chief of police and Captain Parker is from the homicide division. However, as your division's captain is currently unavailable, Captain Parker and I are doing some of his jobs for him. Don't question the decisions members above you may make, even if they do seem *slightly* unorthodox.'

Sam furrowed his brow at this strange remark and caught a glance of confusion Captain Parker too.

'Sir, if you don't mind my asking, what has happened to the missing persons captain?' he asked.

Murdock hesitated. 'He fell ill. Pretty serious condition, he… well, he may not be back at all.'

The man beside Sam chuckled a little.

Murdock turned his head in fury. 'Something to say, detective? I didn't realise I told a joke.'

The man smiled and raised his hands in an amused plea for innocence. 'Nothing, nothing. It's just... well, when you know the truth…'

'What truth would that be, detective?' queried Captain Parker.

'That's he's not ill,' the man responded without hesitation. 'Come on, sir, I've been working on his case! I think it's only fair you tell the new guy.'

'I make my own decisions, detective,' replied Murdock, 'I think you'll find that *I* run this building. I just didn't want to make the new detective nervous, is all, not on his first day. Besides, what's so funny about a missing police officer.'

The man shrugged. 'Well, for starters the guy was an asshole but, I don't know… a captain of the Missing Person's Department going missing? I believe they call that irony.'

'*Enough* detective!' the chief snapped. 'I'm disgusted by your inability to take matters like this so seriously. I'd hope you wouldn't be *glad* about this man's disappearance?'

'Well, I always said you should have fired him a long time ago.'

'If you bring up those complaints one more time, detective, I swear I will-' Murdock paused for a moment and exhaled deeply. 'I would suggest you pipe down, detective. Fast.'

The man sat back in his chair, gritting his teeth in irritation.

'The officer beside you, Turner, is your new partner. His

name is Detective Carlos Rodriguez. He is persistent, annoying, and is always finding novel ways to try to put my position under fire.'

'Sir, I-'

'Don't interrupt me again, detective!' Murdock snapped. Sam saw Captain Parker glancing down anxiously. 'I'm angry enough at you as it is from all those letters you keep sending to the Commander. First, I'm hiding evidence to support your backstabbing *buddy*, then I'm allowing malicious and discriminatory behaviour within the workplace, then I'm hiding information about Captain Adams' disappearance! Soon you'll be saying I'm the damn Phan-'

But Carlos had already stood up and had begun to walk out the door.

'Detective!' the police chief shouted, causing the young man to freeze and to a full one-hundred-and-eighty-degree turn. 'I believe I haven't dismissed you.'

'With all due respect,' he responded, 'I *know* you're hiding things from us. And I only take orders from people I trust.' He walked out, slamming the door behind him.

Murdock turned around and shook his head. 'What a piece of crap. Why shouldn't I just fire him now, huh?' He turned to Mary, who responded neither in expression nor speech. 'Yeah, you're right, we can't afford to lose detectives, even ones like him. Goodness knows nobody wants to work with us after… well… what happened.'

Mary sighed and looked to her feet, a miserable expression on her face.

'Anyway,' he continued, 'you ought to get your gear downstairs. Your office is on the third floor, I believe. Number 12.'

'Yes, chief,' Sam replied.

'So…' he waved a hand. 'Get out of my sight.'

Sam stood up slowly and cautiously approached the door.

'Now!' Murdock shouted.

He hastily escaped the office and shook his head as he looked back on what had just taken place. What was the deal with this Carlos guy, and what cause did he have to mistrust the police chief?

Whatever the case, something did not feel right. Whatever little trust Sam had in his colleagues before that interview had now faltered even further. He'd have to keep his guard up if he'd want to make it through this.

Once he had claimed his weapons and office card downstairs, Sam entered the lift once again. The technology, Sam pondered as he exited the lift to find his office, wasn't the only abnormal thing about this city's police department. The structure of the station was unorthodox, almost like a hotel. How many people was it that worked here? Then he remembered that this was one of the most dangerous cities in America.

He reached inside his right jacket pocket. Between his fingers, he felt the smooth circumference of his father's silver bullet. *Oh Dad,* he thought, *what the hell have I signed up to?*

***

SAM
SEPTEMBER 9TH, 2025
THE TWO SURVIVORS

Sam was apprehensive as he approached his office. He hadn't exactly had the best start with his new partner, and he didn't want things to get any worse than they already were.

'Oh hi,' said Carlos as Sam passed through the doorway, 'did you get here all right?'

'Honestly, no. I'm still getting used to the way people do things in this city.'

'Yeah, tell me about it,' Carlos responded. 'I've been here for pretty much my entire life and I still don't understand it.'

Sam took a seat by the desk and sighed. 'You've lived in this city for your *whole* life?' he asked.

'Hey, it's not so bad!' Carlos responded. He caught Sam's uncertain expression. 'Okay, you got me. Who am I kidding, this place sucks! But I've been in worse.'

'Oh yeah, where's worse than here?'

He shrugged. 'Well, I wasn't born in America. Mexico actually; a place called "El Patio del Diablo." *That* was a worse place.'

'It must have been if you moved to this place!' Sam joked.

He laughed in response. 'Well, my parents weren't exactly doing too well. Dad had to work for some very bad people to earn money and eventually we weren't safe. Criminals, civilians, even cops were planning to rat us out to the big crime-bosses. Mom managed to escape with baby me. In fact, I think I'd say I almost helped her pass the border. As I say, I've lived here ever since.'

Sam nodded as he took it all. 'Blimey, that's certainly one hell of a story!'

Carlos laughed and rubbed his head. 'Yeah sorry… I go on a bit sometimes. I like to be open; it gains trust.'

Sam nodded. 'Yeah, well, don't worry. I can't say I can relate to much of what you said, but I know what it's like to have a father who does terrible things "for his family." It really doesn't help that whole "trust" thing you were talking about when you learn the dad you always idolised was a criminal.'

Carlos nodded slowly. 'Well, I've always thought of trust as something you need to work on. Especially after… Well, you've probably heard the story.'

Carlos was referring to a recent story that had taken the city by storm. It involved a man that, for legal reasons, the media could only refer to as "the Backstabber." This man had lied to and manipulated his partner for the entirety of two weeks until the revelation of the truth led him to murder his partner in cold blood. The police department had been reprimanded, of course, for not identifying such a killer in their ranks. Ever since, it seemed no two officers would ever truly look each other in the eye and trust one another.

'Well, that story's what led me to ask for a job here,' said Sam. He immediately realised how cold that sounded. 'I mean, I don't see it like it's a vacancy. It was horrible what happened. I just acted quickly, knowing how difficult it is to get a job in a police station in these parts. But it was awful what happened, terrible! I mean, what kind of monster would do such a thing?'

'Well, I don't know…' Carlos said plainly. 'You heard me rant in the office a few minutes ago. I'm not even sure I believe we're being told the complete truth about this thing,' said Carlos.

'But you must do!' Sam exclaimed. 'It's everywhere! All over the news!'

'It's on the news? Oh, then it must be true!' Carlos joked. 'But it's so weird how they're covering it up. We're not allowed to say his name to people outside the station. In fact, I can't even tell you because you didn't know him and you're new here!' He twiddled his fingers anxiously. 'I also can't imagine what could have caused somebody like him to shoot his partner.'

'Well, it's obvious, isn't it?' replied Sam.

'What, why he did it?'

'No, why Murdock isn't telling anybody! It's to do with the ongoing court cases. Sometimes they sign these secrecy acts or something to protect the identities of those on trial – hence why the press keeps calling this guy "The Backstabber." Plus, it helps that the general public doesn't know the full details of the case, it'll make them feel safer.'

Carlos laughed. 'Safe? Whoever thought they were safe in this city?'

A deep pit of anxiety stirred in Sam's stomach. 'So, what do you think happened instead if you don't believe it?'

Carlos thought about this. 'Oh, I don't know… I wouldn't say it's all wrong, just that what they're telling us doesn't make much sense to me.'

'Well, why not?'

Carlos sighed. 'Well, they both seemed like such good people. The Backstabber even saved my life.'

Sam raised an eyebrow. 'You're kidding.'

'Not a bit. I've always been a missing persons detective, but I was also a member of the TRT a few months back-'

'I'm guessing the TRT is Nightdrop's SWAT team, right?'

Carlos nodded. 'Stands for Tactical Response Team. I guess I don't strike you as the critical situation kind of guy?'

'I don't know. You seem fairly chilled under pressure; I suppose that always helps. Anyway, you were saying?'

Carlos looked up as if picturing the scene in front of him. 'All right, well one day we were told to go to this hospital – don't ask me to remember its name – and the guys in charge instructed us to evacuate the civilians and search the building. When we got there though, the civilians have already been evacuated. A few of them were missing, but we had no idea about that at the time. We searched the place thoroughly anyway, and for the most part, it was empty. I was on the ground floor with two other guys and my partner.

'Then, the guy who we're talking about, the Backstabber, bursts into the hospital. He says something's up, that we're all in danger and that we need to leave the area immediately. Suddenly, we hear shouting in our walkies, and he charges at me, grabbing me fiercely by the shoulders. He then chucks me into a closet and jumps in after me. Overhead I then hear an immense roar, and above me I can feel this powerful heat. For ages, I lie there with him next to me while this explosion goes on overhead. Rocks and scaffolding rain on our bodies, and there's only so much that our armour can protect. Then it all stops, and the other guy and I are left alone in the small closet. Thanks to physics and a bit of luck, we survived, and I was only left with a damaged right foot. Others… well, they weren't so lucky. My partner, for one…'

'Oh…' Sam said in shocked reply. How else was he meant to respond? 'I'm sorry.'

'Yeah, well, it wasn't your fault. And sorry won't bring him back… so… I guess there's no point, really.'

Sam looked down solemnly. After a few moments, he spoke up again. 'I can't believe he saved you like that.'

Carlos glanced up warily. 'What do you mean?'

'I mean why would a guy like him save somebody else's life, I mean. Part of his cover story, perhaps?'

'I don't know Sam; I don't know if he was a psychopath or anything…'

Sam gave him a concerned stare. 'Apart from the fact that he was later convicted of murdering his partner?'

Carlos shook his head. 'Convicted, there's no proof yet… I'll be honest, I'm not certain he *did* kill his partner. He saved me, Sam, he saved my life!'

'Well… I suppose the court cases haven't gone on long enough for us to condemn him just yet. But don't you think…' He trailed off as he saw the look in Carlos' eye.

'What is it?' Carlos asked him.

'It's nothing. I shouldn't have brought it up.'

'Sam, it's fine, you can-'

'Isn't it suspicious that he knew there would be that explosion?' Sam asked. 'I mean, nobody prepared for it right.'

Carlos looked down. 'Well, he was good at what he did. Analysing stuff, I mean. He warned us that he felt something was up, you know.'

Sam studied Carlos curiously as he processed the story back to himself. 'I bet it was also very brave of him to save you. He probably didn't even know who you were. Right?'

'Yeah? So what?'

'So, why you? All those officers and he risks his own life to save yours. Just sounds odd is all.'

Just then, the telephone on Carlos' desk rang. Both detectives glanced at it inquisitively before Carlos had the mind to answer the call. He almost looked relieved with the change of subject.

'Hello?' he said.

Sam heard a man's voice murmuring on the other end.

'Really?' said Carlos inquisitively, 'yes, we'll be there right away!'

He looked as if he were an active explosive containing a mixture of excitement and shock. He was wearing what was the first smile that Sam had seen all day.

'Well?' Sam asked.

'A case for tomorrow,' replied Carlos. 'A good one!'

***

SAM
SEPTEMBER 10TH, 2025
THE GIRL WHO RAN FROM MONSTERS

'Who would put an orphanage out here?' he thought out loud.

They were driving down a narrow bendy road that cut right through two enormous dry grass fields. Randomly scattered across the grasslands were the many skeletons of trees, their leaves lost in the commencing fall. At either side of them were two valleys of undulating hills, which seemed to rise and fall like waves as the car sped past them.

'Well, I've certainly never been here before!' Carlos remarked. 'I expect it can't be too far away, otherwise we'd be leaving the city.'

Contrary to Carlos' words, the landscape continued to stretch around them for miles. It was as if they were no longer in America, but some vast plain of British country like the ones Sam fondly recalled exploring as a child. The weather would be appropriate for Britain too, Sam noted, considering the thick grey blanket that hung high above them. The clouds were getting heavier, and it seemed a storm would soon be upon them.

'Is this definitely where Murdock said it would be?' Carlos

asked.

'Without a doubt,' Sam replied. 'By the way, I meant to ask; what happened to the other captain, the one you said went missing?'

'Oh him,' Carlos said, a slightly vicious tone in his voice. 'What can I say, he just vanished. Didn't come into work one day. Then he was gone for two, then his wife called in. We tried to find him, but all leads went nowhere. One of the evidence folders even vanished too. Weird stuff…'

'So, he wasn't in that explosion?' Sam asked.

Carlos turned his head in shock. 'No, why do you ask?' Carlos sounded irritated.

Sam frowned. 'Sorry, I didn't mean to upset you. I just thought… you said most of the people in your division died and… I'm sorry I didn't mean it to sound like that…'

'No, it's fine,' said Carlos, staring into the distance rather blankly. 'He was too busy chatting outside when it all happened. Probably bragging about something, the prick. Guess it wasn't his day to die.'

Sam glanced at his partner with caution.

Just then, the car approached a different set of fields, these ones especially bland and lifeless save for the grass that slowly withered upon it. It was as if all colour had been drained away from the landscape, leaving it in an almost grey colour. These meadows were laced with bumps and bends as if an invisible hammer had battered them over many years. There were no flowers, no creatures, no life, and the only object that stopped this area from seeming to be the loneliest place on earth was a small building in the distance. Sam noticed an iron archway in front, with letter beading over it reading:

Nightdrop City Orphanage.

As they got closer, the detectives noticed vines on the wall which firmly clutched the bricks and slithered down to the dead ground below it. The wall itself was tired and worn away and was as colourful as the bleak surrounding meadows. The roof was brown like spoilt coffee and it dribbled over the dead walls which together shared many cloudy windows, through which Sam could just see the outlines of children, bored, upset and lifeless.

'Could they make this place any creepier?' Carlos asked.

'That wouldn't be more possible if the Devil's mother designed it,' Sam remarked.

'Where did you pull that phrase from?' Carlos asked,

'Oh, it was just something my dad used to say.'

They exited the car and slowly made their way towards the thick oak doors of the entrance.

'Ready?' asked Sam.

Carlos looked at him with uncertainty. 'I mean, it's only a care home I guess.'

Sam gave Carlos an *if you say so* face before hitting the knocker three times.

The door creaked open, and they were met with an English woman's monotone voice. 'Good afternoon officers,' said the woman 'I suppose you're here to talk about Sadie?'

As the door opened wider, both Sam and Carlos saw an elderly lady, looking to be in her mid-seventies, whose face was dreary and melancholy, with the skin on her bony cheeks sagging and folding up to make innumerable wrinkles like waves on a rough ocean. She wore a bonnet, a tight waistcoat and a hovering dress, all of which matched the same stormy grey of her aged hair. Her eyes were weary and solemn, as if they had never had the pleasure of witnessing a joyous event so much as a single ray of sunshine.

'Good morning, Mrs…'

'*Miss* Pennyweather. And I think you'll find it's the early afternoon.'

'Ah, so it is,' Sam mumbled, uncertain how he should reply. 'Sadie's the missing girl, I presume? May we come in?'

'All right, in you come,' she responded before opening the door wider and gesturing the two detectives into the hallway.

It was a sea of creaky floorboards, every step on the stained wood uttering a tortured groan as it was stepped on. Sam felt himself cringe from the attack on his ear canal and hurried forwards into the sitting room pointed out to him by the old carer. He looked around warily, as if he were checking for something out of place in this mysterious care home. By the door was a dark wooden stairway which stretched up in a square coil, passing many grimy glass windows along the way. At the tip of the staircase, he could just make out another hall, lined with the curved wooden doors of what he presumed to be the bedrooms of other children. Lowering his head, he saw many dreary paintings hanging off the walls of the corridor; a vase of flowers, piles of books, a golden ram, a skull and a small boy in a dark alley.

The living room was slightly lighter, but seemed ancient, with a dusty oak table and a marble fireplace held in place by a metal grate, beige wallpaper peeling off like dry glue, and three small lightbulbs poking through cubbyholes spread across the ceiling. Crammed against one corner of the room was a small leafy green couch, which directly faced a box vaguely reminiscent of a television.

'Take a seat if you must,' said the well-spoken English tones of the old woman. The two detectives lowered themselves onto the minuscule sofa. The lady herself slowly walked over to her marble fireplace and propped herself against it, her finger resting anxiously on her lip.

'Miss Pennyweather?' Sam asked to gain her attention. 'Would it be all right if you told us a bit about Sadie?'

She hummed in response and pondered thoughtfully for a moment, before finally replying to the detective. 'Sadie was…' she started, 'a troubled girl. Her mother died from an extremely unusual disease – Cryonese syndrome, I think they called it. The doctors were unsure of where it came from, but whatever it was, it was very severe and took an awful toll on Sadie's mental health. Now her father… he looked after her for a while. I suppose his grief corrupted him to turn to temptation because he was arrested in the same month. Killed two people in some kind of heated argument that became a fight at his household. Left alone, with no relatives to care for her, Sadie was forced to live here. She didn't enjoy it more than any of the others do.'

Sam looked down solemnly, deeply disturbed that such a horrific event could happen to a child. He wrote some notes down on a notepad he had pulled out of his pocket and turned his head to Miss Pennyweather again. 'And do you think there's any reason she left?'

The care home runner frowned. 'People leave places for all sorts of reasons. Take it from me, I fled my country just to run from my husband! But I suppose…' A distressed look grew on her face. 'A few weeks ago, the girl started hearing something odd. She said it was as if something was talking to her, she said. When I asked her what she heard, she said it was a man's voice. But not a normal man's voice. She said it was distorted, all "wrong sounding." She said it was cold too, like it felt nothing; not anger, nor joy, nor sadness. Just a cold, robotic drone with the desire to do something evil to her. She told me it said it wanted to get her.'

The look on her face turned from baffled recollection to great sadness.

'But then last night, before what was meant to be her monthly therapy session today, I heard a scream from upstairs. I hurried up the steps as fast as I could and burst into her room. She was gone. I looked all around her bedroom and out the window that she had left open and all I could find was a note on her bed. I haven't seen her since!'

'May we see this note, ma'am?' Sam asked politely.

She reached into her pocket and fumbled about for a folded piece of paper. She clutched it tightly between her fingers as if the last hope of the child's safety in the woman's hands and handed it to Sam.

Sam glanced down at the note. In messily scribbled black ink, it read:

Dear Miss Pennyweather,

I hate to leave you like this, but I have no other choice. The monster is coming for me, and I am not safe to hide from it here. If I'm lucky, I should be able to escape it. It cannot move very fast, and if I can get to where I need to be, then it will never find me.

But first, I have to go and see Mommy. It's been a while, and I think it's something that needs to be done before whatever happens next.

I'm sorry, miss, it's the only way!

From Sadie.

Sam couldn't stop thinking it over in his head. *Go and see Mommy,* he thought. Wasn't her mother dead? Had they already lost?

He slipped his hand in his pocket and felt the curve of his father's silver bullet.

'As I was reading it,' she continued, 'I heard the wardrobe doors slam behind me, and the quick scurrying of feet down the steps. She had been hiding in the closet, waiting for me to come up so she could make a run for it. I ran as fast as my frail legs could take me, but it was no use. She'd fled before I had even made it to the peak of the stairwell. In one last desperate attempt, I went to the open window to call the girl back, but she wouldn't listen. And then, as I was calling and calling… I saw it.'

The detective immediately jumped away from the thoughts and speculations that had filled his heads when she said this. 'It?' Sam asked.

'The monster. The creature. The one she was so afraid of. I thought she was just seeing things but… it was *there* officers; I saw it with my very eyes!'

'Sorry,' said Carlos, 'you saw her monster?'

'Yes. Barely, but yes, I saw it! It had the form of a man, but it was disfigured -and twisted. It stared deeply into my soul with its glowing red eyes, as if it were some higher being. As if I, being a mere mortal, would never understand what it was, why it was there, but it knew me. It almost recognised me. I can't describe it, but it was as if we were connected somehow. Within a few seconds, it fled, but I got a good enough look at it to tell you this, detectives; whatever that girl was afraid of, it was real, and whatever it is, it's determined to follow her no matter how far she goes.'

Carlos looked baffled and terrified, so much so that he closed his eyes. Sam just looked down at the note Sadie had written and analysed it thoroughly, his fist clenching around the bullet in his pocket. Suddenly his brain clicked, and he almost smiled as he discovered what to do next.

'Where was Sadie's mother buried?' he asked the old woman.

'Excuse me?' she responded.

'I think I can find your girl,' Sam replied, 'but you need to tell me where her mother was buried.'

'Well, she wasn't buried,' the care home mistress responded. 'She was cremated, in fact. They scattered her ashes in Dayshine Park, I believe she had a tree dedicated to her in the same spot. Why do you ask?'

Now a smile finally appeared on Sam's face. 'Thank you, Miss Pennyweather, that was all we needed to know. Carlos, come with me, it's time to find that girl.' He ran to the door, Carlos slowly trailing behind.

'But where are you going?' Miss Pennyweather asked in bewilderment.

'Don't worry ma'am!' Sam shouted back in response, 'We'll do everything in our power to bring Sadie back to you! As soon as possible!'

And with that they ran to their car, leaving a very confused orphan mistress at her front door.

***

July 2025

JIM
JULY 9TH, 2025
THE HOME OF THE REAPER

Jim opened his eyes. He was lying in a large stretch of grass, each blade glistening as the radiant sun reflected off the dew that covered it. The sky was like a still lake, so clean that there wasn't a single cloud to stain it.

'Is it you?' said a child's voice.

Jim looked over and saw the figure of a boy who looked just short of six years old. His skin seemed frail, stretched and pale like paper. Patches of dirt and blood covered him; his hair, skin, clothes, even his mouth.

'Jake?' Jim asked as he rose from the wet grass.

'Hello, Father.'

Jim felt like he would cry for the first time in ten months. 'I'm so happy to see you!' he shouted before running up to his son and embracing him.

Jake did not acknowledge Jim's hug but simply looked up to his father, his face expressionless. 'Are you happy?' he asked.

Jim's smile of joy twisted into a nervous smile of concern. 'Of course, I am. Jake, I've missed you ever since that day all those years ago!'

Jake's eyebrows grew enraged. 'Maybe if you tried to protect me, that day wouldn't have happened. Even better, you could have stopped that driver. Think of all the lives that you would have saved.'

The skies were scorched purple, and dark clouds gathered above. The grass suddenly started withering away, the green colours forming into black and the blades crumbling into dust. The same dust was picked up by the air, swirling slowly at first, but then accelerating at a tremendous rate until it was swirling around Jake like a tornado.

'You could have saved me!' screamed Jake.

Jim was distraught. 'There was nothing I could do! He was too good, always a step ahead.'

'You always could have done something,' his son shouted. 'You promised you would do something and now he's back. Think of all the children he could kill now!' The tornado of darkness closed around him and exploded with a mighty roar. Jim saw a figure in the distance, the outline was of man, but it was made of pure shadow. Then, a white truck emerged from the darkness, blaring its horn before it hit Jim. He felt himself tumbling into an abyss.

Darkness was all that remained. He was awake, but it was still so dark. His senses were dampened, and all that happened around him felt like it was part of his imagination. He heard voices, but what they were saying was indistinguishable. The pain in his head felt like the worst hangover he had ever endured, and that was saying something, and his wrists felt hot and sore.

'Anyth… lse?' said a muffled voice.

'No sir, noth… else,' replied another voice, slightly clearer this time.

Jim could tell he was sitting down, but it was hardly in a comfortable position. His arms were stretched far behind him, and his hands and feet were tightly bound. The throbbing in his head was excruciating, and every thought Jim made felt like a knife stabbing into his brain.

'No other weapons, nothing at all? I want to be thorough with this man Lucas! He's clearly going to be jumpy when he finds out we plan to kill him, so I don't want any chance of him escaping.'

Jim felt alarmed. Kill him? Had they already killed Tommy? He felt his body wake up and become alert.

No, he realised. He wasn't dead. He didn't meet his son. It wasn't a bullet that hit him. They must have shot him with a tranquillizer, one with quite some nasty side effects. That explained his struggle to comprehend what was happening. He let out a small moan in an attempt to speak.

'Looks like our friend is waking up,' Jim heard. 'Remove the masks, will you?'

The darkness was snatched away from his eyes and Jim could see a small gloomy room of corrugated iron, lit only by flickering candles on the floor, but the large, overbearing shadows of people diminished the power of even these small areas of light. He tried to move, but to no avail, as he realised that he was on a chair with his upper torso, hands and feet tied up and his mouth taped shut. Whether it was his immobilization, the effects of the tranquillizer, or the ominous room around him, there was something there that made Jim feel uneasy.

'Like the place?' asked a voice in front of him.

Jim shot his head down to see a short, bony man; possibly in his early fifties, with skin as shrivelled as a prune and slick silver hair pulled back at his scalp. The man wore a tight black jumper and jeans of the same description, fitting around his slim yet broad-shouldered body. He held a freakishly wide grin, not down to his mood, but because his left cheek wore a scar stitched tightly down to his lips, pulling up that side of his face.

'You don't like it?' the man continued. 'That's a shame. Personally, I'd want my place of death to be one that I found calm, peaceful, aesthetically pleasing. You know what I'm saying?'

Jim furled his eyebrows to show his confusion, not bothering to speak.

'Oh, I'm terribly sorry. My name is Nathan Blake. Most people know me as the Reaper.' While his lips stayed smiling, his eyes dropped to a look of deep frustration. 'But I expect you already knew that, didn't you, Jim? Would you like to tell me how you found us and why you knocked on our door?'

Jim mumbled through the tape.

'I'm sorry, I don't quite understand you. Could you repeat that?'

Jim regarded the creature before him with an icy glare, to which his captor giggled hysterically.

'You know what, my friend? I'll answer my question for you. My henchmen have searched through the items in your pocket and made some very interesting discoveries.' A woman in a black bandana brought in a miniature table and placed it by the mad Blake. On it were many of Jim's belongings, including his badge, his weapon, his office card and a small flask. Also on the table was a pair of black gloves that lay over the edge, and a pistol, presumably taken from Tommy.

'For starters,' the Reaper continued, 'you're an alcoholic. The flask was a small giveaway.' He stretched the gloves over his bony hands and lifted the flask up into the candlelight. 'Looks like a present, yes? A gift from… your wife?' he looked down at Jim. 'Oh, I see, you're not together anymore, that explains the heavy drinking.'

Jim glared at him furiously. Again, his captor laughed. 'Oh, Jim, you didn't actually think you were the only clever person in the area, did you? And yes, I do know who you are. I believe the press once called you the best detective in the state a couple of years back. Quite the title, I must say.'

Jim wriggled in his chair madly.

'It's no use,' exclaimed Blake. 'Even if you did miraculously get out of those ropes. There's a guard standing right behind you. Anyway, you seem to be impatient, so I'll get to the point.' He paused and stood up. 'I'm aware you probably know that I'm the leader of a highly respected business in this city. We pride ourselves in providing the most optimal drugs in the safest proportions so that people can relax without harming their own lives. For years, citizens of this busy city have stayed in contact with us for our products, and at the same time, we have managed to keep utmost confidentiality to maintain our position.' The man stood up. 'Luckily, people have always been wise enough not to reveal any information about us. Until today.'

'You must understand my frustration, Jim. I built this business from dust. I've provided pleasure for the people of the city. But then two foolish men try to take all my hard work away. So, I've worked out that either one of our customers won't stop talking, or you have one extremely clever customer of mine in the police department feeding you information. Either way, I want to know how you found me.'

Suddenly he ripped the tape off Jim's mouth, causing Jim to gasp in pain. 'You know,' Jim replied, 'for somebody with stitches on his mouth, you don't half talk.'

'I know,' Blake replied nonchalantly, 'it's a common trait of mine. Now, are you going to tell me who led you here or not?'

'We're not here to arrest you,' Jim explained. 'We need information about one of your recent buyers.'

'I don't care, Jim. This whole meet-up puts my business in grave peril. I need information too.'

Jim hesitated for a moment. There was an opportunity here, but one that had the potential to put another person's life at risk.

No, he had to do it. If there was even the slightest chance that the Phantom was involved, then he couldn't stop at anything. Besides, the individual in question was in police custody. 'Then why don't we trade. You tell me the last few customers you delivered your drug to, and I'll tell you who led us here.'

The Reaper laughed. 'No deal, Jim. We have a policy that we never share details about our customers under any circumstances. I've got to say, though, that's pretty dark for an upholder of the law. How about I edit your deal a bit; tell us who brought you here, and I'll grant you and your friend a quick death. Your bodies will be found at the bottom of a nearby gorge, and everybody will think it was a car accident. I may even let you say goodbye to Detective Knightley or whatever his badge says. Don't tell us, and we'll beat it out of you.'

Jim thought for a moment before speaking. 'Show me that my partner's okay, and I'll tell you.'

'Very well,' the drug-boss replied with an eye roll. He nodded his head to a guard behind Jim, who walked away from the sound of things. About a minute later she came back pushing a chair, with the young officer placed on it; tied, bound and taped like Jim with blood surrounding his mouth. He looked to be a mixture of afraid and furious and was looking over to Jim as if lost for guidance. *If the kid dies, it's my fault* Jim thought.

'You're an ass, you know that?' Jim claimed when he saw the state of his partner.

'I'd like to think not,' Blake replied. 'I showed you your friend as you requested. I'm allowing you a quick death. We're not bad people, Jim. We just need to stay off the radar, it's where we belong!' He squatted down to be at eye level. 'So, Jim, I've done what you asked. You do me a favour now. Tell me, how did you find me?'

'You can't afford to kill me, can you?'

'Excuse me?'

'I mean, you care about the confidentiality of this business. I'm willing to bet that if I do anything now, you won't kill me. You won't even have your men lift a gun in my direction. Otherwise, you would have done it outside.'

Blake sighed. 'I hate the smart ones. I'm guessing the threat of torture won't bother you too much either.'

Jim shrugged. 'I've felt enough pain to know that it's just as meaningless as any other feeling.' While he talked, he felt the ropes binding his wrists. They were fairly tight, that was certain. But as he talked, he could feel the end of the piece of rope in the knot. If he could just loosen it a little with some movement, he might be able to break free.

'Well, you're a tough guy, aren't you?' said Blake. 'Then what oh what could make James Griffen give away such valuable information. Oh, I know.' He nodded over to where Tommy was, and Jim saw in his periphery that a woman had just pulled out a knife, resting the blade against one of Tommy's fingers. Tommy struggled and writhed, but it was no use against the ropes tying him.

'You're going to kill him anyway, right?' Jim responded in a flash. 'What difference does it make if he feels a little pain before?'

Blake studied Jim's eyes in an attempt to call his bluff. 'Perhaps I underestimated you, Jim. But that's okay, we've got forty fingers between the two of you to give me a name. And forty toes.'

Jim remained silent. He knew how to identify a liar. Blake was not lying.

'Right, I'll give you to the count of three, then.'

'Hey, come on,' Jim protested. 'Don't harm the kid. It's not his fault we're here, I brought him over.'

'I want a name Jim,' said Blake. 'Three seconds.'

'Blake, be reasonable.'

'One…'

'Blake!'

'Two…'

'Wait, Blake please just listen, I'll give you the name just-'

'Three!'

'The Circle of Saints!'

Blake frowned. 'What?'

Jim thought back to the video that he and Tommy had been comfortably watching just hours ago. 'There's a man working for a group that calls themselves the Circle of Saints. He used your product on a victim of one of his murders. Maybe he's the man who killed my son. Maybe not. He seems to know me anyway, but then who doesn't in this city. We… caught him.' Jim pretended to look defeated in his lie. 'We caught him, and he told us everything about you.'

Blake shook his head. 'No… no, he wouldn't do that. Not a man like him. His partner on the other hand… well, I hear *he's* the wild card. The Circle wouldn't trust him for a minute, not completely.' Brigson studied Jim's eyes for a moment as if looking for a lie. When he seemed satisfied, he turned and slammed his hand on the small wooden table beside him. 'Either way, to think I trusted those dirtbags. Well thank you, Jim, that's all I need to know.'

He nodded to the guards, and Jim felt the cold metal of the barrel of a gun against the back of his skull. He glanced to the right and saw the woman behind Tommy had also withdrawn a pistol and had placed it against his head.

'I'll allow you a quick death,' said Blake. He began to raise his finger.

'Ah, ah!' Jim protested. 'Hold on, I have two requests.'

Blake folded his arms. 'You think I care about how you want to die?'

'It's no trouble really,' said Jim. 'I think you owe us too, given the information I gave you.'

Blake hesitated; his face frozen in contemplation. Then his expression relaxed. 'To most men, I'd say no. But you're not most men, James Griffen. Go on. But be quick, I have business to attend.'

'Well, first of all…' Jim started. 'I want to die first. I don't want my last thought to be of the kid that I took here lying dead on the floor.'

Blake laughed. 'And you'll let his last thought be seeing you dead on the floor, will you?'

'Perhaps he'll enjoy that. We didn't exactly get along earlier, and I was the one who brought him here after all. Besides, I'd much rather be shot by what that lady over there's holding against his skull. Judging by the size of the barrel touching my skull, I'm guessing the person behind me is holding a shotgun, no?'

'Yes, that's right,' said Blake, looking underwhelmed.

'Well, I'd prefer being shot with a pistol of that making over there if that's not too much to ask. I want them to at least vaguely recognise my face when they find me. And I hear it's less painful. Plus, she seems to have steadier hands, I suppose that's why you gave her the finger-cutting job.'

'But Jim, I thought you didn't care about a bit of pain before you die,' Blake mocked. 'One moment it's all tough guy, the next you're so desperate to have it done a certain way?'

'Look, you call yourself the Reaper, the least you can do is respect a dead man's wishes. I gave you the name too, remember.'

'Yes, well, we'll see about that.' Blake rolled his eyes and gestured for the lady behind Tommy to move over to Jim. She did so, and all the while Jim kept his eyes fixed on the knife in her other hand.

As she rested the pistol against his skull, Jim heard the man with the shotgun to not be too far away, perhaps just behind her if he was lucky. Presumably, they'd now aimed the shotgun at Tommy in case of any "funny business." That was all right. Jim would just have to be careful about his next move.

'Right,' said Blake. 'Now all that's sorted, are you happy now, Mr Griffen?'

Jim smiled. 'Yeah, that should do it,' he responded calmly.

'All right then,' said Blake, sitting down in his chair. 'I

suppose you'll be wanting last words too?'

'Yeah,' said Jim, 'Sorry about the mess.'

Jim used all his strength to push himself forwards, tilting his chair so he was well weighted on his feet, and in a fluid motion launched himself back into the lady behind him, tilting his body away from the pistol as he did this. The two fell to the floor, and time slowed as Jim engaged his brain to his surroundings.

Looking around, he saw that the gunner with the shotgun was stumbling back. In about half a second he would overcome his surprise and direct the shotgun away from Tommy, pointing it to Jim on the floor. Even then, the gunner would not shoot Jim immediately but would wait until both the other gunner was clear of his shot and some kind of non-verbal signal of permission had been given by his leader to pull the trigger.

Blake was less predictable. He too was overcoming his initial surprise and was rising from his chair, enraged, his hand reaching across to the small wooden table to grab his pistol. Jim knew that this man would not hesitate to fire at him as soon as he was close enough. That gave him about two-and-a-half seconds from the moment he hit the ground.

Luckily, he had used the fall to grab the knife from the woman behind him, and, if he positioned it in such a way, could use the force of his fall to help slice the cheap ropes binding him. As he landed, he tilted the knife to slide across the back of the chair, freeing him from the ropes around his chest. Blake was beginning his approach now, and Jim used whatever time he had left to thrust himself onto his still tied feet with whatever body strength remained, before leaping forwards to drive himself into the crime boss shoulder first.

As Jim leapt into him, Blake - stunned by Jim's attack - lifted his pistol and pulled the trigger, but Jim was too close, and there was little time for proper aim. The bullet fired as the barrel was pointed against Jim's upper shoulder, and he felt a shot of pain throughout his body as it grazed his flesh. Jim's forward motion from his shoulder-driven leap carried on, however, and both men stumbled to the ground.

The moment they reached the floor, Jim knew he had to act fast. The two armed gunners would hesitate to fire with the risk of hitting their leader, but Blake was picking himself up and reaching for his gun. Jim struggled behind him and lined up the blade of the knife with the rope.

Blake was lifting the firearm to shoot Jim again, but Jim sliced the rope in time and swung his arm around, stabbing the knife into Blake's right wrist. The man screamed in fury and pain and dropped his pistol in an uncontrollable response. In a moment of fury, Jim pushed the blade and the hand it had passed through, to the ground, pinning Blake's now bleeding wrist with it. Seeing the man with the shotgun ready to fire as well as the woman with the pistol up on her feet, he pulled Blake upright before him to shield himself from the oncoming blasts. One shot missed and hit the wall behind him, while another hit Blake's side, causing him to groan in further agony. Jim quickly leaned to the ground, grabbed the pistol, and, without hesitation or inaccuracy, shot both gunners in the legs.

The two collapsed to the ground, the one with the shotgun dropping his weapon entirely. The woman with the pistol vainly attempted to lift her weapon in Jim's direction, but Jim took another shot at her wrist, and her weapon went flying through the air.

Seeing the enclosed room to be safe, with Blake and the gunners wailing and cursing in agony, Jim quickly untied the ropes around his feet and arose. He lifted Tommy's gun from the small wooden table beside him so that Blake could not arm himself and ran to the door, locking it so that no other members of this violent gang would enter. He then walked over to Tommy and untied the ropes.

'Sorry, kid. Normally drug gangs are a little more negotiable in these parts. By that I mean they don't try to kill police officers because they're not arrogant or stupid. Also, what's with the shotguns?' he asked, moving his gaze to Blake. 'Isn't that a little overkill?'

Blake groaned with gritted teeth. 'My men will kill you,' he screamed.

Jim looked down at the ropes on Tommy's chair, which he had made little progress in untying, and rose to his feet. He then placed both pistols that he had acquired under his trouser waist, walked over to Blake and grabbed his wrist. The man struggled and attempted to hit him with his other free hand, but Jim blocked the attack carefree with his forearm. Fighting against the weak yet still struggling mess of "The Reaper," Jim grabbed the blade of the knife and pulled it as slow as he could from Blake's wrist. Blake screamed and collapsed onto the floor, clutching his bleeding mess of an arm, while Jim walked back to Tommy to cut his ropes.

Once Tommy's chest and hands were free, Jim passed him the knife and pistol. Tommy took them silently, before ripping off the tape over his mouth. He did not speak but silently cut his foot restraints.

'Anybody tries anything, and they'll be shot in the legs again,' Jim said. 'Blake, hands on your head.'

Blake, teary-eyed, followed Jim's command, placing his shaky hands on his head. 'What… what is it that you wanted again?' he asked.

'We need to know the name of one of your customers. Somebody using your drugs for something to do with the preservation of bodies or something weird like that…' He sighed, unable to resist the need to say what he wanted. 'He may be British. Male.'

The Reaper glanced to Tommy, more specifically the gun in his hand, before looking back at Jim. 'The preservation of dead bodies. You mean… human right?'

Jim nodded.

Blake shook his head slowly. 'I remember a man saying it was for something along those lines. Something about the healing and activation of the corpse? I didn't question it. And, as you said, he was British.

Jim exchanged a surprised glance with Tommy. 'What was his name, Blake?'

Blake shrugged. 'Why would I tell you that? You're police officers, you wouldn't shoot me unless I was armed. Which I no longer am.'

Jim smiled and chuckled. 'Right. Police officers, of course, police officers.' He shot Blake's left leg, causing the man howl and thrash his fists against the floor.

'Oh, that's right, I'm not a police officer. They brought me back to deal with you, and I can do that however I like, so tell me the truth!'

Blake clutched his wound, tears coming from his eyes. 'He'll kill me if I tell you.'

'Give me the name!'

'I can't! Please!'

'Jim stop!' Tommy protested.

'Shut up Tommy. All right then Blake,' said Jim, 'you just

forfeited the other leg.'

'Wait!' Blake held out his unwounded hand in protest. 'The name of the man you are looking for is Sebastian Brigson. Head of Signision Robotics.'

Tommy and Jim silently glanced at each other.

'Signision?' asked Tommy. 'Are you sure?'

'Why… why would I lie?'

Jim analysed Blake for a moment until he was certain the man was telling the truth. When he was satisfied, seeing that Tommy was focussed on the bleeding body on the floor, Jim subtly placed the pistol he'd acquired under his trouser waist and began to approach the door. 'I'll call an ambulance and some police cars to pick you all up. I recommend you don't resist. There'll be high numbers of them, armoured, and you're going to need that wound treated.'

'I've got people for that. Besides, we'll be gone by then. And don't even think of trying to arrest me now, not if you want to leave here alive. My people will shoot you.'

Jim paused. 'Yeah, I suppose you're right. They'll only let us go if you tell them to, right? And there's no way they'll believe you're doing it out of the kindness of your heart if they see you in our custody.'

'Jim, you're not suggesting we let this guy go, are you?' asked Tommy.

'Listen, the only way we get out of here alive is if he tells his people to. As far as the police are concerned, we barely escaped with our lives, we let them know where to look through an anonymous tip and by the time they got here, the gang were gone.'

Tommy moved closer to Jim and began to mutter. 'What do

you mean anonymous tip? We're going back to the police station, right Jim?'

Jim shook his head. 'Sorry, kid. I know it's been a rough day, but time is of the essence, and if we go back now, they'll arrest me for taking you here and likely fire or demote you for letting me take you to a drug gang.

Tommy swore. 'I should never have come here with you.'

'But you did, because you knew I'd be the only one able to help with this case. Mary knew that too, that's why she got you to bring me in for this one, although perhaps she wasn't sure how far I'd take it. Listen, we go straight to Signision, we question Brigson, we investigate a little, find what we need, and then return to the station. You tell them that I lied to you and drove you to the wrong place, I'll back you up, then we say we barely escaped with our lives but knew we had to keep chasing the lead before somebody else got killed, otherwise our near-death experience would be for nothing. You look good in their eyes, if not a little stupid, and I possibly get an arrest, but hopefully won't have charges pressed against me given how embarrassing that would be for the police department.'

Tommy shook his head, bemused. 'This morning you didn't care about any of this. Now you'll risk an arrest for this case. For me? What changed?'

Jim sighed. 'I made a mistake bringing you my mess, and you could've lost your job or died because of it. I'm sorry about that, and you don't deserve to be punished for the things I do. As for the case, well you know why. Something about that video… look if there's even the slightest chance-'

'I know Jim. Believe me. I know.'

Jim nodded respectfully and pointed to Blake. 'All right Reaper, seeing as we're letting you go, you give your people the order to stand down.'

Blake sighed and brought a communicator from his pocket to his lips. 'This is Reaper. I've let the cops go. They don't know anything and…' Jim looked back and saw the man glaring at him as he told his lie. 'They could be potential customers.'

Jim shrugged. 'Works for me. Tommy, smash the communicator and bind him with that rope. I'll start the car.'

With that, Jim Griffen left the warehouse. Not a single weapon was lifted in either his - or Tommy's - direction.

***

LYNDA
JULY 9TH, 2025
THE LONELY WIFE

The smell there was putrid.

Lynda abhorred hot dogs. In fact, she hated meat altogether; but a promise was a promise. Mary had asked to meet here for lunch, and it wasn't like she could say no. For anyone else it would be different; it would be too easy to say no to a regular person. But not Mary. Mary was too kind.

'What are you getting then?' Mary asked her.

Lynda slowly rolled her eyes from the hissing sausages. 'Oh… I'm sorry Mary, I didn't tell you. I'm… kind of vegetarian.'

Mary cursed. 'I'm sorry, I shouldn't have brought you here of all places.'

'It's not your fault,' Lynda replied hastily. 'I wanted to come. I haven't talked to many people since… well you know.' She shrugged solemnly.

'Yeah, I get you,' Mary replied. 'Look, I know you don't know me as well as you know other people at the station but… have you been all right in the past few years? Honestly? We don't talk much but you always seem…'

'Tired? Bored? Joyless?'

'Your words not mine but…'

Lynda hesitated momentarily before answering. 'Yeah, I'm holding up fine, Mary. Thanks for asking.' They both knew I wasn't true, of course. How could anybody be all right after something like what happened to her?

It was easier to lie about how she felt though. It had always been easier that way. 'Yeah. Yeah, I've been… coping. Getting better, I think. Seeing the positive side of things.'

Mary smiled, although her eyes showed she was uncertain. 'Good,' she said, and propped her back against the wall of a nearby building and looked out to the Hudson. Lynda noticed how beautiful the river was at this time of day, as the sunlight reflected off the jade waters, making it sparkle like a path of jewels. *How can something be so wonderful in a city like this*? she thought.

'I know you're probably wondering why I've asked you to come for lunch so suddenly.'

Lynda smiled. 'I just guessed it was out of pity.'

'Well, you can't blame me if I do feel bad from time to time,' Mary remarked. 'I know you hate the whole pity thing, but you know how well I know Jim.' She sighed. 'But no… that's not the only reason why I wanted to talk to you.'

'What is it?' Lynda asked.

Mary sighed and looked down to her feet. 'Lynda, Jim needs your help.'

She rolled her eyes. To think of the number of times she had tried to help James Griffen. Every day since Jake's death had been worse than the last, with Jim slowly losing his soul to grief, and her beside him, trying and failing to comfort him while she fell apart herself. Trying to save Jim was as pointless as trying to talk to a rock. He'd died the moment Jake did.

'I wonder what it is this time…' she said sarcastically. 'Is my husband drinking again?'

Mary chuckled slightly. 'I don't tend to watch people in bars, Lynda. I'm worried because of this new case.'

Lynda jolted her head in confusion. 'New case?'

A guilty look grew in Mary's eyes as she heard the edge in Lynda's voice. 'The one… we called him to help with.'

Lynda gave a sigh of anguish as she approached the railing beside the river, propped an arm there and rested her head in her palm. She knew this would just make him worse. 'Mary… what were you thinking?'

'I'm sorry, Lynda. It's just the case had us all… clueless, and we needed Jim to-'

'Yeah, I think that justifies it!' Lynda said angrily. 'Bring a grieving father back to the thing that broke him because of a difficult case, that's genius Mary, really smart!'

'All we wanted him to do was to investigate the evidence, Lynda! If you saw the body, you'd know why. It looks just like a suicide, but the corpse-'

'I don't want to know the details, Mary!' Lynda shouted. 'I don't care about the damn details! What I care about is the fact that you brought him back! He's grieving for crying out loud!'

'If two years of grieving isn't enough time then why are you still working for us?' Mary snapped.

Lynda stared at her icily. 'You really think I'd still be here if I had a choice? How the hell am I going to live on my own, pay my rent, buy my food, if I don't work here? It's not like I've got a masters or a different degree, I did criminology! Along with that, I have to worry about my stupid husband-'

'Okay, keep it down-'

'- who is so *horrendous* at letting go of the past that he forgets his wife's entire existence!' Lynda breathed heavily and snapped her head around in fury to look out over the river. Guilt soon crept in… she knew it had been an unkind thing to say, but she'd needed to let it out. 'I'm sorry Mary…'

Mary looked solemnly over the river. 'No Lynda, I am. I haven't even told you the worst of it yet…'

Lynda rubbed her eyes wearily. 'Right. I don't even know the details and here I am getting cross. What's happened?'

Mary shook her head and looked out to the river. 'Jim's gone off looking somewhere with his partner without telling me or Murdock anything. Last we saw of them, they'd talked to the Medical Examiner, and then extremely intelligently decided to put a memory stick left by the killer that they'd found on the body into one of the police computers. He and Tommy proceeded to sprint to Tommy's car and neither has come back for a whole day. Again, I'm so sorry…'

Lynda chuckled, and then desperately tried to stifle it. She then laughed again and looked over to Mary, who seemed a little concerned at her reaction. Suddenly couldn't help it, but she found herself consumed by fits of laughter.

Mary looked at her curiously. 'Lynda, are you okay?'

Lynda couldn't stop.

'You mind telling me what's so funny?' asked Mary, smiling in half amusement, half concern.

Lynda had to force her laughter down for a good few moments to be able to talk. She could feel tears in her eyes. 'Nothing it's just… this is exactly the thing Jim would always have done when he was working here. Except now I don't have to search for him because I'm his wife but because it's my job!' And then she was laughing again.

When she finished, Mary put a hand on her shoulder. 'Are you sure this is okay?'

Lynda smiled. 'It gets me away from the unsolvable mass of missing people that seem to have spiked over the last year. I can leave them to my colleagues for a few days I guess; I'm sure they'll cope just as well without me. Not like we made much progress there, anyway!'

Mary's smile suddenly straightened out as she seemed to remember an additional detail. 'There's one more thing…'

'Another?' Lynda exclaimed jokingly.

Mary cleared her throat. 'The memory stick I told you about. None of our investigators found it, but Tommy and Jim must have found it on the body somehow. It… it seems to have been made by the killer with the intention of patronising Jim.'

'Patronising… Hang on, how would any killer know that you'd bring Jim back for their murder?'

Mary shrugged. 'That's what we've been debating all morning. Either the killer purposefully made it similar to cases Jim's solved before to get us to bring him back or it was slipped in afterwards somehow.'

'I don't understand,' said Lynda. 'When you say this case is similar to one Jim's solved before?'

'Well, that's it. It's probably the same reason Jim's gone rogue. The man in the video seems to suggest that he's… Lynda, you've got to know that if we knew what the killer was intending, we wouldn't have brought Jim back!'

'Show me,' Lynda said plainly.

***

When they returned to the station just half an hour later, Mary showed Lynda the video. Lynda had no idea what to expect, but she never would have imagined it to be as horrendous as it was. Once it was over, she felt a heavy queasiness in the pit of her stomach.

'The man in the video… when he says, "last time?"' Lynda questioned.

Mary had no words.

'And when you say this case was similar to one Jim's done before. You meant…'

'Jim's final case,' Mary admitted. 'Him and the Phantom. This killer - or group of killers, if what the man in the video says is to be believed - they're either imitating the Phantom to provoke Jim or…'

'Or?'

Mary shrugged.

'Mary, Daniel Crockett's dead. I shot him and he fell to his death.'

'I know, I know. Whatever the case, it's clear now that these people want something to do with Jim, whatever that may be, and already they've done enough to set him off.'

Lynda sighed. 'Of course, this would worry Jim. The question is, where would he go next? Could you tell me about the victim?'

Mary nodded. 'His name's Chris Mackledon. He's in his early thirties and he's a lawyer. He had a wife called Sarah, and I think three kids. Sadly, Murdock left me with the task of telling them the bad news. Oh yeah, his best friend's called Mark – I had to tell him too.'

Lynda hummed ponderously. 'What evidence was found at the scene?'

'Train tickets, a wallet, the memory stick apparently, and a spanner next to the body with what was tested to be his blood on it.'

Lynda cringed. 'He was beaten with a spanner?'

Mary shrugged. 'Maybe. There were no signs of a struggle, no reports of any screams from the guards were questioned, no fingerprints on the weapon except the victim's, and the way his hand stiffened around the handle suggests that he was holding it when he died. We all thought it was some peculiar suicide at first. Along with that, the bones are crushed and the body's bruised in such a way that even a bodybuilder with a baseball bat could never achieve, and our medical examiner's suggesting that he additionally received high doses of electricity to his brain.'

'So, the spanner didn't kill him?'

'It may have done, but the evidence suggests that it wouldn't be the only item used on the victim. I have no idea how much of this Jim knows – he didn't stay around long so I think he's only aware of what our medical examiner told him about the drug.'

Lynda was struggling to keep up. 'A drug?'

Mary laughed. 'Sorry, I forgot to tell you, there's some strange drug in the victim's bloodstream. They called it "corpse-shaker" I believe? Our evidence seems to suggest that it was injected by the killer but-' She must have noticed the concerned look on Lynda's face. 'What's wrong?'

Lynda scratched her head. 'In the last year or so my department's been dealing with a large spike of missing people. They're all random people, but some officers have had theories that this huge spike is linked to some sort of kidnapper. We've only managed to find two of them at best, both dead mind you, but... Both of them appeared to have committed suicide, both had some kind of electrical damage to the brain and… they had corpse-shaker in their bloodstream too! We assumed they were addicts but… you don't think these cases could be connected, do you?'

Mary sighed. 'Stranger things have happened. But if they are… well, we're going to need to find Jim. And fast!'

***

JIM
JULY 9TH, 2025
THE EMPTY LABORATORIES

'I can't believe we're actually doing this,' said a slightly nervous Tommy as he crossed the road with his temporary partner.

'Why do you say that?' replied Jim with a smirk. 'We're only possibly exposing one of the biggest technology companies in America.'

As they hopped onto the pavement, both men shielded their eyes from the glaring morning sun, which trickled down floods of light that bounced about from building to building, like a laser in a hall of mirrors. The buildings themselves were like giant glass rods which protruded from the organised black and grey strips of the ground, each of these rods so tall that it looked as if it was their sturdy frames that held up the beautiful cloudless skies on this warm day. Cars in a spectrum of shining colours carelessly bumbled down the long stretch of road, moving at a gentle pace to almost as far as the emerald hills in the distance, and people swarmed the streets as they frantically rushed to their jobs and homes. This was Nightdrop at its best. This was the peace which civilians prayed for every night. Jim was sad that he'd have to break it.

'I still think we should've gone back to the police department. We've been missing for a day! And… my head hurts. Everything hurts.'

Jim stared at Tommy sternly. 'Remember what I told you. We need to stay ahead of *him*. That means no police department and no hesitating. He's probably realised we're onto him already.'

Tommy sighed. 'Just as long as we don't get tranquillized again.'

Jim looked at him and raised an eyebrow. 'Do you ever relax?' he asked.

'Oh,' he said, 'I was relaxed almost every day before I got this job. But then I realised something.' He stopped moving for a moment.

'What?' asked Jim as he stopped with him.

Tommy smiled. 'It gets rather boring after a while.'

Jim laughed and continued walking.

When they arrived at Signision, the cheerful mood had sadly died down. This was it, after all, the place where they would find out what happened to the man at the harbour, or so they hoped. The building itself was grand, much higher than all the others in the city, and stood almost like a pillar of the city's greatness. The sunlight it reflected off its windows sparkled as if it was, like its logo, a fire - surrounded by billions of tiny sparks that each radiated a warm glow.

But instead of seeing the cosy side to this fire, Jim saw the rougher side. The painful side. The one that can burn. If this Sebastian Brigson was his son's killer, if that was the case, then his day of justice would come, and Jim's long-time adversary would finally be put behind bars.

Or worse.

Jim shook his head at the thought. He knew it was wrong to wish death upon people.

But even so…

One of the few laws of Nightdrop that did not differ from those of the state in which it resided was the lack of a death penalty – despite its incredibly high crime toll. If a criminal committed a crime in Nightdrop, no matter how hideous or wrong, the worst they could get was a lifetime behind bars. Jim somehow felt that this would not be enough punishment.

He forcefully repelled the building's glass doors and briskly stepped inside.

'Good afternoon,' he said to a woman at the front desk. He held out his Authorized Voluntary Assist badge, just far and quick enough that she couldn't read its writing properly. 'We're detectives Griffen and Knightley, we're looking for a man who works here.'

'What's his name?' she asked inquisitively.

'Brigson. Sebastian Brigson,' he responded.

Her eyes dropped in fear and immediately her smile became visibly fake. 'Right… of course, I'll send him a message to come down, shall I?'

'That won't be necessary,' said Jim. 'We plan to go up and meet him if that's okay with you? Search the place a little bit too.'

'He's in a meeting at the moment,' she said quickly, her voice wavering. 'And you haven't shown me a search warrant.'

Jim leant forwards. 'No, you're right. Of course, technically without a search warrant, you're not obliged to let us in at all! Now I *could* go back to the police department and go through the hassle of getting one, return tomorrow maybe. However, that's hardly going to benefit anyone! For starters, it's going to slow our job down, potentially leaving time for the deaths of many innocent people. Were innocent people to die in the time it takes for us to get a warrant, well… it would be such a shame if the press discovered that lives could've been saved were it not for the selfish nature of Signision employees.'

The woman looked afraid, very afraid. 'Sir, please! If I let you in now, my boss, he'd… well he'd-'

'You're frightened,' Tommy noted. 'What has Brigson been doing to you? Has he threatened you?'

She shook her head quickly. 'No… no, it's just… Please officers. Sebastian Brigson's not the kind of man you make angry. In fact, he's not the kind of man you ever want to have to speak with in the first place. He's cold and arrogant and… well, *horrible*. The things he says to people, the way he… *shouts* at people.'

Jim sighed and glanced at Tommy. 'Listen,' he said to the woman, 'Some information we recently acquired has led us to believe that Sebastian Brigson is… a dangerous man. A dangerous, disturbed man. We need this guy put away. Now if you like, we can help you, put you in police custody so that you're safe until we catch him. But if we don't go up there right now, more people in this city, including yourself, will be put at risk.'

She bowed her head and started gently sobbing. 'You promise you'll protect me?' she begged.

Jim zoned out and instantly images flooded through his brain. His son's birth, his first day at school, his fifth birthday. That night. The very night he promised to protect Jake.

The night Jake died.

'Jim?' Tommy ushered.

'Yes,' Jim said to the lady as he snapped out of his trance. 'Of course. I'll protect you. Now you get me into the lift to the floors upstairs and I'll give you the number of a friend of mine who works at the police station. Either that or you can get to the station yourself, tell them that Thomas Knightley promised you protection.'

'Thank you,' she said, rising to her feet. She retrieved the lift card soon enough and passed it to them.'

She nodded and ran away.

A few moments later, they were in the lift. Tommy was scribbling something in his notebook.

'Poor girl. Whoever this guy is, he sounds like a nasty piece of work.' He glanced up at Jim and must have spotted the nervous look on his face. 'You all right?' he asked.

'I don't know Tommy,' Jim replied. 'I'm not sure whether to feel happy or not. I mean, this might be him! You know… the guy.'

'The Phantom?' Tommy queried, seemingly careful this time not to call Jim paranoid for suspecting his son's killer to be alive. 'I thought you said you weren't so sure anymore.'

'Exactly. I'm not sure. But when she described Brigson just then? The look of fear in her eyes!' Jim shook his head. 'I don't know Tommy, we're either chasing the guy or somebody who's acting like him to wind me up. Either way, I'm fairly sure I hate them!'

'Well, if it is the Phantom, why be upset?' Tommy asked, as if the idea of the killer miraculously returning from the dead was a vague possibility. 'You'd be onto him at last. You'd finally be able to catch him.'

'I'm not upset,' Jim replied. 'Of course, it would be amazing to catch him now. I'm unsettled is all. I mean, don't you think this has all been a bit too easy?'

'What?' Tommy exclaimed. 'Jim we nearly died an hour ago!'

'I mean to solve!'

'That first case was a nightmare to solve!'

'Don't be ridiculous, I'd worked half of it out a few seconds after leaving the car!'

'Other officers weren't so certain,' Tommy noted. 'The moment there's a lack of evidence, they'll instantly think of alternatives. You'd be surprised how fast other detectives will jump to the first thing that their brains conjure up, *especially* considering the drop in murders this year…'

'There's been a drop in murders?'

Tommy nodded as if it was common knowledge. 'Oh yeah. It's the missing persons' department that's been getting most of the work recently.'

Instantly an image of Lynda flashed through Jim's mind. 'Well, that just makes me even more disturbed. If there have been so many missing people, then why wouldn't the killer have made the last murder look like one? All they'd need to do is hide the body in some abandoned location, and it would look like a drug addict overdosed. If not, why not make the body look like a suicide? Throw it in the water or something. That at least would hide the body for a good while, perhaps increase its time for decomposing before we got it. Instead, they leave the victim out in the open, a spanner in his hand, and leave a message for us in the man's jacket. It's like they want us to solve this case!'

Tommy shrugged. 'I'd say you're worrying more than I do, Jim, and that's saying something. No doubt this guy wanted you to chase him – Phantom or no, he clearly wants a bit of attention – but I highly doubt he'd know where we are now. Hell, even the police department can't find us! You were right! Because we did it this way, we're winning!'

Jim lightly shrugged. It still bugged him, but perhaps there was no point in continuing to dwell on it. 'Guess so,' he concluded.

Finally, they arrived at floor 36, and after the hissing of the elevator doors, briskly strolled into the management team's work area.

The large room was cluttered with straight, evenly spaced desks and clunky computers – each piled high with stacks of paper and random assortments of stationary. The atmosphere was remarkably – in fact, eerily – quiet, each worker either with their head buried in their work or walking sheepishly between the desks with large stacks of documents and files. The moment the officers entered, all heads snapped in their direction, as if startled or bemused as to the reason for their visit.

In the corner of the room, Jim noticed the walls of a small glass office. Peering through the glass he saw that the desk was cluttered and messy, and the drawers of cabinets were all left wide open. The office was not occupied, but a sign on the door instantly notified Jim as to who should be inside. It said:

Sebastian Brigson

CEO of Signision Robotics

'Well, we've found where our guy operates,' Jim remarked. 'The question is… where is he?'

Not a single worker questioned them as they strolled over to the office door. As they went inside, Jim noticed a peculiar smell in the air – a metallic scent, and the smell of burnt material. Looking at the mess of papers on the desk, he noted several overdue or unopened letters of inquiry, company account displays, mechanical part orders and blueprints for vast amounts of unusual looking machinery. Littered around the desk also were almost a dozen mugs of unconsumed coffee, presumably from prior days or weeks given how the milk had separated and risen to the surface. It appeared Brigson had not paid vast amounts of attention to his office.

Jim walked back into the workspace. 'Anybody here seen their boss lately?' he called out.

Silence.

'Don't all answer at once!' he remarked. He pointed at a man near the front. 'You. What's your name?'

'Kyle, sir,' he said, gulping a little.

'Hi, Kyle. Where's your boss? Sebastian Brigson, where's he gone off to?'

He shrugged. 'We rarely see him these days. He's quite… reserved. Used to vanish occasionally, especially at lunchtime, but it's become more frequent in recent months.'

'And where does he go, do you know?' Tommy asked.

The man shook his head. 'No. Normally he just walks off into the corridor and doesn't come back for hours. Just leaves us to get on with our work I suppose.'

'And what would that be?' Jim asked.

'Oh, the boring admin stuff. Managing the accounts, orders, emails to and from potential buyers, that kind of stuff. We're just one of many departments in this building, I suppose it makes sense that the boss isn't always here.'

Jim shook his head. 'No, actually, it doesn't. He's never in his office, how does that make any sense!'

'Oh well…' the man started.

'Listen up!' Jim called out. 'Anybody ever seen the boss go anywhere unusual? Somewhere you wouldn't expect a man of his job description to hang about?'

There was silence for a moment. Then a nervous mumble.

'Or I could just have you all taken into police custody for questioning.'

'The boiler-room!' a woman called out. 'He's always in there, doing goodness knows what. He's the only one who knows the code you see, him and the maintenance people, except they never come and check on it because he never lets them. Always says the problem will sort itself out. And it does, which is the funny thing, except we all know it's him fixing it.'

'Thank you, madam,' he called, before turning to Tommy. 'Are you thinking what I am?' he muttered.

'That this guy's a whack-job? Yeah, I am thinking that.'

'He's hiding something,' Jim pointed out. 'The drugs maybe?'

'What? At his workplace? Gimme a break.'

'Officers!' a man's voice called out from across the room.

Jim and Tommy quickly turned and saw that a young, scrawny looking man was standing at the doorway, his face a mixture of terror and relief. He rushed over to them in a hurry.

'Are you here for Brigson?' he asked. 'Please tell me you're here to stop him.'

'Yes, we are,' Jim replied with a frown. 'What's the matter?'

'The matter!' the man laughed wildly. 'Listen to me,' he said. 'I've seen something, something terrible, and I think he knows I've seen it. You have to help me!'

'Yes, we will! Of course we will,' Tommy assured him.

'What is it?' Jim asked bluntly.

***

A few moments later and they were running down the stairwell. 'Where are you taking us? Tommy asked when they'd descended three flights of stairs.

'The boiler-room,' the man responded. 'That's where I saw it all!'

They approached a white metal door decorated with many caution signs, a keypad bolted to its front. The man approached the keypad and typed in a few numbers, his fingers shaking.

'Brigson's gone for the moment, I think he went for a meeting in the city. My name's Johnathan, by the way. Johnathan Mort.'

After pressing in a few numbers, the door clicked open and Mort strolled through.

'I only know the code because I saw him type it the other night. I also saw… well, I saw a lot of things that night. I was up late, you see, working overtime. I saw him lurking around in the corridors and got curious as to where it is that he actually goes all the time. Made the mistake of following him in here.'

'What did you see, Mr Mort?' Tommy asked.

'I'll show you,' he said. 'Follow me but be as quiet as

possible.'

The room was dark, almost devoid of light save for two dim lights in the ceiling. The air was thick, warm and moist. It was radiated by the numerous pipes which twisted and coiled about the walls, and at the back was a large red boiler, which Mort approached quickly and started to crawl around.

'There's a hidden space behind here,' he told them. 'Must've been left over from when they built the place. At the time I was following him, I supposed he might have been coming here to have a smoke, or maybe he was having some sort of affair with a colleague, I don't know. What I saw was so much worse.'

They followed him through the small gap and squeezed into the space behind the boiler, which was about the size of a prison cell. The floor was coloured with all sorts of unusual dried puddles, red, black and brown. Although it was dark, Jim could see that Mort's face had changed into that of confusion and terror.

'It was here! It was right here; I saw it just the other night!'

'What was here, Mr Mort?' Tommy asked.

'The machine. That medical contraption!' Mort exclaimed.

Jim furrowed his brow. 'A contraption? What do you mean?'

'It looked like some kind of suit for a human to wear. It was completely white had these two glaring blue lights on the head, which I assume were meant to represent eyes or something? It was the inside that terrified me though. There were these…' it seemed like he was struggling to think back, '…needles. Sharp needles on tubes that looked as if they were meant to inject some kind of drugs into the wearer of the suit. I know it sounds crazy, but you've got to believe me, I know what I saw!'

Jim immediately thought back to the pinpricks in the victim's body and the drug in his bloodstream. 'I'm not doubting you yet, Mr Mort. Please continue.'

Mort's face scrunched up as he tried to think back. 'Well after that, I… I saw…' His face morphed into horror. 'I saw Brigson dragging someone. It was a woman's body, middle-aged I'm pretty sure. It looked like he was putting them into the suit. He must have heard me then because he instantly turned and stared straight at me. I tried to run but was hit hard in the face by a man holding some form of weapon.'

'There was another man?' Tommy asked. 'What did he look like?'

'Look, I don't know, Man! It was dark, and it all happened so fast. The next thing I remembered though, I was slumped in my office, and Brigson was standing above me. I questioned him about what I saw, the machine, the body, the man that knocked me out. Brigson just gave me this cold stare, said I was clearly insane. Told me… I was high.'

'High?'

'Yeah. He told me he'd found some drug in my possession. "Corpse-shaker," he said.'

Jim glanced at Tommy. 'So, you're an addict?'

'No! That's the thing. I'd never taken a drug in my life, but there he was, accusing me. I threatened to go to the police about it, but he warned me that you lot would think I was crazy, and then that you'd search my house and find some of "my drugs" there. I told him I didn't have any drugs. He just smiled. At that point, I realised what had happened. Brigson was trying to blackmail me into keeping my mouth shut. He knew I'd seen something, something he didn't want the police to know. That night I went to my house and sure enough, I found a box of needles under my bed, with a note saying that there'd be traces of the stuff all over my house. I would've said something sooner, but I was afraid people wouldn't believe me. When I saw you two here today, I thought I'd be able to show you, but… the machine's gone! It's vanished! You must think I'm crazy.'

'No, Mr Mort,' replied Tommy. 'We believe you. May I ask a question?'

'Of course.'

'You suspect this man killed somebody, yes? You saw him dragging a woman's body. But instead of threatening to kill you, or getting rid of you altogether, he just blackmails you? I hate to be blunt, but if he is a murderer, why not just kill you? And why keep you hired here?'

'To avoid further suspicion?' Mort suspected. 'Perhaps me missing, as well as his current disappearances around the workplace, would cause my colleagues to ask questions. Plus…' Mort hesitated. 'He said something else. Said he… *needed* me for something. Something important.'

Jim pondered on this. 'Perhaps it's because he wanted you to be here for when we arrived.'

'Don't be ridiculous, Jim,' Tommy reasoned. 'Otherwise, he wouldn't have blackmailed the guy in the first place.'

'No think about it, Tommy. What if Brigson *wanted* this man to just tell us? Just us! Thomas Knightley and James Griffen alone. He'd need to keep him alive so he could answer our questions, but equally, he couldn't have had him rushing off to the police station to tell them too early.'

'Jim that's insane, why would they want us and *only* us to know about this?'

'I don't know…' Jim whispered. Maybe it's like what I said in the lift. This has all been far too easy, Tommy. We know from the video that Brigson knew I'd be involved in this, right? Maybe his whole intention is to bring you and me right where *he* wants us to be.'

'And he knew you'd go off the book like this? Go into Signision without the police department?'

'He could've made a reasonable guess. Most members of the public would know with enough research that I don't like involving others in difficult cases. If he were the man I suspected he was earlier, then he would know better than most. So, if he were smart enough, he could predict that I'd try to investigate this building without Murdock or Mary's authority.' He approached his partner. 'This is worrying Tommy. I feel like we're just puppets in this, being pulled about by somebody else. Him and whoever he's working with. Perhaps he wants us to find him?'

'Or maybe,' said a deep, resonant British voice in the dark corner of the room, 'the man you are talking to is higher than a kite.'

The voice's owner emerged from the darkness, revealing a tall and slender person with deathly pale skin and squinted black eyes behind narrow glasses. He wore a once white, burnt, chemical stained lab coat that looked as if it had been fed into the gears of a machine. He put his hand out, expecting Jim to shake it. 'Sebastian Brigson,' he said, 'a pleasure to meet you.'

Jim stared at the outstretched hand cautiously, as if it were a kind of weapon. As for Mort, his face wore an expression purely of fear and dread, and he slowly shuffled back, pulling Jim and Tommy's coat sleeves to indicate his urgency to leave.

Brigson shot his hand back and placed it into his coat pocket, 'Ah, I see. I'm guessing he's told you the story, has he not? The one about me working on some secret project in the pipe room?'

'Well, you are in this very room with peculiar stains on your lab coat,' Tommy replied.

Brigson merely laughed. 'And I also see that you believe him! How extraordinary, and you call yourselves men of reason…'

'Do we call ourselves that?' Jim asked. 'I believe we call ourselves detectives, and it's a detective's job to listen to what petrified workers have to tell us about their rather suspicious bosses.'

The curious man smiled. 'Well, perhaps your job should also be to hear what the suspicious CEO has to say about his petrified worker, hm? Do you seriously think that I was working on a secret project in here? I think you'll find that I'm just fixing the boiler. Have you noticed how considerably chilly the upstairs rooms have been? As for the oil stains, one of our machines broke down recently. It's extremely annoying how we have to wait a whole month for temporaries.'

'Couldn't you call a plumber?' Jim asked, very suspicious.

'I could,' the man replied, 'but I find modern-day plumbers very clumsy. Last time we had one, he caused a flood in one of the labs upstairs. It destroyed so much machinery, you'd be shocked if you saw the cost of repair.' He rubbed his hands ponderously. 'If you'd like to know why my colleague is accusing me of such things, I could probably make a presumption, but first I would very much like it if you told me why you are here.'

Jim glanced at Tommy and then back at Brigson and answered. 'Well, this morning a body was found at St Mark's Harbour. It looked a strange suicide, but it turned out somebody had brutally murdered him and stolen one of the harbour's boats. According to our Medical Examiner, traces of the drug cylopatonine were found in the man's bloodstream. We did some digging and discovered that you've been ordering some very large batches of the stuff. Have any way to explain yourself?' Jim had made sure to leave out the part with the memory stick so that Brigson might let it slip that he knew something of it.

Brigson, relaxed as a man on the beach, just shook his head in what looked like some strange sort of shame. 'Jim, do you mind if I talk to you privately?'

Mort looked at him in utter terror as he walked over to the wall.

'Now Jim,' Brigson said quietly, 'I know that you only just met me, and that trust is extremely difficult after what he just told you, but I am not the bad guy here. You see, for a few months now, Mort has been going a bit… delusional? Should we say? He's been saying mad things about how I've been working on a secret project in here, but really, I've just been doing the plumbing. Initially I assumed it was down to the drinking, but now that you inform me that somebody has been buying "corpse-shaker" in my name, I'm starting to get a good idea of what's happening here.'

Jim smiled, 'that's an amazing cover story, but how do you explain the corpse-shaker in the body of the victim we found?'

Brigson pondered on this. 'Jim, was I the only customer that Blake was allegedly selling that drug to?'

Jim frowned. 'No.'

'Then why are you so certain it was me? Or should I say, why are you so certain it was Mort, given he bought the drug in my name.'

Jim cleared his throat. Would he bring up the fact that Brigson had similar attributes to his son's killer? Or that he suspected Brigson was The Phantom in the first place? He decided what he would say. 'That receptionist downstairs. She seemed quite afraid of you.'

Brigson laughed. 'Are you sure it wasn't the madman,

possible drug-addict, standing behind you that she was afraid of Mr Griffen?'

Just these few words infuriated Jim more than he had ever known. The man was either a very good liar or worse, telling the truth. Despite this, Jim kept his cool. He knew what had to be done. 'Well, we'll see, won't we? You're both under arrest. On suspicion of murder and drug use. We will take you back to the station for interrogation if that's all right with both of you.'

Tommy threw over a pair of handcuffs to Jim, who snapped them around the wrists of Sebastian Brigson. Brigson only responded with a look of annoyance and mild amusement.

Tommy then pulled out another pair of handcuffs and approached Johnathan Mort. 'I'm sorry Mr Mort, I'm afraid we're going to have to arrest you too on suspicion of drug use and wasting police time, just in case Brigson is telling the truth.'

'But I'm innocent!' Mort replied as Tommy snapped on his handcuffs.

'Perhaps,' said Tommy. 'But I'm afraid the *rules* say we can't trust either of you until you've both been questioned properly.' He winked at Jim. Jim requited with a sarcastic smirk.

***

September
2025

SAM
SEPTEMBER 10TH, 2025
THE EYES OF A MONSTER

'Remind me why we're here again?' Carlos asked.

They had just parked the car by the side of a lonely road, before briskly walking along the endless grey pavements. Sam was determined as to where he needed to go, his walk quick and certain. Carlos, however, seemed clueless as to why they were here, straggling behind and gazing around to understand his surroundings.

Sam rolled his eyes. 'Did you read the same note as I did?'

'Yeah.'

'And what did it say?'

Carlos tilted his head up as if to think back. 'That she was going to see her mother. But her mother's dead. That could mean…'

Sam smiled. 'I thought the same when I first read the note. Don't worry though, that girl was smart. She wanted us to know where she was, but she couldn't let "the monster" know. So… "I'm going to see mommy" probably means...' He turned to his left and gestured his arms outward to the park he was facing. 'She went here.'

Carlos looked up at the massive blue sign above him. 'Dayshine Park?'

Sam nodded. 'Her mother's ashes were scattered here, so we can assume she'll be here as well.'

The detectives jumped over a low black rail onto a large sea of autumn leaves, decorating the ground like brightly burning flames. Great trees sprouted from random areas of this fiery floor and brushed the misty grey sky with their half leaf-covered branches.

'Sam, this park is massive. How the hell are we meant to find the site where one woman's ashes are scattered?'

Sam squinted through the thick sea of fog that had engulfed the two of them, turning once or twice to check the area in which they were standing. 'We'll need to find some sort of tree or bench, possibly old, highly likely to stand out. If we're lucky, it'll have a plaque by it too.'

Carlos looked at him, baffled. 'That was a lot of uncertainty for one sentence. Besides, do you think we'd just find her hunched by a tree?'

'She's probably not here, Carlos. A young girl thinks she's being chased by a monster. Do you think she'd stay out in the open?"

'Then why the hell are we here?'

'Because,' Sam replied, 'I have a hunch that she left us a message. To help find her.'

Carlos thought about this and nodded slowly. 'A hunch?' he then asked.

'Yep,' Sam said, 'but let's face it, what other leads do we have? We better start looking before it gets dark.'

'It's pretty dark already!'

Sam sighed and pulled two torches out of his pocket, throwing one to Carlos. 'Here, I found these in the car. Call me if you find anything.' He walked off into the heavy grey, leaving a bothered Carlos behind him, motionless.

'Okay then,' his partner shouted, 'I guess I'll do this side of the park.'

Sam laughed quietly. This would take a while.

***

'Sam, this is ridiculous!' Carlos shouted a few metres away, barely distinguishable in the mist. 'Completely and utterly ridiculous! Two hours of carefully analysing every single damn tree in this damn park. I can see why everybody loves this job so-'

Sam saw him freeze in front of a large oak tree. A smile slithered onto his face. 'Sam, get your ass over here. I've found it!'

Sam ran over to his partner and spotted a golden plaque nailed into the tree. It read:

In Loving Memory of Clara Williams.

Beloved mother and wife.

May she rest in peace.

'This is it!' Sam exclaimed.

Carlos shot a look over to him. 'Yeah, thanks man, I'm well aware this is it, I'm the one who…' He stopped mid-speech and crouched down over the dirt. He burrowed through about a centimetre and revealed a small tea-coloured ball of scrunched paper. He unfolded it to reveal a scrawled handwritten message.

'She's left a message for us,' Sam stated. 'What does it say?'

Carlos read out the letter.

Dear Sadie,

I know I haven't written in a long while, but you must forgive me; the less close other people thought we were, the better. My only regret about giving myself over was leaving you on your own, but the law is the law, and despite my intentions, I had to pay for my crimes. I do hope you find it in your heart to forgive me.

I now fear that one of these men is looking for me, or rather the stone, once again. I was warned about this by one of the new inmates, so I made my escape, and now I am on the run. You must understand why I couldn't come to see you now that I am outside of jail. The risk on your life would be far greater than you could imagine.

If you do find yourself in danger, Sadie, come straight to me at our special spot. Do not go to the police! It is my belief that some of the bad people chasing me are working at the police department, and they'll come for you if it means getting to me and my dangerous possessions. I could not risk losing you.

Good luck, my little petal,

Dad.

Sam frowned. 'I don't like this at all… What he said about bad people in the police department?'

Carlos shrugged. 'He might have been mistaken or something?'

Sam eyed him carefully. 'Well,' he said, 'you know what we have to do now, don't you?'

'Find her dad? Yeah, this should be fun. At least we know he's an ex-convict with the surname of Williams.'

Sam laughed. It couldn't be. 'Michael Williams?' he proposed.

'The famous escapee? Could be. It wouldn't be the weirdest thing to happen in this cit-'

Suddenly they were interrupted by a whirring noise a few metres behind them. Both officers immediately swivelled round to face the origin of this sound. They squinted, pressing their eyes through the heavy fog.

Carlos spotted something. 'Hello? Who is that?'

Sam quickly saw it too. It was the outline of a person, but it was unusual. Disfigured. As well as this, it was unusually tall and large in shoulder span. But there was something else. Something was illuminating this creature in the grey fog. Dug into its head were two luminescent, glaring red eyes.

In the space of a few moments, his throat had become sandpaper, his legs ice blocks. 'I thought Sadie was… exaggerating about the eyes.'

But Carlos didn't hear him. His face was deathly pale, blending well with the surrounding mist, and he just stared in horror at the creature. 'S-S-Sam! Look at its arm! Look at its left arm!'

Sam looked down to the left arm of this beast, and he too was flooded with the fear that Carlos had felt. It looked as if this figure had half its forearm cut clean off, and that it was replaced with numerous, spindly, thin tentacles, tangled in each other's grip. Every so often, tiny flashes of fiery white lights would buzz from one of these tentacles, flickering and dancing in the air before they fell to the floor like sparks and fizzled away into nothing.

The officers were frozen in fear, but the creature kept on plodding - heavy feet thumping against the forest floor. Every time it moved a leg, the creature made a strange whirring noise, as if its joints were old and creaking.

'W-what do you want?' Sam asked in a desperate attempt to be brave.

The creature stopped and tilted its oval head, slowly analysing him. It replied with a deep scratchy groan. 'You know what I need, detectives. You already know who I'm chasing. Even amateurs should be able to work that out.'

Carlos screamed, terrified. 'What... *are you?*'

The creature made some grunts reminiscent of laughter. 'Carlos Rodriguez? Scared? How could a man be so scared after all the hell you've gone through?' He made a sort of laughing noise when he saw Carlos' face. 'Yes, I know everything about you. Who you are, where you're from, what you're hiding. Oh yes, I know your secrets, just like your former captain. Such a shame that he was killed before he could tell everyone. I hope you won't do the same for me!'

Suddenly an enraged Carlos whipped out his gun and shot repeatedly at the beast. Sam gazed in shock as Sadie's monster kept on walking towards them, slowly at first, but gradually increasing in pace.

Sam decided he should probably have done the same, so he too started shooting at the creature, but even double the firepower did not deter the raging monster. Realising their guns were no use, Sam tugged Carlos on the shoulder and sprinted out of the park. Carlos was hesitant, but followed all the same, and tried his best to limp at Sam's pace until they reached the edge of the park. They could hear the creature's continuous groaning and whirring, but eventually, it began to sound fainter to them. Once at the edge of the park, they jolted over the outer fence and made for their car, ready to get as far from Dayshine Park as possible.

For a while, none of them decided to talk but instead

collected their thoughts in the long drumming of the rain.

'So,' Sam said, breaking the long silence, 'do you get things as weird as that all the time?'

Carlos laughed. 'You'd be surprised.'

***

SAM
SEPTEMBER 10TH, 2025
THE MYSTERIOUS EMAIL

'I'm telling you, Captain; we know what we saw!'

They were back at their claustrophobic office, having just driven through half an hour of rain. Both detectives were shivering, and Sam for one felt cold and shaken. Murdock seemed bemused by the detectives' story.

The chief smirked, his eyes rolling in disbelief. 'What's your partner got you taking, Turner? Same stuff as him? Your delusions are just as crazy, I'll give you that!'

'I'm telling the truth!' Sam exclaimed, glancing back to Carlos for support. Carlos slumped back on the office chair in silence, staring entranced into the distance.

Murdock shook his head and approached the door. 'Well, it would seem Rodriguez isn't piping up for once. Perhaps a monster in a park is too much of a stretch – even for him. I dread our next encounter, detectives…' And with that, Murdock briskly strolled out of the office.

Sam threw his arms up into the air in frustration and slumped into the chair in the corner of the room. 'Thanks for the support, Buddy!'

'Yeah, don't mention it,' Carlos said, still entranced.

Sam scowled in quiet disbelief. 'Could we just talk about what happened for a second? You're being awfully quiet about the whole thing!' Sam asked.

Carlos slumped into the office chair. 'What more is there to say I guess…'

'How about, "what was that thing?"'

Even after replaying the moment several times in his head, Sam still couldn't comprehend what had happened at the park, or what it was that he saw. For some reason, the notion of it being a human seemed far more absurd than any alternative, but Sam wanted it to be true. For all his life he had followed the facts and stuck to logic – not once holding onto superstition, or the belief of something that could not be proven. Now that he had seen something unexplainable in the flesh, however… well, he didn't feel too certain about anything anymore.

Carlos shrugged. He was staring intently at the office computer screen, madly clicking around the pages that he found. 'Sadie's monster, I guess, why does that matter?'

Sam was stunned. 'How are you being so nonchalant about what we saw? Didn't you see its eyes? I know you saw its arm!'

Carlos sighed. 'People get shocked about things because their experience of the world tells them what they saw wasn't possible. You get shocked when you see what looks like a monster in a park because you've never seen anything like that before in your life.'

'And you have?' Sam queried.

'No. But I just figure that if I see it, it can't be impossible, therefore I should stop being so damn worried about it and get on with what needs to be done.'

'Well, won't understanding what that was help us find Sadie?' Sam proposed.

'Not when we know barely anything about what it was we saw. I doubt we'd find much about a child's monster on an internet search, and two detectives can't exactly go around *asking* about it either. What we need to do now is find Sadie's dad so we can find Sadie. Feel better?'

Sam glared at Carlos in annoyance. 'No, not really.' In truth, Sam knew his partner was right; he did need to focus on what was important. 'Her dad. Is he who we thought?'

Carlos nodded. 'Michael Williams it is. Who knew we would be chasing the daughter of the most wanted man in this department?'

Two months ago, around the same time as the conviction of the "Nightdrop Backstabber," there was the Williams escape. Michael Williams was locked away at Stormfeld Prison in the October of 2024 for stealing a large sum of food from a local supermarket. It wasn't a major crime, allegedly he was doing it to help his daughter, but it had earned him a full year behind bars. But on the same day that the Backstabber was taken to the prison to stay between court trials, two months before he would have been freed regardless, Williams went missing - vanishing in the dead of night with another inmate. Some said the two events were connected, but people were told not to jump to conclusions, especially when barely any details were known about the original escape.

'Yeah, why is it we're tasked with finding the daughter and not the man himself?' Sam asked, bemused.

'We've got better guys for that job,' Carlos replied. When he saw the look on Sam's face he backtracked. 'Not that we couldn't pull it off, Sam, it's just you're new and I'm crippled.'

'You've got a bad foot.'

'Exactly, crippled.'

Sam laughed. 'So, can we contact the prison? Ask around?'

'Yeah, Murdock's sorting that out for us. He may be a completely self-centred jerk, but he's quite persuasive.'

Sam nodded in amusement.

'I'm sure the other guys working on Williams' case won't mind,' Carlos continued. 'So far they've been stumped on the whole thing so anything we find will be good news for them.' He sighed. 'By the way… we're probably going to have to work out how some of the escape was done to find Williams, right?'

'Yeah…'

'Well, you know how people offer to help you in return for favours. I was thinking… perhaps… we could ask to talk to the Backstabber?'

Sam sensed something was up. 'Why would you want to do that Carlos?'

Carlos looked anxious. 'Well think about it, people have been suspecting for a while that the Backstabber's arrival at the prison and the escape were linked somehow. Perhaps he'll have some useful information that can help us.'

Sam raised an eyebrow.

'Why are you staring at me like that?'

'Because I know why you want to talk to this guy. Carlos, I

know he saved your life, but one good action doesn't just take away all the bad that he's done.'

Carlos frowned. 'You don't *know* that he's done anything wrong!' There was a razor-sharp edge to his voice, and Sam saw a fuming red rising in his cheeks.

'Okay, Carlos, let's talk seriously for a minute. I never knew this Backstabber guy personally. Hell, I don't even know his real name, but what I do know is that he was filmed killing a guy, his confession was recorded by his now-deceased partner, he led a bunch of police officers to their death, and witness accounts mentioned him falling prey to "outbursts of anger." Sure, he saved you, but how do you know that he didn't just do it to look innocent? The facts don't lie, Carlos, they just don't, and if I'm honest, I hope that man gets three life sentences.'

He instantly saw that he'd said too much. Carlos looked as if he were about to throw a chair in his direction. 'How can you say that?' his partner questioned madly. 'How can you talk about the facts after what you saw and heard today? I looked up to him, Sam! I would have followed him to hell and back after he saved my life.'

And then the penny dropped. All the remarks about the old missing persons captain, the defence of the Backstabber, the lack of surprise when faced with Sadie's monster, and the reason the Backstabber had saved Carlos in the first place all came together now. Suddenly Sam's partner looked so much more different to him than the kind, open man he had met at the start of his career. 'To hell and back?' Sam asked.

Carlos looked slightly taken aback at the way Sam had said that question. 'Yes.'

Sam smiled through the sudden rage that had just filled up inside of him. 'You know, that's so strange. First, that monster mentions something about you having something to do with the absence of the old missing persons captain, and then you continue to stick up for your "friend" who just so happens to be a convicted murderer. Why don't we dig a little deeper? What if the reason why you're so chilled out about a little girl's monster appearing in a park is that you know something that I don't? How does that sound, Carlos?'

Carlos glared at Sam disgustedly. 'Completely delusional. Sam, are you out of your mind? I'm just a detective, like you!'

'Then perhaps you'd like to tell me a bit more about the last missing persons captain.' Sam approached his partner closely, so that they were barely a hair apart from each other. 'Tell me, Carlos, what did your old captain do for you to hate him so much?'

Carlos cleared his throat and glared into Sam's eyes. 'I can't believe you seriously believe that… thing in the park. But I tell you what, he was half right. One thing always bugged me about the old captain; he always stuck his nose in areas where he shouldn't have. It would be such a shame if someone I worked with were to do that again!' Carlos rose and stormed out of the office.

Sam breathed out heavily as the door slammed. He wasn't finished though. He had to check he was right. Luckily for him, Carlos had left in such a rage that he had forgotten to log out of his computer.

Sam walked over and closed down all the open web browsers still left on the screen. Then he opened up everything he needed. File storage, email, notepad. If Carlos had written anything suspicious, he needed to know. Then he proceeded to the search bars, typing in anything that could help him, such as "Backstabber" (a futile effort that only ended in dozens of news reports), "disaster" (Sam knew it was a long shot, but there could have been information about Carlos' injury), or even "Sadie." Finally, after typing in "Graham," the name of the old missing persons captain, Sam found what he wanted.

It was a chain of two emails, between Carlos and the captain himself. Sam studied each message carefully, trying intensely not to miss any details.

The captain's first email began like this:

I have discovered your little secret. I saw what you were doing last night, and it repulses me. I am ashamed that one of my detectives has fallen from grace in such a way. Yet if you're lucky, I may decide not to tell the others about this.

All you need to do, detective, is two little tasks for me. Every week, you bring me a sum of money from your wages. A decent wedge will do, considering how much I know you want to keep this quiet. In addition to this, you will be my eyes and ears, telling me everything that people say and do in this police department. Nothing gets past me. Should you fail to do this, or tell anybody about my message, I tell everybody you hold dear. Every man, woman and child in the city will know the truth, after all, I'm sure this will be big news.

Make the right decision Carlos,

Your captain.

Carlos replied in six words:

You've messed with the wrong man.

Sam sat back and rested his hands on his aching head. *Okay…* he thought, *they're both twisted bastards.* His head was whizzing, unsure of what to do, what to say. Would this be enough evidence to put forward? What if he was wrong, or worse, right? If Carlos had done something atrocious to the captain, and if even an experienced police officer couldn't stop him, then how could Sam?

You have the upper hand, Sam thought. *He doesn't know you've seen the email.*

He knows I'm on to him though, the other side of Sam's brain replied. *God, I wish I'd kept my mouth shut!* Perhaps Carlos would refrain from doing anything to Sam, lest it would look too suspicious. *He can't know I'm on to him. I just have to pretend I just freaked out after seeing the thing in the park and he'll think everything's okay.*

He heard footsteps outside, before the slamming of a door and the revving of a car engine. Looking out the windows Sam saw Carlos getting into his car, a dark look on his face, before beginning to drive away.

I need to follow him, Sam thought. *I have to know what he's up to.*

And so, he did. Sam sprinted downstairs to the car park as fast as he could. And then it was one detective chasing after another.

***

SADIE
SEPTEMBER 10TH, 2025
ON THE RUN

How much longer?

Sadie gasped for air as she stopped again, this time in a dark gloomy alleyway. She was lucky no strange people were drinking here this time around, but the area still made her afraid. It was getting dark now, and there were graffiti eyes on the walls that seemed to be watching her every move.

She had been running on and off for over a day, unaware as to who she was truly running from. Was it the monster? That thing was certainly frightening enough to send most eleven-year-old girls far away. Or was it the detectives? Her father had warned her that most of them were dangerous, and that if they found her, they may ask her about where the known convict Michael Williams had escaped to.

Or perhaps she was running to something; her father himself. It had been months since she'd been able to see him last, and even longer since she had given him so much as a hug. Prison rules were strict when it came to meet-ups, especially with kids. For long lonely nights, she would think about her father. Where he was, what he was doing, if he was safe from police and criminals alike. Sometimes she would dream about seeing him again. Running onto that field to find him standing there, his arms wide open, ready to embrace her with open arms.

But she'd have to get there first. And that meant travelling ten more miles with a monster at her heels.

Sadie could never work out how it always found her, but it caught up nonetheless. If she ran, it would walk, if she stopped, it would walk. Stop for too long, even in the remotest of locations, and the monster would never be too far behind. She'd certainly had a few close calls, like the time she had to jump off a first-floor balcony to escape it, only to have her fall broken by a canopy. Or the time she tried sleeping in a one-way alley and awoke right before it got to her. You could never be too careful in Nightdrop. Sadie couldn't at least.

Suddenly a large crash sounded from behind her. Sadie jolted around, expecting to find the red-eyed monster waiting there. Fortunately, she only saw a small raccoon climbing out of a dustbin.

'Hey little guy…' she beckoned the creature. 'Come on over here.'

The raccoon glared at her warily for a few moments, before plodding closer towards her. At first, it hissed when she put her hand out, but curiosity got the better of it, and soon it was sniffing her all over.

Sadie giggled when it did this. 'I suppose we're not too different,' she said to it. 'Both of us are forced to eat scraps and run away from those who are bigger than us…' Now the raccoon was affectionately rubbing its face on her trouser leg. Sadie didn't think she'd ever seen one so friendly.

There was a loud rumble, and the creature jumped back slightly. Sadie heard it too but knew exactly where it came from. 'I'm just hungry,' she told the creature. She had been hungry all day, only once stopping to eat some scraps from a dustbin. That had certainly been a mistake, considering the stomach-ache that followed for hours afterwards. She soldiered on though, driven by the fact that she was being chased by a murderous monster. It would be a good distance away now – perhaps she had evaded all together! Part of her doubted that, however. No matter how far the place, no matter how obscure, the monster always seemed to find her.

'You're not safe,' she told her racoon friend. 'Everywhere I go, this thing follows. Do you really want it to catch you when you're not fast enough to even catch me up?'

The creature just stared into her eyes, almost mournfully.

She sighed. 'That means go. Get as far away from me as possible.'

With a small whine, the racoon tried approaching her once more.

'Go!' she shouted.

The animal almost glared at her, but there was sadness in its face too.

Sadie shared its feelings. This raccoon, this dumb street animal knew exactly how she felt – what it was like to be chased away and treated like vermin. But she wouldn't lead it to slaughter. *It probably won't live long without me anyway*, she thought.

Just as she considered changing her mind, a gunshot resonated from behind and a bullet passed straight through the animal.

Sadie screamed and turned. There, at the back of the alley, stood the monster. Most of its body was cast in shade, but she could still see its worst features. The pale body, white as bone, the twisted tentacles on its left arm and the glowing crimson eyes that shot a penetrating gaze in her direction.

'Why would you do that? You sick freak!'

The creature tilted its head in what was almost confusion. 'What? Kill a street animal?' From its throat came a horrible airy wheezing noise, almost reminiscent of laughter. 'Animals are animals, girl, humans are humans. Not that it makes a difference to me when I need one dead.'

'And what are you then?' she questioned. 'Are you an animal or a human?'

The machine paused for thought. 'I was human once. But I don't think I class as animal *or* human anymore. I'm... superior.'

'You think you're some kind of god?' she questioned mockingly.

'No,' it replied. If it had a mouth, it would have been smiling in that very instant. 'I was thinking more... the Devil.'

The creature began to stomp fiercely towards her, sending panic through her nervous system. For a few eternal moments Sadie could not move – her body frozen like a corpse. Fortunately, the rational side of her brain kicked in, and adrenaline soon followed. The moment her limbs loosened up, she bolted away from the monster, leaving its grasp just centimetres away from her arm.

It could kill me right now, she thought. *Even if I run, it could disintegrate me like how it disintegrated that raccoon.*

But the machine didn't disintegrate her. Instead, she carried on running, one step after another. Even when she was blocks away, Sadie would not stop. After passing a post office, she spotted a bridge spanning over the river. *Once I cross that I'll stop*, she thought. *I'll be safe then.*

Once she was merely halfway across, however, Sadie grabbed the railing and brought herself to a sudden halt. Her stomach lurched and soon she was retching over the bridge, all while attempting to gasp for oxygen. *No*, she thought. *Don't stop, it's not safe.* Then the world started going fuzzy and grey, and she felt her limbs fall under her like they were made of paper.

When she came back into consciousness, she was still alone but was clueless as to how long she'd been out. Sure, she was still alive, but the monster always seemed to know where to find her. How would she stop it from finding her again?

I have to find Dad, she thought. *He'll know how to stop this thing. He'll keep me safe.* She looked to her right. There, across the river, was the forest. Although most of the area on the other side belonged to the national park, there were a few acres of land belonging to the city where construction was perfectly allowed. The farm would be over there, the one where her father was hiding the stone. That was where she needed to go.

And then she heard the whirring once more.

'Go away!' she screamed as she spotted the monster on the city side of the bridge.

The monster seemed to pay no attention to her but instead brought out what looked like a large, luminescent, indigo blade. Sadie had no idea what it was, but it danced and flickered in the dark as if it were made of purple fire. The monster glanced up at her almost mockingly before bringing the blade down on the metal of the bridge rail.

What followed was an awful hissing sound, accompanied by the sight of smoke and molten metal oozing from the cut being made. The blade was melting the rail, slicing through it as if it were a vegetable.

She then understood.

Without hesitation, Sadie began to sprint to the forest edge of the bridge. The loud hissing continued behind her like a massive snake, threatening its prey. Glancing back, she saw that the monster had already cut through the entire rail and was slicing his knife through the base. *If he cuts that, I'm dead,* she thought, as she glanced over to the raging river below the bridge.

So, she kept running, her footsteps pounding over the resounding base of the bridge. The hissing too continued, pushing her fear – making her move faster. Eventually, however, the hissing began to quieten, and the end of the bridge was getting closer. *Just a few more steps*, she thought. *Just a few more steps and I'll be over.*

The bridge collapsed from beneath her.

In her blind panic, Sadie flailed her limbs in all directions, desperately searching for something to grab. A single moment before she hit the water, she caught a broken segment of railing from the bridge and swung viciously into the river's icy depths.

It hit her like a freight train, the icy cold waters excruciatingly painful against her young body. For what felt like years, Sadie clambered tightly onto the segment of railing, her face barely above the water, choking for air. She was floating at a rapid rate, and she knew that she would die within minutes if she didn't find a way out soon.

The railing hit the bank for a single moment, but a moment was all she needed. She launched herself at the bank with whatever strength remaining within her and grasped for something, anything. Her foot slipped beneath her, and for a second she thought she was a goner, but then her hand found a root in the river cliff, and she was able to keep her toes above the water. After a fit of spluttering and a long clamber to the dry land, Sadie had made it out of the river. She was safe.

Not for long, she thought. She glanced back at the bridge and noticed that the monster was no longer there. *There are other bridges*, she thought. *It's still chasing me!*

So, after barely any time to recover from her close meeting with death, Sadie ran again.

***

July
2025

JIM
JULY 10TH, 2025
THE SECOND MURDER

Once again, Jim woke to the loud hammering of Thomas Knightley at his door. He groaned drearily.

'Good morning, Jim! How did you sleep?'

Jim tried to think back to his sleep last night, or even the previous evening, but nothing could be plucked out of his memory. 'I'm… not too sure.'

'Ah!' Tommy expressed with understanding. 'Makes sense – another heavy drinking night? You know, you really need to stop going to the pub every night.'

'How do you kn-'

'Oh. Who's that?'

Jim turned around to see a small, scrawny looking, brown-haired boy. For a good while, Jim couldn't put his finger on who this boy was, for his facial features and bodily proportions were far more disproportionate from the boy he once knew. 'Daddy?' the boy asked.

Jim stood motionless and shocked at the sight of his son. Suddenly, two shadow-like arms broke through the wall and grabbed the boy firmly by the arm and shoulder.

'You could have saved me,' he said in a strangely calm voice, before being pulled away into the wall.

'Jake!' Jim shouted, running to where his son was. He looked around as the house rumbled, bits of the ceiling crumbling. He could see that the sky had turned purple and felt the wind was lashing out against him.

'You're too late, Jim,' said Tommy. His eyes were completely black. 'Why didn't you save him?'

The figure of Tommy burst into wisps of darkness. Behind him, the headlights of a truck shot bright beams into his eyes, while the truck's horn blared fiercely. He heard a huge crunch above him and looked up as the ceiling of his house dropped down onto his body.

Then all that remained was darkness. 'I will return, Jim,' said a British man's voice. 'I will return.'

He immediately jolted upwards from his bed, his forehead dripping with sweat. His house was fine, Tommy and Jake were not here, and it was a Thursday. Jim cursed as he remembered the events of the day prior. Mary had approached him when he reached the station and had asked him to hand his badge back. He'd then begged her not to make him leave, pointing out the progress they'd made in getting Brigson and Mort, and that confronting the drug gang had been a mistake. She'd sighed and said he was lucky that she didn't try to arrest him, but ultimately dismissed him, asking him to hand his badge in at the front desk.

There was a noise which he was too shocked to understand. It was a beeping… or a ringing.

His phone.

He hopped out of bed, walked over to his phone and answered the call.

'Jim. Where the hell are you? Did Knightley not pick you up?'

Jim frowned.

'You only just woke up? Don't you know what happened?'

Jim realised it was the captain's voice on the other end. 'Jeez Mary, it's only…' he checked the time on the phone and frowned, 'eleven… are you still mad at me for going missing the other day?'

'Jim, it's not always about you! Check your damn TV! Listen, I've got to go, but I just wanted to check that you knew.' She hung up the phone.

Jim sprinted downstairs to his living room and turned on his television. The first channel that came up was the Nightdrop City News Channel.

An elderly lady on the television was speaking, '-and it had these shining blue eyes. It stared at me like it was looking into my soul or something.'

Jim read the title;

Police Department Infiltrated, Suspect Murdered.

***

Jim arrived to see the police station surrounded by a swarm of journalists and reporters, some in front of cameras, some writing in notepads, others looking up in shock at what had happened. By the main entrance, Jim spotted a smashed window, so utterly shattered that it looked as if a giant could have walked through. There was something else. Directly in front of the chaotic crowds, blocked only by striped police tape, was a scarlet puddle of blood. Jim sprinted over to another officer who was writing notes. The officer glanced up at him solemnly.

'What happened?' Jim asked.

The officer continued to stare at him glumly for a moment or two, before starting to speak. 'There was a break-in… well, a breakout. A man in a mask and… well, something that all of our witnesses are struggling to describe, got into the police station last night. Four men and five women were incapacitated and… they took some people.'

'Who?' Jim asked. 'Brigson?'

'No,' the man replied, 'Johnathan Mort and… that other woman.'

Jim felt a headache coming on as anxiety rose in his body. Johnathan Mort. One of his two only leads. Taken by something… he wasn't sure what. And that receptionist, the one he'd promised to protect. She'd been kidnapped, just like that. 'Where's Brigson?' he asked. 'Is Brigson still at the police station.'

'Yes,' the man replied, 'still in custody, but he won't talk. The only thing he's said is that he wants to talk to you.'

Jim's head was racing. *Why wouldn't the Circle rescue Brigson if what Mort said was true?* 'Well that can hold,' Jim replied. 'Whether they want me here or not, I'm going to help find Mort.'

The officer looked down to the ground and made a small sigh. 'Jim,' he said before a long pause. 'They found him.' There was a silence between the two as Jim stared at him, puzzled. 'Him and that woman working as a receptionist. They were found on St Matthew's Lane. Skin cold. Eyes wide open. Small… pinpricks in their neck.'

Jim just stared at the officer with a blank expression. 'No,' he said. 'I… no. Th- they can't. They can't…' Jim tried to find his words, but all that came out was a jumble of stutters and mixed letters. His head felt like a lead weight, while his body felt flimsy like paper. He slowly rocked. Back and forth. Back and forth. Before falling backwards, the world around him darkening as he fainted from the shock.

Everything was dark now. He heard many voices. Tommy. Mort. Brigson. Jake. That receptionist who he'd promised to protect. They were all muffled, but he could tell that they were saying the same thing. 'You failed.' He had failed. He couldn't stop failing to protect the people around him There was nothing he could do to save Jake. To save Mort. The receptionist or even the man at the harbour. Jim had never helped anybody.

His eyes flickered open. A deep rage consumed him, and he immediately knew exactly what he'd do next. 'Jim?' the officer asked. 'Are you all right?'

Jim pushed himself off the ground, wiped the dust off his body and looked towards the doors of the police department. Before he could go in however, he heard the hum of a police car. He turned to see Tommy, Mary and another woman that he knew all too well stepping out of the vehicle across the road. Tommy gave Jim a look of pity and sadness, but Jim merely looked down to the ground, took a deep breath, and turned away from them to talk to the officer. 'Make sure the medical examiner scans both this blood and the blood of the victim, do you understand?'

'Yes sir,' the man replied.

'And don't call me sir,' Jim added, 'Even if I was still a detective, I'd have no higher authority than you, officer.' With that, he headed into the police department and walked directly towards the interrogation room.

Jim was quick to find Brigson inside. His head was bowed but donned a sinister, icy smirk. Jim looked down to see a small device which was transmitting and recording everything that happened in the room. He switched it off, along with the cameras displaying multiple videos on the monitors to his left, and walked inside.

Brigson did not look up. It was as if he'd been expecting this to happen. 'Mr Griffen…'

'All right then, Brigson,' Jim said. 'Nobody knows we're in here, so as far as I'm concerned, I can do whatever the hell I like. So, tell me. What do you know about this thing everyone's talking about? The one that killed Johnathan Mort?'

Brigson smiled. 'If you get me out of here and take me back to Signision,' he said calmly, 'I'll show you.'

***

'So, are you going to tell me what's going on,' Jim asked as they walked down the winding corridors of Signision Robotics, 'or am I going to have to force it out of you?'

Brigson chuckled. 'Oh Jim. I promise you; you won't believe a bit of what I tell you.'

'Try me!' he snapped.

Brigson rolled his eyes. 'All right then, I'll spill everything. A year ago, this company was in the process of developing a new medical machine, a robot capable of scanning, identifying and treating any medical problems that an individual might have had. It was new and unheard of and even gained intrigue from the military for me to develop a weaponized version for the battlefield, with an A.I. capable of identifying and shooting the enemy while saving and healing its allies. It could even be worn as a suit, with a bulletproof shell, arm guns and charged energy beams, meaning even the wounded could fight. It was genius… but then the Circle came…'

Jim furrowed his brow. 'The Circle of Saints?'

Brigson nodded sadly. 'Yes. A few months ago, while the machine was nearing the end of its development, they came to me, believing they could use the machine for a "greater purpose." They even offered me a great deal of money for it too, but I, being an honest man, refused.'

Jim frowned suspiciously.

'The Circle of Saints, however, are not a group to be denied, and so they stole my project. One of them must be an expert in computer programming because it seems they have found a way to confuse its code. Now, if the machine sees any human being except for any of them, it will kill them. I assume that's why you found so much cylopatonine in the body you were investigating.'

'So, you admit to owning the drug?'

Brigson laughed, 'Of course. The healing properties of that chemical are incredible. It was essential that we had some for our project. Sadly, Mort got a little too familiar with the stuff – I wasn't lying about what I said earlier, you know?'

When they reached the entrance to the boiler room, Jim thought over all that had been said. 'Hang on… if you used corpse-shaker for healing people, then why did they give it to the body?'

Brigson smiled. 'That's the golden question, Jim. And I think I have an answer.'

Jim opened the door with suspicion and the two-walked in.

'Do you know much about the Circle of Saints, Jim?'

'I know that they're that religious group who supposedly

founded the city. I didn't think they really existed though. What was it they were looking for again, a magic stone?'

Brigson laughed. 'Not all stories should be taken at face value, Jim. The stone that they look for in the story could give its holder eternal life and magnificent power. It's a metaphor. They want eternal life and power, that's all. It's pretty obvious once you look at their motto. *"Perire finite non est."* Death is not the end.'

Jim stumbled as his foot tripped on a loose grate in the floor. The room was dimly lit, and it felt like there were dangers all around. 'What are you suggesting? That they're trying to raise the dead?'

Brigson gave Jim a cold stare.

'You can't be serious.' Jim was shocked to find a grave look on Brigson's face. 'It's not possible!'

'It doesn't need to be possible if it's being tried by lunatics,' Brigson responded calmly. 'Let me show you what I'm talking about.'

They kept walking through the maze of pipes until they reached the boiler that Jim had seen earlier. They stepped behind it and found themselves in the cell-sized area once again.

'This was where I used to keep it!' Brigson said, almost in awe of his recollections. 'It was beautiful. After the majority of board members decided to shut down the project, I worked on it in secret here. Improving the weapons, adjusting the healing, reprogramming its A.I. over and over. Here, you can look at the file.' Brigson approached an almost completely hidden vent in the corner of the space and pulled it straight off. He bent down, pulled out a dusty coffee-stained file and handed it over to Jim. On the front, written in bold capital letters, was one word. "**LAZARUS.**"

Jim opened the dusty old cover to reveal a set of numerous photographs bound together. The first was an annotated drawing of a body that could have been defined as humanoid, were its features not so obscure and out of proportion. The torso was abnormally large, seeming to tighten around the back as it stretched all the way around. Contrastingly, the limbs were long and spindly, as if they belonged to a mechanical spider, attached to the torso by a small cylinder tube and a few thick wires. The feet were boot-like, large and rounded, presumably providing much room for the foot of the individual inside. And the head was a peculiar oval shape, which was divided in two by a line that cut straight through the centre lengthways- as if it were made from two large puzzle pieces that were welded together and stuck onto the neck. What Jim found the most disturbing, however, was what was on the head. Two perfectly circular eyes, equally spaced from the line in the middle, with minuscule black cameras in the lowest inner corners. As Jim stared at them on the diagram, he felt the peculiar feeling a child might have when alone in the dark. The feeling of haunting that can make a person toss and turn infinitely in the night-time. The feeling of demons entering one's mind, and a monster grasping at one's soul.

Jim quickly turned the page and saw another diagram, this time revealing the machine when opened up. Both halves of the face were folded out and back, and the body was opened up, with half an arm and half a leg open at the edges of each torso. Inside were numerous syringes and wires, each protruding from the back. On this drawing, annotations linked to the wires and syringes said things such as, *contains adrenaline*, *contains morphine*, *contains cylopatonine.*

Jim rubbed his forehead. 'This can't be…'

'Possible?' Brigson asked. 'What's impossible about an android killing a lawyer? Machines have been on the rise for years now Jim, it was inevitable that one day someone would mess with its code and-'

'Lawyer,' Jim said.

'Excuse me?'

'You said lawyer. You shouldn't have known that the man was a lawyer.'

Brigson's face straightened.

'And… Mort said he saw you dragging a body into the machine… and now Mort's dead.'

Brigson turned to the wall in frustration and laughed. 'Damn… I am a terrible liar, Jim. I really ought to learn from my colleagues.'

The penny dropped. 'The Circle of Saints didn't steal your invention, did they?' Jim asked. 'They paid you a large sum of money and you started working for them.'

Brigson smiled. 'Yeah, I did. It didn't take too much money, actually. The whole prospect of keeping my project from the destruction of others was enticement enough. After all, you'd do anything to protect your child, wouldn't you? Now I get to work on it while getting paid to do so.'

'By experimenting with dead bodies?'

'Well, I'm not the one who killed them. My partner, he does that. I just put them in the machine afterwards.'

'You're a monster!'

'Why so Jim?' Brigson asked. 'Worse things have been done in the pursuit of science.'

'And that makes it all right?'

'If the end outweighs the means, then yes I believe it does!'

'They were good people!'

'How do you know; you only saw the last three!'

Jim stared at the mad scientist for what felt like a millennium of silence.

'Oh… you didn't know.' Brigson started cackling maniacally. 'You thought that dumb lawyer was the first murder? No, of course not, we've been doing this for months!'

'Months?'

'Well, yes… hasn't your wife been telling you about the huge spike in missing people recently? Then again, I suppose you haven't talked to her too much since-'

Then Jim was ploughing into Brigson like a wild boar. He thrust the scientist against the wall, his hands closing around the scientist's throat.

'Then why didn't you just hide these bodies, huh?' Jim asked. 'Why did you leave them out in the open for us to find when you could have disposed of them like the others?'

Brigson smiled. 'Because we needed your attention, Jim. Why else would we make his suicide so obscure? It was to bring you back.'

'For what?'

'The end of all our plans. The grand conclusion. The *Rebirth of Nightdrop*.'

'Jim!' shouted a woman from behind him.

It was a voice he knew too well. 'What are you doing here Lynda?'

She stepped forward. 'How about stopping you from murdering our only witness?'

He looked around behind him and saw that she was standing beside Tommy and Mary, who both shared her look of concern. 'I'm interrogating him.'

'I'm not sure that's the way you're meant to do it,' said Mary.

'Well, in case you'd forgotten,' Jim replied, 'I'm *not* a police officer!'

'Which is why you shouldn't be touching *our* witness!' Lynda shouted. 'Look at him, Jim. Look at yourself.'

Jim took a huge breath out as if he were just drowning and lowered shaking hands. 'He's all yours,' Jim said to the detectives.

There was a small silence. Tommy began to speak. 'Well. Now that's done, I suppose-'

He must have heard the noise when he stopped mid-sentence, as Jim had heard it too. A whirr, and then a thud. It was the same noise, over and over, repeating itself and increasing in volume each time. Whirr, thud. Whirr, thud.

Jim glanced at Brigson on the floor, who rather oddly now seemed to be laughing. It was a wicked laugh as if amused of something horrendous approaching.

'Did I do well?' Brigson asked, raising his voice so it stretched down the room. 'I don't know about you, but I think he's ready.'

Jim saw Lynda shoot a confused look in his direction, to which he shook his head to say he didn't understand either. Then he turned again to Sebastian Brigson. 'What's going on?'

Brigson attempted to stifle his laughter. 'What's going on? You're about to scream in dread is what's going on...'

'Oh crap,' said a voice from behind.

Lynda and Mary all swung round to see Tommy pointing his gun at something so shocking to witness that it made Jim stop breathing altogether. For the thing in front of them was not a human. This thing had a completely disproportionate white body, an abnormally large torso, spider-like arms, great, heavy, boot-like feet and two cold, emotionless, soul-penetrating, blue eyes.

This was the machine that Jim had read about.

This was Lazarus.

It slowly approached them, step by step. Tommy took a few steps back and fired shots at the thing, but it was unhindered, and continued to move towards them at the same slow pace.

Jim pulled the gun he stole from Blake out of his trousers and pointed it at the machine too, but he knew there was little point. The machine just kept on moving.

Now Lynda pulled her gun out, and then Mary. All were trying to shoot this monstrous creation. All the bullets merely deflected off its impenetrable white shell. Suddenly she seemed to have an idea. She aimed her gun to where many tubes lay exposed between the legs and the feet and shot a bullet right through the pipe in the right leg, causing a great hissing sound while steam and chemicals spurted all over the floor.

The machine tilted its head and looked straight at her as if she had angered it. It then looked down at Tommy, who tried to pull the trigger of his gun, but only to find that it had run out of ammunition. The machine quickly advanced towards him and picked him up by the throat, looking at him briefly, and throwing him across the room to its left, right into three metal pipes hanging down from the wall.

In anger, Jim decided to throw his weapon at the mechanical monstrosity before him, apathetic as to whether it would do any good. The machine barely noticed him, but instead lifted its arms to point at Mary and Lynda. Two canisters popped out of the side of its arms and released a white spray into the air, causing both detectives to collapse instantly as it was inhaled into their lungs.

'It seems guns didn't do much for your friends there, eh Jim?' said Brigson wickedly.

Jim looked around at his colleagues' motionless bodies. Lazarus was ahead of him, looking cold and devoid of emotion.

Jim glared at Brigson. 'Whatever you're doing, whatever you're planning, I promise I will stop you!'

'Will you, Jim?' asked Brigson. 'Because if you don't mind me saying, you've done…' he paused, 'an *excellent* job so far.'

Jim felt a fierce prick in his neck and pulled whatever hit him out to find what looked like an anaesthesia dart, shot into his throat by the machine. As his legs collapsed like folding paper, and his head turned lighter than air, the last thing he saw before everything went dark was the scientist before him - cackling like a madman.

***

JIM
JULY 10TH, 2025
THE WRONG DECISIONS

He sat in silence on his chair, his arms crossed and looking down onto the blank wooden desk before him.

As Jim glanced up, he studied the people with him. Tommy leant awkwardly against the wall, staring far off into the distance. Lynda was slumped in one of the spare office chairs, her arms folded, staring angrily at Jim. Mary just strolled around the room awkwardly, looking as if she felt out of place as an inevitable argument approached.

After the events in the Signision building, all three had been unconscious for a good half an hour. They all felt like they'd been hit hard on the head with a brick and took a while to recuperate and pick themselves off the ground. When they had finally made it out of the pipe room and down the elevator, they soon realised that none of them would be fit to drive. They had been forced to call the chief, who was of course more than happy to take time out of his lunch break for them. After a large scolding and some explanation from Jim about the case, what followed was an awkwardly silent car journey, no words but the muttered curses in the driver's seat.

Tommy was still wincing from the pain in his back. While it wasn't even fractured, let alone broken from the huge blow against the pipe, he still needed painkillers from the medical office.

'You should really get that checked out,' said Lynda in a worried tone. Clearly, she had spotted his pained face too.

'It's all right,' Tommy replied reassuringly. 'Just aches, that's all. The machine went easy on me, I guess.'

'You're lucky it didn't kill you,' Jim replied. 'In fact, I don't see why it didn't kill any of us… we all know something about the case…' Jim shrugged. 'Then again, I suppose four missing police officers last seen at Signision would look pretty dodgy.'

Lynda glared at him. '*Three* missing police officers. Or did you forget that you're not working with us anymore?'

'What are you talking about?' Jim asked moodily.

'What am I talking about?' Lynda replied. 'I'm talking about you going off with Tommy to hunt a drug gang! I'm talking about you taking a man out of police custody. I'm talking about you strangling the same man near to death, what did you think I was talking about, you ignorant asshole?'

'Lynda-'

'No! You listen to me now, Jim! You're *not* a detective anymore. You made that choice two years ago! Meaning you have no right to run around chasing criminals. Mary only called you in, if she even should have called you in, to solve a murder. *Not* to point guns at criminals. You don't get to do that.'

'You realise this is all exactly what Murdock said,' Jim moaned.

'Obviously he didn't say it *clearly enough* considering what you did today!' his wife shouted. 'You've just lost our only remaining witness as well as risking all of our lives. God knows how long it will be before the press realises that our whole case has been jeopardised by a drunken idiot!'

'Our case?' Jim asked. 'Sorry, I didn't realise you were involved in all of this?'

'That's where you're wrong,' Lynda replied. 'Three of the people we've managed to locate over the last few months have been found dead with corpse-shaker in their bloodstream, and then according to you, Brigson himself said something about my missing persons cases all being down to him. Oh yeah, there's also the fact that my husband is strangling suspects and tampering with evidence like a lunatic. I'd say I'm *pretty* involved, what about you James?'

'Hang on,' Tommy started, 'you two are married?'

'Not now, Tommy,' Mary whispered.

'I was invited by Mary to investigate this case,' Jim protested to his wife. 'You just barged your way into it.'

Lynda seemed to ignore the latter part of the sentence. 'Well, Mary and I both agree that bringing you back was evidently the wrong choice. You were instructed to help solve the murder, not chase the criminals! So, I'm ordering you to go home. Go home and continue living out your pathetic existence of sleeping and drinking.'

This caught Jim off guard. 'You're firing me…' He looked over at Mary for support, but she just frowned at him guiltily.

Lynda sighed. 'You can't fire somebody who isn't properly working for you. As a police officer, I'm asking you to leave.'

'But I know far more about this case than any of you!'

'Then you will write a summary of all the information that

you've gathered so far.'

'And if I refuse?' Jim argued.

'Then we'll arrest you for wasting police time or withholding valuable information. You'll want to get started; I don't want to see you here when we get back from Brigson's house.'

Jim frowned. This was all too much to handle. 'Brigson's house?'

'Detective Knightley's idea,' Mary pointed out with a smirk. 'Perhaps a good one for once!'

'Oi!' He crossed his arms with a smirk. 'I have good ideas…'

Lynda shrugged. 'It does make sense. Considering we know he's guilty of something, he's probably our only *remaining* lead…' Lynda glared at Jim. 'Every inch of Signision is being searched as we speak, so the next logical place to look is his home. Come to think of it, I better collect the warrant.'

Jim's wife started to leave the office; her eyes fixed away from him. As she passed, Jim placed his hand on her shoulder to stop her and leaned near to her. 'Lynda,' he whispered, 'why are you doing this?'

She stared at him blankly, but her emotions were as clear as blue specs on a white canvas. 'Because it's my job, Jim.' She walked away.

For a while, nobody talked or moved. Jim just stared lifelessly out the window, reflecting on the mistakes he'd made.

Mary then sighed behind him. 'I forgot to tell you,' she said to him. He turned to see her looking at the floor in sad recollection. 'We found the boat from the harbour. It wasn't much use to us except for the footprints leading to the bridge over the river, but… well, I thought you'd like to know.'

Jim smiled appreciatively. 'I'll see you round, Mary.'

The captain nodded, and she too walked away.

Tommy approached Jim slowly and patted him on the shoulder. 'I'll try talking to her.'

Jim laughed. 'I'm shocked, Tommy! I'd have thought you'd have wanted me gone by now!' Glancing out of the office window, he spotted his wife leaving the building in a huff. 'Lynda's a feisty one. I could never persuade her, and I know her better than most.' He smiled. 'I appreciate that though, kid.'

'Well… I just don't want the job to become dull all of a sudden after the hell you put me through these past few days.' Tommy nodded in his direction. 'I hope I'll see you soon, Jim.'

Jim nodded with a smile, unsure how to say goodbye himself. Luckily for him, he didn't have to. Tommy too had left the room.

Jim strolled to the desk and slumped down before it with a sigh. The I.T. department had deemed the computer safe to use since the virus risk from the memory stick incident, but this was the first day since then that they could actually use it. Jim laughed as he remembered it, but something felt sad within him. Why was that? On the morning Tommy had retrieved him, he would have done anything not to be involved in this job.

Jim typed a few words on the computer, explaining how he was woken, what Tommy told him, what he was met with at the harbour. Writing it down, following the learning of new information seemed to help him process what must have happened. One of the Circle of Saints, most likely Brigson, used the machine to kill the victim, before throwing the victim inside the mechanical suit to bring it back. It was crazy – in fact, everything that Brigson told him was insane – but it did give Jim some inner relief. Now that he knew this group was real and behind it, he no longer had to worry about the previous possibility.

How are you so sure the Phantom isn't helping them? The doubting voice inside his head asked him.

Because he's dead, he thought back. *Lynda shot him.*

Perire finite non est, remember?

Of course Jim remembered. The whole motive of the group causing these murders was to try to find a way to bring back the dead. Even their motto meant "to die is not the end." As hard as Jim tried, he could not stop himself from thinking back to that night when Lynda had shot the Phantom. Would bullets have been enough?

I'm getting paranoid, he told himself. *Why do I always get paranoid?*

It's not paranoia, Jim, it's desire. Be honest. You want *him to be alive, so you can kill him yourself!*

Jim shook his head and continued to write, not caring about the Phantom or his son for a few peaceful moments.

And then his phone rang.

Jim pulled it out of his pocket curiously, hoping it would be Tommy, or Lynda, or Mary telling him they wanted him back. Instead, it was an unknown number, one that he didn't know, but certainly recognised. This person had been calling him repeatedly over the last few days, and each time he had chosen not to pick up the phone. Perhaps they'd leave him alone if he did so now.

Accepting the call, Jim placed the phone to his ear.

'Jim?'

He recognized the voice immediately. He put his hand to his head, so overwhelmed with emotion, namely regret and sadness, as well as a glow of nostalgia, that he had completely forgotten how to string two words into a sentence. He sighed. This was becoming one hell of a week.

'Jim? Are you there?'

He just managed to croak out a few words. 'Where are you?'

'I'm at St Luke's Hospital. Look, Jim… I know you've hated meeting people since that day, but something's wrong with-'

'I'll be there,' he said, before hanging up the phone. He took a few moments for himself to absorb what had just happened before walking back into the office and shutting down the computer.

It was truly typical. Something like this happening in a week already filled with so much pain and despair. It was as if fate wanted him to suffer, to atone for the sins of his past.

Why now? he thought. *Why would my sister call me now?*

***

September

2025

SAM
SEPTEMBER 10TH, 2025
LOOSE WORDS AND OPEN EARS

'Did anyone follow you?' the mysterious man asked hastily. 'Anybody at all? I need to know!'

'No,' Carlos replied. 'Nobody followed me, although I've got to say my new partner's turning out to be a bit of a risk.'

Carlos' "new partner" was just around the corner of that dark Nightdrop avenue, listening in to every word that Carlos and the mysterious man were saying. He was right. Carlos had been up to something, and now he would know just what.

'How so?' the mysterious man asked.

'Well…' Carlos explained, 'two days in and he's already suspicious. He knows how I survived the accident, and he knows why I've been fighting to keep… damn it, can't I just say his name?'

'*No* Carlos!' the other man urged. 'The verdict may be days away, but the case isn't finished yet! If you say his name, then you break the secrecy contract that you've all signed and could be arrested in contempt of court. How are we going to get our *friend* out if we're already in prison with him?'

Sam's ears pricked up. *Get who out?* What were they planning?

'Right…' Carlos said unimpressed. 'Well anyway, Sam knows I've been trying to clear *his* name for a while now, and already he's suspected that I helped the guy blow up that old hospital. He's probably going to make another mistake now, like reporting me to the Murdock. I'm so sick and tired of all these idiots in the police department.'

Sam heard the strange man sigh in exhaustion. 'This is worse than I thought. If he were to tell anyone about this, even if it were just the food staff then… well, it would make this situation way more complicated than it needs to be.'

'Why?' Carlos asked.

'*Why?*' the other man repeated, bemused. 'Because if what he says gets to court, then not only will you be in a mess yourself, but our chances of helping G- *"the Backstabber"* will decrease significantly!'

Sam poked his head around the corner, praying that they would not spot him. There, in the darkness, he spotted the bodily outline of Carlos and the strange man. The strange man was lean, not too tall (yet much taller than Carlos), wearing what looked to be a grey suit – although the colour was difficult to distinguish in such low light. Sam wished he could see the face of this individual, but it was dark, and the man was facing away from him. All the detective could go by was the gentleman's brown hair, medium height, and deep voice.

Carlos tapped his foot on the ground anxiously. 'So, what should I do then?'

The mysterious man shrugged nonchalantly. 'Tell him the truth.'

'What!' Carlos exclaimed.

'You heard me.'

Carlos shook his head. 'You can't be serious? Does that include the whole bit about me sneaking off to see you every night? What about the other thing, huh? Should I tell him about that too?'

'You can say it, Carlos.'

'I'd rather not! Do you seriously expect me to tell him all of this? I met him yesterday!'

'Carlos, he's suspicious. If you can get him to join our cause, then he won't be a problem anymore. He may even be an asset to our team.'

'A team of two?' Carlos asked.

'There are more than two of us in this battle. Trust me, Carlos,' the man replied.

Carlos looked up to the night sky. 'And what if he's not so compliant? What if he threatens to tell the world the truth like the captain, but then actually does it?'

Sam shuddered as he heard the old captain referenced in this way. So it was true then? The last captain had known something.

'Then…' the mysterious stranger replied. 'Let me deal with him.'

Carlos began to shake his head anxiously. 'Oh God, this has all gone so much worse than I thought it w-' He paused and was suddenly looking directly at Sam's peering head.

Sam jolted away instantly, but it was too late. He could hear Carlos telling the other man that somebody was watching them. Whether they saw his face or not, it was hard to say – it was dark after all. Regardless, Sam picked up his feet and sprinted off, making sure Carlos and this other man wouldn't get a better look at him. He splashed through puddles up the long hill and turned away the moment he saw another street. Just to be safe, he kept on running and turned again, before finally stopping in the middle of a street he had never seen before.

Panting, he placed his hands on his knees, bending over to catch his breath. He needed to find his car, and quickly. Before Carlos did, at least. Once he had re-oriented himself, he made his way down a different set of streets from the ones which he had run up, making sure not to cross paths with his partner.

After many minutes of backtracking and attempted navigation, Sam finally spotted his car down the road. He sprinted down towards it; determined to do what he planned next. He would make sure to tell someone immediately, be it Murdock or the homicide captain (he wasn't sure he could trust anybody else in *his* division anymore, and this was possibly murder). Unfortunately, a problem arose quickly, as standing before the bonnet of his car was Carlos Rodriguez.

'How's it going, Partner?' said Carlos, his arms crossed.

'Not so great,' Sam replied, fighting off the rage within him. 'First day on the job and I'm already hearing tales of betrayal.'

Carlos shook his head as if ashamed. 'What you heard back in that alleyway was both out of context and none of your business?'

'None of my business?' Sam asked, seething. 'Your friend, "dealing with me" is none of my business? Whatever you did to our last captain, that's *none of my business?'* He laughed. 'We're meant to be partners, Carlos. We were meant to trust each other! I *wanted* to trust you!'

Carlos stared at him fiercely, his eyes like sharp needles. 'Well, I suppose things don't always go the way we want them to.'

'No,' said Sam as he reached for his holster, resting his hand on his weapon. 'I suppose they don't.'

Carlos looked down at the weapon in surprise for a moment, before raising his hands defensively. 'Listen, Sam. I know I've been dishonest and suspect, but just give me a few minutes and I can explain what I've been-'

'Before your partner gets here, you mean? You don't need to explain anything to me anyway, you lying prick! You're planning to break out the Backstabber, you and your friend. I know there are more than two of you planning it, I know there are no longer people in the police station that I can trust, and I know you helped the Backstabber kill all those previous officers, despite all the one-dimensional sob stories you've given me about your dead partner. I'm going to the police station to tell them all this, with you alive or not, so I'd recommend you get out of the way of my car.'

Carlos merely stared at Sam for a few moments before stepping in front of the door. 'I'm afraid I can't do that Sam.'

Sam felt his hand shaking, and the rage rising within him.

'I'm warning you, Carlos!'

'I know you are Sam, and I'm warning you that you might just have to shoot me because you're not leaving here until you let me explain what's going on.'

Both officers gave each other icy stares for a good while, unsure how to act next. Sam felt a conflict within him. He knew he couldn't shoot his partner, but he had to get away before the mysterious man returned.

'Screw it,' he muttered with a sigh. He lifted his gun and swiped it at Carlos' face, causing it to smash into his nose with a crack. Carlos screamed in pain and collapsed to the floor, his hand covering his bleeding nose.

Sam bolted up and grabbed his partner by the ear, yanking him on his feet and throwing him to one side. By Carlos time he'd made it to his feet, he was too late. Sam was already in the driver's seat and driving away.

Sam pressed a button on his monitor, and a loud beep followed. 'Call Edward Murdock,' he said.

The car accepted the request, and the phone rang for a good few moments. After many repeated ringing sounds, somebody finally picked up on the other end.

'Hello?' said a woman's voice.

This took Sam aback. 'Hi… uh… who is this?'

'It's Captain Parker, I'm standing in for Murdock while he's out.'

Sam sighed in relief. Captain Mary Parker was one of the few police officers that he trusted. He had met her several times, especially in his interviews, and would likely need her help now. 'Mary, thank heavens! I'm sorry to call you so late. It's Sam. You know, Sam Turner? The new missing persons detective?'

Mary was silent for a few moments before she finally realised. 'Oh! Sam! I remember now. Sorry, it's been a crazy day. What can I do for you?'

'I need you to come to my place,' he said simply. 'I'll give you the address in a second but... I think my partner's up to something.'

***

SAM
SEPTEMBER 11TH, 2025
THE SECOND BACKSTABBER

Sam reluctantly entered the lift to the third floor, incredibly uncertain of what would happen next. Close behind was the homicide captain, Mary, an unsettled look on her face.

Telling her at his house the night before hadn't been easy, and Sam could still tell she didn't completely believe what he was saying. 'Say again?' she'd said. 'Your partner - who you met just yesterday - is conspiring to release a known convict?'

'I know, it sounds crazy! But Captain, if there even is the slightest risk that he's not to be trusted, how can we just sit here? Can't we just ask?'

So, they would ask him. Perhaps arrest for questioning was a better way to put it, but Sam knew what he'd heard. *It's like what Sadie's father wrote*, he thought. *There are bad people in this department.*

Mary sighed. It had been said that Captain Mary Parker hadn't been the same since those horrific events two months ago, and Sam could tell just by looking at her. Her face was pale and sullen, and great purple bags rested beneath her eyes. 'Sam, if we're wrong…'

Sam raised his hands in exclamation. 'How many people did the Backstabber kill, Mary?'

'*Captain!*'

Sam ignored that. 'Twelve police officers were killed in that explosion he created. Three more were elsewhere. As for regular civilians…'

He saw that Mary was shaking her head in stubborn silence.

'All I'm saying is… isn't doing the right thing and being wrong better than not doing anything at all?'

And then Sam saw something which genuinely surprised him. A tear was rolling down the captain's cheek.

'Oh… Captain I'm-'

'No!' She wiped it away quickly. 'No, no, it's fine. It's fine. It's just…' She looked him in the eyes. 'The Backstabber… he wasn't a detective. People… they don't know that.'

Sam frowned. 'What? You don't mean…'

'I know, the press always says those kinds of things, but the press got their facts wrong. He was a regular man who we… *I'd* called in to help us. He was only able to kill all those people because I gave him the power to do so.' She rubbed her eyes. 'So if I'm reluctant to do this… it's because I've made mistakes before. I don't want to make another.'

The elevator stopped with a ding. Mary led the way in a hurry, seemingly to escape the icy conversation. Sam followed her closely behind as they approached his office, his hand centimetres from his pistol. He didn't want to use it, but bad things always happened at Nightdrop.

They finally reached his and Carlos' office door. Sam turned his body away at an angle to hide his silhouette in the translucent glass window, while Mary pulled her pistol up, poised closely behind him. His fingers reached into his pocket momentarily, quickly rubbing his father's silver bullet for luck, before he gently clasped the golden doorknob. He decided it best to take out his weapon, just in case.

He took a deep breath as adrenaline rushed through him like a river. Finally, he spoke. 'Carlos? Are you in there?'

There was silence for a good few moments, and Sam wondered where his partner had gone. *The people at reception said he'd come in today.* Finally, Sam got a reply. 'Sam? I didn't expect you to speak to me so soon. Come on, I've wanted to talk to you.'

Sam sighed and closed his eyes. 'Are you armed?'

More silence. 'Oh… you're arresting me, aren't you? No, Sam, I'm not-'

Sam twisted the doorknob and burst into the room; the pistol pointed at Carlos. He was ready to fire, his brain analysing what was before him at a rapid rate. Mary followed him quickly, her weapon up too.

But Carlos wasn't ready to fire back. Instead, he just sat there, his eyes focussed on his partner. 'I told you, you're making a huge mistake.'

Sam laughed. 'Well, so help you if I'm not. I told you I'd stop you. Captain?'

Mary approached Carlos carefully, her weapon poised well. With her left hand, she pulled a pair of handcuffs from her belt and quickly fastened them onto Detective Carlos Rodriguez's wrists before he had the chance to do anything else.

'Is there anything you'd like to tell us before Mary takes you into questioning?' Sam asked.

Carlos closed his eyes and hummed. 'Let me think… How's *go to hell?*'

Sam shook his head in disgust. 'You were my partner. I was meant to be able to trust you.'

Carlos laughed. 'You *can* trust me, Sam! You just choose not to!'

Sam approached him in fury until his face was just inches from Carlos's. 'Don't you say that. I heard what you said in that alleyway, I *know* what you're planning!'

'Really?' Carlos asked. 'Because that's your problem, Sam Turner. You heard me, but you didn't listen.' He gestured his head to the door. 'Come on Captain, I believe I have some talking to do.'

Mary approached the door, her hands firmly holding Carlos' shoulders. As she left, she gave Sam an uncertain look, and Sam felt the doubt creeping in again. *Was I correct? Please say I haven't made a huge mistake.*

He approached the desk, curious as to what Carlos had been doing. There, right before the computer, was a small warrant, the one allowing Sam to investigate the disappearance of Michael Williams. On it was a small yellow post-it, with three-minute words. *Speak to Jordan.*

Jordan? Sam thought. *Is that someone at Stormfeld? The Backstabber, perhaps?* None of it made sense. Why would Carlos leave a note for himself? Unless…

What if the note is for me?

Sam knew he couldn't trust his partner, yet for some reason, this note intrigued him. Either this was Carlos attempting to prove his innocence or to manipulate Sam. Either way, it would be useful for working out this mess.

That's what I'll do, Sam thought. *I'll find Williams, and I'll find this man.*

As he approached the front doors, he found the captain waiting for him once more. Her foot was tapping on the ground impatiently, and her arms were crossed when he saw her.

'Your partner's all locked up until his questioning. Where are you headed exactly?' she asked him.

Sam shrugged. 'A girl is missing, and the best lead I have to find her is the whereabouts of her father… meaning I need to go to the prison he broke out of.'

'And leave me here with *your* partner? Your mess?'

Sam sighed. 'I'm sorry Captain, this has all piled up at once, and today is the only day I can get to the prison.'

'Fine. That's fine, things always happen at once. A double-crossing partner, a missing girl, a broken bridge at the Hudson. Hell, a man in a taxi was shot in broad daylight this morning by some woman in a bandana.' She smiled kindly. 'I wasn't much help to the others, anyway. I'll question our suspicious detective and… you find that girl.'

Sam nodded. 'Thanks, I appreciate it.' He noticed the sad look in her eyes. 'Hey, are you all right, Boss?'

Mary shook her head. 'No Sam. I'm not all right. Two months ago, a lot of shit happened to me and my colleagues. Everything that happened, the case, the explosion, the "*Backstabber*" I… It's been hard to cope with. Lost a lot of friends too. Some dead, some retired, some missing, some… convicted. This whole thing about *your* partner being suspicious? Well, it's just brought a lot back is all.'

Sam frowned. Had she known the Backstabber well?

Mary shook her head. 'You be safe out there all right, Sam? I don't want anything happening to one of our new detectives.'

Sam nodded warily and pushed open the doors. Two rogue officers in two months. It was no wonder Mary was struggling. As for all those friends she lost…

The lieutenants.

There were two empty lieutenant spaces in the police department, or so Sam remembered over-hearing a couple of days ago. One was a man who'd been killed in the explosion, and the other a woman, presumed dead after the collapse of a church.

And they still haven't found her body, he thought. *One of our own and the best guys in the department can't find her. Are they even still looking?*

He prayed the same would never happen to him.

***

July
2025/1885

LYNDA
JULY 10TH, 2025
THE FOUR APOSTLES

Lynda knocked once more on the hard oak door of the tiny cottage. 'Excuse me? Is anybody home? This is the police! If you're in there, open up!'

She, Tommy and Mary were standing in front of a small stone-bricked cottage – an abnormal sight in Nightdrop - that was so dull and bland, it would have ultimately been ignored by any passers-by. The bricks were worn away, now a dusty brown like the colour of rust dirt. Its windows were likely once white but had now gone a strange beige colour, the frames becoming slowly consumed by strange green moulds and the glass so dirty and uncared for that it was almost opaque. The roof was also a mess, with tiles missing in all sorts of areas, as well as a wind-beaten chimney and a gutter that was falling to bits. Perhaps the very reason Brigson lived here was to be left alone by the rest of the world, to live in a place that both frightened civilians and blended in.

They waited another few seconds before Tommy shouted. 'Okay, we're coming in.'

He took the house key that he had been given out of his

pocket and slotted it into the keyhole. With a turn and a click, the door opened, revealing a dark, dusty beige corridor, illuminated only by the rays of sunlight streaming through the tiny square window of the door and the light from the slightly ajar door in front of them. The cottage had a peculiarly strong smell of oil about it, making Lynda's nose crinkle up like tissue paper.

'Anybody home?' Mary asked in a raised voice. After a few moments of no reply, she turned to Lynda, gave her a nod to say *that settles it* and said, 'I suppose we should start searching.'

'Yeah,' Lynda replied, looking around the corridor. 'There are seven doors, so perhaps if we search two rooms each, and then rotate so we've all searched each other's rooms. We can do that one at the end.' She pointed at the living room.

'Sounds like a plan,' replied Tommy. 'Although we should make sure we can secretly contact each other, just in case we find him in one of the rooms pointing a gun at us.'

'That's what our micro-recorders are for,' said Mary.

'What?' Tommy queried.

Both Lynda and Mary looked at him hysterically. 'You… don't know what a micro-recorder is?' Lynda asked.

'Yeah, it's probably one of the most important bits of police technology that there is,' Mary furthered, 'did they not teach you about them at the academy?'

Tommy held up his hands in self-defence. 'Look sorry boss!' He glanced at Lynda. 'Bosses. Maybe somebody in the station should have told me about this.'

Lynda sighed. 'Maybe you've just forgotten. Take out your badge and tap the logo.'

Tommy slowly took out his badge, tapped the logo and opened it up. Inside was an ID code, his computer password, a small piece of paper with a strange circular symbol on it and a small almost transparent semi-sphere, no bigger than the top of a thumbtack, sitting inside a clear bag.

'Do you know what this is?' asked Lynda, pointing at the semi-sphere.

'No,' said Tommy in confusion. 'I was told about all the other stuff but not this. I didn't even know it was there!'

Lynda shrugged. 'It's something we use to send distress signals to each other. Stick it to your hand and it's barely visible. If you press it, not only will it alert other officers on your case to your location but will also record what's going on too. You can edit who receives your distress signals on the police database too, but right now it would alert Mary and I as we're on your case, as well as sending messages to the phones of any family members on your emergency contact list. Pretty nifty when you're kidnapped.'

'That's certainly exciting,' said Tommy. 'Wish I'd stuck this to my hand before going into Blake's warehouse. Criminals don't know about this?'

'Only the smart ones,' Mary remarked. 'Bit weird you didn't know about it though,' she added. 'How long have you been here again?'

'Look, I'm still alive, aren't I?' Tommy reflected.

Mary nodded. 'Alive and smarter than ever, Mr Knightley.' She smiled. 'Should we get to work?'

Tommy smirked and saluted her jokingly. Lynda just rolled her eyes and got on with the search.

***

A few hours later, Tommy came into the kitchen to check on Lynda.

'You want some help?' he offered. 'I'm just about done in all the other rooms.'

Lynda sighed 'No Tommy, it's all right. I'm done too.'

'Found anything?' Tommy asked.

'Not a single wood-shaving,' she replied. 'Something's got to be in here somewhere!'

Tommy laughed. 'You know what I find weird?'

'What?' she asked.

'That this guy lives in one of the few bungalows in the city. I mean seriously, isn't that so weird? Somebody in *this* city not being able to afford a second floor?'

Lynda just stared at Tommy and crossed her arms.

'Sorry,' he said more seriously. 'I just try to lighten the mood from time to time, especially with… well, you know. Hey, by the way, I was wondering if we could talk about-'

'I'm not bringing him back, Tommy.'

Tommy glanced at her in shock. 'Okay… Wow, was I really that obvious?'

Lynda shook her head and turned back to the oven. 'He's caused far too much danger already. Aiding witnesses, entering restricted areas, tampering with evidence… In fact, let's just talk about all the bad things that you've *let* him do for a second! You even gave him the address to the drug group, which I have no idea how you got given you didn't even-'

'Look, Lynda, Jim's a stubborn guy-'

'Then you should have arrested the prick! You're lucky that Mary and I haven't decided to call you off this case, so don't you go telling me who to bring back or not!'

'Everything all right in here?' Mary asked sheepishly by the door.

Lynda rubbed her eyes. 'Yep. I'm just chatting with your new detective. He thinks we should bring Jim back.'

'All right, all right, I get it,' said Tommy.

'Well… I mean he's got a point,' Mary added.

Lynda shot a fierce gaze at her.

'I only mean he was a good detective.'

Lynda laughed aggressively. 'Yeah, he was. He *was* a good detective, two years ago! Now, though? Now, James Griffen's just a semi-stable middle-aged man with a drinking problem and the inability to follow the rules. Unless he magically improves his ways in the time it takes us to solve his case, we're not bringing him back, and that's final!'

They both stared at her with almost sad eyes. Lynda felt infuriated. 'We're *not* bringing him back!'

There was an icy silence for a short while. Lynda breathed in and out heavily. This was her case now. She wasn't going to let it be ruined for her by her stupid husband. Not again. Not ever again.

Tommy broke the silence. 'Why… don't we search the living room.'

Lynda lifted her head and nodded.

They exited the kitchen. 'You know, it's weird,' Mary remarked. 'This place is unnaturally tidy. It looks as if it was cleaned especially for our arrival.'

Tommy turned to her startled, 'you're not saying you think he's been here since that machine-thing knocked us out?'

'Oh no!' she exclaimed. 'I was exaggerating. By the looks of it he may have had an obsession to keep everything tidy, but I'm no psychologist.'

They were hit with the sickly fragrance of honey the instant they entered the cosy room. Light streamed through the dirty glass door to the patio in front of them, making the shelves stacked with what must have been hundreds of books glow in the midday sun. Underneath the shelves were small cabinets, and in the centre of the room was a grand oak table, decorated with wooden phoenixes on each leg.

'I have a degree in psychology you know,' Tommy blurted out.

Mary laughed. 'No kidding! You should be the expert then. Do you think Brigson was a looney?'

Tommy shrugged. 'A guy kills a few people with a machine in an attempt to cure death? What's so crazy about that?'

'Can you two focus, please?' Lynda asked.

'Sorry Boss, we'll get to work right away.'

They began to search, Mary in the furniture, Tommy in the cabinets and Lynda in the bookshelves. Many of the books were biblical, with each small book being devoted to sections of the old and new testaments. Other books included "Advanced Mechanics,

Book Three," "Cogito Ergo Sum: A Study of the Consciousness and the Brain," "Homo Mechanicus: Humanity's Future in Machinery" and a strange laminated manuscript titled, "The Fabled Element; An Examination of Arconium," written by Brigson himself, stamped "EPCAS," "Confidential," and "Not to Be Removed" at the bottom of the front page. But out of all the books, one stood out to Lynda the most. It was a small blue book titled: The Circle of Saints.

'Hey guys, check this out!'

Tommy and Mary walked over and stared at the book in her hands with blank expressions. Neither of them seemed too surprised. 'What?' Tommy asked.

Lynda glared at him for being so thick. 'Have you read the title?'

Tommy laughed. 'Of course I've read the title, it's a kids' story about the city.'

Lynda stared at him in bewilderment.

Tommy gave her a querying look. 'You don't know. The Circle of Saints is the alleged story of how the city was created. About the settlers? And the magic stone?'

Lynda shook her head slowly.

'Blimey Lynda, how long have you been in this city?'

'That's beside the point,' Lynda ushered, quickly changing the subject. 'The point is, why *would* they name themselves after a kids' story?'

'Not the story itself, but the people within the story,' Tommy replied. 'The religious group who find a deadly rock with the power to raise the dead. They believed it was a gift from God, but then they end up using it for evil, so a man steals it with the intent to destroy it.

At the end, there's a bit of a cliff-hanger when the Circle vows that they will not rest until they find the rock again. Their choice of naming did concern me at first, but then Jim told me not to worry about it.'

Lynda rolled her eyes, slightly amused. 'Well, for once he had some sense. I'm not going to get all frightened about a magical rock.'

'It may just be a story, but most stories have their roots and do contain *elements* of truth,' said Mary. 'The stone in the story granted power and eternal life. So, if the Circle are real, or if this group is copying them, I suppose it makes sense if that's what they're looking for.'

'According to Jim, Brigson said the same thing, and we all know how reliable *he* turned out to be. But if it were true…' Lynda started. 'Well, I suppose there's the chance that this group we're dealing with could be decades old!'

'If they're not imitators,' Tommy added.

Lynda nodded slowly. A thought hit her. 'Hang on, did you say they were a religious group?'

'Yeah, so what?'

Instantly, Lynda ran over to the bookshelf and piled all the biblical books onto the floor.

'Lynda, what are you…'

She was rummaging through the different biblical books when suddenly she noticed something inside the gospel of John. About halfway through was a little green note attached, with the word "*Rebirth*" on it, written in red writing.

Lynda walked towards it and picked it up. She opened it at the page the note was stuck to and saw instantly that numerous words and letters were missing:

[43]When he had said this, Jesus called out in a loud voice " , _ome out! [44]T_e dead man came out, his h_nds and feet wra_ped in strips of lin_n, and a c_oth around his face.

Jesus said to _hem, "Ta_e off the grave clothes and let him go."

'And you accuse us of messing with evidence!' Tommy exclaimed.

Lynda showed the book to her colleagues. 'Why are all those letters missing?' Tommy asked as he read it. 'There's a word gone near the start.'

'I don't know, but surely it has to mean something!' Lynda exclaimed.

'And "*Rebirth*?"' Mary asked.

Lynda pondered on this. 'Do you think there are any notes in the others?'

'Well, it's worth a try.'

For a while, they flicked through hundreds of pages of many books and found nothing. Finally, Tommy's hand leapt into the air.

'Aha!' the young man exclaimed. 'Look in here.'

Lynda gathered with Mary next to him, glancing at what was in his hands. She was looking at the inside of the front cover of St Matthew's Gospel, and there, Tommy pointed out, was the outline of a square indented in it. Lynda pulled out the square card, which was a flap in the inside cover, revealing another green note inside, with the number two written on it.

'Well, how does a hidden note help us?' Mary asked

He did. And sure enough, in all of their front cover there were flaps, and under each flap was a note with a number.

'Oh my God!' she exclaimed, putting her hands on her head in excitement.

'Tell us, what is it?' Mary asked eagerly.

'The numbers aren't random,' said Lynda. 'I think we know where the next murders will be taking place.'

***

JIM
JULY 10TH, 2025
THE HOSPITAL

Jim slammed down the accelerator, forcing the car to go as fast as the law allowed it. He was determined to get to the hospital as quickly as possible. What he had heard on the phone – or rather who he had heard on the phone – made it clear to him that this was an emergency.

He was glad that he didn't have to tell his colleagues what was going on – especially Lynda. He had a past that he was quite ashamed of and telling them about it wouldn't have made the matter any easier. Ever since he had lost his son, he had been sent into spiralling grief. He had disconnected from everybody - his wife, his parents, even his only remaining sibling. Jim knew at the time that his family would understand, of course; that they would leave him to grieve and get on with life if that was what he so wished. After all, they all knew what it was like to lose family, with Jim's father and older sister leaving their lives at separate occasions. It had reached a point where they would only ever call him in a serious situation, one where Jim was needed urgently. Would he soon lose *another* family member?

He parked outside St John's Hospital, a towering building, identified by its giant blue logo of an eagle with a heart at its chest.

Jim swung the glass doors open, dodged past all the many doctors and staff in the area, and made his way to the reception desk.

'Hi,' he said. 'Have you checked in an Eliza Griffen recently? I'm Jim, her older brother.'

The lady nodded and looked at the screen in front of her. She tapped some keys before addressing him. 'Ah yes. She came to Nightdrop after finding news of a possible treatment for her mother-'

'Her mother?' Jim exclaimed. 'Is Mom all right?'

The lady looked pitiful. 'I'm not the one who can tell you that, Mr Griffen. The disease that she has is said to be quite rare and peculiar, but I assure you that our best doctors are doing everything they can to help her.'

Jim was worried this would happen. 'Where is she?'

'Floor Six, Ward C.' She handed her clipboard and pen towards him. 'Could you please sign your name he-'

But by the time she had finished the word here, he had signed his name and was making his way to the sixth floor. He gritted his teeth anxiously. Was his mother okay? What if this was the last he would ever see of her?

When he had made it to the corridor on floor six, he braced himself for what was to come. He had not seen anybody in months. His mother. His sister. They were all such distant memories. Jim approached the corridor fearfully and swung open the doors. There, sitting in one of two black chairs outside the room, sat a tall woman with long, silky, smooth black hair, a naturally pale and even face, small curved lips and two fiery hazelnut eyes.

'Elly,' he said sadly.

The look on her face was torn between surprise, sadness and

annoyance. 'Jim,' she said dully. 'You came.'

'Of course I came!' he exclaimed. 'Elly, what happened to Mom?'

Her face seemed to break down slightly from its firm expression of keeping it together, and Jim noticed his sister's eyes glisten more than usual as she spoke. 'Well… she started having these fits of coughing. At first, it seemed perfectly normal, but they happened again and again, and it just got worse and worse until she was struggling to breathe. Then she started getting pain in different places in her body; starting in her lungs, then spreading to her chest, and eventually her liver. Anyway, we went to the doctor. We thought maybe it was cancer. Maybe there was a chance but… oh Jim, they said she might only have a year left.'

She ran to him and embraced him firmly. Jim heard his sister silently sobbing at his chest, and he felt her tears dampen his shirt. While he knew he looked strong on the outside, he felt very close to doing the same as his sister. Mixed in with his sadness were feelings of regret and guilt too. He had abandoned his entire remaining family for two years. And while he lost himself grieving for what had happened to one of the ones he loved, he had missed out on a whole twelve months that he would never get back with his mother.

The two released each other and sat down on the chairs by the door. For a while, neither spoke verbally, but in wordless silence and emotion that they were feeling. Finally, Elly talked.

'I don't blame you by the way,' she said.

Jim turned his head to her and listened.

'For not talking to us, I mean,' she continued. 'I remember Jess doing the same thing after Dad died.'

She was referring to their older sister. After their father's death, Jess Griffen had left the household for good. Jim didn't blame her; she was escaping years of icy silent dinners and heated arguments. The only issue was that she never communicated with any of them. No texts, no calls, not even a letter. The only time they saw her after then was the day she was buried ten years later, her death being of unknown causes, and her funeral full of mysterious people that Jim had never met in his life.

'I still regret it though,' said Jim. 'I should have learned from her – I should have known that there was a chance I would never see you again if I kept pushing you away. Jake's death should have brought me closer to you, but instead, it just brought me further apart from everyone I loved…'

There was more silence again.

'Jim. I hope you don't mind me asking,' said Elly, 'but ever since… that night… what happened between you and Lynda?'

Jim looked at his sister, turned his head back to the ground and cleared his throat. 'We gave each other some space,' is all he said.

After a brief pause, a nurse approached. 'She is ready to see you now,' the nurse spoke.

'Thank you,' said Elly.

They walked into the patients' ward, which was so white and clean that it looked as if it was cleaned that very morning. There in the bed in front of him, was a short lady, sound asleep, in a light blue hospital gown, with silky grey hair, pale blue eyes and a soft, wrinkled face.

'The doctors say she's very weak,' Elly confided quietly. 'The doctors showed me the x-rays – it hasn't spread too much or far for now so maybe there's time but… she's old Jim, and even if she could have chemo, they told me her prospects wouldn't be great. They said…' Her eyes were watering, but she tried her best to compose herself. 'They said it was likely a matter of if over when.'

Jim nodded slowly. 'How long?'

Elly shrugged. 'Depends on the treatment. Anywhere between months and a few years.'

Nora's eyelids fluttered open, and she turned her frail head towards Jim. As if she believed she was still asleep, she clenched her eyes shut and opened them as wide as she possibly could, her pupils dilating slightly at the sight of her son.

'*Jim!*' she exclaimed in a slightly croaky Irish accent, streams of joyous tears making rivers down her face. '*Is that you?*'

'Yeah, Mom, it's me. It's actually me. I'm so sorry I left you…'

And they talked. Talked about the time they had missed together. Jim told her everything since his son's death. Him splitting up with Lynda. The drinking. Moving into a tiny little house, all alone, with no friends or family to talk to (unless you counted those who knew him at the police department, like Mary, who helped him in his grief, and Barry, his old partner, who had retired around the same time that Jim did). He told her what he was allowed to about the new case. How he had thought it was his son's killer, how he was very wrong. He nearly told her how he almost killed a witness, but he wasn't willing to tarnish his mother's impression of him anymore; not now, at least. He didn't tell her about the machine either, considering how unsure he was of the machine's role in this himself; what exactly it was, who was controlling it and what it was truly for. It didn't matter now though, that case was done for Jim.

'I'm sorry we didn't help you, Jim,' his mother spoke softly. 'We knew you needed space, and we thought you would recover quickly. By the time we realized that you were drowning instead of recovering… we didn't know where to find you. You wouldn't answer our calls. When they told me that I had a year to live, I moved over from Boston to Nightdrop, in the hope that you would still be there. Your sister's smart, she thought you might not answer if a call was from us. So, she called you from the hospital telephone.'

Jim smiled a little. 'You were always the smart one, Elly.'

She smiled back.

The clock on the wall chimed six o'clock.

'That's visiting hours over. I hate to leave you so soon Mom, but I promise, I *will* visit you every day from now. And I mean that. You hear me?'

She nodded frailly. 'I know you mean it, Jim. I ought to be getting some rest myself if I'm truly honest. Do come and visit me though, won't you Jim? Please.'

'Yes,' he said. 'Of course.'

Outside the room, Elly bade him farewell. 'Jim, please come back. I know what this is doing to you, but she loves you and-'

'Four people, Elly. How many more? How many more after her do I have to watch die?'

Elly looked down in a half-understanding-half-irritated sort of way. 'Jim, life isn't some perfect world where we all sing songs and live joyful lives together. People die, okay? And-'

'You think I don't know that,' he said with a raised voice. 'You think I don't know the toll of being alive. Watching those around you die. You don't even have a son! You wouldn't know what it's like losing somebody made from your very heart and soul. Your DNA and your spirit. You have no clue, so don't you dare bring me all the way up to Saint Luke's damn hospital and give me a lecture about…' His voice trailed off as something clicked in his brain.

'What is it?' Elly asked, detecting the drop in his voice.

'Saint Luke's Hospital…' he repeated.

His sister seemed slightly worried. 'Yeah, that's what they call it.'

'*Saint Luke's* hospital.'

'*What about it?*' she asked in annoyance.

'St Luke! St Matthew, St Mark, St Luke, and St John!'

'The four apostles, so what?'

'St Mark's Harbour. St Matthew's Lane. St Luke's hospital…' He kissed his sister's forehead, half excited, half nervous. 'But that means... Listen, Elly, I have to go. Don't come into contact with anybody, and if something bad happens, lock yourself in Mom's room. I promise you I'll call you later!' Jim suddenly found himself sprinting to the stairwell.

'But where are you going!' his sister shouted.

He stopped and poked his head around the door. 'Back to the job I always despised.'

***

LYNDA/TOM
JULY 10TH, 2025/JULY 27^{TH,} 1885
A ROCK AND A PROMISE

Just as they were rejoicing from their discovery, her husband entered the office.

In an instant, all of Lynda's joy had been sucked away, leaving only frustration inside of her. Simultaneously, both her colleagues went silent too, and she knew why. They weren't mad at Jim, presumably quite the opposite – they were just frightened to how she would react.

'Right then,' Jim remarked. 'Glad you're all happy to see me…'

Lynda glared at him in icy fury. 'What the *hell* are you doing here!'

Jim grinned like it was Christmas. 'I've worked it out!'

Lynda crossed her arms. 'Please, go on.'

Jim rushed over to the table and brushed all the maps they had laid out aside. He replaced them with his own map of the city, before pushing thumbtacks into various locations on the grid.

'What on *earth* are you doing?' Tommy queried.

Jim looked up and grinned. 'Both sites where we've found bodies have something in common. There's something that links the two of them in a way so subtle that it slipped right under our noses.'

Lynda crossed her arms. '*What* could that possibly be?' she asked, a hint of sarcasm in her voice.

Jim didn't notice her tone. 'They're all named after saints! *Saint Mark's* Harbour, *Saint Matthew's* Lane. If they're going to strike anywhere soon, it will be named after a Saint, meaning it will be in one of *these* locations.' He gestured to twenty or so thumbtacks pinned onto the map.

Lynda shook her head in silence.

'What is it, lieutenant? Have I left you speechless from my detective skills? Regretting asking me to leave now?'

She smirked and lifted the map that she and her colleagues had worked on just ten minutes prior. On it were not twenty locations highlighted, but two. St Luke's Hospital, and St Luke's Primary School.

Jim cleared his throat in slight irritation. Lynda could see Tommy holding in hysterical laughter to her right. 'Huh… you worked it out?'

'M-hm. You're not the only person with a brain in this city, Jim.'

Jim frowned. 'And how are you so certain that the Circle are going to strike in only one of *two* locations? There are *twenty-six* places in this city named after saints. Trust me, I did my research.'

Lynda smiled. 'That is correct, Jim. But only *fourteen* are named after the ones who wrote the four main gospels. And only *two* of those are St Luke.'

'How do you know it's going to be St Luke?'

Lynda picked up the pile of books that they'd found at Brigson's house and dumped them to face him on the desk. 'These are the books we found at Sebastian Brigson's house-'

'Brigson's house! You shouldn't have those, they're evidence!'

'Oh, quit your whining, unlike you I asked Murdock, and he's given us special permission to give them further investigation. Now, on the inside front cover of each gospel is a flap concealing a number which directly correlates with the order of the murders. Inside Mark's is the number one. Matthew's, there's a number two. Luke, number three, and John… well, hopefully number four won't happen.'

'There was also this funny page,' Tommy pointed out. 'One with a bunch of missing letters and words, and a note saying *"Rebirth."* Creepy, huh?'

Jim seemed extremely zoned out. 'What's wrong?' Mary asked him.

He shook his head. 'It was something Brigson said. Not important now. Why are the letters rubbed out?'

'I don't know,' said Mary, 'you can guess some of them I suppose but right now, there's something else we need to focus on. Look at the notes in the flaps.'

They watched as Jim picked up a book and read the note on the inside front cover. 'Yeah, it's just a number.'

'Is it?' Lynda asked. 'Look below it.'

Jim squinted at the note, and suddenly his face widened. 'It's a date. Do they all have dates on them?'

She nodded. 'All except for John, and the dates match perfectly with the killings.'

Her husband squinted further. He was holding Luke's gospel. 'This one says tomorrow, 10:25! Lynda, there's going to be a murder tomorrow!'

Lynda smiled. 'We know. Murdock's already on it. In the morning, two groups will be sent to evacuate the school and the hospital. All the evacuees healthy enough will be taken into police custody where they will be questioned and examined. Anybody too sick will be sent to St Bartholomew's Hospital on the other side of the city. Then, by 6:25 tomorrow, every other remaining TRT member in the department will be sent to the two locations, ready for the Circle and whatever they have planned.'

'Are you sure this is the right thing to do though?' Jim asked. 'I mean, come on, the person in the video did say he would always be a step ahead. Why would Brigson leave details of a murder in his own house for detectives to find unless he wanted you to?'

'Let's not be paranoid, Jim,' Tommy ushered.

'No, I'm serious! How do we know this is going to be safe?'

Lynda sighed. 'Let's say they did plan this, that this is some little game of theirs. We go in tomorrow, and they're ready for us. Maybe there'll be some Circle members or that machine. Either way, it won't matter. Murdock knows how dangerous this *could* be, so he's throwing in thirty-five of his best trained, fully armoured, most skilled officers to deal with the situation. With those numbers, the Circle can try their hardest.' She put a finger up. 'But you know what we should be asking?' She pointed at Jim. 'How did you get in here?'

Jim shrugged. 'For starters, I haven't finished writing all the information from the case.'

'You haven't f- Jim, I don't know if you realise how tight a schedule we're on here!'

'Yeah, well, I had a little family emergency.' He looked at her with lost eyes. 'Mom's sick.'

Lynda glanced down in guilt. 'Oh…'

He shrugged. 'It's fine. Happens to us all in the end. Some sooner rather than later. I better finish off that document though. May I?'

Lynda hesitated. Finally, she nodded that he could stay.

Jim walked over to the desk and swapped with Tommy in the computer chair. Tommy strolled over to the window so he could look out to the passing cars and pedestrians. 'So…' he asked. 'How much time do we have until we roll out?'

Lynda paused and glanced at her watch. 'Oh… about seven hours. Mary maybe a bit less. You guys might want to get some sleep.'

Jim laughed. 'Not me! Tight schedule, remember?'

Mary laughed. 'I won't be sleeping for a bit. It's only, what? Nine twenty-five? And we don't exactly have any more cases to solve, so… how about we do something to pass the time.'

Lynda smiled. 'If you like. Any suggestions?'

'Food would be nice,' Jim remarked.

'Not you, you're working,' she said firmly. 'Anybody else?'

Tommy raised a hand. 'I have an idea.'

'And what would that be, Detective Knightley.'

'Well Lynda, seeing as you haven't heard the story of the Circle of Saints, I figure we should tell you.'

'You *haven't* read about the Circle of Saints?' Jim exclaimed. 'I used to read it to Jake all the time!' His face straightened out a little after he realised what he'd said.

Lynda paused for a moment, taken aback. This was the first time Jim had mentioned Jake to her in over a year. She smiled a little. 'Hey, well... Tommy didn't know what a micro-recorder was!'

Jim laughed. 'Yeah well, *that* doesn't surprise me.'

'Anyway...' Tommy started. 'Who wants to hear it?'

Lynda nodded. 'Go on, detective.'

Jim put out a hand, gesturing Tommy to continue. Mary smiled and ushered him to tell it.

'All right then,' said Tommy. 'About a hundred and thirty years ago, long before this city, or most cities in this area, this whole land was covered in huge forests. Despite all the settlements and towns surrounding it, it was almost as if this place had never been touched before; like it was shielded from the outside world and the destruction of mankind. But one day, in the late July of 1885, that all changed...'

***

'Now come on and *face* it Tom!' shouted the small, pudgy man. 'We're all gonna die out here. There's no food! No water! What is it that you're exactly hoping for?'

Pastor Tom turned to Billy. Instead of his good friend, he saw a petrified child in a grown man's body, desperate for protection. They'd been walking non-stop for days, a whole town's worth of people living off scraps, and as much food as what a family would eat in a fortnight. Nobody knew what caused the town fire. Some said it was an arson, others said it was the work of a vengeful God. It made no difference. Decades of work and improvement on that small, isolated area had been consumed by flame and turned to ash in a single night. It was enough to lower anybody's spirits.

And now they were stranded; lost in an endless ocean of yellow grass. Every step was becoming agony in their soles, and they were cooking under the glow of the blazing sun like ants under a magnifying glass. Soon it would be night, and the night was always worse. Night was when wolves came out, and wolves never relented to take their food. Some nights, packs took their pickings, an old washerwoman, a skinny farmer, perhaps a helpless little baby. It didn't matter who they were, nor how much life they had in them, the victims were always bones the next morning.

'We're all dying, Tom!' Billy screamed. 'Dying! And all the people ever do is fight or grieve for the children who couldn't make it past the flames. Nobody has an idea of where we all meant to be going! We were the only town in miles, and soon our corpses will *litter* this field. It's hopeless!'

Tom glanced pitifully into Billy's dark watery eyes. He knew only one thing to say because it was his job to say it. Even if it were all lies, he had to keep the people calm. 'I believe that the Lord God will protect us, no matter what happens, Billy. Every hour I pray to him. And every hour, so does the rest of the village. We all pray to our Lord and Saviour to help us, and if we pray hard enough, I truly believe he'll save us.'

'How could you know that!' Billy protested. 'Did God save us from the fire? All those children stuck in their homes, *screaming and burning!* If God really cared, he'd send us a miracle right about now!'

And that was when a trail of green fire blazed in the sky.

***

'Sorry Tommy,' said Lynda, 'You've lost me. Who are these people?'

'Oh, right!' the detective laughed. 'According to the story, they were a bunch of villagers whose town had been burnt to the ground. For days they walked in search of somewhere to stay, but they were hopelessly lost. People starved and died - some were even driven to kill and eat the flesh of others. Nasty stuff.'

'This is a kids' story?'

'Just *a* story, all right, Lynda? A fun thing that the early people in this city made up to attract attention. Loads of places have them, you've got Warsaw, Copenhagen-'

'Murphy's Lake,' Mary added.

'So you do,' Tommy remembered, 'now that's a story and a half-'

'Okay, I get it!' Lynda exclaimed. 'Continue from the green streak in the sky, please.'

Tommy rolled his eyes. 'Anyway, so the villagers were praying for a miracle, and this is what they got…'

***

'Great God almighty!' exclaimed Billy as he saw the green streak across the night sky. 'Good Lord, forgive me for doubting your greatness.' He collapsed onto the ground; his hands clasped together. 'Oh, Lord! Oh, Lord! It's a miracle!'

Tom smiled in wonder. In truth, this shocked even him, but he couldn't let that show. The people needed somebody to lead them, to give them the strength to carry on. 'Did I not tell you we would get a sign? That if we prayed enough, we would get a miracle like this?'

'You did!' shouted Billy. 'Oh, you did, and you were right! Lead us, Tom. Follow that streak in the sky that the Lord has sent us and lead us to righteousness.'

***

'Of course, everybody was religious in those days,' continued Tommy, 'the most prominent belief in the area at the time being Christianity. Naturally, the townsfolk believed this comet, or whatever it was, was a gift from God to save them. So, for hours, they walked, following the green streak of light that was left in the sky. And finally, after many miles, they saw the streak stop…'

***

'See there!' Tom shouted to the townsfolk. 'The rock has landed not too far ahead. We are nearby, friends!'

There was an erumpent cheer from the men, women and children as they continued to walk the last few paces. Onwards they marched, never ceasing, never slowing. Finally, they reached a clearing in the trees.

Before them stood a large crater, surrounded by dozens of charred wooden trunks. The smell of burning was in the air, and the smoke around caused his eyes to water. He raised his hand, gesturing the townsfolk to cease movement as they approached this unusual sight, before edging forwards himself. Finally, he saw it, buried at the lowest point of the crater.

At the base of the crater lay a pool of sizzling molten metal, a weird kind which seemed to reflect light in a twisted kind of manner. Around the centre of this pool, the sizzling was most ferocious, with large amounts of metal quickly fizzing and darting to the sides.

Finally, something began to rise from the centre of the pool.

It was a rock, but not the typical kind found in mines or by mountains. This rock glowed like a candle or a firefly, but in an eerie, shimmering sort of way. The light produced by the strange stone was a warped green, the kind one would expect from burning copper (a sight he knew all too well when the village blacksmiths went into flames). It was something else about this stone that unsettled him the most, however, and that was the way it sounded when he approached it. It was the sound of breath in the cold, echoes in a cave, whispers in the dead of night when one is alone and nobody is there to comfort them. It was the sound of dread and death and emptiness, and equally, it was as if there was no sound at all.

'Rejoice' he proclaimed, his voice wavering in a nervous uncertainty. 'God's gift!' But when he reached down, he felt his hand burning from the heat that surrounded it. *I am forbidden to touch this rock,* he thought. *The Lord forbids me. It is the Lord, isn't it?* He rubbed his pained hand and turned to the townsfolk.

'Whatever gift our God in heaven has sent to save us, it is clear he does not feel that we're ready to take it. This is clearly a gift of great power, and only the pure can be trusted with such. Therefore, we must absolve ourselves from sin before we can wield this rock's strength. From this day forth, we shall build our new home in this habitat that the Lord has given us, a strong and proud nation that will last millennia, so that we may serve him for the duration of our lives. Every day, we shall pray to him, and when the time is right, we shall let him into our hearts and souls, and wield the power of his mighty gift.'

Tom smiled as the whole village brought up a triumphant roar of approval. Provided this area was good enough, they could start anew here, and perhaps with enough worship, prayer, and hard work, they would be able to experience the power of God's rock.

If it is a gift from him, the cynic in Tom's mind whispered. He shook the thought away. Why else would it appear in their time of need? What would any demon possibly gain from their wellbeing?

Each day, as the townsfolk prayed and prayed and prayed, spilling their thoughts and emotions and identities out to this rock before them, the rock began to reach out, feeding off their hearts and minds and burrowing deep within their consciousnesses.

***

'And so,' Tommy continued, 'on that first night, they explored the area. They found a lake full to the brim with pure, fresh water, and many animals including deer, squirrels and wild goats resided nearby. In their provisions, they still had some wheat and whiskey, and the many trees surrounding them proved sufficient for building shelter. Within the first week, each member built a house surrounding the stone, certain members of the group being allowed closer depending on what they believed was the strength of their faith. Nobody touched this crashed artefact, however. Not until one day, when a member of the city craved its power for himself. The day when the city realised that if anything, this rock was sent by something closer to the Devil.

***

'What are you doing Billy?' Tom asked, dismayed.

Billy turned around in a flurry, like a young child caught in the act of doing something horrendous. His soft face became a beetroot and his speech became a slurry of sounds that Tom just about managed to grasp the understanding of. It seemed to be something of a quickly made excuse to do with straying off the path. Tom didn't believe a word of it.

'Billy,' Tom responded, 'I'm not going to try to pretend I understood close to half of what you just said, but I know it was pretty damn pathetic. You were going towards the stone weren't y-'

'Shh, keep your voice down!' Billy exclaimed. He was greeted with a look of disappointment. 'Look,' he explained, 'yes, I was going towards the stone. But you'll understand why if you let me explain what happened last night.'

Tom felt obliged to warn Billy there and then. To call the other townsfolk and seize his friend before they were all put in danger. As each day passed, Tom grew less and less certain that this rock was a gift from the Lord at all. Every time he did so much as look at the thing, he felt a sense of malice and wickedness, a feeling as if the rock was staring right back at him. But for whatever reason, Tom wanted to hear what Billy had to say. It was the last poor decision he would ever make.

Billy's eyes lit up in excitement. 'Oh Tom, you're gonna love this!' He pointed a fat finger at his minuscule wooden cabin a few metres away. 'I was just sleepin' in my cabin, Tom. Nothin' too outa the blue. I was very tired from all the farmin' yesterday, and so I was in some pit-deep sleep. But then there was a bright light Tom! A bright white light that exploded before my eyes and woke me up. And as I looked up, my hand not so far from my face,' he made a gesture with his right hand, like he was blocking out the sun, 'who do I see Tom? Why I see my dear sweet mother in the form of an angel. And she says, "We sent that stone for you, Billy. For all of you. Touch the stone and the Lord God will give you a drop of his almighty power, and you and your villagers shall be the ones to cleanse and prepare the earth for the future to come. Hold that stone in your hand, and you shall have limitless power. Hold the stone, and you will be immortal."'

Tom looked at the beaming fat infant standing before him with great concern. He couldn't simply pass the dream as false. Perhaps the Lord had sent his mother. But it didn't feel right. In fact, ever since he had spent all that time praying to get into the land, nothing had felt right. It was like a worm had wriggled its way into his mind, feasting on his thoughts and feelings, stealing all his treasured memories and sharing gleefully in all his horrific ones. And it, whatever it was that had managed to burrow and plant itself deep inside his mind, was growing. Slowly at first but accelerating. And over time the stone which had seemed at first like a beautiful miracle was now something which he could not trust deep inside of him. It seemed whatever demon that had reached inside of Tom had grown far faster in Billy and was now twisting his grief and beliefs against him. This had to be stopped. This was so wrong, so very wrong.

'You- you're not happy, are you?' his friend asked in a sad tone.

'Look Billy I just don't-'

'I don't get it,' Billy exclaimed in a raised voice, his voice reverberating and choking slightly. 'I just don't get it at all! One minute it's all "whoop-dy doo the stone is a gift from God," but as soon as I'm the one who has an experience, you get all concerned.'

'Look, Billy, as each day passes, I grow warier and warier that-'

'The stone's not safe,' Billy shouted, 'yeah we know. Well, it seems for once that I know something that *you don't!*' His face was now boiling in anger. 'I have to wield that stone, and unleash the powers within, but if you don't agree, then I suppose you'll have to go!' He instantly swung a left hook at Tom's jaw.

Tom tasted the blood in his mouth as the world blended into a sea of grey. His feet lost all weight before lifting off the floor. Pain reverberated through his body as he smashed into the ground below him, and for a few seconds, everything went black.

When his eyes opened, he saw his friend start to run, and so Tom picked himself off the moist spring grass. It took a knock to the head, but now he knew for certain. Whatever could make Billy - sweet little innocent Billy - do that, was not anything good; but a trick from the Devil. Without thinking, he gave a shout for Billy to stop, to which there was no response, before pulling out his pistol and pulling the trigger, the bullet aimed towards Billy's leg. But it was too late. His old friend had dived to the ground a second before he pulled the trigger. The bullet whizzed over before the man's fat hands grasped the stone tightly, and green light exploded all around.

Tom's body was embraced with a soothing warmth as his body immersed in this wave of light. All anxieties were washed away with it. It felt as if the light was filling up inside him, bringing a strange tingling sensation to every point on his skin. There was something so unusual about it – it was as if the energy that now bathed him was somehow alive.

Infinite eternities later, but likewise in no time at all, Tom saw a vision that was not the light. Something penetrating his mind. A plan. A horrific plan to bring chaos to this planet. He saw a field. He saw a box. Inside, he saw the stone. He saw the rest like a progressive story; the ghost-shaped itself into a knight; the knight became the monster. A fierce woman and a little girl were caught in this monster's grasp, and the only creature that they could trust, the one with an eagle's head and lion's legs, was caged in a storm. A tyrant king and an alchemist were unmasked by two unlikely heroes, and the monster led an army of criminals and traitors to take the kingdom. And that was only the beginning.

As monsters and beasts of all kinds, battles and violence unheard of, chaos and bloodshed, rocks and spears and wars that would change the world forever flashed before Tom's eyes, he slowly felt his grip on reality drain away. Everything was going mad, chaos was unfurling, and only a few would dare to try to stop it.

And then the vision stopped.

The ground hit hard against Tom's back for the second time this day. His senses were returning to him now, and his memory of what had just happened was fading. One thing was clear in his mind though, that stone was dangerous. He rose to his feet and rubbed his eyes - only to see his good friend Billy crouching on the floor, making strange whimpering noises which could have passed as sobbing.

'Billy?' he inquired.

Billy responded with a strange croaking noise.

'What's wrong? What are you trying to say?'

'*So much…*' he attempted to respond.

'What is it, Billy?' Tom asked.

Billy stood up, his back facing Tom. '*So… much…*' he turned to Tom, and Tom was instantly hit with shock and panic. Billy's eyes were now completely jet black, and tears were streaming down his wide cheeks. With a fierce effort, he finished his sentence, '… *power!*'

Tom slowly walked back from his altered friend, who was now advancing towards him rapidly. He saw the green rock clutched between Billy's fat fingers and finally understood its malicious abilities.

'That rock's gonna kill you, Billy,' he shouted. 'Maybe not physically, but it's gonna eat your heart and soul away until your body becomes its vehicle. You know that it's evil Bil-'

Billy suddenly sprinted forward at a faster rate than Tom had ever seen even a horse run at. Before Tom could realize what was happening, Billy's right hand was clutching tightly around his throat.

'*You can't see the future!*' Billy shouted. '*I see the finest of the human race unified as a strong, immortal army, on the surface of this planet. Then the*

Others shall come, and they shall provide us with great gifts. We shall serve Them, and They shall reward us, and we shall grow to conquer it all!'

Tom wriggled under Billy's immense strength like a dying worm in the sun. Billy was his friend – no – his best friend; Tom knew him better than himself. His family, other friends, past lovers – even his favourite possessions and worst fears. This was not his best friend, but a demon wearing his skin. Tom's only hope now was to bring back the real Billy.

'Billy,' he choked. 'This. *Is. N-not. You!'*

Billy looked down at his victim as if he had only just noticed him. He stared coldly at Tom for an eternity, as if searching deeply for something about him. And finally, Billy spoke eight words. '*It seems your existence is no longer necessary.'*

Billy raised the stone and clenched it tightly. A beam of green energy fired in Tom's direction.

Tom's body exploded into green light.

***

'… he blew up his best friend.'

'What?' Jim queried, his head jolting up from the computer screen. 'I don't remember that in my version of the story.'

'Well, in the one I know; his best friend's body is ripped to shreds. Again, it's not the nicest of stories.'

'And what's this got to do with saints?' Lynda asked.

Tommy sighed. 'Well, that's to do with how the story ends. You see, now that this villager had the power of this demonic stone, he effectively had control over the entire village.'

'*Village'*

'Yup, this is years after they first arrived, they've settled down now. Anyway, for about half a decade more, this madman ruled over the village with the stone in his hand, and they obeyed. After all, they weren't ready to be destroyed either, and some of them had begun to turn rotten themselves. This, says the story, would have continued to this very day, had one woman not changed things forever.'

'And who would that be?' Lynda asked, her arms crossed.

'Nobody knows her name, or what she may have looked like, but the people allegedly called her the Cloak of the Night. She led a rebellion against the mad villagers, killed the holder of the stone, and hid the stone away for nobody to find it, allegedly using the metal from the meteorite to contain it somehow. Some tales even say she discovered how to destroy it. And from then on, regular, sane people took control of Nightdrop, a town named after the rock that dropped there in the night-time.'

'But… the wicked ones weren't finished. Even if the stone was destroyed, or even if it never existed in the first place, they would not give up on what they started. They wanted the city, they wanted the country, in fact, they wanted it all. And they wanted to live forever. So, believing themselves to be saints chosen by the stone, they called themselves the Circle of Saints, and would live in hiding for over a century until an opportunity arose…'

Lynda looked at him impatiently, waiting for what came next.

'That's it,' said Tommy with a shrug.

'That's it?' Lynda exclaimed. 'That's the whole story? I expect the writers could have milked that for a while.'

'Some people believe it to be true, you know?'

Lynda laughed. 'Well clearly, we're dealing with the bodies they leave behind! I mean, come on; a stone made by demons? A "secret" organisation that has a whole story named after them.' She turned to Jim and Mary. 'Don't you guys think it's a little -'

They were both fast asleep.

For the first proper time in a long while, Lynda burst out laughing.

'We're stopping a murder tomorrow and you're reading me a kids' story!'

Tommy chuckled. 'Tell me about it. Maybe we should get some working on this case, God knows they'd solve it faster than I could.'

'Oh… I don't know.' She smiled. 'I doubt they could tell a story as well as you!'

'Yeah…' Tommy shook his head in amusement. 'Wasn't life so much simpler back then? When we were kids?'

Oh man, she thought. *The things I'd do to be a kid again. Things were so much simpler back then.*

***

September
2025

SADIE
SEPTEMBER 11TH, 2025
THE COMPANIONS OF A MONSTER

For the first time in the last two days, Sadie didn't wake up to its bitter cackling.

Instead, she found herself alone, buried amongst the fiery autumn leaves on the forest floor. Up in the trees, birds were singing for the early morning, as if nothing bad had ever occurred in this world. They had no idea what the real world was like, not like Sadie did, but it was a welcome sound nonetheless.

The girl picked herself up, brushing the leaves and dirt off her now ragged and torn grey dress. She frowned guiltily as she saw how her clothes looked. Miss Pennyweather would have killed her for looking in such a state back at the care home. But that place was far in the past now, along with any fears of her old mistress.

Having re-oriented herself, Sadie followed the path to her father again once more. She wasn't too familiar with these woods, but the general direction of where she needed to be going was clear to her. *Keep the river slightly right and move deeper into the woods.* That was what the last map she had checked suggested, anyway. The problem would come when she couldn't see the river anymore, however. How would she know where to go then?

I suppose I could always leave a trail behind me. Like Hansel and Gretel.

But what of? Not leaves, there were plenty of them in the forest. She couldn't use food either – the squirrels would get at it. Finally, looking around, she spotted a pile of rocks. *They could work.*

With pockets and hands alike, she could probably carry about thirty stones. If she dropped one every twenty paces from the moment the river was out of sight, that would give her a good few metres before she'd need to restock. Keep doing that enough, and she may just get there.

If I do ever get there.

She stopped and nearly kicked herself for being so stupid. *Don't put stones out, you idiot, you'll only tell the monster and detectives where you're going! Why give yourself away when you may have lost them both for good.*

Sadie sighed. It had been foolish of her to leave notes for Miss Pennyweather and the detectives, and she'd regretted the decision ever since making it, but how else would they know she was okay? She knew what Miss Pennyweather was like. She may not have been the softest woman, but somewhere underneath her uptight exterior, she did care for her children.

Sadie's sense of security faded with the light as she went deeper into the forest. The river would be miles behind now, along with all civilisation and any chance of help. *As if they could have helped me.*

Somewhere amongst the trees leaves rustled and a few twigs snapped. Sadie's limbs locked, leaving her planted in the ground like one of the many trees surrounding her. She could feel beads of sweat running down her forehead and began to shake uncontrollably. It could have just been an animal. What animals lived down here again? Deer? Squirrels?

Wolves?

Her father used to tell her stories about men who'd turn into wolves. 'Down in the dark forests,' he'd tell her by her bedside, in lands long forgotten by human minds, barely touched by human feet, lived the wolfmen. Most days and most nights, they took on regular human form, travelling in large groups and hunting their food with spears and bows. As long as you didn't bother them, they wouldn't bother you. But all that would change on the night of the full moon. For, on one night every month, these regular men and women would undergo a horrible, excruciating process, and become vicious monsters, who'd rip you to shreds, tearing you limb from limb.'

Michael Williams would never shy away from a frightening tale – perhaps it was his way of toughening her up for the real world. Sadie had liked them, though. She'd always felt exhilarated when she heard a spook tale.

I'm not feeling too exhilarated right now.

She distinctly remembered the last night he'd read to her. It was a chilly night in October 2023, back in his old cottage by the river. He was reading "The Plight of the Vampire Child," when there was a knock at the door. Her father had told her to keep quiet while he checked it out. Greeting him at the entrance of the house had been three tall gentlemen, their outfits blue, cuffs in their hands.

'Michael Williams, you have the right to remain silent. Anything you say can and will be used against you in the court of law…' Immediately the men had started snapping cuffs around his wrists and dragging him away to the back of their car. She remembered how she'd screamed that night. For her dad to come back. For the police to let him go. Perhaps they would listen to her if she screamed loud enough. Or perhaps not.

'Be brave, Sadie!' he'd shouted as they pushed him into the confines of their vehicle. 'Be my brave little girl!'

I will be, Daddy. I will.

Sadie was sick of this. She was sick of being so afraid of everything. She'd been running away for days; nothing should have frightened her anymore.

'What do you want!' she shouted into the forest. 'If you want to take me, go ahead. Seriously, take me now for all I care, *kill* me if you want! You haven't tried it yet, but I'm sure you could give it a go if you plucked up the courage! Just do it!'

There was no reply.

Sadie slumped onto the ground and put her head in her hands. Maybe she was going insane. Hadn't she heard that fear could make people crazy sometimes?

Or maybe I just want to be home again.

She picked herself up once more, her right hand clenched tightly around one of the rocks she'd gathered earlier. *Next time he comes for me, I'll be ready*, she thought. *I hope he comes. Even if I hit him just once, it will be worth everything.*

For hours she continued down those dark woods, nothing to keep her occupied but her thoughts. Every so often she'd hear a sound - maybe an animal, a deer perhaps – that would cause her to freeze, her rock ready again in her palm. After endless steps through the dark, the branches above her lessened in number, and more of the midday sun began to peer through. At last, Sadie saw the field.

Stretching for miles across, it glowed like the Tuscan sun.

Rows and rows of burnt tall grass filled the landscape, the majority of it nearly twice her height, and in the distance, about four miles away, stood the familiar abandoned cottage that she'd visited as a child.

How didn't they find you? How did you stay hidden for so long?

The house had been abandoned since long before she had been alive, long before her father had even moved into the city. He'd discovered it one day as a child, just a few years older than she was now, during an exploration of the forest. Something about it must have intrigued him because he kept coming back for years after. He'd bring his friends, his wife, even Sadie herself a couple of times. It was as if something was there that he needed to check on - an item that he'd looked after since the first day he'd arrived there.

Maybe it was that box. The one he didn't want me to touch. It was the reason he escaped prison. So he could stop dangerous men from…

In that moment, Sadie understood everything. *The thing outside my bedroom could have killed me so many times, but it didn't. It just scared me. Taunted me. Drove me to find Daddy. And that's exactly what it wanted.*

Sadie began to run back, back into the dark forest that she'd spent hours trying to escape. If she was quick, it wouldn't find her father or the thing he was trying to guard. She could go back, cross the river, lead the monster somewhere else, *anywhere else.*

Her course was blocked by two grown-ups in obsidian black clothes and bandanas. They had just emerged from the nearby bushes and were both holding rustic looking shotguns. Sadie heard footsteps, and sure enough, six or so more men and women were walking around her, surrounding her from all sides.

And then she heard the whirring.

She'd never seen her monster in the light before, but that didn't change the rate at which her heart pumped or the dread that made her skin crawl. Something did interest her as it emerged from the dark forest, however, and that was the identity of this thing that had chased her for so long. Everything about it - its limbs and body and head and arms – was not organic, but simply mechanical. She had suspected such after the bolt that hit the raccoon and the bridge incident, but now she could see it all. What she had once thought were tentacles trailing down from its left arm was, in fact, a tangle of loose wires, sparks flying off in random directions every so often. Between each of its unnaturally long limbs and its broad-shouldered body was a long metal tube, large enough to fit a human arm within, along with an assortment of smaller transparent vessels, which she noticed were pumping all sorts of strange-coloured liquids and powders. Its shell was an ivory white, with areas of chipped paint all around, and its bright crimson eyes were only so bright because they were two electrically powered spotlights with cameras in the corners.

The machine made its typical horrific screech of a laugh as it saw her as if she was some stupid dog doing tricks for it. For once she understood its amusement. Through fear and her love for her father, it had manipulated her to lead it right where it needed to go. Just metres away was a house holding all the power in the world, and it only needed to chase a child to find it.

'Hello Sadie,' it said enthusiastically in its deep, scratchy British voice. 'Allow me to introduce you to "The Children of the Reaper." They may not be as smart or handsome as my good self, but they have similar motives and it helps to have the extra firepower. Right, Nathan?'

Another man appeared to the creature's left. He was tall and bony and had a long-stitched scar pulling up the right side of his face. His body was covered with slim-fitting black clothing, and it seemed his left eye was suiting the colour scheme. 'Just get on with it, you sadistic monster,' he groaned, as if bored.

The creature laughed. '*Sadistic monster!* That I am. Tie her up ladies and gents. She's more useful to me alive.'

One woman pulled out a large length of rope, and suddenly Sadie was being pulled around forcefully from all sides. They started with her hands, pulling the rope so tight that they began to feel numb. Then they moved onto her mouth, tying it tightly so little noise would escape. Finally, they cut a length of rope and looped it around her neck, tying a knot at the back of her head to make a kind of makeshift noose at her end of the line. The other end of the rope was given to the creature, which tugged her body back forcefully many times as if she were some dog pulling ahead.

'See Sadie?' it said condescendingly. 'I did catch you in the end!' It tugged at her once more, causing her to fall on her back and wheeze.

The creature chuckled in the usual fashion. 'I could do this all day Sadie, I really could, but more exciting things are on the horizon. You and I - or rather just *I* - have a weapon to collect. And your daddy's going to help me get it!'

***

SAM
SEPTEMBER 11TH, 2025
STORMFELD

Sam slammed the door of his car fiercely, the icy air howling around him; blowing ferociously through the baked maroon grass surrounding the dull mossy walls of the prison before him. The walls towered over all surrounding buildings and landmarks and were tipped with tangles of barbed wire to ensure the futility of escape. At each corner was a guard tower, each equipped with a spotlight and a guard - always on the lookout, armed with a firearm.

Sam breathed heavily and approached the entrance, determined in his task. He had to find that girl, or what good would he be?

Following several security checks and a long line of questioning, he found himself being escorted by two large prison guards to the warden's office. He was rather shocked that there was a possibility he could be any kind of threat - after all, he was not a reasonably strong man and any weapons that he had were taken from him. What would or could he possibly do that would be deemed dangerous?

The sun blazed over the courtyard like a hovering flame. Such warm weather was unnatural at this time of year. Nonetheless, dozens of the prisoners dotted around the area could be seen shirtless or dripping with sweat. Some were lying under benches just to gain some cover from the sweltering heat, and Sam noticed a few acting rowdy, trying to gain his attention. *Thank God there's a fence,* he thought. Heat and police officers were two things guaranteed to stir up a crowd of convicts.

He was extremely relieved to be inside once more, and now he found himself looking down a long grey corridor. Looking through windows of adjacent corridors, he saw large rooms filled with many cells, several occupied by bored-faced inmates and melancholy cons. There was something about this prison which seemed to suck the joy out of the air, leaving a rather uncomfortable sensation inside of him. After a number of twists, turns and steps, they finally made it to the warden's office. The guards made sure to stay as close to Sam as possible as they entered the room. It seemed they really had no faith in "upholders of the law."

'It's okay fellas, you can leave him here with me,' said a man across the room. He walked briskly over and gave Sam a firm shake of the hand. 'You must be Detective Turner. My name is Warden Peter Locke, I very much appreciate your coming here.'

The warden of Stormfeld Prison was a large, stout fellow, with stumpy legs resembling what Sam had grown to call eggplants. He wore a black pinstripe suit which took on the shape of a large balloon when wrapped tightly over his plump peach of a body. Balancing at the tip of his broken looking nose was a pair of small circular spectacles, and on his head, lay curtain-like, oily black hair with a bald cap at the scalp.

'Sam, please, and I'm happy to help after the other officers…' He failed to think of the right word. 'Well, quite frankly they gave up I suppose.'

The warden hummed in sympathy as the guards strolled off from behind. 'Well, it stumps me! Come, please, sit down.'

In the small, cluttered pigsty that was Warden Locke's office, was a wide birch table, a chair at each side. As they took their seats, Sam took a moment to examine the area he was situated in. In the entirety of this cramped room, there was one single window, which streamed in just enough light to allow him to see the outlines and dim colours of the furniture. On the walls hung many picture frames, full of photographs, poetry, soliloquies and newspaper clippings.

'So, detective… or Sam, I should say. I must ask… what has led you to come here when so many others have failed?' He squinted. 'Not to say that you are not good, detective, it's just… well, we've had several seasoned officers come here before and they've all tried and failed to understand any of this. Williams seems to have gone completely off the radar, and the means of his escape are unbeknownst to anyone! What makes you think you can solve this, a puzzle that has stumped officers for months, in one day?'

Sam sighed. 'I'll be honest Warden, the answer to that question is because it doesn't concern just Williams.'

The warden looked puzzled. 'No? Who else? The other inmate who escaped? The prison staff? Or are you one of the ones who believe Mr G-' He stopped himself and smiled. 'The "Nightdrop Backstabber" is involved in all of this?'

Sam shook his head. 'No sir, it's none of those people. The person in danger is Williams' daughter, Sadie. She's on the run, being chased by… well God knows what it is that's chasing her, but the point is she's in trouble. We know she's on foot, and we know she may be looking for her father, so if we knew where she was going-'

The warden put a hand up. 'I understand. You would be able to find her, and Williams with her. Well, I suppose that's as good a reason as any.' He frowned. 'Peculiar… I recall a past officer questioning Williams' daughter on his whereabouts.' He shrugged. 'Perhaps she was a good liar. Now I suppose you'd appreciate it if I were to tell you the details regarding Mr Williams' escape?'

'I'm all ears, Warden,' Sam responded.

'So, I was having my breakfast with the wife and kids, as you would, when suddenly I hear sirens go off. The sound was coming from the prison – we could hear it because we live just under a mile away - and so I pulled on my suit fast as I could and go and went to see the problem; that problem, I would soon find out, being the breakout. The night before, you see, Williams had been put in solitary for fighting with an inmate. He was to spend the rest of the night in there to teach him a lesson. Wasn't the first time he'd fought either, oh no. He'd been fighting on a multitude of occasions ever since his first day here. It was usually with the same person too, funnily enough! But that night, when he and this prison brute who he'd been fighting named Cody Busher were put in, both escaped. The next morning, all that was left was two great big holes that would have taken years to dig in the walls of their confinement blocks.'

'Both confinement blocks?' Sam asked, a notepad and pencil in his hands.

'Oh yes, not just Williams. Busher also escaped. Funny that. You wouldn't have thought Williams would help the guy considering their long-standing rivalry at the prison. Two months later, and we don't have a clue of how two sworn enemies both managed to destroy the walls of their solitary confinement blocks in one night, with the only trace of them being the half-eaten porridge bowl that Busher was given that evening. After breaking the walls, they'd have found themselves in the piping areas. There, they made another hole, this one right through the metal of the pipe that travels all the way to the Hudson.'

Sam reviewed what he had written down for a good few moments. In the deafening silence, he processed what could destroy concrete walls and metal piping in one night.

'I'm guessing the holes aren't there for me to inspect anymore?'

'Afraid not,' the warden replied, 'but we have photographs.' He pulled out two rectangular cards from his draw and slid them across to Sam.

The two photographs showed holes in the walls of a dimly lit room, large enough to fit a horse through. In each of the photographs, next to these holes were large mounds of rubble. That was all he had to go on. The story of a warden and two pictures of holes. *What the hell can I do with this?* he thought. He lifted the picture closer, scanning it for any minute details or interesting discoveries, but all he ended up finding in addition was the dinner trays of each inmate.

'How're you doing there?' the warden asked wearing a concerned expression.

'Fine, fine,' Sam lied. *This is hopeless. Completely and utterly hopeless. A child needs my help and I'm stood here looking at photographs.* 'Is this all you have on the escape? No sightings of Williams or anything?'

The warden shrugged. 'We sent a team off to find him, but it was only hours after the escape that we actually discovered they were missing. Solitary has no cameras, you see, and it's rarely checked. I mean, the only thing that gets in and out of there is the food.'

Sam banged his hands to his head in frustration. *Could they have smuggled something in their clothing?*

No, he reasoned, *they would have been checked beforehand. Besides what could be small enough to hide from a guard but big enough to cut through both stone and metal?*

The warden shook his head. 'The last news we had was that Cody Busher was spotted on a flight to New Mexico. By the time the authorities got to the airport, he'd already left. We now have officers searching for him all over the place in the area, and given the state of things, Williams could be with Busher right now.'

'No, no, no…' Sam moaned. 'Sadie's father distinctly told her to find him in his letter to her. "Come to our special place," it said. What father would expect their child to walk to Mexico if they were in danger?' He looked at the photographs again. It was just holes and dinner trays.

The warden sighed. 'Well, I'm sorry detective, I really am. I wish I could help you more than that. I did tell you; this has stumped many detectives before you.'

Sam groaned. It reminded him of a time he was once talking to his father during math homework. '*I can't do this!*' he'd shouted in fury as he'd slammed the pencil on the table.

'*Hey, hey, it's all right,*' his dad had told him. '*Sometimes you've just got to take a step back. Open your mind. Breathe. Treat the problem like you already know the answer and then stress won't affect your thinking. That's how I solve crimes, I'm sure it'll do good for your homework.*'

Open your mind. Breathe in.

He took a look at the photograph one last time, and finally, he spotted it. It was a subtle difference, but an important one nonetheless, one that changed everything.

Like a fast-running stream, the facts shot into Sam's head piece by piece as Sam picked up all the details. The dinner on the tray, the timing of the fight, the direction of the rubble, it all fell into place so quickly. One deduction progressed to the other so swiftly and elegantly that Sam was having difficulty catching up with himself. Finally, his brain made a conclusion that he could not refute.

'Warden,' he blurted, 'was there a chef that retired recently?'

The warden stared at him in stunned silence. 'But how did you-'

'We'll get to that later,' Sam declared, but first tell me, what was the name of the chef that retired?

The words choked out of his mouth, 'Brendon Lyan. Why?'

'Brendon Lyan…' he nodded slowly. 'Okay, that's good, very good. So I was correct then?'

The warden looked bemused. 'Yeah, but how, and why is his retirement important whatsoever?'

Sam seemed to miss the question. 'And it was Cody Busher who only ate half of his porridge, correct?'

The warden rolled his eyes, 'why, yes, but is that really necessary?'

'Warden,' Sam remarked with a smile, 'it's the most necessary detail in this whole case. I didn't get it before, why the other detectives chose to stay in this disgusting city, but now…' He beamed from ear to ear. 'Williams ate all of his dinner, Busher didn't. The rubble in Williams' block was facing away from the camera, down the hole. The rubble in Busher's was inside the cell, facing the camera. This is hardly a coincidence, Warden sir. You see, if the rubble patterns are facing opposite ways then that means one wall must have been broken on the inside of the cell and one on the outside. If it was an outsider who freed these two prisoners, the rubble for both walls would be on the same side, either outside the wall or in the cell, depending on the means used to break the walls.

The fact that they are not suggests that one of the prisoners broke their wall from the inside and broke the other prisoner's wall from the outside.'

'Hang on a minute,' the warden protested, putting his hand out to stop him, 'these guys are sworn enemies. They were fighting since the day they arrived here, you can't be trying to say that one broke the other out.'

Sam smiled. 'So they arrived at this prison together, did they?'

'Yes,' the warden exclaimed, 'but they didn't know each other!'

'I expect not,' said Sam, 'but if you were facing a long sentence in prison and a guy approached you saying that he had a plan to get you both out, providing that all you had to do was pretend to hate him for the next few months, wouldn't you go with it?'

'I don't follow, are you suggesting they're friends' said the warden. 'And that they'd been planning this escape for months?'

'Perhaps not friends, just two men who wanted to escape,' said Sam. 'I'm going to assume that the man who orchestrated this plan was Williams, due to knowledge from Sadie that he was hiding something very dangerous, and that he needed to be ready to escape at any time. Should this thing that he'd been hiding be discovered, he'd be ready to escape instantly. He must have known that the quickest way out was through the pipes and that the closest area to the pipes was the solitary confinement blocks. To get there, he'd need to get into trouble. Specifically, he'd need to get into a fight. That's what Busher was for. With me so far?'

'Just about,' said the warden.

'Now think. If they had just fought on the day of their escape, the guards would wonder why two prisoners who rarely talked were suddenly having a brawl. Williams couldn't risk Busher giving away their escape plan on the day of their escape! So, to avoid that risk, they fought since day one. Sure, the guards asked questions initially, but this would be ages before the escape, and Williams could keep Busher in the dark until a more convenient time. Eventually, the guards would be used to their fighting, used to the fact that Busher and Williams simply "hated" each other, so Williams and Busher would no longer be questioned every time they attacked one another. Then on the day of the escape, Williams and Busher would fight once more so that they could be thrown in solitary with barely any questions asked.

'Now, back to the solitary blocks. We know one prisoner broke out from the inside, but the question is how, as then we'll know who did it. Explosives would make most of the rubble blow out of the cell, while tools or chemicals, needing to take longer, would cause the rubble to shower down into the cell block. For starters, we can eliminate tools. No criminal could smuggle a tool into solitary that would be large enough to destroy a wall in one night. Maybe a small tool could be brought in, but it would need the aid of chemicals to weaken the walls. We can rule out explosives, as there were guards within earshot and it would be too risky, leaving us with chemicals, likely acid given the speed in which he would need to break down the walls to ensure ample time for escape. If it was acid, whoever broke the walls from the inside would have the majority of the rubble left inside their block afterwards, as opposed to outside of it, meaning the one with the acid and possibly a small tool in hand would be…'

'Busher,' the warden finished as he began to catch on.

'Exactly,' Sam remarked. 'Busher broke the wall from the inside and then broke Williams' cell wall from the outside in the pipe corridor. But the question is, how did he get the chemicals and possibly a small tool into his cell?'

The warden gave him a blank expression.

Sam smiled. 'The half-eaten porridge!'

'The *what?*'

'Yep,' said Sam with a smile, 'the half-eaten porridge serving, as opposed to the fully eaten porridge on Williams' tray. A small acid bottle and some kind of tool could fit easily inside. As to how they got in there, well, Williams was clearly in no rush. This whole plan was for *if* he needed to escape, not when, otherwise why leave it to two months before your sentence ends? I assume he had many connections on the outside who he could pay to buy the acid and possibly the tool. Then all he'd need to do is bribe a chef to put it in Busher's meal. Any chef working in a prison, seeing what this place was like first hand, would need a great deal of money to be persuaded to do such a thing, enough at least to retire from, and get as far away as possible from a place where there would possibly be an escape in the near future. That was why I asked you whether a chef had retired recently. Your answer confirmed my theory.'

The warden, a baffled look on his face, attempted to recap what he had just been told. 'So, Williams tells Busher that he can get both of them out one day as long as Busher keeps having fights with him when instructed to. A year later, something to do with this dangerous object you kept mentioning makes Williams want to escape, so he briefs Busher, gets a load of outside guys to provide some highly acidic chemicals, and *then* bribes a prison chef to put the acid bottle and maybe a tool in one of the porridge servings next time he and Busher are thrown into solitary for fighting. Later on, the two fight, get thrown in solitary, Busher uses the acid and maybe a tool to break out of his cell, and destroys Williams' cell wall from the outside. The two men search the pipe corridor, find the sewage pipe leading to the Hudson, break into it with the remaining acid and hey presto the river takes them miles away from the police that can bother to look for them.'

Sam nodded.

The warden rubbed his head in dismay. 'I have to say, that is quite the escape.'

Sam shrugged. 'A man will do anything if he has the motive to do it. The next problem is to find out where that chef went. If anyone but Busher knows where Williams is hiding, it's him. What did you say his name was again? Brendon Lyan?'

The warden had a deeply upset look on his face.

'What's the matter?' Sam queried. 'You're not feeling bad about the escape, are you Warden?'

The warden shook his head. 'No Sam… No, it's just I didn't tell you while you were so excited but… Brendon Lyan's dead.'

Sam stared at the warden blankly. 'What?'

The warden sighed. 'He was murdered just two weeks ago on his way to the airport. Some woman in a bandana came up to his taxi and shot him in the chest. Have you not heard the news? I think he was moving to Canada, but what do I know. I'm sorry to have to tell you this…'

Mary told me about this, he thought. *They're covering it up. Whoever's chasing Sadie tried to cover up Williams' location. That way they'd reach him before we did. And if Williams was right about the police station not being trustworthy… perhaps that explained how the Circle discovered Brendon Lyan.*

He hit the desk with brutal force and closed his eyes. 'Great. Well, I suppose I'll have to investigate a murder n-'

Suddenly a tall man came bursting through the door, his skin dark, a confident smile on his face, wearing a cream and white suit. Under his left arm was a large assortment of files. 'I'm so sorry to burst in on you like this warden, but I need to speak to Mr Turner immediately.'

The warden was flabbergasted. 'What in the-'

'Sam, listen to me,' the man interrupted, 'time is running out for all of us! You *have* to come with me now.'

Sam approached him slowly. 'That voice…' It seemed so familiar. When he worked it out, his heart was racing, and he so nearly hit the man straight in the face. '*You! You* were the one talking to Carlos in the alleyway! You said you'd deal with me!'

The warden stepped forwards confused. 'Sorry, *who* are you?'

The man shook his head. 'Calm down, all right? I know what I said, but you've got this all very wrong. I am not the bad guy, far from it, but you don't need to believe that yet. All you need to know is that Sadie is in great danger and that if you come with me, I can tell you how to find her.'

Sam didn't believe it one bit, but it would be quicker to hear this man now rather than arrest him. The clock was ticking, and he'd need to find Sadie fast.

'Fine. I'll come. You're right, she is in danger, and there's nothing I won't do to stop that from being the case. But *first*, I need you to tell me something. Who the hell are you?'

The man laughed. 'I'm… many things. My name is Jordan Ellington. I'm your partner's boyfriend and colleague, but more importantly, I'm the lawyer to the one you call the Backstabber.'

Speak to Jordan, Sam remembered. It could still be a trap though. 'Oh yeah, now I trust you even more. You're in a relationship with one backstabber and a lawyer to another! How fitting. And now I suppose you want me to talk to him, to believe his story. Tell me, how on earth do you expect me to believe a man when I don't even know his name.'

Jordan shrugged. 'Well, I don't suppose such legalities matter if we lose this fight. Come with me, Sam, and I promise you, you'll find out everything. Who he is, what he did, and the chaos heading for this city. But it needs to be now.'

Sam hesitated for a few moments and glanced to the warden, who looked both baffled and flustered at this current time. He turned his head back to the lawyer. 'You said something was coming to the city. Like what? A storm?'

The man shook his head. 'An army with the power of life and death in their hands. And it's being led by the Devil himself.'

***

July
2025

JIM, LYNDA
JULY 11TH, 2025
ONE STEP AHEAD

'All right, everyone!' Murdock declared in the heat of a debriefing. 'Today we get the rare chance to do what many officers dream of. Today we get the chance to beat a killer at his own game.'

He plodded up and down along the front of the beige-coloured briefing room, fiddling the whiteboard pen anxiously between his fingers. On the board behind was a crudely drawn bird's-eye view of St Luke's Hospital and St Luke's Primary School – two areas full of vunerable, almost helpless citizens, any one of whom possibly at risk to the Circle and their machine.

Jim slumped wearily on the desk. While he was deeply concerned for the safety of his family, he had no idea why he needed to be here, when he could have been looking after them, checking that they were all right. He wouldn't be with the Tactical Response Team after all. Murdock, Lynda, even *Mary* wouldn't allow that.

'Initially,' continued Murdock, 'we will have two teams evacuating the areas, led by Captain Parker at the school and Lieutenant Stevens at the hospital. The next two groups will take over, allowing the first groups to lead all civilians to safety while both the hospital and the school is being thoroughly inspected. The civilians will then each be questioned thoroughly, and those who we deem suspicious will be taken into custody for further questioning. For the duration of this operation, you will be communicating with these…' Murdock gestured to a box of small black devices before pulling one out. 'These are state-of-the-art comms devices; each and every one of you should be equipped with one. I'm sure you'll be familiar with how to use it from your training but allow me to give you a quick run-down.'

It went like that for what felt like hours. All the while Jim was groaning inside from anticipation and dread, fearful for the safety of the ones he loved.

Finally, after asking for a quick word with Tommy, the chief told them to roll out. Immediately, dozens of officers laden in protective uniform emerged from their seats and headed downstairs for their duties.

'What did he want you for?' Jim asked Tommy when he finally emerged from his talk with Murdock.

'Oh, he was just making sure he knew every detail. You know how stressed he gets. Tries to run the whole thing.'

'Well, he does run the whole thing,' said Lynda, coming up behind them like a ghost. 'Unfortunately,' she muttered.

Jim sighed as he entered the lift. 'Well… I guess I'll see you both later.'

Lynda gave him a cautious look. 'What will you be doing when we're gone?'

Jim smiled. 'Oh, you know. Writing upon the case, anxiously awaiting a call from my family, boring civilian stuff.'

For the first time in a long while, Lynda warmly smiled at her husband. 'See you later, Jim.'

They both exited the lift swiftly, Tommy nodding as he went.

'Hey…' Jim called.

Both detectives swivelled around quickly.

'Don't…' He looked down to his feet. 'Don't die or anything.'

Tommy held a thumbs up. 'We'll try our hardest. Imagine how lame that would be. Dying at an elementary school!'

Jim laughed. 'I'd rather not see that on anyone's graves.'

The last thing he saw was the faces of Tommy and Lynda before the doors closed to a shut.

Jim did not press the microphone button in the request of going up any floors. Instead, he waited a good few moments until he could see Tommy and Lynda leaving at the end of the corridor through the transparent glass doors. Once they were gone, he hit the "open doors" button and trailed them from behind.

'Okay Team, re-group at the vans!' Jim heard a woman shout on the other side of the blue corridor doors.

The vans were on the other side of the building. That meant Jim could reach his car at the front car park and head down to the hospital. He couldn't afford to be seen - Lynda wouldn't go easy on him if she knew he was "getting involved again"- but he had to see his family. He had to know they were safe after abandoning them for so long.

Once in his vehicle, he strapped on his seatbelt and quickly left the station. For the next half an hour, he carefully drove down the backroads of Nightdrop city, being sure to shield himself from view should a police van be nearby. One time his heart was racing as he found himself in a long line of traffic when the vans came driving past, but luckily, they passed him without any hesitation. Even if he was spotted, he wasn't exactly their top priority.

When he finally arrived outside the hospital, he felt an icy shudder down his spine. It was so tall that just being under its shadow felt like he was entering the early evening. The wind rushing through the partially open window was icy as it kissed his face, and the clouds were a miserable grey. In the distance, he saw numerous people pacing in and out of the building. There were the officers - with their hard jackets of dark blue, and their black helmets that left them barely distinguishable from one another - and then there were the people. Dozens of men and women, young and old, some walking with a cast, sitting in a wheelchair or even connected to an IV drip, filed out of the building in an orderly fashion, the masses being split into groups and sorted into different vans.

Jim parked on a close road and squinted to view what was going on. It seemed all the civilians had been successfully rounded up now, with the vans driving off to their respective areas, bringing the greatly sick to further hospital care and the healthy for police questioning. He couldn't see his mother or sister, there were many people after all, but their absence concerned him. *Where are you? Elly? Mom?*

He checked his watch. It was 11:30 – exactly eleven hours before the murder was scheduled to take place in Brigson's gospel book. It was slightly disconcerting that Brigson had left the Circle's plans in a biblical text, but perhaps he was trying to be discreet. But then there was the question of why he needed to write the times down in the first place. A bad memory? Putting them down just in case? That didn't feel like Sebastian Brigson.

For some peace of mind, Jim pulled out the radio

communicator. There had been so many in the briefing room earlier – of course, Murdock wouldn't have seen him take one. For the briefing they would have one officer broadcasting to all vans – if Jim was lucky, he could listen in at the right time, make sure everything was going smoothly. After a flick of the switch and a few dial turns, he finally tuned in to the other officer's frequencies. 'Yes… we're looking for a male named Sebastian Brigson,' said a woman's commanding voice. 'He's about an inch taller than me, brown hair, a scar across his right eye and walks with a limp.' There was the sound of some rustling of paper as well as a confused murmur. 'According to these records, we should also be on the look-out for a weird kind of… robot that Brigson apparently uses to kill his victims. It's… white, about six feet tall, has long thin limbs, large boots and two glowing blue circular eyes. Everyone understand?'

There was a murmur of agreement over the communicator.

'Ok Team,' said the squad leader, 'roll out and form up!'

Sure enough, each officer exited the remaining vans one by one and formed into numerous groups. Jim assumed each group would initially hold a floor once it was checked thoroughly. Then, they would follow several search procedures, ensuring no civilians, innocent or guilty, or dangerous items were left in the hospital. This search would go on for hours, ensuring that nothing remained to put the hospital, or the civilians nearby, at any risk.

Outside, a few officers remained to keep people away. Jim recognised one distinctly. His name was Graham Adams, the captain of the Missing Persons Department. Beside him, several other officers were posted by the police tape, answering questions and preventing people from danger.

Out of nowhere, Jim's phone began to vibrate in his pocket. As he pulled it out, he noticed Elly's number on the front. He'd forgotten to call her. How could he forget?

He accepted and placed the phone to his ear, only to hear many muffled sobs.

'Elly?' he asked in a panic. *'Elly, are you okay?'*

He heard her cry just before she spoke, but the words that she said to him were not hers. *'We... have your beloved mother and sister, Jim... We warned you not to try to trick us...'* The phone hung up.

Jim collapsed into his seat in shock and dropped the phone. They took them. Elly and his mother, his only remaining family. Why? Who would do such a thing?

A better question is how? Every man, woman and child was escorted out of that building by a police officer. How could anybody get my family out when the place is under complete police supervision?

There was only one logical explanation, and it was one that Jim dreaded.

He left the car and sprinted into the hospital.

***

'All right B Squad, roll out!'

Lynda pulled on her collar to allow some cool air to her body. Protective as these suits were, a suit made of lead would be more comfortable to move in. Sweat poured down her face in beady droplets, and her breath was long and heavy, steaming up her dark visor so that her visibility was like looking through fog. *How am I meant to catch a killer in this?* she thought to herself.

Lynda jumped out of the van onto the warm concrete, her boots smacking against the floor. In her hands, she carried a carbine, one of the new ones recently donated to the station. If the suit didn't make her feel like lead, the firearm certainly did, this time morally too. If she had to use it, it would be in self-defence, or to protect the life of another. She would not risk killing anyone just to stop them running, even if they were a murderer. That just wouldn't be right.

As they marched in through the side entrance, Lynda spotted another officer, dressed exactly like her in every respect, briskly approach her. The officer placed a hand on her shoulder, pulling her to the side while the others marched in.

Lynda did not recognise this individual immediately. The helmets on these suits were far too concealing, but their identity was all too clear once they lifted it off, revealing a tumbling cascade of frizzy hair.

Lynda reciprocated, making her face clear to her colleague. 'Morning Captain. I'm surprised you even recognised me in this thing.'

Mary laughed. 'You're a pretty tall woman, Lynda! The evac's all done, and every kid *and* teacher has been registered three or four times.'

'Excellent.' She grimaced. 'Time to stop this in its tracks. If there's anything to stop that is…'

'Well, I do hope not…' Mary nodded to the door. 'You better get to work. If all goes to plan, I'll see you tomorrow with some leads.'

'And if it doesn't?' Lynda asked.

Her colleague hit her on the shoulder. 'Hey! Be optimistic for once! Everything will be fine, I promise.'

Lynda nodded slowly, forcing a small smile between her lips. 'That would be nice.'

Mary held a hand up in a small wave. 'I ought to go, got to drive a van halfway across the city! See you round.' She ran across the road back to one of the evacuation vans.

The moment Mary was out of sight, Lynda's smile dropped. It was astonishing how well Mary managed to keep positive in a city so full of disgust and corruption. What was there possibly to be smiley about when three men and women had already died? Even the weather was awful.

She's had it easier I guess, she thought. *One of the lucky ones.* Thinking back, Lynda wasn't too sure she knew anything about Mary's past at all.

In a few moments, she found herself escorting large groups of children and teachers alike through the school, surrounded by fellow officers, all of whom dressed in dark blue, armoured uniform and black helmets. She hadn't a clue of where Tommy was – most likely he was in a separate group patrolling around the school, but she couldn't be sure who was who with all the gear and helmets that they had to wear. It unnerved her that she couldn't identify a single one of her colleagues. It was as if anybody could have been under those masks.

'Excuse me, officer!' shouted an elderly teacher in the middle of the group she was escorting. '*Please*, nobody's listening to me!'

She brought her head closer. 'What's the issue, madam?'

'There's a little boy. Christopher, he's called. He was put on my register, but now he's gone missing. He kept asking me if he could go to the toilet, I'm assuming that's where he must be!'

Lynda nodded slowly. This kind of thing happened all too often. 'I promise you I'll find him, madam. What does he look like?'

'Short, about waist height, brown, straight-combed hair and round glasses.'

Lynda nodded and brought her communication device close

to her head, "B Squad, this is Lieutenant Griffen, we have an unsupervised child roaming the school grounds, requesting patrol groups to search immediately. Do you copy?'

The voice that replied was Tommy's. 'Copy, lieutenant, could you give a description?'

She did so and lowered her device. 'I promise you we'll find this boy, madam.'

'Oh, thank you! Thank you!'

Lynda strolled out of the school gates over to the black evacuation van and knocked on the driver's door window. When he opened it, she spoke. 'There's a lost kid somewhere in this school, I'm going to go search for him. You all good here?'

He held two thumbs up and nodded.

Lynda bolted to the school, apathetic to whatever regulations told her she couldn't. Once inside, she turned to face a long corridor with a pin board and a flight of wooden stairs to the right. Climbing the stairs, she sighed in relief as she found a sign for the toilets. After climbing one more flight, she finally found the toilet doors, only to see another officer standing there already. He was tall and thin, presumably male, and for a moment, Lynda thought he may have been Tommy. It was only when he spoke that she noticed the difference. This man's thick American accent was far deeper, and she shuddered to find it nearly recognisable.

'Don't worry, ma'am, I've got him,' the man said. Lynda saw that a small, brown-haired boy was wrapped under his arm. The boy looked guilty, as if caught doing something wrong. 'This one was writing stuff on the walls of the toilets while everybody else evacuated as they should have done.'

Lynda looked at the man carefully, unable to see his face

under his helmet visor.

'Do I know you?' she asked, certain she recognized his voice.

'Well… not extremely well. I'm a CSI assistant as well as being TRT qualified. Artie Webber?'

Lynda thought hard for a moment. 'I don't think we've met,' she said finally.

'Well, it's nice to meet you,' the man said to her. 'I better be getting this boy to the rest of the school, excuse me.'

'Oh sure, yeah.' Lynda moved out of the way against a wall.

Artie Webber, she thought. Now that she considered it, that name did sound rather familiar. *Artie Webber, Artie Webber…*

The man was halfway down the stairs with the boy when she remembered. Artie Webber was a roboticist who had just won the Nobel Peace Prize. And the voice of the "officer" she was just talking to, belonged to…

'Brigson.'

Lynda shot down the stairs, sprinting at nearly impossible speeds considering the weight she was carrying from her armour. Brigson, his face behind a visor, was beginning to run now, dragging the boy from a tight hold around the wrist. At the base of the stairwell, Brigson turned a full one-eighty around the bannister, running away from the office and making his way further down the corridor. Lynda trailed behind, screaming into her communicator for back-up. When he reached a set of large double doors to his right, he smashed his foot through one, and proceeded to climb out, still dragging the boy tightly by the arm. As she followed through the same shattered hole, she saw the man reach a white van with sliding side doors, before he proceeded to open up the back, revealing a space full of computer machinery and monitors.

'Stop right there!' she shouted.

He cackled. 'Really?' he asked as he slowly turned around to her, pulling his helmet off in the process, revealing his pale, calculating face. 'I never thought police officers actually said that.' He savagely pushed the boy that he was holding into the open van.

'Don't lay a finger on the boy you son of a-'

'You don't need to worry Lynda,' Brigson said smoothly. 'Just call your backup, and the boy will be fine. Even if I did manage to take him, I wouldn't be the one laying any fingers. That's my partner's job.'

Lynda gave him a puzzled expression. 'Your partner? You don't mean the machine?'

'No, I don't!' His chest moved up and down vigorously as he laughed again. Everything was one big joke to Sebastian Brigson. 'Lynda, I do love my creation, but it's certainly not a person!' He shook his head. 'No… I mean the man who got me this uniform.' He gestured to his body. 'What, you thought I made it myself?'

The young boy began to shuffle behind him. Suddenly Brigson whipped a gun out and pointed it at his head. '*Don't* you move!'

Lynda shook her weapon. 'I'm warning you, Brigson. Drop the weapon or I'll-'

'Shoot me? You realise this armour's bulletproof. Shoot me and I'll kill the kid!' He turned his head to the boy. 'Get back inside!'

Lynda saw the boy's terrified expression. 'Hey… Hey, look at me! It's going to be okay…'

Brigson was not amused. 'It's not, your brains are about to splatter onto the walls of my van, sad to say for my computers. Get to the back.'

The boy shuffled backwards. Lynda gave him a nod as if to assure him he could trust her.

Brigson sat in the van. 'So what is it Ms… Griffen? It's still Griffen, isn't it? After what's happened between you and Jim?'

Lynda ignored the attempt to provoke her. 'How many are there in your organisation.'

Brigson shrugged. 'Straight to the questioning, fair enough…' He grimaced. 'I couldn't tell you the *exact* number of people in my organisation, Signision is a very large company, after all, I'd say there-'

'You know which organisation I meant! The Circle of Saints!'

'Oh, the Circle?' he gasped in a cartoon fashion. 'But- But I would never be in league with the Circle! Oh dear me no! I'm just one of their pawns, somebody they use quickly who can easily be disposed of. It's why I said I have a partner, not *partners*… The Circle of Saints organise these killings, but it's me and my partner who do the dirty work.'

'You seem to respect *your partner* a lot!'

Brigson laughed. 'Respect him? He terrifies me! You imagine working with a serial killer day in and day out. It would be horrible! Then again, I suppose you already know exactly what my partner's like.'

Lynda frowned. 'What are you suggesting by that, Brigson?'

He laughed. 'You'll see. It shocks me how little you know about your male friends… and your *husband* for that matter.'

Lynda was shocked. 'Jim's not a killer! He's just a little…

shaken, that's all!'

'Really?' Brigson looked a bit confused. 'Well correct me if I'm wrong, lieutenant, but your large spike in missing people - the ones you evidently discovered to have been taken by us - when did they start again?'

'The start of 2024. Why?'

'Oh! That's… what? About half a year after little Jakey died. I suppose grief would take a while to… sink in. And what about the police uniforms? Where do you think I got those?'

She laughed at the ludicrous nature of it all. 'Not from Jim! He's not even a detective!'

'Yet he tries so hard to be… *and* has been spending a large amount of time alone at the police station. Weird, huh?'

Lynda shook her head in determination. *He's manipulating you*, she thought. Yet… a part of her felt uncertain.

Suddenly the backup groups came through the door behind Lynda, all their weapons pointing towards the scientist.

Brigson pulled out the terrified boy from his van and swung him across to Lynda. 'Here, take him,' he said. He's not the one we want, anyway.'

Two officers grabbed the boy by the arms and escorted him away. The rest kept their weapons poised.

'Well,' he said calmly, 'I've done what's needed to be done. I think it's best I'll be off.' He nodded in the direction of one of the visor-covered officers.

Lynda was furious. 'You're not going anywhere you-'

Suddenly a loud blast sounded behind her, the sound so loud

it left her ears ringing. Her eyes began to water uncomfortably, clouding her vision even further than the visor, but it seemed that one of the officers behind her was clutching his vest on the ground, another with his gun pointed in the injured officer's direction.

'What are you-'

The words barely left her mouth. The officer who'd shot the first colleague had already lifted his weapon to aim at another, before blasting a bullet straight through their exposed neck, causing blood to spurt onto Lynda's visor. Her only remaining able colleague rushed in at the gunner, but in the time that the charge took, the gunner had already dropped their weapon and had begun retracting a knife from their trouser waist.

The slash was clean and quick.

In this time, Lynda had managed to recover from the shock and lift her weapon towards the traitor. Before she could pull the trigger however, she felt a stabbing pain deep in her back, launching her and her weapon forward.

The floor did not hit harder than the bullet, but it hurt nonetheless. She could feel some dampness in the area the shot had hit. *Blood*, she thought. *Did it penetrate my armour?* she thought.

The officer who had shot the bullets had run right past her body, straight into Brigson's van. As she rolled around, she saw the twisted euphoria on the scientist's face.

'What do you think of him? My partner?' He opened the driver's door. 'You thought the machine was the only other danger, didn't you? You were so far from the truth. A puppet is only as dangerous as its controller. I want you to remember that.' He jumped in and slammed the door, the window still wide open. '*Perire finite non est*, lieutenant.' And with that, the van sped away.

Lynda shook her head wearily. So Brigson had help. But who? It couldn't have been Jim, could it?

It was almost too much to lift the communicator to her lips, the pain in her back growing overwhelming. '*Two officers down, more backup nee…*'

She shut her eyes.

***

'No, no, no…' Jim muttered, lifting the Communicator to his lips. 'This is Jim to all of B Squad. This is a trap! I repeat: this is a trap! The Circle knew we were coming here! They-'

He found his path to the hospital blocked by a vaguely familiar face.

The man was old looking, perhaps old enough for retirement, with wispy silver hair and spectacles balancing on his nose's rim. 'Griffen!' he shouted. 'What the Devil do you think you're doing with a police communicator!'

'Sir, you have to listen to me! The Circle know we're here, they know we're-'

'I've heard much about your delusional fantasies, Lynda tells me all about them, believe me! I'm not having you march into this hospital and muck things up for us.'

Jim spotted two more officers in dark visors approach from behind, their weapons resting comfortably in their arms.

Jim lowered his voice. 'Sir… I just got a call from my sister. She tells me she's being taken somewhere; she doesn't know where!'

He smiled. 'Yes, yes… the evacuation process can be confusing Jim, but as an ex-officer, you should know that they'll be safe in the confines of the-'

'They're not *going* to the police department! The Circle have taken them, meaning they know exactly what's going on over here!'

The captain sighed. 'Griffen, I'm not taking any more of this. Hand me your communicator and let us do our jobs. We may not even arrest you for interference if you just walk away now…'

It was a futile effort and Jim knew it. He slowly lowered the communicator into - what he could only assume to be the missing persons captain's hand.

The captain lifted the communicator to his mouth, eyeing Jim cautiously. 'This is Captain Graham Bennett instructing you to ignore the previous comments made through your communication devices. Griffen's at it again!'

The two officers behind the captain laughed, and the man himself began to chuckle.

A static response resonated from the communicator in the old man's hand, followed by a woman's voice. 'Uh… sir. This is Detective Barker, do you copy?'

He brought his communicator up in concern. 'Copy detective, what seems to be the issue.'

'Well, there's this… thing up here. At first, I thought it was some medical device - it was so still - but… it looks a hell of a lot like that robot you described to us…'

There was silence. The captain looked to Jim fearfully. He was about to bark a command into the communicator when noise erupted from the speaker.

The sounds of screams and gunfire.

***

'… she all right?'

The world was a mess of grey. Words around slurred into one another like mixing paint.

'… will be. Perhaps we should…'

In and out. In and out she faded. Sometimes there was the pain. Sometimes there was just nothing.

The doors of the van slammed shut.

'… about the others. What's happened to them?'

'Two de… thers injured.'

Lynda tried to access the deepest confines of her memory, but all that came was her name, and the familiar face of a man she'd once searched for. Who was it? Mark? Arnold? Will?

'*Tommy*,' she groaned, remembering.

The young man bent over her, his eyes scanning her face with concern. 'She's… awake, I think?'

The thought lingered in her brain for a moment. It was a thought of similarity; between two faces she knew well. But it was gone in a flicker.

'Lynda…' Tommy asked. 'Lynda, can you hear me?'

Opening her eyes wider, she saw she was being overlooked by two men in police uniform. Surrounding her was a large amount of hospital equipment, and she appeared to be covered in a red blanket.

She sat up and gasped. Memories were re-emerging. '*Tommy*.

Tommy! Brigson… he escaped. His partner… They killed-'

'We *know* Lynda, it's all right. Everything's all right.' He pushed her gently back down into a lying position. 'The children have been evacuated, and we're taking you to a hospital now.'

'The other officers? What happened to them?'

They stared at her for a while. Then the other man whispered something into Tommy's ear.

Tommy crouched low. 'Lynda, I promise we'll explain everything to you once you're at the hospital.'

'Jim! Where's Jim?'

Tommy smiled and nodded. 'Jim's fine, he's at the police station now.'

'Actually, officer,' the other man interjected. 'I got a report about a minute ago. Jim's outside St Luke's Hospital. And apparently, something's gone very wrong…'

***

'You heard that. You have to warn them. Please let me help you.'

The missing persons captain did not reply, but merely stared through Jim, all the way to eternity; utterly unresponsive. Clearly, he was not used to these kinds of situations.

Jim took a glance at the other two officers. They were running inside. He took the opportunity immediately and chased in after them, the pistol he had stolen behind his trousers.

Down the large corridor, Jim saw five officers, two of which the ones who he'd talked to earlier. They were all staring fearfully at the elevator.

'Officers, you need to get out of here.'

One TRT member at the front removed their helmet, revealing long brown hair and a pale face. Tears were rolling down her cheeks. 'It's going down floor by floor…'

Another set of bullets and screams were heard from the communicator.

'Come on, we all need to get out now,' Jim repeated with greater urgency. They didn't even glance in his direction 'Seriously, I'm not letting you all die here today. You have families!' Again, no response. '*Children! Think about your kids, dammit!* You want them to grow up without a mom or a dad?'

'No, Jim!' the woman at the front of the group shouted back. 'Of course I don't! But what choice do we have? We know your sob story all right? We know you suffered from losing your son. We get it. But if we're not going to put up a fight against these criminals, then more people will die, and more families will be destroyed. I'm not going to risk that even if there's only the smallest chance of destroying this… whatever it is! If I die here today, at least my kids will know that their Mom defended this city when she got the chance, instead of giving up like so many others.' She turned her head to him. He could see her crying. 'You go, Griffen. You shouldn't even be in this mess in the first place…'

Jim shook his head. 'I can't let it happen to you like the others.'

'You need to learn something, Jim!' the woman snapped. 'People die! You can't prevent that. You can't reverse it. Death is fixed, and when it happens, even if you think you could have done something, it doesn't matter because it happened anyway. The most important thing is making your death count, and I'm sorry Jim, but I'd rather have a death today that counted than living the rest of my life regretting not trying to end this right here, right now.' She wiped her face and placed her helmet on. 'Let me have this one…'

An officer behind raised a hand. 'Me too.'

'And me.'

The final two raised their arms, and Jim understood. There was no persuading them now. But he wouldn't leave them to die on their own.

'Count me in too.'

They turned their heads. 'But you're not even a detective. You're unarmed!'

He pulled out Nathan Blake's pistol from his trousers. 'We're all as good as unarmed against this thing. Just aim for the pipes in the joint areas, maybe its eyes and… Well, it's like you said. It's better to die here than regret it forever.'

They nodded and faced the elevator. The number above it told them it was on floor two. More screams from the communicator confirmed such.

Then the screaming had stopped. There was one floor remaining. The one on the ground.

As the red "one" on the screen above the lift slowly disintegrated to make room for a large "G", the officers raised their weapons. Jim felt his thoughts halt completely, and suddenly he could feel, see, hear everything. Time slowed down, and just as the elevator reached a "ding", he noticed a supply cupboard behind the group of officers to his left. *What was it they always said about confined spaces at the academy?*

The doors crawled open, but the machine was not standing in the lift. Instead, there was a small round device with wires crawling out of it at all ends. It made a strange humming noise, which steadily began to increase in pitch like a toddler ready to scream. It was a bomb.

By the time this had become apparent to Jim's conscious mind, he was already charging towards the supply cupboard, his hand quickly grabbing a nearby officer to join him. He was unaware of whether he had warned the others. His body had detached from his brain and time had slowed down, making him feel like he was running through thick cream. In an instant, he launched himself and the other officer to the ground as they reached the inside of this confined space, and in the last moments before the explosion, turned his head to where he had just been. The door was closing, but through the remaining crack Jim saw men and women all rushing away. Some had noticed just after him and were in the process of running to the doorway, while some were slow and had only just begun to flee. A sad part of Jim knew they would never make it and doubted he and this man would make it themselves. Jim closed his eyes as the door closed behind him and listened to the roaring blaze that began to consume the corridor…

Heat, sound and smell became overwhelming, as Jim felt his body being cooked like an egg. All around was an orange blaze, and soon rocks rained down from the now collapsing hospital. In a moment of panic, Jim tightened into a ball and braced his hands around the back of his head. He knew this was barely protective. Even a helmet could be penetrated in a second if a piece of rubble was large enough.

The sound grew more unbearable as the chaos ensued, but soon Jim found that he was no longer receiving it. His eardrums were evidently damaged, despite his best efforts at covering the sound. The rocks kept raining and the fire still blazed. Jim felt himself begin to sob violently.

I'm coming, Jake, he whispered. *I'll be with you soon.*

You don't belong in heaven, his son replied in his mind.

The black was welcoming.

***

Lynda burst into tears when she saw the footage on the television.

In seconds, the once-grand hospital burst into a ball of flame and smoke. Glass shards sliced through the air like small needles, and the fire raged upwards like a ravenous worm, consuming anything solid in its path. After a few moments, the building's supports weakened, and over fifteen floors of metal and stone plummeted to the floor, leaving a thick cloud of soot in its wake.

'Turn it off,' one of the nurses behind her begged. '*Please*, this isn't doing the patients any good.'

The screen closed into black, and Lynda found herself sobbing even more. Just hours ago, she had lost Brigson and three colleagues. Now, she had lost Jim and so many more.

Why did you have to run in there? she thought. *Why couldn't you have just stayed at the police station like I asked?*

She looked around, her vision a teary blur. The room was packed with other patients, some sitting quietly in gowns, some squawking away about their scheduled operations. Others were confined to beds and wheelchairs, with IV drips lodged into their wrists. One thing was clear – there were too many patients and not enough doctors.

'Oi!' a man shouted to a large nurse nearby. 'When are we

going to get treatment?'

'Where is my son!' an elderly woman with a stick cried. 'I can't find my Wilf!'

'I demand that I get a phone call *now!*'

'We all deserve compensation!'

'Why aren't you listening to me?'

The nurse was overwhelmed - frantically trying to calm the group to no avail. Eventually, the poor woman backed out of the doorway and made her escape.

Lynda dropped her head in hopeless loss and screaming and arguing ensued around her. She was welcomed by a warm sleep

She must have dozed off for a while because after what felt like moments, she woke to a dark room with half the people from before all gone. Before her was Tommy, his face solemn, but somewhat relieved.

'Lynda? Thank God, I thought you'd never wake up.'

She rubbed her eyes. 'Tommy…' She shook her head to wake herself up. 'Tommy what's the matter.'

He smiled. 'Good news.'

***

Pain. Jim was fairly used to the feeling at this point. The pain hurt. But the pain was good. Pain meant alive.

At this moment, everything was dark. Silent. Jim's conscious thought was fuzzy.

He had thought he was dead until the pain seared through his spine. Why couldn't he be dead? Why couldn't this end?

Because it never ends, Jim. Your suffering will never end.

So many died because he had failed to save them.

How many have suffered because you tried *to save them? Because you tried to distance them to keep them "safe." Nora Griffen. Elly Griffen. Lynda Griffen.*

'Stop it…'

Others too, people who've been gone a long time. Your best friend, Adam. Your cousins Leron and Grace. Your uncle Chris.

'Stop…'

Even your darling son before he died.

'Stop it!' Light flooded into his eyes like water entering a sinking submarine. Jim was certain that he had not been breathing a great amount over the last few seconds, whether it was the burning ache in his lungs or the great croaking wheezes that were being produced by his mouth. He coughed mightily in a futile attempt to bring up the soot currently cluttering his insides.

He was lying flat on the ground, with about a half a metre of clearance between his head and the rubble above. The whole room was a wreck, filled with broken supports and singed tools. There was a sickening stench in the air that nearly induced Jim to vomit – a culmination of combusted cleaning chemicals and singed flesh.

Jim heard a moaning produced from a man next to him and turned to find it was the officer he had tackled into the closet the moment he saw the bomb. He had heard that confined spaces were the safest to be in during an explosion but had never even dreamed that he would have to test the theory first-hand. The officer proceeded to take off his helmet, revealing the pained face of a young olive-skinned man with jet black hair.

'*Argh.*' The single noise that left the man's mouth.

Jim inspected him from the head down. The man's foot was horrifically crushed, like a tin can, by a metal pipe protruding from whatever ceiling was left of the collapsed room that they were in.

'Are you all right?' Jim asked, slightly concerned by the broken, flattened, bloody state of the man's foot.

The man gasped for air before speaking. 'Just… *stings!*' He turned his head toward Jim. 'It's you! You…'

'Shh, don't talk too mu-'

'You saved my life! You saved me!'

He shook his head. 'Yeah, well, I couldn't save you all…'

The man gritted his teeth from the agony. Jim glanced over to the foot once more. Although it was incredibly burnt and bruised, it did not seem to be bleeding out. The heat and pressure of the pipe that currently held it may have had a part to play in that. 'Don't worry, kid. That's not going to kill you for as long as it takes to get out of this place.' He surveyed his dark surroundings, searching for a weak spot in the surrounding rubble.

'How are we alive…' groaned the young man.

Jim shrugged. 'The one thing that seems to have stuck from the academy. You're more likely to survive a collapsing building in a confined space. The nearby door frames provide a sturdy structure and the walls are closer so are more likely to fall onto each other and hold each other up, as well as being able to stop larger bits of rubble. Still needed a hell of a lot of luck though. Perhaps it wasn't our time.'

The young man seemed to be studying him. 'What… what's your name?' he asked drearily

'Jim Griffen….' He turned. 'You?'

'Ca- *argh.*'

'Don't worry! I'm sorry, I shouldn't be asking you things.' He found some loose bricks piled on a support beam above. If he could move those, he could get them out without the rubble collapsing. 'I think I've just found us a way out. You wait here, a doctor will be on their way, I promise!' He pushed the bricks outward, revealing a promisingly large beam of light to stream down into the room.

Jim dusted his hands and prepared to jump up. Just before he did, however, the officer began to speak again.

'Carlos,' he said. 'My name is Carlos Rodriguez.' He held his hand out for a shake.

Jim shuffled over and took it. 'Nice to meet you, Carlos Rodriguez,' he said. 'You hang in there all right? Help's on its way.' Carlos collapsed, exhausted, as Jim walked over to the hole, jumped up, and yanked himself out, sliding to the surface like a worm.

Before his eyes was a world of despair and desolation. The sky was thick and grey, a murky soup shielding the entirety of the city from the sun's gentle rays, but whatever light that was left revealed an atrocity that would scar history. A vast plain littered with rock, metal, machinery and black heavy-duty armour clung onto lifeless, doll-like bodies. Hundreds surrounded the area; their faces grim, their mouths frozen. Ambulances had already begun to culminate, but the faces of doctors leaving the vehicle suggested they wouldn't have much to find.

At the centre of this disgusting litter, on all the motionless, morose, heartlessly-created objects, Jim spotted a dusty white figure. It was lying curled on its side, the majority of its lower body held down by rocks and metal. The figure lifted an arm from the mess and clamped its black hand onto a large support that lay across its body. It lifted it like a child would lift a block of wood.

The figure slowly emerged from the ground, rocks falling off its body as it did so. It stood firmly on its long slender legs, before turning to Jim as if it knew where he was crouched. It did not attack him. It did not even approach him. It did not care. Instead, it stared with a gaze that seemed to pass through him; the eyes piercing blue as ever. It looked at him as if he were now as much of a problem as the charred, broken bodies that lay scattered around them. Because they, whoever controlled it, had not just killed Jim Griffen. They had broken him. And that was so much worse.

The machine turned left and walked onwards. Nobody was in its path, nor would it have been forced to worry if anyone was. If an explosion like that didn't even leave a dent in its shell, then what would?

It's over, Jim thought. *It was over from the start. There's no beating these people now.*

He fell to his knees and sobbed.

***

September 2025

SAM
SEPTEMBER 11TH, 2025
THE DEATH OF A GOOD MAN

Sam analysed the lawyer carefully as he followed in his footsteps. His pockets seemed to be empty, and a weapon in the hat was doubtful. Besides, they were in a high-security prison. How would a man like that possibly get a weapon into this building?

The criminals manage it all the time…

'The Backstabber…' Sam pondered. 'Mary told me he wasn't actually a detective. Is that true?'

Jordan glanced back, hesitated, and finally nodded. 'Not when he was arrested, he wasn't.'

Sam chewed on this for a while as they continued down the corridor. 'Would I know him?'

Jordan shrugged. 'May do. He was quite the celebrity a couple of years ago. Considering how well this has been kept a secret, I can only assume that people had forgotten about him when he was arrested a few months ago.'

'And who is he to you?'

They stopped before the door to the questioning room. Jordan froze, his hand clenched firmly on the handle. 'To me, he's just a client. To Carlos, though… To Carlos, he's a hero. This man saved Carlos in an event that killed dozens. He could have run away and made it out, but instead, he risked his own life. This man is everything to Carlos, and Carlos is everything to me, so yeah, I'll protect him with my life if necessary.' He pushed in a few numbers on the combination lock and pulled down the handle. Both he and Sam strolled through the door before Sam heard a pained grunt from behind.

'Oh, I'm so sorry, Warden.' Sam had been so engrossed in the Backstabber that he had completely forgotten the large man was even following them in the first place. He rushed to hold the door open, which seemed to have trapped the man's fingers.

'That's quite all right…' the man said, red-faced and slightly flustered. 'If you ask me, detective, to me this seems to be an awful waste of time. I haven't brought you down here to be talking to the Nightdrop Backstabber, you're here to solve the Williams escape-'

'Which I have!' Sam exclaimed. 'But while your case is solved, mine's gone pretty cold, and the only lead I seem to have besides questioning the prison chef's entire family, who I doubt will have been told anything, is a man in this very prison telling me that he has every answer I need to find the little girl and determine the guilt of my partner. It could be a trap, but quite frankly the benefits of this not being one heavily outweigh the dangers of any said trap that I may face, so for the love of all things good let me do my damn job because quite frankly you owe me a favour!'

The flabbergasted Warden stood there lost for words.

'Sorry, that was a bit harsh,' Sam admitted. 'It's been a long few days.' Sam proceeded into the room. Before him was a huge set of screens and two speakers surrounding one large glass window, which he could only assume to be a one-way mirror. Peering through, he saw a single grey table, surrounded by three chairs, two empty on one end, and one occupied by a strongly built, brown-haired man, with an unshaven jaw, and a scar under his right eye.

'Is this him?' Sam asked the lawyer.

Jordan gestured to a door to the right of the glass. 'Come on,' he said. 'It's time you learnt the truth.'

Sam turned to the warden. 'You stay here, Warden. If things get hairy, call for help.'

The warden nodded miserably.

Jordan opened the door, and Sam promptly followed through. It was the definition of claustrophobic, the concrete walls so tightly packed into each other that he felt there wouldn't be enough air for the three of them. Everything in here was grey, whether it was the walls, the furniture, or the prisoner's jumpsuit. Sam took a good look at the man in the chair, making sure not to miss any details. He looked weary, with large violet bags under his eyes. His right eye was decorated with a scar, and his left arm was in a bandage. There was no expression on his face, except, perhaps, mild panic. Aside from that, he looked dead to the world; pale, ungroomed, unreactive.

Jordan pulled out the seats from the other end of the table, and both he and Sam took a place in one. Sam stared a while at the prisoner on the other end in silence. The other man requited, but his stare was more inquisitive than examining.

'So…' said the man in the jumpsuit. 'You want to hear what I have to say?'

'I give everyone a chance, but only one,' Sam shot back. 'You're going to answer everything I ask you, right here, right now, because quite frankly I have a little girl to find, and time is running out.'

He shook his head. 'If I'm correct, time's already run out, but that doesn't mean you can't save her. Ask away, but please don't waste my time. Ask the right questions.'

Sam shuffled back into his seat and folded his hands over each other. 'First things first then… Why were you working with the police force?'

'They couldn't work out what was going on. The case they had on their hands was very similar to one only I could solve a few years before. I'd been a detective a couple of years before, you see. I was the best they had, they needed my help, so I helped them…'

Sam sighed. 'Did you kill your partner?'

'In a way, I suppose you could say yes.' The man didn't even hesitate.

Sam raised an eyebrow. 'Why?'

The man before him looked amused. 'You haven't even asked the simple stuff yet… Like, what's my name?'

'I know who you are, sir. Jordan's right, you were a celebrity back in the day. I'm surprised more people don't know *you're* the Backstabber.'

The man laughed. 'It's a stupid name really, what the press calls me. They don't know what happened that night. Why I did what I did. I may have killed him, but I am *not* a backstabber.'

Sam smiled. He had this man ready to spill everything. 'Then help me understand. What happened that night? In fact, tell me everything. The murders, the case, your partners, everything. And then tell me how Sadie fits into all of this.'

The man nodded. 'All right then. I better be quick, because time's running out and it's a pretty long story.'

Sam gave him a lying smile. 'Take your time, Mr Griffen.'

Jim nodded. 'It all started with the harbour…'

***

July 2025

JIM
JULY 13TH, 2025
CONFESSION

Empty.

Like the beer glass before him, this was exactly how Jim Griffen had felt since the explosion. He and Carlos had to be taken immediately to Bartholomew's Hospital down by the river. There, he had stayed for two nights, while his head and right leg were treated, and it was also there that he had found out the truth. That he and Carlos were the sole survivors of that explosion at St Luke's. Of course, Jim was hardly surprised. There were many explosives capable of taking down a building like that. The only thing that kept people safe was the fact that terrorists normally didn't have or use them.

I underestimated them. They planned this. They wanted my family. They wanted all those officers to be killed in that hospital. They lured us in like fish on a reel.

Jim held up his arm for another glass. The pub was a dimly lit, off-smelling area, with creaky wooden surfaces and glasses barely washed. The hygiene rating of this place was a low scorer, leaving the area nearly empty on weekdays. That's what would draw Jim here. He didn't care about the cleanliness or the upkeep, so long as he had some space to think.

When the large, bearded bartender slammed the third pint on the counter, Jim felt his body shudder, and he was instantly plunged into memories of fiery chaos. When he lifted the glass his hand shook, leaving the beer to spill all over the counter.

'You okay, Buddy?' The bartender asked. Quite frankly, it was the most considerate thing Jim had ever heard leave his mouth.

The nurses had warned Jim about this. He hadn't obtained any serious injuries… except those within him. "*Traumatic experiences can stay with people for a while.*" They weren't damn kidding. 'Yeah… Yeah, I'm good thanks, Dez. Long day, that's all.'

'Yeah, it's been a pretty messed up few weeks. You hear about that explosion?'

Jim closed his eyes and nodded.

The bartender sighed. 'Tragic, isn't it? You know I was right there! Just a few blocks away I was standing. Man… what a world.'

Suddenly images of screaming officers and charred corpses flew into Jim's mind. All those people, men and women with lives and families and memories and dreams. They were all dust now.

And the machine isn't.

The thought deeply bugged Jim. How was the machine perfectly intact? All the human bodies were cooked, an overwhelmingly-sized hospital reduced to nothing but hot rocks and glass shards. But the machine? Perfectly fine. Bullets? Explosions? They must have been as harmless to it as apple pips to a person. Could it even ever be destroyed? *You've done it this time, Brigson. I hope you're proud.*

And what had happened to Elly? Or Mom? Were they safe? Or had the Circle taken them away from him too.

God, let them be alive. You can take my soul, but you can't take my family. Then there'll be nothing left living for.

This is what had kept Jim up through those bitter, eternal nights. The physical pain in his body was nothing.

After two hellish days at the hospital, Jim had headed straight for the bar. He had no care of whatever damage he would cause to his physical or mental health. The others were all dead. How could drinking a few pints let worse happen to him?

So for hours, that is what Jim Griffen did. He continued to drink, pint after pint. At the point where one more would surely make him throw up, pass out, or both, a familiar woman walked through the door.

'Lynda?' Jim asked.

She laughed. 'How much have you had to drink exactly?'

Jim recognized that voice.

'Who… are you?'

She sat down, and suddenly it all came into focus, her vine-coloured eyes, at this moment wearing a worried look, reflective sparkling teeth and black curly locks. 'Jim, you do recognize me, don't you?'

Jim had a drunk smile. 'Sorry, Mary. I can see you all right now…'

Mary gave a concerned smile. 'Jim, you know you shouldn't be drinking this much straight out of the hospital.'

'Out of hospital!' the bartender exclaimed. 'Ma'am, I deeply apologise; I had no idea!'

Mary raised a sympathetic hand. 'It's okay,' she said.

'It's not okay…' Jim slurred. 'You should have given me more…'

Mary sighed. 'Jim, why are you doing this to yourself?'

Jim gave her an unusual look, somewhere between amusement and confusion. 'Why do you think, Captain?'

'I need to hear it from you, Jim, you know I do,' she said. When he just stared at her and said no more she spoke again. 'Jim, I was here for you then, and I'm here for you now.' She moved her head to gain eye contact. 'What's the matter?'

Suddenly tears appeared in Jim's eyes and he started to tremble. 'I…' he started. 'I… killed them all, Mary. I should have seen it coming, I should have worked out that it would be a trap, that they wanted us to go there. But instead, I was reckless… and angry… and I followed the damn Circle all the way. I didn't work it out in time, and now… now they're all dead because of me…'

Suddenly he felt a cold hand on his shoulder, and jumped around, startled to see Tommy standing behind. 'Woah, where the hell did h- he come from?'

Tommy chuckled and grabbed a seat by him. Lynda too appeared and grabbed another at the end of the bar, a sympathetic, sad smile on her face. 'Jim, we've been here behind you the whole time,' he claimed. 'How much have you had?'

Jim shook his head. 'I don' know…'

Lynda looked down at the counter. 'Look Jim… you and I have had rough times. We've had some fights, and you've done some pretty sucky things, mind you. But I'll tell you one thing, what happened tonight? *That* was less your fault than it was for *any* officer in the department.'

Jim shook his head vigorously. 'No. No, no, no, you see they wouldn't have been able to work it out. They're stupid. *People* are stupid. Only I could have stopped this, and I failed…'

'Listen up!' Tommy suddenly commanded in a sharp tone. 'Just because you're one of the best detectives there is, doesn't mean that you deserve punishment every *damn* time you miss something. You're not a superhero, Jim, you're just a man! And a man like you shouldn't have to carry the weight of the world on his shoulders.' He hit Jim friendly on the back, causing some minor acid reflux. 'Just think of what you did today! Because of your phenomenal mind, you saved a man's life in an event that was meant to wipe out every TRT member in that hospital. Now ain't that something to be proud of?'

Jim mumbled. 'Yeah, I guess.'

Mary smiled. 'He's right, Jim. You didn't kill those people. You couldn't have prevented all of their deaths, but you prevented one man's life from ending. That's one more family member, friend or colleague that you've just kept in this world because you risked your own skin to save him. That's more than most officers could say, I'll tell you that.'

Jim shrugged. 'I know, I know. I just… I just thought we were finally onto something. And now dozens are dead. My family's missing.'

Lynda reached over and squeezed his right hand. Her palm was warm and caring. 'Hey… I promise you, Jim, if there's one thing we will do, we will find your mother and sister. What the Circle did yesterday was the last time they will *ever* get close to the ones we love again, and now we're going to stop at nothing to get them back. I promise you!'

He looked into her eyes and instantly felt assured by her determined gaze. 'We?' he asked.

His wife reluctantly grinned. 'You saved a life today, Jim. That's better than most detectives would ever be. Plus, they are your family. Of course I'll let you in on things.'

He nodded in confidence. 'You're right. We were too distant. We fought too much. If we're going to do this, it needs to be together…'

Tommy gave him a heavy pat on the back, while Lynda grabbed his glass and gulped down some beer. Mary just looked wistfully out into the distance.

After a few moments of deep thought in the group, several beers arrived on the counter. 'On the house,' the bartender bellowed. 'This is three more customers than I usually get anyway!' Tommy took a sip and gagged from the taste, causing Lynda to giggle next to him. She then proceeded to lift hers and gulp it down so quickly that it didn't touch the sides. Mary, however, just glanced at her glass and smiled, her eyes showing her to be light-years away.

'You okay there, Mare?' Lynda inquired.

Mary smiled and chuckled. 'No, it's just… well, it's just us four… reminds me of a time I was out drinking with my partner one time…'

Jim frowned in curiosity. 'You had a partner?'

She glanced at him in amusement. 'Well, yeah… I wasn't always a loner, Jim! A few months before you came, about a year before your lovely wife, I was a homicide detective like you working with a guy named Alex. We were…' she laughed. '*close* if that's what you'd say. Our minds tended to think alike, it's why we always solved cases so damn quick. And most Friday nights, after finally solving that week's big case, we'd normally hit the bar…' She stopped as she looked over to the focussed looks of her colleagues. 'Sorry, I get terribly distracted sometimes.'

'No please,' Lynda urged, 'carry on.'

The captain smiled. 'Ah fine… There was this one night where we'd finally caught this nasty pain in the ass that the press had been calling "the Eel." She was a piece of work to find, I'll tell you that! Got her name from all the times she'd slipped through our fingers. Took us a few months before we finally got to her.

'So, that night, we got *particularly* wasted. I mean I was pretty bad - a couple quickly downed pints, a cocktail or two. But Alex? That kid didn't know where to stop! By the end of the evening, he was wearing his shirt on his head, standing on the table, belting out country music in his worst country accent.' She giggled ferociously, a few tears, Jim noticed, welling in her eyes.

'As you can imagine,' she continued, 'the chief was not happy when word got out about this. It was,' she put on her best scratchy Murdock shout, '"a disgrace to the entire department who have sworn to defend this city," yada yada yada. Alex was tidying Murdock's office and clearing his emails all week!'

A slight sad twinge quivered around the corner of her lip. 'Those were good times… He was a good friend to me you know… I just wish I'd been a better friend to him...'

Jim raised an eyebrow. 'What happened?'

Mary shrugged. 'Well… one day, without any prompt whatsoever, he just upped and left. Didn't even say goodbye…'

Lynda choked her beer down in horror. 'He just left you?'

Mary tilted her head and shrugged. 'Look… Alex was a troubled guy, you know. He had this warm, funny exterior, but…

sometimes I'd just catch him. I'd walk into our office, and he'd just be sitting there, motionless, looking sadly out the window. He never talked about his past much, my Alex. About his friends, family, anyone! And then one day, just a few weeks after the bar, Murdock hands me this note. Says it was from my *old* partner. Inside, all my best friend has to say is "Dear Mary, I'm sorry I had to leave. From your friend, Alex." That's all he put. I tried calling him a few times, but his number had been terminated and passed on to someone else. I asked if there were any relatives I could talk to, but there was only his aunt, and she told me he hadn't said anything to her either…' Mary sniffed. 'And that was it. He left me. And all this time I keep thinking to myself… what did I do wrong? How could I have helped him? Why did he leave me so suddenly without even saying goodbye? Sometimes I lay awake all night, clawing at my mattress, wondering if he… well… if he'd kill-' The words froze in the captain's throat as she hung her head and began quietly sobbing.

Lynda left her stool and walked over. She embraced her partner fiercely. 'Hey, hey…' Jim watched his wife gently pat the captain's back. 'It's all right Mary, it's okay…'

They stayed like for a good half of a minute, two officers in each other's arms, forgetting about the mess that life had dealt them. When they released their embrace, Mary's eyes now dry once more. She sniffed a little before speaking. 'Anyway, since that day I promised I would always be there for people. I know Alex was troubled, and I know that even if I had said more, it might not have helped. All the same… I don't want anything like that to happen again. For somebody to feel so lost and alone that they set off and leave their life and loved ones behind, one way or another. It's horrific, and people, especially Alexes, don't deserve that…'

Lynda nodded. 'You know… all this time I thought you had it easier than us. Sometimes I'd even get mad because I thought the reason you were so positive and helpful was that you were lucky enough not to feel loss.' She shook her head. 'I was so wrong, Mary. You're the strongest out of all of us. You helped us through all we went through and we never took the time to think about what you were going through. What kind of friends are we…?'

Mary shrugged. 'Don't be so hard on yourself, I never even made it clear to you. You know, sometimes I think I should stop living under a mask and actually tell people how I am…' She took a sip of beer. 'I guess that's just not how I operate. Since Alex, I've always had this fear of losing people, so much that I'd do anything to make them all right again. Sometimes I think I try too hard and just mess it up…'

Jim lifted his head and sighed. He felt surprisingly sober all of a sudden, a feeling he wasn't too accustomed to at eleven in the evening. 'That isn't true, Mary. I know you've helped me....'

She looked up, the corners of her lips rising hopefully. 'I have?'

He shrugged. 'Well, of course. Remember that time my first partner broke his back? You were there for me then. Or that time I had to shoot that armed criminal to protect that old lady. You… well, you *and* you,' he pointed to Lynda, 'were there for me that day. And then when Jake…' his voice cut off. He cleared his throat. 'When Jake was… *killed.* I know I didn't show it, I know I didn't give you the appreciation you deserved, and I know I certainly wasn't there enough to help *you* Lynda but… I was in a dark place; and although I didn't show it, you, *both* of you through the light to help get me out.' He sighed and gazed at a dent in the counter. 'And yeah, I doubt I'll be the same again after what happened that day, but it could have been a lot worse. You two saved my life, you know that? You always have done…'

Mary nodded with closed eyes, her face acceptant and radiant once more. Lynda wore a puzzled, pleasantly surprised smile. Perhaps she'd previously thought he'd never appreciated her support all those months ago.

And then, as if something had just clicked at the moment, Jim realised there was something which needed to be said.

'Guys…' he started. 'While we're on the topic of being open, well… there's something I've never *really* told anyone.'

They all glanced at one another, then brought their focus back to him. 'Go on…' his wife ushered.

'Well… do you all remember Marcus Arwick?'

They all nodded, and Tommy spoke. 'Yeah, you said he was the one you were certain to be the Phantom. All the murders could be traced back to the night his wife and daughter were killed in a drunk driving accident or something…'

'Yeah… yeah, that's him. Well… my theory wasn't too implausible. I mean I know it wasn't him in the end, but the first murder was the drunk truck driver himself, then it was the driver's friend who was sober in the vehicle at the time, then it was the boss who hired him to be a truck driver a few weeks before despite numerous strikes on his licence, and then it was the judge who'd given him far too short a sentence for a similar incident about a half a year prior in the April of twenty twenty-two, when the same driver intoxicatedly drove into a parked car, severely injuring the woman in the driver's seat. Well… the only reason I bring this up is because the Phantom made one murder that doesn't seem to fit the pattern at all. One that seems to make no sense whatsoever…'

Lynda closed her eyes. 'Jake…'

Jim nodded. 'I doubt we'll ever know why the Phantom, or Daniel Crockett as we found him to be, decided to target those specific people; why he put his life on the line to avenge someone else's family. Perhaps Crockett was a close friend of Arwick's, despite what evidence suggests. Perhaps he was tired of this society and decided to use the death of a random woman and her child as a motive to try to fix it. Or perhaps he just wanted to kill, so targeted those people to make us chase the wrong guy. It doesn't matter. What does matter, is the fact that every single murder the Phantom committed links back to the deaths of Marcus Arwick's family. And that includes Jake...'

Tommy frowned. 'I don't understand. What could Jake have done for the Phantom to target him?'

Jim shook his head. 'Not what Jake did. What *I* did.'

His colleagues glanced at each other nervously.

Jim was silent for a few moments while he collected his thoughts. 'December the seventeenth, twenty twenty-two... It was my final day of work before my holiday. I wasn't even meant to be there that day; I just needed the extra pay to afford a present I'd wanted to buy Lynda for Christmas. On my way home I was stuck in a bit of traffic, and I was meant to be going with Lynda to see Jake's nativity. So, I took a backroad, probably going a bit too fast in my haste to get to the play. On my way, however, I see another vehicle. It's large, white, and has the logo for that famous chemical company on its side, you know, the one with the bear. The person inside was probably going a bit too fast as well, swerving left and right a little. Now sadly being a police officer, you're obliged to do your job right, even when you're rushing to your child's first nativity performance. So, I flick on the sirens and signal for the man to slow.

'He did, although not without some reluctant continuation in his drive. It was as if he was expecting me to carry on driving and leave him alone. Anyway, once he stopped, I noticed that there were two men in the car, the one in the driver's seat looking rather wild. I asked them if they'd had anything to drink. "Yes," the driver said. "A glass or two." Clearly, this man had gone far over the limit, and so with reluctance, I told him I'd have to bring him into the station. I'd started ushering him out of the vehicle when he suddenly said something that grabbed my attention.

'"Well, hold on now, officer!" he said. "I wasn't doing no harm or anything. You see, the motel I live in is just five minutes away." At this point, he pointed his finger ahead of him. I will at this stage point out that there was a motel just a few minutes away from the exact place I'd found him. "You see, I was just having an old-fashioned Christmas Party with my friend here. I wasn't planning on drinking too much, but you know how things can get a bit carried away. I would walk home, but would you look at the state of my friend here? So, I offered to drop him off just a few blocks down the road. It's why I took this backroad you see, so I wouldn't be putting anybody in no danger! I swear to you, officer, his house is just a few blocks down there!"

'At this point, I looked at his friend. "Is this true?" I asked. He gave me a wild look and smiled. "Yessir! Just down the road, sir!"

'"See," said the other man, "I've got a family I ought to be getting home too. My wife's cooked us up a lovely Christmas meal and I need to go see her. Please officer, please don't bring me to jail over a few pints!"'

At this point Jim raised his beer glass, examining it as if examining the state of the world itself. 'And… I believed him. Maybe I wanted to. Maybe I was so damn desperate to see Jake in that play that I let him go. But I soon found out that I did the wrong thing. That man had lied to me. Because half an hour down the road, his truck smashed right into the car of Rachel and Susie Arwick.' A salty tear tugged down his face and landed with a bitter taste on his tongue. 'I couldn't bring myself to tell anybody, especially when the Phantom came about, with all his connections to that one night. And so then, when the Phantom killed Jake, I understood. Somehow, through various methods, be it some surveillance footage, or a witness by the road I pulled him over at, Daniel Crockett discovered that I let a drunk driver go, leading to the deaths of a woman and her child. In return, following whatever sympathy he had for that poor family, he ended my son's life. So yeah, Lynda. I do blame myself. Not just for Jake, but for Rachel, and Susie, and the driver, and his boss, and his friend, and that judge, and all the pain that Marcus Arwick would have felt following his family's murder. I've held that guilt for well over two years now, and let me tell you, there's not one *night* that Jake doesn't haunt my dreams, nor one where a white truck doesn't flash before my eyes, carrying enough guilt to burn my soul into ash. You asked me why I blame myself, Lynda, and it's simple. I'm the reason Jake's dead. And every day I find myself wishing that the Phantom had killed me instead like with all the other victims…'

There was a stunned silence. Even the bartender, who must have overheard the conversation, froze in his place, mid polish of a beer glass. Jim felt concerned as he saw the look in Lynda's eyes. They weren't angry, neither were they sympathetic. They just stared at him. They gazed at him blankly, as if she'd had such an overload of information that her brain couldn't physically compute what had just been spoken. On his left, Mary rubbed her forehead in bafflement, completely uncertain what to say. Behind his wife, Tommy gazed down sadly at the bar, his eyes looking bothered by something.

'And you never told anybody…' Lynda asked. 'Not even me…'

Jim shook his head. 'I just… I couldn't live with the shame. Maybe I figured it would go if I never spoke of it. But it came back to haunt me… and ended everything good left in my life. And I deserve it, you know… I killed that woman. I killed that kid. Maybe not directly, but *I killed them.* And what does that make me, huh? I spent months chasing the Phantom because he killed people, while I hid the fact that I'd killed two people of my own. Who knows, perhaps it was the other way around! Perhaps *he* was chasing me! Whatever the case, I deserve a fate worse than death, and I just thought if I could have just helped you catch this new guy… well, maybe I'd be making things right.'

Mary nodded solemnly. 'Jim… granted, you didn't do your job that day. What you did was a *stupid* thing. But to blame yourself for that woman and girl's deaths? That's just preposterous. The man in that truck *lied* to you, Jim, and you chose to believe him. And that's okay. You thought you were doing the right thing, that he'd get to go home, back to his family, and you'd get to see Jake's pantomime with your wife. Who wouldn't choose that option? I'm not saying it was the right one, God knows it wasn't, but you're only human Jim! And humans make sloppy errors, which every so often can build into chaos, but that's not to say that's what they intended. The point I'm making is that you're *different* because you didn't want those people dead! You wanted the best for everyone. You're *not* the Phantom, Jim! You're a good man!'

Lynda nodded. Tommy, on the other hand, was motionless.

Jim shrugged. It wasn't their judgement that made a difference. It would be Arwick's, wherever he was. 'Well… I appreciate you being so understanding,' he said politely. 'It's good to get it out.'

'You know we're always here to listen,' Mary said kindly. She spotted Tommy staring down the bar motionlessly. 'What about you, Mr Knightley? Anything to share?'

Tommy suddenly snapped out of a day-dreaming trance and grinned. 'Ah… I'll save my confessions for tomorrow. It's getting late, and I, for one, am exhausted!' He rose from his stool.

Jim nodded. 'I'm with Tommy here, I'm beat. Let's pick it up in the morning…'

'God, is it a *Monday* tomorrow?' Mary exclaimed. 'In all seriousness, we are going to bring all of these son-of-a-bitch criminals to the ground. Our top priority tomorrow is finding your family, Jim, we promise you.'

Lynda put a hand to his face. 'Agreed! First thing I'm doing is asking around my department. Anything that can help us find your family, I'm getting it.'

Jim smiled. 'I appreciate it guys. I'll catch you in the morning. I'll even be up nice and early for you all.'

Lynda grabbed his right hand and looked him in the eyes. 'I'm so proud of you for telling me all of that. I know it must have been hard.'

Jim shrugged. 'You're my wife, you ought to know.'

She nodded a little, perhaps taken aback slightly by the realisation that they were still married. 'Well, I'll see you tomorrow, yeah?' She joined with Tommy and followed him out the door.

Mary walked past before turning and holding out her hand. 'You coming with?'

Jim nodded. 'In a minute. I think I may just stay here for a little while.' He saw her concerned face. 'I'm not going to drink anything, Mary…'

She smiled. 'Well, okay… Look if you ever need anything…'

Jim smiled. 'You bet.'

She playfully saluted him. 'See you round Griff!' Mary too left the room.

Jim felt lighter all of a sudden. It was peculiar, the effect that these three people had on him.

They're all I have left, he thought.

And that's who my enemies will always target.

***

JIM
JULY 14TH, 2025
THE SILENT PARTNER

'Daddy?'

Jim arose in the same dark field that had haunted his dreams many nights before. In front of him seemed to be his son, but the field in which they were standing was now so dark that he could hardly see the boy's face.

'You made a mistake, Daddy,' Jake continued. 'You should have arrested that driver. You shouldn't have left me alone that night you chased the Phantom. I would be alive if it weren't for you.'

'Jake, stop this!' Jim shouted.

'You couldn't protect me, Dad. But now you can avenge me.'

The boy pulled out a semi-automatic pistol and held it out on his flat palm. He then nodded to something behind Jim.

Jim turned his head to see the shadowy figure of a man, the same figure he had seen the night his son was-

A scream blasted out behind him, and he turned to see that

Jake had disappeared. All that remained was the pistol lying on the floor. Jim lurched towards it in rage, spun like a top and shot the darkened figure square in the head.

The figure stumbled but did not fall. It stared deep inside Jim, leaving an icy feeling inside his heart. 'You can't kill death, Jim,' it said, and in a moment, Jim was blasted with darkness.

***

His eyes shot open. He was drenched in an icy sweat, but that did not matter. His head ached from the night before, but that did not matter. What did matter was the time. Half-past two in the morning, three and a half hours before he was planning to wake up. Somebody was calling him on his phone.

Instantly his hand went to his phone. The name that popped in his head was *Elly*, and for a second his heart was filled with hope. Instead, he found it was Lynda.

'Lynda, what is it?'

'Jim, I'm at the police station.'

'W-what why?'

'Please come as soon as you can, it's important.'

'N-no no Lynda wait,' Jim shouted down the phone. 'Tell me what's happened. Is it Elly? Mom?'

'It's Tommy,' she said in a wavering voice. 'He's been… taken.'

Jim hung up the phone and rushed to his uniform, before bolting outside. Then the realisation hit Jim; his car was by the bar.

Seeing a truck parked on the road, Jim jumped in front of it, his hand gesturing it to stop.

He pulled out his A.V.A. badge. 'Sorry, police things,' he said, exasperated.

'Are you kidding me?' said the driver, who seemed to be wearing some sort of strange silver costume.

'No,' said Jim, 'I'm not. The fancy dress party can wait thank you very much. Now could you please shift your ass out of the damn van?'

The man sighed. 'You know what? I can run!'

Once in, Jim slammed his foot on the peddle with the greatest force he could muster and drove the fastest route to the police station. When he arrived, he saw Lynda and another woman by the reception desk. They were staring at the monitor on the desk in horror.

'Lynda, thank God! What's happened to T-'

Jim picked up on what they'd seen. The computer showed Tommy bound and gagged on a small wooden chair. The surrounding room seemed to be cramped and dark, like a cave or basement of some sort. The look on his face was pure terror, and at the bottom of the screen there were seven words:

FINAL MURDER. CAN YOU PREVENT THIS ONE?

Beside it was a countdown timer, currently at two hours, forty-five minutes, and thirty seconds.

'How did you see this?' Jim asked Lynda.

'It was Becky who saw it,' she replied, pointing to the receptionist. 'She'd come in early to do some work and found that it was on every screen in the station.'

'Every screen?' Jim asked, aghast. He looked around to see

dozens of officers staring horrified at their screens. 'How did you know to call Lynda?' he asked the receptionist.

'I saw you three together,' she replied in a trembling tone. 'I knew Lynda and Mary the best and… I wasn't going to risk calling Murdock.'

'Why?' asked Lynda.

'Because he frightens me,' she said quickly, nothing else to add.

Lynda turned back to Jim. 'Mary's on her way right now. Any ideas?'

'I need to find out where Tommy is,' said Jim. 'Lynda, get one of the computer crew to look at this, see if they can locate where this is coming from and whether it can be traced.'

'On it. You try to work out where he is, I'll get Murdock to assemble a TRT as soon as possible to rescue Tommy by the time-'

'*No* TRTs!' Jim demanded.

'What?'

'Last time we sent a Tactical Response Team to deal with these guys, half of them were killed. You think I'm going to let that happen again?'

Lynda threw her arms up in frustrated bewilderment. 'So what then? We let them kill him?'

'No…' Jim muttered. He knew what he needed to do, but he also knew Lynda would never let it happen. 'You know what, you do what you think's necessary, I'll call you if I find anything.'

'You promise?'

He avoided eye contact. 'I promise.'

***

Jim slammed the office door open so powerfully that it felt like it would surely break and ran over to the books on the table. Surely the answers had to be in there somewhere.

'St Matthew, Mark and Luke have already happened. Meaning…'

He grabbed the gospel of John from the table and opened the flap inside the front cover. The notes inside did not have a date like the others, just the number four and a smiley face in the corner. He rummaged around the desk and finally found the map of the city, the one where his colleagues had highlighted every location with a Saint's name. There were seven locations named after Saint John.

Jim threw the book down in rage and put his fists to his head. *How am I meant to work out which one's Tommy? And even if I do find it, what then? They want us to find Tommy. They'll trap us like they did last time. What's the point?*

But he's in danger… He's your friend…

Jim needed to think fast. He looked over the books again, checking for anything he may have missed. Then he remembered.

Around the centre of the gospel of John, a green note stuck out the top, the word "*Rebirth*" scrawled onto it in red writing.

'Of course,' he said with a gasp.

This had to be it. Jim flipped straight to the page and was greeted by a typical biblical passage:

[43]When he had said this, Jesus called out in a loud voice " , _ome out! [44]T_e dead man came out, his h_nds and feet wra_ped in

strips of lin_n, and a c_oth around his face.

Jesus said to _hem, "Ta_e off the grave clothes and let him go."

Jim studied the text over and over, curious as to what could help him. Every time he looked; the missing letters caught his eye.

What are the missing letters?

He gathered a pen and paper and started jotting them down. The missing word was obviously Lazarus - a little biblical knowledge from high school helped with that. Following this was a missing C. Then it was a missing h. Following this were the letters a, p, e, and l shortly followed. '*Chapel…*' he muttered. Following this were the letters "T" and "K." '*T, K,*' he now whispered under his breath. Finally, it clicked. T.K. stood for Thomas Knightley. The Circle had been planning this the entire time. He ran back to the map. Seven locations in the city had St John in their name. Only one was a chapel.

Jim pulled the truck keys from his pocket and rushed downstairs. He knew the Circle were expecting him to go, but he couldn't just leave Tommy (*or* his family if there was even a chance they were there too). Equally, he couldn't tell Lynda. He knew full well that this was a trap - sending Lynda with a TRT in there would just lead to more deaths. No, this had to be him, and him alone.

After about fifteen minutes, Jim arrived at the weary, derelict church building. The sky was reasonably light, and so irradiated the hideously cracked stained glass windows, giving them an almost supernatural luminescence. The great wooden entrance to the building was covered in moss and decay and seemed to produce a foul smell which made Jim's nose slightly twitch.

Jim felt vulnerable. He was unarmed and didn't have a shred of armour covering him. That problem was rectified, however, with the semi-automatic pistol lying on the church steps. *Tommy must have dropped this*, he thought. Hesitantly, he raised the pistol with his right hand and slowly proceeded to the door, which swung open with little effort as he pushed it. With the firearm poised, he proceeded into the nave of the building, where all the wooden benches were either flipped or broken in two. Then Jim saw what stood in the centre of the room.

It was the tall, mis-proportionate figure that Jim had seen twice before on two separate but tragic occasions. It was not facing him, but Jim knew that on the other side of its head were two disk-like eyes through which it would see. It was the machine.

Jim aimed his weapon right at the machine's back, but the hideous creation seemed to ignore him. Slowly, Jim approached its menacing figure, and yet it did not shift from its original position. Finally, he was about a meter away, and as he moved around the tall robotic figure, saw that the eyes were not glowing blue as they had done so many times before, but rather were not glowing at all. In curious bafflement, Jim pondered on how such a thing could be turned off; but then remembered that his friend was in danger and let the thought pass. He proceeded to search through the old church, the choir stalls, behind the organ, the side chapel, but there was no sign of Brigson or Tommy anywhere.

Finally, Jim spotted two stone doors towards the back of the building. He cautiously crept up to the doorway, and upon pushing the doors open, found a set of stairs leading downwards toward a crypt. He quietly proceeded down the many steps and soon saw shadowy figures emerge from the room below, in addition to a familiar, deep, British voice.

'I don't know, Mark. This just feels too risky…' Brigson sighed to the lack of a reply. 'All I wanted was to work on my machine. Not all this… mess… Are you sure yo-?' His voice froze, and he began to laugh. 'Ah, it seems our guest has arrived. Come down, Mr Griffen. Make yourself at home…'

Jim walked down the remaining steps, his weapon at hand, and saw in disgust the room before him. It was only the size of a regular bathroom, with grimy black walls as its supports. There was hardly any light, the only source being a single dangling bulb in the centre of the ceiling. Below this bulb was a small wooden chair, occupied by a bound, bruised, unconscious Tommy, who was facing a small camera on a tripod. This camera was wired to one of three monitors at the edge of the room, and watching these was none other than Sebastian Brigson in his chemical-stained lab coat. Now though, his expression was different. Where-as before he was manically laughing, now he seemed upset, almost angry.

'Hello Jim,' he said simply. 'Glad you could join us. Have you had a nice trip?'

Jim just pointed his weapon at the man. 'Get on the ground now, Brigson.'

'Oh…' He seemed genuinely surprised. 'They told me you'd be unarmed! Said not to worry if you got mad.' He shrugged. 'I don't suppose I should worry, considering you have to worry about police law. You can't shoot me until *I* have a weapon myself.'

Jim smirked. 'Yeah, well, you and I both know you never really cared much for what the police say.' He heard a whirring and in his peripheral vision he saw the camera turning to face him. Now everybody at the police station would see him alone, his weapon poised at Brigson.

'You want to repeat that Jim? Go on, I know you do! They won't mind! You know this is the only way to stop me.' The scientist laughed. 'Oh… this makes perfect sense. They lied to me, Jim. They *lied* to me… My part of the plan's done now, so they gave you the means to dispose of me. We're all just puppets in their game, I suppose. How fitting…'

'Stop talking!' Jim demanded. 'Why are you filming this? Why are you filming all of this Brigson, what do you aim to show the police station?'

'The kind of man you are!' Brigson smiled. 'You're a vengeful, homicidal maniac, James Griffen. And I promise you that you will end at least two lives tonight. First, you'll kill me. Then… you'll kill your partner.'

'Tommy?' Jim shook his head and laughed at the absurdity. 'Why would I kill Tommy? He's my partner! My friend!'

'No, he really isn't. You despise the man in that chair over there, you've told the world that on many occasions. You know his death will further your own selfish plans!' Brigson was clearly enjoying this. 'I shouldn't be surprised; you've been unstable ever since your son died!'

'What are you talking about?' Jim shouted.

'I'm talking about you, Jim! I'm talking about the psychopathic, murderous wreck that you really are!'

'I'm not a *murderer!*'

The gun fired.

Jim didn't even feel his finger tug at the trigger. All he felt were the thick red droplets that sprayed across his face, and the fierce tremors of the weapon in his hand. Brigson fell and lay still on the floor, a gaping, bloody hole above his left eye. Blood leaked into a body-sized puddle.

Jim collapsed on his knees and dropped the weapon. To his side, the camera dropped, and the monitors by Brigson's corpse all shut off one by one.

Jim bowed his head and shut his eyes, leaving only darkness. Silence was all around, save for his shaky breathing. This wasn't possible. He didn't pull the trigger – he couldn't have!

There was a clap to his right.

He lifted his head and frowned.

Another.

Jim opened his eyes. His breathing became faster, more fearful. What was that noise?

More clapping. Slow and inconsistent. A single man's amused applause. Jim turned his head. He was met with a wicked smile.

Thomas Knightley shook off the ropes that seemingly bound him, and stood from his chair, now giving Jim a standing ovation. His face was glowing with what looked to be malicious pride.

'Tom-'

'Ah ah ah. Don't speak. You'll ruin the moment!' His clapping was faster now, the applause building in a vicious crescendo. His smile twisted again, this time into an enraged glare, his eyes studying Jim with disdain as if he was some hideous parasite.

'I don't… I don't understand.'

'There you go talking again, why have you *always got to talk?*' Something was different about the way he was speaking. His accent…

Tommy pulled an odd-looking device from his pocket and pressed a button on its surface. From far up the chapel, Jim heard the familiar whirrs of the machine approaching the stairwell.

'If I'm correct, your family should have been found by now. I assure you; no harm has come to them... yet.' His accent was British.

Definitely British.

Then it clicked in Jim's mind. 'You…' Jim said hopelessly. 'Lynda told me that Brigson mentioned having a partner.' He brought himself to his feet. 'It's you? No…'

The man Jim knew as Tommy threw his arms up in the air as if it was so obvious. 'Well, yeah… Come on Jim! The obscure mentions that I'd lost someone? My lack of knowledge in most aspects of police work? The fact I was able to work out Nathan Blake's location so quickly? You really thought I'd questioned that drug addict? Nobody would be able to pull answers like that from a Child of the Reaper in such a short space of time!'

Jim gazed at the man he'd known to be his partner, terrified at what he had now become.

'And how else was the Circle meant to guide the police department to that hospital? *I* was the one who suggested that we searched at Brigson's house, and *I* was the one who shot all those officers behind Lynda at the school! They didn't even notice I was missing either. All I had to do was jump out of the van at a convenient point and run back. All this time, I've been guiding you all to be exactly where I needed you to be. In fact, *I* was the one who suggested to Mary that we bring you in for the case! It was *me* who put the memory stick in the first victim's jacket! And *I* rigged that pistol on the floor, so you would shoot my partner straight through the head when it was activated.' He glanced over to the scientist's corpse. 'Got it on camera too. Good old Briggy, he always did his job well. Shame he became pretty useless towards the end, but at least he got to weaponise his tin man a bit before he left…'

'I trusted you!' Jim exclaimed, rising to his feet. 'I thought of you as my partner. My friend.'

'You thought of Thomas Knightley as a friend,' the man

replied with a smirk. 'But he was just a personality. A character I invented from a past long gone.' The man laughed in amusement. 'You were always so good at sniffing out the bad guys, Jim, just not the ones right under your nose. And that's why I've already won!'

The machine was just behind Jim now. He could hear it had stopped, and he could feel its arm move to point towards his neck.

'Won what, Tommy? All this murder and deceit - to what end?'

'You know what Jim? I think I might just tell you... But let's get the basics right first.' The man enthusiastically raised the device in his hand once more. 'My name is not Thomas Knightley.'

The machine shot the tranquillizer into Jim's neck. As his legs gave way under him, he frantically ripped the micro-recorder from his right palm and stuck it on his inside left cheek.

'My name… is Marcus Arwick.'

***

LYNDA
JULY 14TH, 2025
THE LAST LAUGH

'What do you mean he just left?'

The woman at the reception desk flinched away. 'I don't know he… he just ran out of here.'

Lynda raised her hand to her mouth and bit her finger in anxiety. 'It's always the same. He finds out before me, he goes in alone because it's *too dangerous*, and then he nearly dies. Why did I marry him again?' The receptionist stared at her with fearful eyes. 'Yeah, don't answer that…'

'Lynda!'

Captain Mary Parker burst through the front doors of the building; her face afraid. 'Is it true about Tommy?'

She nodded wearily. 'And Jim's gone off to chase him.'

Mary sighed. 'I wouldn't have predicted *that*. Have we got any leads?'

Lynda shrugged. 'Clearly, my husband has some. Perhaps he

left something in the office? The tech guys are also investigating where this video feed is coming from. I talked to them just now. They told me the Circle have put a virus into our system via a memory stick. The message on all the screens is being transmitted to that.'

'A virus? But that means the Circle had to have entered the police station sometime in the last few hours. How the hell did they pull that off?'

Lynda nodded. 'Same way I believe they got that bomb setup in the hospital, or that rogue officer at the school. Sure, the machine could have been hidden away at that hospital a while back, but I figure the bomb would have been noticed by at least one of your squad if it was put there before you entered. And no outside members could have possibly put on police uniforms and hidden with us at the school.'

'You're saying there's an inside member…'

Lynda shrugged. 'Possibly multiple inside members. Two, at least. It would explain a lot.'

Mary nodded slowly. 'Well, that's something we can't afford to worry about right now. We need to get to Jim. Fast!'

Lynda's phone began to ring. It was one of the officers tracing the signal. She answered it.

'You've got it?' she clarified. There was more talking. Lynda eyed Mary. 'Okay, we're on our way!'

***

The vans screeched to a halt, and one by one the officers spilt out onto the moonlit street.

They were beside the river; the waters sparkling like blue

sapphires under the night sky. Up ahead, she spotted the dark outline of the abandoned "St John's Steelworks." Lynda was struggling to count the number of abandoned buildings in this city – perhaps it was a sign of Nightdrop's decline.

Their boots clopped against the floor as they quickly marched to their destination. Lynda prayed she would find her colleagues in here before it was too late. Jim was known to make rash decisions, and she remembered how he'd nearly killed Brigson at Signision.

There were several blue entrance doors dotted across the building. The officers didn't even have to try to break them down – it seemed every single one was left unlocked. Lynda entered around the front of the building, walking into a room full of conveyor belts, large metal basins and furnaces. There was little light, only that of the moon streaming through the high glass windows. The air was dry and cold, and silence hung all around.

There was a sudden cry for help.

Dozens of lights flickered on above, and the whole room was stunningly lit. Lynda looked for the source of the scream, and saw a dishevelled woman, with tangled brown hair and a bruised face. Her body was tightly bound, and she was seemingly attached to the conveyor belt.

Mary cursed behind her. 'That's Elly Griffen.'

Lynda covered her mouth in shock. They'd finally found Elly. But that meant…

'Where's Nora? Jim's mother.'

Right on cue, there was sobbing from the corner of the room, and Lynda turned to view its origin. Nora Griffen looked less harmed than her daughter, but her face was still in great distress. Her mouth was gagged, and her hands and feet bound by large cuffs to a metal chair. There was still an IV drip in her arm, and Lynda instantly remembered that the poor woman needed hospital treatment.

There was a loud crackling noise all around, like the start of an announcement on an aeroplane. In the corners of the room were large loudspeakers, all transmitting the same audio. 'Hello, officers.'

The voice was Brigson's for certain. It had the same amused British accent. 'The fact that you can hear me means you've accidentally activated our tripwire. Well done. You may have just killed yourselves…'

Suddenly there was a fierce whirring in the room. Several machines were starting to activate.

'The Circle didn't need us to do this; the hospital was enough for them. My partner and I, however, thought it would be… amusing, to have a little celebration to mark the end of our great plans!'

'As you can see here, two hostages from the hospital lie trapped in this awful mechanism. When this recording finishes, the machine we have built here will activate. If you would trace the conveyor belt that dear Elly is tied to, you will find it reaches a… *fiery* conclusion.'

Sure enough, following the belt up its incline, at the end was a large furnace, looking as if it were beginning to warm up from the orange glow that emitted from its open door. Following on from the other side of this boiler was a long chute, presumably intended to funnel away the molten steel. This chute twisted and turned until it reached its broken-off end, directly above Nora Griffen's head.

'And I suppose I don't need to tell you what happens if the furnace is used. Good luck officers…' The speakers cut off. Nothing happened for a few moments, and Lynda surveyed the trap analytically. On further inspection, she noted Elly to be bound to several steel bricks. Bricks that would melt and pour down the chute should they ever reach that furnace.

Brigson's voice came back. 'Oh, and one more thing. This machine is timed for the metal to reach the end of that chute in seven minutes. That's two minutes to get Elly off the conveyor belt, five minutes of blasting in the furnace and one minute for the metal to travel down the shoot. Once that time is up, we haven't given you much time to get out of here before our explosives blow you all to pieces. If you think this is all a little sadistic, get used to it. This is the world now. I'm tired of pretending I'm a good man, and as you'll soon learn, doing the right thing will just bring you misery. Have fun!'

The belt began to move, and Elly screamed for help once more, writhing madly as she began to move. Lynda bolted straight to her, along with three other officers. The poor girl's body was wrapped in a total of three chains, each held by a padlock. A note was taped on her torso reading, "*the key to freedom lies in hearts of steel.*"

While the other officers tugged at the chains, Lynda stepped back and thought. Hearts of steel. That couldn't mean…

The moment it clicked in her brain, she sprinted to the large metal basin by the doors at the back and shouted for help. Another officer came and hoisted her up, fiercely clutching back her foot so that she did not fall in. Sure enough, inside was a single metal key.

'The keys are in the basins!' she shouted. Carefully, she lowered her body, hooking her feet to the edge to avoid trapping herself inside. She yanked the first key from the bottom and pulled herself out, before throwing it over to Mary.

The homicide captain fumbled around with the key for a second, but finally a click was heard. 'It worked! Hurry!'

Elly was halfway to the beginning of the incline on the conveyor, but luckily another officer had already found his way to another basin by the wall at the back of the room. In haste, he jumped in to retrieve the key.

There was no response for a few moments. Finally, he shouted, 'I've got it!'

Suddenly there was a loud clunk and the sound of a claxon. Brigson's voice spoke again. 'Uh oh, forgot to mention that I wouldn't make this easy. Sorry, I really should have warned you.'

Suddenly a hatch in the wall above the basin began to swing slowly open. To her right, Lynda heard a scream and the frantic steps of officers as the belt began to speed up.

'What's going on!' the man in the basin shouted as the hatch was half open.

Lynda gaped in horror as she saw the bright orange fluid begin to pour out of the hatch.

'Oh no. What is that? Get it away from me, get it away!'

Lynda ran to the basin. The man's arms were flailing frantically. 'Somebody let me out!'

The pouring molten steel began to quicken into a thick glowing stream. The man was frantically trying to hoist himself over the edge, the key tight in his right hand.

Lynda jumped and grabbed his arms, desperately trying to pull him up. 'I've got you. Push yourself up.'

He was screaming even more. 'I'm slipping. Please help. Get me out of here!' The basin was about a quarter full now, the man's feet barely missing the surface.

Lynda tried ferociously to pull him out, but it was a futile effort. The angle was horrible, and the man too heavy.

'I'm not going to make it…' he said hopelessly. 'Take the key. Take the key.' He was waving the key frantically.

Lynda took it, but continued to pull him up with all her strength. 'You are going to make it! Listen to me, we're going to get you out of-'

But the man seemed to slip, and suddenly Lynda's grasp of him was lost, sending him plunging into the orange liquid. His shrill screams and pained writhing stayed with her even when his body had been fully submerged.

But then she remembered Elly.

Jim's sister was beginning the slow incline to the furnace now. Meanwhile, Nora was sobbing in her chair, while another officer attempted to remove her handcuffs. Lynda ran to Mary and handed her the second key.

'Do you see the third basin anywhere?' she asked the captain.

They looked around and saw only the two they'd entered recently. Then Lynda had the initiative to look up. The third basin looked the biggest and hung high up in the warehouse. Beside it was a grated metal platform, leading in from a large set of stairs. Lynda knew what she needed to do.

'When I shout, you've got to be ready to catch it!'

Mary nodded, the signal for Lynda to get moving.

Lynda made her way to the foot of the stairs and proceeded to run to the top. They didn't feel very secure – rust coated most areas, and the entire stairwell shook as if seconds from collapse. About halfway up, she felt her foot brush past something, and the voice in the speakers played once more.

'That's very high, detective! Careful not to… *slip.'*

Suddenly a strange liquid was projected by a hole in the wall and began to spray on one of the metal support beams holding up the stairs. Lynda didn't feel concerned at first. What could a bit of water do?

'Lynda! Run!' Mary shouted. 'That stuff's corroding the metal. It's not water, it's *acid!'*

'You've got to be kidding me!' Lynda muttered. She bolted up the remaining stairs, which began to feel less stable by the minute. Once on the metal walkway, she saw the basin up ahead, a large gap between it and the edge.

She cursed. It was too far to just step onto. Taking a few deep breaths, she prepped herself to run.

'Lynda, the pole's about to collapse!'

She looked back and saw a shrivelled, thoroughly dissolved pole, trembling as it struggled to take the shared weight of the walkway. Lynda shifted her gaze forwards and set her eyes onto the basin.

What if Brigson's trapped it? she thought. *Will liquid metal pour into this one? How will I get down, anyway?*

None of that mattered now. The only way forward was jumping, whatever the cost. She sprinted forwards.

She leapt.

The platform became loose and dropped behind her, the whole thing collapsing from one broken beam. Time froze as Lynda found herself gliding through the air, the weight of her body pulling her down every unit she moved forwards. The large metal basin was close, but it was becoming too high.

She reached for the edge of the basin. Her fingers just caught the rim.

Her legs painfully smacked against the bottom and for a few moments she was helplessly dangling in the air. The floor was far lower than it had seemed before now, and with a glance, she saw Elly halfway up the upwards incline leading to the furnace.

It's all right, she thought. *Imagine you're climbing out of a pool.*

Her arms felt as if they were burning hotter than the furnace themselves and sweat now rolled down her face in thick beads. Lynda mustered all the energy she could fathom to pull herself over just a few centimetres.

Her left hand slipped.

Now only her right arm was hooked onto the basin, her left dangling down below her. Her heart pumped faster than a machine, and she gasped as she saw the floor below.

I refuse to die tonight, she thought.

In a moment of rage and determination to survive, Lynda swung her right leg up, just high enough that her foot reached the top of the basin. Hooking it over, she managed to get half her limbs on the inside. One final push was all it took for her to hook her body completely over.

She gasped in relief for a few moments and found the key lumped under her back. She jumped up and screamed at Mary. 'Now!'

The key flew in the air for a few moments, and Lynda jumped to her feet to check if it had reached its destination. Looking over the edge, Lynda saw that Elly was just inches away from a fiery demise, but she sighed in relief when she saw the captain fumbling over the last lock... For a few heart-racing moments, it seemed the key was surely stuck before the lock finally clicked. Elly rolled out of her chains and fell off the platform, moments before it entered into the blazing inferno.

Lynda sighed in relief. Nora too was stood up, after the other officer managed to release her from her seat and was now having the IV drip removed from her arm. Everybody was safe…

Until Brigson's voice began to play again. 'You'll want to be getting down, officer. Here, let me help you.'

Suddenly the chains which suspended the basin began to drop fiercely, sending Lynda crashing down to the floor. *I knew this would happen one day*, she thought. Closing her eyes, she embraced the quick death that rushed towards her.

And then the basin stopped.

She opened her eyes once more, to see Mary running over to her as the basin dropped the final few inches to the floor. 'I'm not dead,' Lynda said, amazed.

'Not yet. We found the remote that controlled the basin. We were going to lower you down ourselves until Brigson did it for you. Still, you will be dead in a few moments if we don't get out of here.'

Lynda crawled out and followed her partner in haste. The other officers had seemingly begun to evacuate, making her and Mary the final ones out. Brigson's voice played one last time.

'See you another time, officers. *Perire finite non est.*' The man laughed over the loudspeakers.

They were just a few metres away when the building was blasted to smithereens. The force of the explosion propelled them forward and Lynda could feel the heat onto her back as it happened.

The roaring continued for a good few moments before at last everything was silent. Lynda and Mary found themselves on the ground, their suits singed, their bodies aching.

'Well, I wasn't exactly expecting that kind of experience tonight,' Mary joked.

Lynda pushed herself off the floor and offered a hand to her partner. Up ahead, the rest of the Tactical Response Team and Elly gazed at them in awe.

'Are you all right?' Lynda said, looking over the hostages carefully for any signs of serious injury.

Nora, who had been sat down while she showed symptoms of shock and exhaustion, nodded wearily. Elly was shaking, but eventually ran over and embraced Lynda fiercely, sobbing over her shoulder.

'Hey… it's okay. You're all okay now.'

The early morning sun was beginning to rise, and Lynda could hear the sound of sirens, declaring the arrival of the ambulances. Nora and Elly made their way to the vehicle that would hopefully take them to the correct destination.

Lynda approached the other officers. 'Tail that ambulance. Make sure it reaches St Bartholomew's and nowhere else. Then talk to Murdock, make sure we get protection for Nora and Eliza Griffen.' They nodded and set off.

Lynda turned to Mary, who seemed panicked and exhausted. 'I'm guessing we're not finished,' Mary remarked.

Lynda shook her head. 'No. No, we're not. Brigson sent us here as a distraction; clearly, he just wants Jim on his own.'

'How could he have been so certain that only Jim would go?'

Lynd shrugged. 'Because only Jim would sprint into a hostage situation on his own. Perhaps they set it up so we'd only be able to track the signal once Jim reached the church. Anyway, you look pretty shaken, you sure you want to continue?'

Mary nodded in certainty. 'Definitely. Jim and Tommy are in danger.'

Lynda nodded in agreement. 'Last time I saw him, he was heading to the office. If we're going to find out anything, it'll be there. But could you do something for me first?'

Mary frowned. 'Yeah sure.'

'Find a woman named Lucy Green. Her husband died in that factory…'

Mary looked back in solemn thought. 'Zach. I remember him.' She sighed. 'I'll tell her. Don't go running off to find Jim without me though.'

'Of course not,' Lynda lied.

What was wrong with her? She was becoming like her husband. But after that experience, Lynda didn't want Mary in any more danger than she already was.

I've got to find Jim alone, she thought. *This is as much about me as it is about him…*

And if I fail. We'll both see Jake together…

***

JIM
JULY 14TH, 2025
THE BIRTH OF A MONSTER

'Jim…' said the darkness.

'Jim… wakey wakey Jimmy.'

The darkness was brightening into a blurry mixture of colour, like the surface of an artist's paint board. There was still a vast majority of black smothering this colour, but it was slowly dying away. In front of Jim's was something large, something part reflective white, part fierce jet black. Beside it was a smaller figure, a mix of blue and black. Jim soon discovered that this was what made all those wicked noises which invaded his head and forced his brain to work hard and understand them. He wanted to just sleep. Sleep and escape from this cruel world. Was anything even left for him?

'Jim?' said the blue-black figure.

After great effort, Jim finally made a responsive groaning noise.

'Ah! Hello Jim, awake at last!'

Jim wriggled about madly. He was tightly chained to a chair, barely able to breathe, let alone move. On his chest, and by his wrists, padlocks kept him bound firmly.

The man Jim had once known as a friend strolled forwards. 'Obviously, I've emptied your pockets…' He pointed at a small table to the right of the blurry black and white figure. On it seemed to be all of Jim's pocket items, a notebook, a pen, a pack of mints, his badge and…

What's that? Jim thought. *A weapon.*

There was a semiautomatic pistol lying on the surface, its barrel pointing in Jim's direction. It must have belonged to this man who Jim had once known as Tommy, perhaps to kill him and end it all for good. It was calling out to him. So near, yet so far.

The man walked over to the counter and inspected Jim's items. 'None of it would've been useful anyway! I've also taken and wiped your single micro-recorder too, in case you're planning to send any messages, and put you in chains this time, not ropes. I'm a tad more cautious than those idiots at Blake's warehouse.'

Jim suddenly remembered his final actions before falling unconscious but knew he couldn't act on them yet. His aching body struggled in its seat. 'You…' he just about managed.

'Me…' the man mimicked in a similar croaky voice. He laughed at his own humour for a while. 'Oh Jim, I've been waiting so long for this! You, Jim, were always my greatest challenge because I knew that if I could beat you, I would become unstoppable! And now here you are, in my grasp, my entire plan complete. Well… save for one thing. We've still got to complete this guy,' he banged the black and white figure, 'and then… well, I think I'll have the right to upgrade from "Phantom" don't you?'

Jim's vision became clearer now, and suddenly he understood what was in front of him. They were upstairs, in the nave of the chapel, between the old wrecked choir stalls. The black and white object seemed to be the machine, but it was different from normal. The front of the head was split open down a vertical line in the middle and the entire head was pushed back as if it were looking upwards. The wires that normally surrounded the neck still held the head and torso in place, but the neck itself was split in half and opened from the centre. In fact, the torso, arms, legs and boots all had their front halves opened up. The inside of the machine was jet black, like a windowless room with no light source. Along the inside hung many transparent tubes, some thick and long like an eel, while some were more like tubes from hospital machinery. Most tubes had reflective needles at the end. Jim also noticed the presence of many wires on the inside of the body, some of these connected to a metal frame at the head which seemed to encompass where a skull would sit. This gave Jim the impression that they were used to electrocute the brain in some way, as with the many victims of this case. Some wires lead to the arms, and Jim saw that they were connected to concealed weaponry, like the firearm which killed his colleagues, and the hands, possibly a weapon or a defibrillation device for when the machine was made for the battlefield and hospital.

Next to the opened-up machine was the young man that Jim had met just days ago. The same young man he had come to trust and respect. The young man who betrayed him. Tommy, or perhaps Marcus, was wearing a smile, but unlike the one which Jim was so used to seeing. This grin was malicious. Satisfied.

'I don't…' Jim croaked. 'I don't understand… You're not the Phantom. For a start, you claim to be Marcus Arwick, but you don't look anything like him.'

His ex-partner chuckled. 'Jim, why do you think Lynda could never find me? It wasn't just the fact I shaved off all that beard. My first murder was that truck driver, do you remember? I threw his body into one of the barrels of acid that he was delivering, but the fight didn't exactly go smoothly. I ended up with a face full of acid myself. Burnt my hands too, hence the lack of fingerprints! It was easy enough to hide after that acid stripped most of my identity from me. This here,' he pointed to his face. 'It's all reconstruction. Quite a good job too. I wouldn't have been able to afford it myself of course, but that's what the Circle are for.'

'But that's the thing, you didn't even kill that truck driver!' Jim exclaimed. 'Even if you're Marcus Arwick as you say, you're not the Phantom. I used to think you were, but you can't be. He was a different man, a surgeon I didn't even know about. He's *dead…*'

Arwick leaned against the machine, looking pleased with himself. 'Why? Because your wife "shot me?" Because they found a body by your apartment? Your wife shot Daniel Crockett, a British surgeon, coincidentally the same one who gave up on my little girl far too early.'

Jim frowned as he remembered. If "Tommy" really was Marcus Arwick, that meant Jim was partially responsible for his family's death. A pang of guilt hit him deep inside.

'Back when I was on my virtuous spree of vengeance, taking out all those responsible for the deaths of my wife and daughter, I came to a bit of a stalemate with the police. I knew you'd probably worked out who I was by then, and I still had two victims to go. So, I thought I'd disappear, right after killing you and Crockett.'

'It was easy enough. Crockett had a family. A son like you. A bit of blackmail's all it takes for someone to commit murder, even the murder of a kid. I gave him a costume and a script of what needed to be said, told him his son would die if he didn't go through with it, and he did all the work for me. Lynda shot him and the Phantom was dead to the world. Piece of cake.'

Jim shook his head. 'I should have guessed. It was so simple.

I thought maybe he was a friend or a guy looking for an excuse to kill. But you had it all figured out…'

Arwick tilted his head in half-agreement. 'Well… almost. If I had, I wouldn't be stuck here, would I? My *actual* plan was to kill you at the warehouse but… backup tracked you. I've made sure not to make the same mistake this time – one of our guys at the police department had eyes on you; made sure you would figure out to come here on your own, while the rest of your team was preoccupied. There were a bunch of ways we could have got you to come here, but I'm glad you finally worked out the Bible thing. Meanwhile, he pretended to track the signal I sent and led the police to the wrong warehouse. The rest of the police will now be on a mad goose chase, trying to save your family, while I sit here and talk to you.' He leant casually against the machine. 'You see, unlike you Jim, I *learn* from my mistakes. I wasn't able to kill you back then, but the result now is *far* more glorious. Besides, I had the joy of Jake's death to keep my anger at bay until now.'

Jim tried lurching at him in anger, but the effort was futile.

Arwick wasn't deterred. 'Really? You have the audacity to get angry that I *indirectly* killed your son? If I remember correctly, my family would have been fine if not for your mistakes!'

Jim calmed down, and the guilt hit again. 'I didn't know…'

'No. You didn't. But you *did* know you were breaking the rules of your job, I believe. Isn't that why the rules are there? To stop these kinds of things?'

'You think I haven't thought about that?' Jim shouted. 'You think I haven't had nightmares every night because of what I did?' He got no response but a blank, non-convinced expression. 'At least I feel remorse, you son of a bitch!'

'Yeah, well, I didn't deserve what I got. You did. And I didn't directly kill your son, anyway.'

'No,' Jim remarked. 'You just blackmailed a guy into doing it for you. You didn't just kill him out of anger, you planned the death of my son!'

'*You killed a kid too!*' Arwick screamed. 'My kid… My little girl. For years, you've been ready to kill me for what I did, well how do you think I felt Jim?' He nodded at Jim's silence. 'You get it now? You're not so innocent, James Griffen!'

Jim chewed on this for a while. How different was he from Arwick when he looked at it? They were both just two guilt-driven fathers. He rolled his tongue in his mouth and felt something hard stuck to his cheek. It was the micro-recorder he'd attached before falling unconscious. Perhaps it would help him.

'When did you find out my part in… what happened to your family?' he whispered.

'Oh, ages and *ages* ago, back when I still cared.' Arwick turned around to face the other end of the chapel, giving Jim time to press the micro-recorder and spit it between his lap. 'I told you it was a brutal fight with my first victim, but once I had that truck driver up against the barrel of acid, he told me *everyone* I should have killed instead of him. It's funny what people will tell you when under threat of-'

'Back when you "*still cared*"?' Jim exclaimed. 'You don't still care about your own family's deaths?'

Arwick looked rather miffed that he had been interrupted, but humoured Jim nonetheless. 'Oh, I did care, Jim! Right at the start, way back when it first happened. I cared so much that it drove me mad to the point that I only had one goal. To kill those responsible! To be honest, I thought that first murder would bring me some closure, but instead… it left me craving for more. In his panic, the driver was pleading that there were others far more responsible. So, I got around to finishing them all off. It became my purpose. Every murder satisfied me, but it was never enough. I became… hungry. Desperate. Addicted. I think I'd forgotten *why* I was doing it around… murder three?'

He crouched down so he was at eye level with Jim. 'You know, I don't always lie. I told Lynda I did a degree in criminal psychology – that bit was true. Not once did it occur to me that I'd end up like one of the loonies but thanks to a little help, here I am! I believe there's a monster that grows inside all of us, just waiting for the right moment that will weaken all the sanity that keeps it locked away. I've been trying to fish yours out for a while now…'

'So I'm some experiment to you then?' Jim provoked. 'Brigson had…' he nodded to the opened machine, 'that *thing* over there and you have me. Is that what this whole thing's been about?'

The man hesitated before shaking his head. 'No. No, I wish it were, but unfortunately, I have a debt to pay.'

At last, Jim understood. 'To the Circle of Saints.'

Arwick nodded.

'So they exist then?'

'Well of course they exist!' he shouted, throwing his arms up in the air. 'I certainly couldn't pull off an operation of *this* magnitude, but the Circle? They've been building in strength and number for a long while. They have fingers in pies all over this city, and soon they'll be in a position to take it all down!'

Jim didn't reply. He was hoping Arwick would continue. Arwick pulled out one of the flipped-over chairs in the centre of the church and brought it by the machine, before slouching into it with a sigh.

'That shooting at the warehouse on the night your son died. Turns out, I left a little more behind than I anticipated. A blood sample was left on the scene, belonging to none of the officers in the building. It was only a matter of time before they traced it back to me, and my whole effort to disappear from the world would be blown through the roof.

'Luckily, somebody got to it before the other police officers could.' He grinned, once again knowing something that Jim didn't. 'Your medical examiner.'

'Tessa? Why would she help you?'

'The same reason Murdock did, Jim. Because they wanted to recruit me…'

The penny dropped. 'Murdock and Tessa…' Jim started. 'Are part of the Circle of Saints?'

'Yep. Didn't you wonder why she hated me so much when I "first met her." She never cared for me much. But Murdock? He thought I was an incredibly valuable asset. Ever since their creation in the late 1800s, the Circle have been looking for a new way to carry out their work. To fulfil their quest of gaining eternal life, and this time, they aimed to achieve it through a certain medical-robotics machine.' He pointed to the open contraption. 'I always thought it was horseshit of course, but what choice did I have?'

He stood up. 'So, they hid the evidence, and after weeks of the Circle searching, found and kidnapped me from a street corner. Took me to this very spot. Here, Murdock presented me with two options. Help Brigson kidnap and dispose of victims for his robotics-related experiments or face eventual arrest. I chose the former of course - besides I'd get to do a bit more of what I did best…'

Jim shook his head. 'That spike in missing people across last year. That was all you?'

Arwick shrugged. 'Not all me. Some were legitimately missing, but yeah, I put the work in. Gave me something to do I suppose, else I'd probably end up putting a bullet through my brain.' He saw Jim's scornful face. 'Oh, don't give me that look, Jim, the Circle's been doing messed-up crap for years! You've probably worked on cases of their mess without even realising it.'

Jim nodded slowly. This was good. Arwick was giving him what he needed. 'Then what was all this?' Jim asked. 'Clearly, the experiments were over.'

Arwick looked uncertain, as if in the realisation that he'd already told Jim a lot. 'You ask a lot of questions, Jim. Any reason for that?'

'Well, seeing as I'm going to die anyway…'

Arwick laughed. 'Who said anything about dying?' He glanced at the machine. 'But I suppose the truth is safe in your hands. Even if it gets to the right people, only one man would ever believe you, and he'll be dead soon.'

Jim frowned. They weren't going to kill him? What could they possibly have had planned?

'After a few months of experiments, Murdock and the Circle realised our good old robo-buddy over here wasn't working the way the Circle intended. It was such a shame considering the lengths Brigson had gone into engineering it. Luckily, hope was on the horizon. A guard at Stormfeld Prison, one working for the Circle, overheard a rather interesting piece of dialogue from one of the prisoners. The prisoner's name was Michael Williams. He was on the phone, asking somebody to check on a certain "dangerous rock" every so often, lest it would fall into the wrong hands…' Marcus sat there for a while, letting that one fact sink in. 'I know, crazy right? I thought the same when I first joined the Circle. The rock from the story? That can't possibly be real!'

Jim shook his head in doubt. 'You're insane. You're telling me that you believe an actual rock with that power exists, a rock from a fairy tale!'

'No Jim, I know it exists. The Circle have done their research and with Brigson's help, it's rather extensive. Scientific types call it arconium, and it's one of the rarest materials found on this planet, perhaps in the known universe. Its scientific properties are so unusual that it doesn't even classify as a proper element! I believe we left a paper on it for you to find at Brigson's house.'

Jim thought back, attempting to recall a paper of the sort.

'Anyway, the Circle were convinced. Just to check, they glanced at Williams' criminal file. Before he was a criminal, witnesses reported him disappearing often from time to time, going into the forest across the river to do "goodness know what."'

Jim thought about that. 'That is strange.'

'Strange enough for Murdock to change plans entirely. He knew if he could get that stone, the Circle would be unstoppable and would be able to take the city, starting with the police department. So, his new objective was to get to Arwick, while mine and Brigson's was to weaken Nightdrop City Police Department just enough so that when the Circle did get the stone, we could launch an attack from inside and outside simultaneously.

'Some help from Murdock, and I managed to disguise myself perfectly. He got me a fake identity and managed to hire me for the police department. On top of the shave and facial reconstruction, I had my hair dyed blonde, wore these stupid shoes that made me look taller, put in some coloured contacts every day and changed my accent. Thomas Knightley was born. You'd be surprised how little cops recognise faces from files when you change the right bits.

Especially you and Lynda.

'Then all that remained was for me to direct you all the way I wanted. That whole affair with Blake was unexpected, of course. Sure, I knew his address and ultimately led you there, but Brigson had forgotten to let him know that it was all part of the plan. Whoops. On the flip side, that whole hospital school thing?' He clapped twice, slowly. 'Superb! When it got to that day, we made sure to split the groups so that the school contained all the Circle members working for the police department. That way, we could ensure the deaths of over half of the non-Circle TRT members in the police force. The essential roles filled by the people we hire next will almost all be Circle members, at least until there are no more Circle members to hire, and then, when we finally have the stone, the *Rebirth* will begin, and we can take this city.'

Jim looked at his captor in silence. Suddenly he began to laugh. He laughed and laughed, and soon he was in tears. Marcus was at a loss for words, probably not accustomed to being laughed at. That just made Jim more amused.

'So that's your plan! Get the magic rock and take the police station? That's the big reveal! To think I was afraid of you, that I thought you were my intellectual equal!'

Arwick looked angry. 'You won't be laughing in a minute Jim, I assure you.' He reached into the machine and flicked a switch. Suddenly all the inside wires began to lash out violently, and certain areas started to clamp open and closed. From the head of the machine came the buzzing of electricity.

Jim's laughter stopped. 'I see. This is the final part of your plan? To kill me in your machine?'

Marcus shook his head slowly, his expression unchanging. 'No… you were always so slow, Jim. The machine brings people back. We *kill* them first. They're lucky enough not to feel the dozens of needles, the clamping, squeezing metal, the thousands of amps of high voltage electricity directly to their brain. But you will, Jim. Mark my words, you will.'

He walked behind and began to push Jim's chair closer to the machine until the wires were reaching out just millimetres from his face.

'You see Jim, my plan had a second half to it. Ever since the beginning, I've seen so much potential in you. Your outbursts of anger, your tragic childhood, the loss of your son. I thought if I could push you enough, I could make you into *me*. Think of it as another attempt of achieving immortality. But alas, you always pushed back against your dark side. That's what always fascinated me. The light inside you keeps fighting back…'

He pushed the chair even closer. Jim pulled his head back as the needles on tubes whipped closer.

Arwick grabbed the back of Jim's skull and yanked it forwards. Jim felt a wire quickly slice him across the right eye, causing him to grunt as great amounts of blood trickled out and impaired his vision.

'So *this* time,' Arwick continued. 'I built a case against you. Already I've recorded you at the pub, saying *you killed them all.* Just now I recorded your crippling guilt in response to my family's deaths. I filmed you shooting Brigson, and there were numerous witnesses to your prominent outburst of anger. Like me, you're a guy from the outside posing as a cop, and you were even the only survivor at the hospital, although I'll admit I did *not* plan for you to go running in there!' He pushed the chair forwards another inch. 'All this combined with your impending madness, your knowledge of my whereabouts, my talks to the police, Circle members feeding members of the jury lies and… well the moment you and I walk out of here, they'll all think this was done by you!'

He pushed the chair even closer. Needles whipped furiously about on Jim's face, and the metal shell clamped fiercely. Above all this noise, Jim just heard the sound of clinking metal from Arwick's hands. *Keys*, Jim thought.

'And finally, Jim, you will become like me. James Griffen, the Nightdrop Betrayer.' He brought the keys closer to Jim's back and wrist, ready to unlock him and push him into the contraption. 'Or something along those lines.'

As Marcus attempted to unlock the handcuffs, he tilted the chair forwards slightly, and suddenly the micro-recorder slid from Jim's lap and onto the floor. The cuffs clinked open, and Arwick had put the next key in the padlock as Jim quickly stamped his foot over the micro-recorder to conceal it. Too late. Leaving the key in the padlock, Arwick crept over to Jim's foot and kicked it aside, revealing the recording device underneath.

'You've been recording me. You son of a-'

But Jim had unlocked the padlock with his free hand, and now stood up, free of his chains. He grabbed the chair and swung it at Arwick's face, causing the villain to stumble back a few steps.

While Arwick was dazed, Jim took the time to unlock his feet. But his enemy was wiping the blood from his mouth and was approaching him quickly.

Arwick was now fishing into his back pocket. After a few moments, he revealed a small knife. 'You're going to wish you'd fallen into that machine.'

Arwick stepped towards Jim slowly, dragging out each footstep to make the anticipation linger. Meanwhile, Jim picked up the chair from the floor, ready to defend himself again. Finally,

Marcus was in attacking range. Jim picked up the chair and swinged it towards his head. This time his enemy ducked under the swing, before coming back up to stick the knife in Jim's throat.

In a moment of panic, Jim dropped the chair and darted backwards. Marcus lurched at him with the blade again. This time Jim slid to the right, hitting the knife-wielding left hand in the process. The knife clattered on the ground and slid across the floor, while the Phantom attempted to maintain his balance just in front of the machine. A few moments passed between them, as they saw the knife lying just metres away. Finally, as if in direct synchronisation, they both darted for the weapon.

Jim darted forwards and hit the ground first, his right hand clenching the hilt of the blade. Arwick soon followed, collapsing his weight on Jim, causing him to wheeze for breath. Jim felt pain sear in his wrist as Arwick grabbed it tightly, his nails digging into Jim's flesh. Jim refused to give up the blade. He lifted his left arm to push off his captor, but the man spotted it quickly and pinned that down too. Now it was a wrestle for control of the blade, Arwick strongly tugging at Jim's wrist so that the blade in Jim's hand would slash at his face. Jim pushed back in an attempt to get the sharp knife-edge closer to his enemy.

It was like this for a few moments, two men fiercely fighting for control. Finally, in a single swift action, Jim mustered his strength and unexpectedly pushed the knife round to the right, spinning the blade upwards and slashing it across his antagonist's eyes. Marcus countered this in an instant, vengefully plunging the blade into Jim's lower back. Jim groaned in pain and thrust his head towards his enemy's skull. The instant that Arwick loosened his grip from the blow, Jim clenched his right fist, spun and delivered a hook to Arwick's jaw.

They rolled over, Arwick on the ground, and now Jim was looming over Marcus. He shot his thumbnails forward, digging them into his enemy's eyes. He could feel blood and tears rising, covering his grimy thumbs. He was still aware of the pain in his side, but that was quickly diminishing, as Jim focussed on finishing off his captor.

But Arwick wasn't done. His knee rose straight into Jim's groin, causing the ex-detective to double over from the pain. Arwick grabbed Jim's hair and smashed his skull into the stone floor, over and over again, before finally releasing him, causing the ex-detective to collapse feebly.

The world became fuzzy and grey for a few moments, and Jim swore he heard the cry of his son. Fists pummelled down in all directions and he couldn't tell what was real anymore. All he saw before him was a shadow with a face of rage, sending fists like bullets down to crush his battered body.

Each punch shook him intensely, and each shake loosened the blade wedged in Jim's lower back, sending a searing acute pain up his side. It was more refreshing than cold water, and suddenly Jim felt a second wind of rage and determination fill within his chest. He took the knife beneath his fingers and slowly began to slide it out his lower back. He could feel his flesh sliding against the metal, but that did not deter him. Marcus' punches were getting heavier and harder, and it was only a matter of time before unconsciousness ensued.

Finally, the blade clattered out. Jim clutched it tightly as Arwick's fist rose once more, before slashing it across the first layers of skin in his enemy's throat. Marcus ceased his punching and stumbled back as he attempted to wheeze in air, giving time for Jim to arise. Both of their faces were painted in thick red blood, Jim almost half-blind from dried blood and swelling in his right eye. Both men now watched one another with caution.

'Any deeper on that cut and you would have killed me,' Marcus croaked with a smile.

Jim nodded. 'I know that's what you'd have wanted! I'm not going to become your "legacy."'

Arwick shook his head. 'Face it, Jim! You would have burst into laughter if I'd died then.'

Simultaneously, one charged towards the other, and in moments they collided. Marcus groped Jim's neck in his left hand, his fingernails digging deep. Jim wriggled and squirmed like a worm cooking in the sun, trying his hardest to yank Arwick's fingers off with his left hand. His right, in the meantime, was making desperate swings with the knife at Arwick's turned body. All were futile efforts. *There's one place I can still hit*, he thought. He'd lose the knife, but what options were left? He plunged it towards Arwick's wrist.

And missed.

Arwick, with a face of triumph, shot back his left arm and brought his right forward, knocking the knife out of Jim's hand and catching it himself. Jim caught a few gasping breaths before the knife now came slashing at his own body.

The silver glimmer of the blade flickered before Jim's eyes like an eel, but he had instinctively leant back to avoid his face being cut. Soon after, Marcus thrust the blade in Jim's direction, causing Jim to jump backwards. Marcus' right arm then shot at him as if to hold him in place, but Jim was too fast and grabbed the arm while turning to avoid the following knife jab. As the knife ended up just before his knee, Jim snapped his lower leg up, kicking the knife out of Arwick's hands and straight behind him.

Suddenly, a foot ploughed into Jim's stomach, causing him to grimace in pain and foolishly release Arwick's arm. Before Jim knew it, a fist had smashed into his face, and as far as he knew at this point, at least two of his teeth were very loose in his mouth.

Time slowed down, and Jim decided on one thing clearly in

his head. He would fight until the end. Even if given the chance to run away, he would make sure this man either ended up in jail or dead. The Phantom would not slip through his fingers again.

Jim charged in rage straight to the monster's waist, his tackle so ferocious that it managed to push Marcus almost the full way to the open machine before both men collapsed onto the floor. Marcus took out his free hand and sent two nails directly into Jim's eyes. Jim, in retaliation, started hitting and clawing away at Marcus' face. Marcus, now laughing, did not release his hold but started to dig his nails in harder. Jim, in one final attempt to stop himself from going blind, started using his right hand to fumble around on the wooden cabinet by the machine. He felt his badge, then his mint packet, then his wallet, and finally what he was looking for. Arwick's pistol. Quickly he grabbed around the handle, pulled it down from the wooden table and swung it across Arwick's face.

There was a loud crack as the Phantom's head swung to one side, his limbs dropping weakly. Jim stood up shakily just as Arwick made noises of stirring and took a step back. As his enemy arose from the ground, blood dribbling from his forehead, Jim pointed the pistol straight for the man's head.

The silence was deafening. Arwick was now standing before the open, still writhing machine; his face bruised and bloody, his hair wild and grimy. He gave Jim an unimpressed look. 'You're going to try to shoot me when you can't see the hand in front of your own bloody face, Jim?' Arwick taunted.

Jim's hands trembled uncontrollably.

'Don't tell me you're having doubts! First rule of murder, if you're going to kill someone, you have to commit to it! Come on, lemme help stir your rage. I killed your son. I pretended to be your friend and proceeded to kill a bunch of your colleagues. I lured you here so I could torture you and frame you for all of this. Why wouldn't you shoot me?'

Jim hesitated. His hands lowered. 'Because it's not right.'

Arwick looked irritated, giving off a groan of boredom reminiscent to that of a six-year-old. 'How boring! Have you ever considered not being the good guy-?'

Jim raised his gun to his enemy's head and pulled the trigger.

Just a click.

Jim tried again twice, but no bang was made.

Jim pulled the trigger over and over, and nothing came out the other end. It was empty.

Enraged, Jim threw the gun on the ground, sending a reverberating echo through the chapel. When it finally caught up to him what he had nearly done, he suddenly felt sick, and queasily fell to his knees.

Before him was a rare sight. The Phantom looked surprised. The look of shock slowly twisted into a beaming smile. 'You… did it…'

Jim glared up at his superior.

'You shot me.' He chuckled. 'You actually shot me, well… would have done.' He walked over to the pistol and lifted it off the floor, before walking back to his spot before the open machine and propping it on the wooden table. 'That one was just for show, I wouldn't risk putting a loaded one on display.'

Jim's enemy walked around to the back of the robot and flicked a switch, causing the machine to shut down into a motionless slumber. He then seemed to tear something off the machine's back in the process. When he came back to his original spot before the machine, he was holding a different, presumably loaded, pistol in his right hand. 'I didn't want to have to use this Jim. I did kind of need you alive and crazy for the police to think you're me but… well, you have been rather uncooperative. Better you die and my experiment fails than you being a pain in my arse for the next part of the plan. In fact, what difference does it make if you're alive or not? Provided I find and kill whoever you sent that message to, Lynda and Mary I'm guessing, and destroy their micro-recorders, I can tell the world I escaped *your* clutches and that you, the real killer, died.'

Finally, Jim could see his enemy clearly. He did not see Tommy or Marcus. Instead, what stood before him was unrecognisable. A brutal, malicious being, which didn't fit in with the natural world that Jim knew so well. It was in every sense a monster; it terrified him. The irony was that this monster looked like a viciously beaten version of the sweet, naïve persona of Tommy that Jim had met earlier this week - but he had not been frightened by him then. It seemed at this moment, the sight of this man now represented something far worse, something far more frightening. But what scared Jim even more, was the fact that he was becoming the same. He couldn't let that happen.

'I'm sure your evidence will be enough with me dead,' he said hopelessly to his enemy. 'You've achieved your task. You've made me a monster. Now go on. Take your alleged stone. Take the city. Make more monsters out of people. Just finish me off.'

Arwick nodded, almost respectfully. Jim bowed his head and closed his eyes.

'Thank you for co-operating Jim. And thank you for the fun.'

There was a loud blast.

***

Jim's brain was curious as he stared through the darkness. Nothing felt too different from when he'd been alive. Not yet.

Has my body even hit the floor? Has the bullet even reached my brain?

Thoughts came and went, speeding past like cars on a highway. Images of his mother appeared. Images of his sister too. *There wasn't enough time…* he thought.

There was plenty of time, Jake replied at the back of his head.

And there still is.

Jim's eyes shot open when he heard violent hissing and horrendous spluttering. What he saw was Marcus Arwick, both eyes and mouth wide open from shock and pain as if he were doing a silent scream. His hands were clutching the left side of his neck, which Jim now saw was bleeding rapidly through a huge gash.

The harsh hissing was coming from the open machine behind Marcus, which appeared to have been hit by whatever had torn through Arwick's throat, presumably a bullet. Inside the machine, all the wires and syringes whizzed around in the air hideously like the tentacles of an octopus, while the metal cranial frame hummed slightly from the many thousands of amps of current running through it.

In the agony from his wound, Marcus stumbled backwards. This was, in fact, a fatal mistake.

The moment Marcus's body was in range, one of the many needles of the machine's tubes and wires came into contact with his body. This caused him to gasp, and his face to contort in agony. Following this, another syringe tube shot into Marcus' body, then another, and another, until his back, legs, arms and neck were all impaled by the miniature blades.

Following this, something rather absurd happened. The tubes that had injected themselves into Arwick not only started to pump their many chemicals into his bloodstream but seemed to pull him closer to the machine as if he were a puppet on strings. This was when Marcus found his voice, and suddenly a painful, fearful, rage-filled scream emitted from his croaky throat.

'*No!* Not *me*!'

Closer and closer he was pulled backwards until he was just centimetres away from the doom that awaited him.

'Jim!' he shouted. 'Jim! You have to help me! This machine, it will-'

The machine vigorously tugged him back even further. Jim looked at his adversary, shocked. Almost satisfied.

'Jim! Please!'

Suddenly Jim snapped back to his senses and rushed forward to help, but it was too late. Just as he approached, the screaming Marcus Arwick was pulled into the innards of the machine.

The moment his head came into contact with the metal frame, his body twitched and writhed like a recently-caught fish, and the smell of burning was apparent in the air, with smoke rising from Arwick's hair. More screams were escaping the man's throat, but these were slowly becoming different, almost unnatural. In an instant, the arms of the machine flipped back around and clamped so tightly around Marcus' arms that Jim even heard the audible crunch of the man's bones. The same happened with the legs and torso, too, Marcus' own body being crushed and replaced by the shiny white exterior of the expressionless machine. Soon, the only human feature remaining was Arwick's screaming, shaking head, but in an instant both halves of the machine's face clamped around his skull, revealing the glowing blue eyes that pierced through Jim's soul.

The machine, or rather Arwick, or rather the monster lurking inside Arwick, began to twist and turn in agony. All three states, android, human and monster were now indistinguishable from each other as they danced in pain. The fire of their shared agony melted one into the other, making them one malicious entity. The agony continued for what felt like an eternity, the machine's eyes now flickering from blue to red over and over. Repeatedly, it screamed in a synthesized voice. 'Error. Measurement malfunction. Error. Measurement malfunction. Continue assessment? Continue assessment? Error.' The words got faster, higher-pitched, and the eyes flickered faster. White sparks started to fly in all directions, and all sorts of weapons were being activated and deactivated; purple blades shooting from the creature's wrist, arm-guns ejecting and occasionally firing over and over. At last, the figure made a final reach towards Jim, the menacing eyes a flickering crimson. Then it froze, defeated and dead, and the glowing eyes faded to darkness.

For a brief period, Jim stared at this combined husk of a murderer with wordless bewilderment. The Phantom was finally gone, and Jim was alive. But then… who shot Arwick?

Slowly, he turned. Slumped on the ground by the altar, dishevelled and exhausted, was Lynda, her pistol frozen in her hands.

Jim shook his head in shock. 'You could have shot me!' he exclaimed.

'*He* could have shot you!' she retorted.

Jim stumbled over to his wife and collapsed into her arms, exhausted and in pain. They both slumped to the floor, weary but grateful to be alive.

'Lynda, Tommy… He killed our son.'

'I know,' she said quietly. 'I know, but he's gone now!' She looked over to the frozen figure of the anguished machine. 'It's gone.'

Jim looked at her and smiled. 'You saved me.'

'I suppose it's kind of an obligation at this point.'

Jim chuckled, and then, in the spur of the moment, turned and kissed her.

When they pulled away, she looked into his eyes, confused. 'Didn't quite expect that.'

'Tell you what, next time you save my life I'll give you another,' said Jim with a smile. 'Guess you heard my message then?'

'Yeah…' Her smile straightened out. 'I did.' The slap to his shoulder came suddenly. 'God, you always have to go in alone!'

'You would have been killed if you came with me!' Jim exclaimed.

'*You* would have been killed if I hadn't!' She shook her head. 'I heard what you said. "Just do it…" Jim, please don't pretend you had that situation under control.'

Jim looked at the machine in silence. She was right. He had almost died.

'Look… I've been rash. I've been stupid, but you're right. I can't keep doing this alone.'

'Then don't. We're here for you, Jim. We always have been. Promise me that *whenever* you need help, you'll come to us.'

He nodded. 'I will. Of course I will…'

'You promise?'

Jim froze. *Promise me, Dad…* 'I…'

Just then, Jim heard the familiar whirr of police sirens, and there were numerous flashes of blue through the windows of the church.

He grinned at his wife. 'I can always rely on you to bring back up. I've got a lot of explaining to-'

'I didn't.'

'What?'

'I… didn't call back up.'

Jim frowned in suspicion. 'I suppose the I.T. guys must have traced the location then?'

'No, we traced that a while ago. Apparently, the signal was redirected at this weird steel factory and then that blew up so…' Her face grew wide. 'Oh my God, your family! They're a little shook but…' She beamed. 'They're alive! They're safe!'

Jim stood in shock. 'You… you found them?'

She nodded. 'They… I'll be honest, they weren't treated kindly. But they're fine now. They're in our protection.' She looked at the machine and smiled. 'And he's finally gone!'

Jim lent her a hand and pulled her off the ground. 'He may be, but the group he's working for, the Circle, they may take a bit longer.' He heard the sirens cut off outside. 'I shouldn't tell you now. Just in case. We've got some work ahead, I suppose.'

Lynda nodded slowly. 'I know. Just-' Her phone began to ring. 'I better take this; it may be important.'

She put it to her ear, and her face dropped.

Jim mouthed, *who is it?*

Lynda looked up and smiled with a shaky nod. 'Oh, just Tim,

the I.T. guy. Go outside and get to an ambulance, I'll meet up with you in a bit.'

Jim nodded as she put the phone to her ear. He made his way to the main doors of the chapel, stumbling as he only now remembered the stinging pain in his back. Just before he reached the doors, his phone too began to ring.

Jim laughed. All that bragging and Arwick had forgotten to take his mobile phone off him.

But as he pulled it from his pocket, something instantly felt awry. The phone didn't belong to him. As for the person calling. It was Murdock.

Suddenly memories flooded back, and Jim recalled what Arwick had told him.

He answered.

'Hello Jim,' said the voice. 'I see you survived. It was only as we intended.'

Jim pushed open the door and began to walk out. 'What do you want you lying son of a-'

He froze as he was greeted with dozens of officers hidden behind their cars, their guns poised in his direction.

On one of the car bonnets stood Murdock, a megaphone in his hand. 'James Griffen, I want you to keep talking to me on the phone, can you do that?'

Jim looked around at the many weapons facing him and reluctantly nodded.

Murdock put down the megaphone and brought his mobile to his ear. 'Arwick wanted you framed, so he framed you himself.

The "evidence" against you was released to the entire department while you were unconscious. Of course, the original plan was to *fake* his death with this whole explosion and secret tunnel out we had in mind, but you went and killed him for us. I'm so proud.'

Jim shook his head. 'They'll never believe your lies.'

'Look around Jim. They already do…' Jim looked. The faces of the officers were completely convinced, some even hurt. Jim's heart broke when he saw Mary in the centre, her eyes streaming with tears, her face convinced, and her weapon poised.

Jim shook his head. 'Not for long. Lynda has Arwick's confession. As does Mary, as do I. On our micro-recorders.'

Murdock sighed. 'You *got* me there. Except… well, it's such a shame that Captain Mary Parker can't seem to find hers. Perhaps someone took them. And isn't your micro-recorder inside the chapel? Isn't your wife *also* inside the chapel? The chapel rigged with explosives?'

Jim pondered on this for a moment. Then the penny dropped. He screamed in protest and turned to run back into the building behind him.

Then it blew to pieces.

A fierce blaze erupted from behind the door, sending it slamming into Jim, launching him through the air, accompanied by the sound of shattering glass and crumbling stone. Jim was thrown down the steps into the crowd of police officers as the building went up in a blast of fire and crumbled to the ground.

Lynda…

He hit the floor in seconds, his surroundings a blur. The door was crushing him, and he felt his right arm bend in a horrid angle behind his back. His legs felt hot and singed.

Lynda.

Jim scrambled to get back on his feet as the noise of the explosion died, but soon he was being yanked by his arms and legs, officers urging him to remain calm, their firearms inches from his face. He screamed for his wife, pleading to know her whereabouts, but nobody paid him any response, thinking *he* was the cause of that explosion. Only Mary seemed to pay any attention to his comments, her face sad and confused.

The church, meanwhile, was a mess of crumbled stone and burning wood. Lynda was not in sight.

'*Lynda! Please,* somebody, help her.'

And then Edward Murdock blocked his view, his face stretched by a pleased smirk. 'What do you care? You were the one who killed her.'

Jim looked around in hopeless despair. Finally, he realised he had lost. Arwick may have been dead, but it was the Phantom that got the last laugh.

They brought him into an ambulance, surrounded by several armed officers. Soon he was lying on a bed, and they were injecting some sort of fluid into his neck.

This is it, he thought. *This is where my story ends. The Circle will find what they're looking for, and then they'll take the police department.*

Tommy was just the persona of a madman. Lynda was dead. Mary believed Jim was guilty. What friends were left to him?

I expect the Circle will kill me once my guilt is proven, he thought. *They'll kill anybody that stands in their way. Even if we're in prison.*

Jim's eyes were becoming heavy, but a spark of an idea flew in his mind. It burned fiercely until it flourished into hope. He had the advantage – there was nothing left to lose. So why not use it?

I'm not the only one they plan to kill at that prison. The Circle's plan involves getting to Michael Williams, the man who allegedly has the stone.

But if I got there first.

Right before he fell into unconsciousness, Jim had one thought left on his mind.

I'll honour you, Lynda. I'll honour you, and everyone who died. And then I'll be ready to meet you and Jake.

Find that convict at the prison. The one that needed the stone to be protected. Find Michael Williams.

And then perhaps the Circle would never get that stone.

***

September 2025

SAM
SEPTEMBER 11TH, 2025
BREAKOUT

Sam put his hands on his head and leant back with a sigh. His head ached ferociously, unsure how to take all the information he'd received. For two months, he'd believed the Backstabber to be guilty. He hardly knew any details of the case, but he'd been convinced. Now… he wasn't so certain.

'You all right, Sam?' Jordan asked carefully.

Sam shook his head. What was true anymore? 'And so, you told Williams?' he asked Jim. 'That's why he escaped just weeks before his potential release, he knew the Circle wanted him dead because *you* told him?'

Jim nodded. 'Look, I don't know about a green rock that fell from the sky, but clearly they're convinced Williams has something they need. I had nothing left, except to stop them from getting to him.'

Sam shrugged. 'Or you told him to escape so he would be an easier target for the Circle.'

Jordan laughed. 'You kidding? Michael Williams is pretty

much off the grid. Why else would the Circle be using his daughter to get to him?'

Sam's head shot up. 'Carlos told you about that?'

Jordan nodded. 'He told me everything. Even… what you saw in the park.'

Sam shuddered from the memory. A thought occurred to him. 'The creature. The almost human-like one with sparks flying from his left arm. Glowing red eyes.' His head shot up. 'That couldn't be…'

Jim's face was grave. 'I feared just as much when Jordan told me. I've been trying to get out of this hell-hole for so long for that very reason but… the evidence is too overwhelming.' He sighed. 'Arwick could be alive.'

Sam stood up in a panic. 'But that's not possible. You said he's dead, the machine killed him.'

'No,' Jim countered. 'The machine saved him. Think about what it was designed for, to heal sick people. It may never have been able to bring people back from death but to prevent them from dying. That bullet wound in his neck; it could have healed that. The explosion? Well, I saw that thing at the hospital, it takes a lot to destroy the armour of that monstrosity.'

Sam chewed on this. It was too unbelievable to be a lie. He'd seen the machine himself; he'd heard the horrible things it had said. That thing was chasing Sadie. Why would Jim be on its side if it was his child's killer?

And if this was all true, then that meant Carlos was innocent too. His partner, who had trusted him. And what had Sam done? Thrown him into questioning with Captain Williams. *Perhaps she'll believe him…*

'Prove to me you're not lying.'

'I'm sorry.'

'Tell me something, make me certain that you're telling the truth. I have to be certain.'

Jordan seemed flabbergasted. 'Sam, we already told you, the evidence against Jim is overwhelming-'

'For a jury, yes, but not me. I saw the machine with my own eyes, I know what kind of evil it is, and I know a little girl needs our help.' He focussed his eyes onto Jim. 'Convince me.'

Jim nodded. 'My wife. I may not have been good to her all the time, but… I loved her. She was always there for me, especially when things got tough. Tell me, why would I kill her?'

'A psychopath would.'

'Does a psychopath lash out in anger from the death of his son?' He looked around. 'I mean seriously, most of the evidence against me rests on my emotional instability after Jake's death. If I cared about my son, why wouldn't I care about my wife?'

Jordan nodded slowly and smiled. 'I should use that in court.'

Sam nodded. 'Okay, that's a start. Now, Jordan,' he turned to the lawyer. 'Do you trust Carlos with your life?'

Jordan didn't hesitate. 'Of course. I'd die for him.'

'Did he… did he kill the old captain of the Missing Person's Department?'

Jordan shook his head. 'The missing person's captain was a homophobic bastard who planned to blackmail Carlos. Carlos grew up in a very prejudiced community. He didn't want anybody knowing about… us. The captain, well, he wanted money. But no, I don't believe Carlos would. He's not capable of murder. Anything that creature may have told you, it would only be because Carlos was supporting Jim and being a pain to the Circle.'

Sam nodded confidently and looked down at the desk. What was he doing? Believing a man accused of murder? *The law's not black and white, I suppose.* He put a hand into his pocket and felt the silver bullet. *The ones who you think are good people can turn out bad...*

He clenched the bullet tighter. *But perhaps the reverse is possible too.*

He stood up. 'Jim? I'm going to give you something I haven't given to anybody in a long time. My trust. Perhaps there is more to you than meets the eye...'

Jim's eyes widened with surprise. 'You... believe me?'

'Many wouldn't, I know... But if there's one thing I learnt in life, it's that people aren't always as they seem. And sometimes that can be for the better.' He laid his arms on the table. 'All right everyone, our current situation is this: Jim's in prison, Carlos is in questioning, acting-deputy-chief and captain Mary Parker doesn't believe any of this and pretty much the entire police department could be the enemy. So...' He smiled. 'What's the plan?'

Jim raised an eyebrow. 'I guess we do what we were always going to do... I tell you how you can find Williams and you stop the-'

'That's not what I meant,' Sam replied plainly.

'What do you mean...?' Jordan wondered.

'I mean, how are we going to get Jim out.'

A silence hung in the room.

Sam looked around. 'Well? Any ideas?'

Jim was speechless. Jordan held up a hand. 'Hold up a minute. You're saying you want to get Jim out today? Today? Despite all the evidence against him and… oh yeah, the law?'

Jim spoke up. 'Sam, this is ridiculous! Fine, I didn't kill those officers, but nobody believes me! The only way I can get out is if a miracle happens at court, or if you stop the Circle for good and get a confession.'

'And how are we going to do that, Jim?' Sam rose from his chair and began to pace around the room. 'You said it yourself, the Circle are literally *in* the police department and, most likely, members of the jury at your court case. We don't know who we can trust, and if what you say is true, they're going to kill you pretty shortly anyway!' He pointed to Jordan. 'I know this is probably against most of what you both stand for, but what we have here is *way* past the law. Right now, the legal system is being upheld by horrendous, sick people. The kind of people who would murder dozens and kidnap children. The kind who would experiment on innocent civilians to further their own agenda. And they're being led by a serial killer in a military machine.' He turned back to the convict. 'We need as many people who know the truth as possible, Jim, and we need you especially. You've seen Arwick and the machine the most. You must have an idea of how to stop it. We need to get you out of here.'

Jim shook his head slowly. 'Even if you can, I don't know if I should…' He looked up for some response. 'Sure, I didn't kill Arwick, but I pulled the trigger of a gun aimed at his head. I didn't kill Brigson intentionally, but I wanted to. And all those other-'

'For the love of God, would you shut up!' Sam cried. 'You *might* have done this, and you *would* have done that, and you *inadvertently* did something else, but did you actually do any of the things you're supposed to be guilty of? You feel bad for not seeing the hospital trap coming? Well, hindsight's a wonderful thing Jim but *nobody* saw that coming. What you did was amazing though. You saved a good man's life. And in the end, one life is better than none. All I'm asking of you now is to do that again. You think you're a bad person, but the past is the past. Imagine how bad you'll think you were if millions died because you didn't let that past go for once.'

Jim closed his eyes and froze sullenly. Nobody dared speak.

'All right… I help you with this. But after that? Well, we'll see if there is an after that.'

Sam smiled. 'All right then. First of all, where's Williams now?'

Jim shrugged. 'Beats me. He wouldn't tell a soul about any of his personal life. Not even me.'

Sam slammed his fists on the table. 'You don't know! Please don't tell me I wasted four hours for nothing when I could have been using it to find-!'

'Hold on a minute! Calm down!' Jim exclaimed. 'Do you always get this worked up? I don't know where Williams is. But I know how we can find him. It's why I've been telling you my story; you need to believe all of it for my idea to make sense.'

Sam sat back and exhaled deeply. 'Go on.'

'Edward Murdock.'

Sam coughed violently, both him and Jordan leaping forward in their seats. 'What?'

'Think about it, Murdock's the only Circle member we can be sure of. If we want answers, he's our guy.'

Jordan clapped sarcastically. 'That's… genius Jim, that's great. But how do you propose we get *you*, a known convict that everybody believes to have killed *dozens of police officers* into a police station?'

Sam laughed. 'You're missing the big picture. How do we get him out of a prison?'

Jim sighed. 'Look, you guys wanted me to help you, well that's my plan! If you think there's a better way, now's the time to talk!'

Sam was speechless as to what to say, so instead slumped forwards and shrugged. He looked to Jordan, but he had nothing either. 'You're right,' he admitted. 'Murdock's our only shot. But first, we've got to get you out of here. Come on Jim, I know you probably haven't given it much thought, but we've got a lot to work with here. He's a lawyer, I'm a police officer, and you're the smartest guy in the city. If any group of people could get out of a prison in a day, it's us.'

Jim nodded and stared at the wall behind Sam for a while as if processing all this information. Finally, he zoned back, and looked over to Sam. 'Okay… well, I have a plan to get us out of here. It's a little risky but… again, what other options are there?'

***

When he'd finished explaining, Jim smiled for what was the first time in a long while. 'Well if it fails, I'll just be back to square one. I've got nothing to lose now. The question is, are you two ready?'

In the space of a few minutes, all three men had planned the escape. It was far from flawless; in fact, they were far from certain it was going to work - but they had to try. Lives were at stake.

Sam and Jordan looked each other in the eye. 'So what if we fail?' Sam proposed. 'Better to fail at trying something good than succeeding in doing nothing at all.' He turned to Jim.

Jim cleared his throat. 'All right… let's get out of this hell-hole. They can't hear us, so you'll need to exaggerate until they open that door,' said Jim.

'Gotcha,' Sam replied. 'No time like the present I guess.'

Sam arose in his chair and leant over, his arms adjacent to the table, his face up close to Jim's. In his peripheral vision, he spotted Jordan, a look of trepidation on his face.

Sam furrowed his brow in false anger. 'So I just talk and look angry?'

'Yep. Although, maybe shouting would be best. Jordan, be ready to get the warden in here. You ready, Sam?'

Sam sighed. 'No, not really. But what choice do I-'

Jim's skull smashed into his nose like concrete. Sam felt the crunch and stumbled back as his eyes began to water irritably. Blood poured out quickly, staining the upper half of his shirt.

'Warden!' Jordan screamed as he opened the door. 'Warden! Guards!'

Sam watched the supervising guards rush into the room, their batons armed. According to Jim, the volts of electricity running through those beaters was enough to make any substance inside of you run out of either end quicker than a white water rapid. 'Basically,' he'd said, 'don't get hit.'

Behind them was Warden Locke, his face twisted in angst. Sam felt bad for what he'd have to do. The warden had been kind to him.

'I think we'll be taking you out of here, Griffen,' one of the guards sneered, rolling his hand around the baton.

The second guard approached Jim slowly. Sam noted the

apparel of the guards at this prison – black uniforms with emblazoned caps on their heads. *That won't hide a face easily,* he thought. The guard unlocked Jim from the handcuffs attached to the table and put new ones on his wrists. In a few moments, she was standing, Jim's arms firmly in her grip.

They began to tug him away, and Sam caught the look in his eye. It said *do it.* And then the plan was in motion.

'Get back, he's got a knife!' Jordan screamed.

The guard jumped back in caution for a moment, just enough time for Sam to make a move for the other guard closest to him. The other guard's attention was focussed on Jim, so didn't see Sam's hand flying for his wrist. In an instant the baton was on the floor, giving Sam the time to scoop it up and swing it at the guard's leg. He trembled for a while before passing out quickly.

Meanwhile, the guard by Jim had caught onto the situation and reached for her radio for backup. The warden too had begun to leave the room.

'Warden, I swear! Leave now and there'll be a death in this prison!' Sam hadn't meant it to sound so harsh, but it had the right effect. The warden froze in place.

The guard was still speaking on her radio when Jim pushed her forcefully into the wall. Sam took the opportunity and sprinted forward; his baton ready. She too was out like a light.

Sam panted for a few moments. 'Backup's coming, we need to move fast. Jim, I have a plan. Put on the uniform of that guy over there and lie face down on the floor, you'll understand in a sec.' He turned to the petrified warden. 'Warden, I'm so sorry. I couldn't actually be any sorrier. I didn't mean the whole death thing, I just needed you to stay.' The large man now looked more confused than worried. Sam patted him on the shoulder. 'When you wake up, get the hell out of the city. I promise you, if this all blows over and I'm still alive, I will make it up to you tenfold!' Jim was finishing buttoning up the guard's shirt. Backup would arrive any minute. 'And I'm sorry for this too!' Sam rammed the butt end of the baton into the warden's forehead, feeling heavy with guilt as the poor man fell to the floor.

He stepped back and messed up his hair as Jim lay face down on the floor, as if asleep. 'Jordan, just so you know, Jim's escaped.'

'What?'

Dozens of guards entered the room, but all they saw was three knocked out guards - one de-clothed - the unconscious warden - a large purple bruise on his forehead -and Sam and Jordan, both injured.

'Thank God!' Sam exclaimed, wheezing. He put his hands to his ribs to signify pain. 'Griffen. He stole a baton. Beat us up quite a bit. Only person he let off was Jordan.' Jordan shrugged in a matter-of-fact sort of way.

Sam pointed to the de-clothed guard. 'He took a guard's uniform and ran…' He panted and pointed right.

'He's heading for other cells?' asked the front guard.

'Said he'd be freeing other prisoners,' Sam wheezed, breathing heavily between each word.

The guard cursed. 'Tully! Juby! Help these men. The rest of you; follow me!'

All the guards ran down the corridor, the complete opposite direction from the B-wing exits, leaving only two others in the room. The moment the remaining officers were alone, Jim sprung up and dealt with one, and Sam knocked out the other.

They left the questioning room one after the other, before proceeding to exit the observation area. They were greeted with a large stretching white corridor.

'The doors are definitely that way?' Sam checked, pointing left down the corridor.

'Yeah,' Jim said assuredly. 'Trust me, I've looked enviously down this corridor enough times to know where the doors are.'

'Fair enough,' Sam said with a shrug. 'All right, let's go.'

The three men ran left down the corridor. About ten metres ahead of them lay a ninety-degree right turn which would have them facing the exit. After that, they would have to walk around the quad fence and hope that Jim would not be recognised. All that would be left would be to exit through the main building and drive away as fast as possible in Sam's car.

After making the turn, the officers spotted the B-Wing exit. As near as it was, it seemed so much further with the guard blocking the door. Jim had warned them about this man, the one with the register. Sam and Carlos put on a limp as if injured, while Jim pulled his hat lower to cover his face.

'Hey,' said the guard. 'You ought to be sorting out that Griffen guy. What are you doing here, man?'

'I'd ask you the same thing…' Jim said in a gruff voice, looking at the man's badge, 'Gerald. But I know how important your… uh… *door-keeping* duties are.'

Gerald shook his head slowly. 'I always hated you guys with your attitude. Who are these men anyway?'

Jim chuckled and hit Sam on the shoulder. 'This is the *amazing* detective that was talking to Griffen before he beat their asses in.' He gestured his thumb towards Jordan. 'And *this guy's* currently under arrest as far as I can tell for suspicion of aiding a convict. I heard he was always fond of the *Backstabber*. I've been asked to get them out of here before the situation gets worse. Don't want a cop in a building full of escaped convicts.'

The doorkeeper squinted. 'I see… so that would be…' he looked down at his register. 'Officer Turner… Mr Ellington… and?' He glanced up at the disguised Jim.

Jim was silent for a few moments. Sam felt his heart racing from panic. 'You don't recognise me?' he asked, buying himself time while his mind scrambled for one of the guard's names.

The doorkeeper laughed. 'Man! I see dozens of screws each day. Do you know how much brain-power it would take to remember all those faces?' He ducked his head in an attempt to see Jim's face a little clearer.

'Bet you don't use it much,' Sam muttered quickly, just loud enough that the man would hear it and move his attention from Jim.

'Excuse me, detective?' He glared at him icily.

Sam shrugged and grinned as if it was just some playful banter. 'I mean… you stand by a door all day, that isn't going to need so much brain-power, right?'

The officer was fuming, his head about to burst from the look of things. Quickly Jim swept in as he seemed to remember he had a nametag. 'Redding!' Jim interrupted. 'Officer Redding.'

The doorkeeper glared at Sam, gave Jim an annoyed glance and checked through his clipboard. 'You got a first name or…?'

Jim looked around nervously. 'Oh, *come on* man, you still can't remember?'

'Never mind, *Andy*, I can read the clipboard.'

Jim exhaled slightly in relief, nodded at the doorman angrily and proceeded outside.

'Hang on a minute!' the doorman shouted, causing Jim to freeze. 'I forgot to check your I.D. Andy.'

The three men froze and turned. Jim coughed. 'Blimey; you really are persistent!' Jim approached the man at the door, an exhausted, but frustrated look smeared on his face. 'What's your name again?'

'Why would I tell you that?' the man replied jeeringly.

Jim smiled and made a full turn anti-clockwise. 'Oh, you know, just for when the warden's mad at us for the police department giving this prison a bad rep. I mean, not only was one of their finest detectives beaten, but he wasn't being allowed to be taken to medical care thanks to a persistent, annoying-'

'Okay, okay! I'm just doing my job. Warden can't punish me for that.' At this point, the doorkeeper tried to look Jim in the eye, leading Jim to turn his head slightly to keep his face shielded.

'Okay then…' the man said cautiously. 'You go on now, I should probably check on the situation in the cells, anyway.'

Walking quickly away from the B-Wing, Sam noticed the main building across the prison yard. Having seen both the sniper towers and fellow inmates just behind the yard fence, Jim lowered his head as he walked past.

'Jim,' Jordan hissed. 'How are we meant to walk right out? Won't they kinda recognise you?"

Jim pointed past the wire fence to a man that neither Sam nor Jordan seemed to recognise. The man was very much like Jim, broad-shouldered, and arms thick, but his face was rather dissimilar. This man seemed to be a few years younger than him, with buttery blond hair, pale navy eyes and the tattoo of a dragon on his exposed left shoulder.

'Got any money?' he asked.

Sam and Jordan stared at him in bafflement for a while, but eventually fished out their wallets, emptying whatever they could and handing it to Jim.

Jim then subtly approached the fence by which the inmate stood, causing him to squint in confusion. Once the man finally recognised Jim, Jim put a finger to his mouth, showed the money in his hand, posted it through the fence, and whispered something indistinguishable. The man nodded, turned around to the guys a reasonable distance from him and shouted, 'Thirty dollars a man! Go for the screws!'

Suddenly all the men, about six, ceased whatever they were doing and followed the blond man with the money. In a place such as Stormfeld, money ranked just below freedom in a prisoner's list of priorities. After a short period of assembly, four of the men were gathered into a circle, surrounding two men in fighting stances.

'Come on,' Jim urged. 'Let's get out of here.'

'But Jim?' Sam asked as they approached the doors to the main building. 'What hap-'

'I paid the guys thirty dollars each to start a fight. Should cause a bit of a riot and distract some guards long enough for us to knock out some people by the doors and bolt outta here.'

Upon entering the building, all three men heard a loud shot out in the courtyard. That, however, would be the least of their concerns, considering they now found themselves in a grimy beige room speckled with guards in their muddy grey uniform.

With his eyes glued to the concrete floor, Jim plodded dead

ahead down the tight corridor. Sam, wary of onlooking eyes (although most were attempting to peek through the corridor's small windows to see the cause for the gunshot) decided he would put on his injuries once more to help make it past.

How many steps more would it have to be before they could escape this hell? Ten? Thirty? Fifty? Freedom was so near.

Finally, they saw the front office before them. The rows of benches around the circumference and in the centre. The petrified and angry faces of the recently convicted. The guard at the desks behind a glass panel in the wall, collecting and handing over the possessions that made these convicts free men.

The men slowly approached a woman behind the glass pane. Jim pulled down his hat forcefully and spoke in his usual gruff voice. 'These are detectives Sam Turner and Carlos Rodriguez. They were here earlier to talk to Jim Griffen and well… there's been a bit of an incident. I've been instructed to get them out of here as soon as possible.'

'Of course, I understand,' said the woman calmly. 'I'm afraid I'm going to need to see your I.D. though.'

Sam fished out his I.D. card and slammed it down on the counter. Jordan followed suit. The woman looked at Jim with a penetrating, expectant stare. 'Would you mind getting my gun please?' Sam asked to buy them time.

After what felt like an eternity, the woman returned with Sam's firearm. He placed it safely in its holster.

Jim coughed. 'I'm sorry, miss, but I have to get this lot out of here.'

'And I'm sorry too,' she insisted, 'but *I need* your I.D. sir.'

Suddenly all heads turned as sirens blared across the prison.

The other guards must have realised that Jim was not where they were told he went.

Sam seized the moment and pulled his gun out, aiming them for the locked glass front doors. The bullet smashed the glass in an instant, and they ran like their lives depended on it.

In a blur, ignoring the shouts, protest and shots behind them, Sam, Jordan, and Jim all raced to the police car. The moment they reached the doors, Sam turned to see a swarm of grey and orange, guards and convicts, rushing at them like a high tide. They jumped in and slammed the doors, just as the mob seemed like it would come into contact, and sped away the moment the fists of the guards came upon the roof.

Luck was on their side. For now. If not for the other convicts that had attempted to leave the premises, they would not have driven away so easily. Once they had shot through the dense forest and reached the bridge across the Hudson, the men were certain that they weren't being followed.

Following a small chuckle from Jordan, then a quiet complimentary laugh from Sam, all three men had ended up in erumpent merry laughter. Whether through luck, skill or destiny, a detective, a convict and a lawyer had managed to escape a high-security prison with less than half an hour of planning. None of them believed they had performed such a feat in their entire life. For a golden minute, all three were the smartest men in the country, on the planet in fact, and each revelled in their glory.

That was until they heard the sirens.

Jim cursed. The police had found them already.

Sam squinted, and in the distance, saw the white speck of a police car, parked horizontally across the road. It was placed in such a way that it took up the space of the entire lane, and none of the three could think of a method to get past.

'Well this is it, fellas,' Jim shouted, punching his hands on the bonnet. 'Stopped by one officer in a car!'

In silence, the men hung their heads in disappointment. All their efforts had suddenly become futile. Sam, who was driving, eased his foot off the accelerator and slowed to a halt before the parked vehicle. How would they stop the attack on the station now? Would this officer believe them?

But then something highly unusual occurred. Instead of pulling out their weapon, the woman standing by the car (whose face was indistinguishable in the sunlight) gestured at them to hurry towards her.

Taken aback, Sam shielded the sun and took a closer look at this officer's face. Although he could not see much, he realised how familiar this woman looked. Her hair, skin, and eyes, although not completely visible in the glaring sunlight, looked strangely familiar.

Another officer, this one a man, left the parked vehicle. His hair was black, his skin olive, and he had a mischievous, almost impressed grin on his face. It took a few seconds for Sam to process, but Jordan's outcry confirmed it.

'Carlos!'

The lawyer jumped out of the car and ran to embrace his partner. Sam and Jim left slowly too, Jim awkwardly looking to the floor as he approached the other officer.

'Well, if it isn't Detective Timewaster,' said the woman, her eyes sternly fixed on Sam. 'And his partner,' she looked at Jim, 'who I believed to be a murderer for two months.'

Jim sighed. 'Mary, look-'

She held out her hand. 'I know, I know, Carlos told me everything.' She grinned. 'How ya doing Griff?'

She ran to hug him, her eyes welling. 'I thought I'd lost you!' She said as they hugged. 'I thought it was all my fault.'

Sam approached Carlos carefully. He was met with crossed arms and a mildly irritated face. 'Hey…'

Carlos nodded. 'Hey… How was the investigation? I was just part of one myself.'

Sam looked up guiltily. 'Carlos look… I shouldn't have jumped to conclusions, I know that. I… I suppose I have trust issues.'

He laughed. '*Yeah.* I guess you could say that!' He smiled sympathetically. 'But… I understand that not everything was made quite clear. And with the whole…' he nodded to the ex-convict, 'Jim thing, I wouldn't be surprised if trust was a little hard. I suppose… well, it would have been a little easier if I was more honest to you.'

Sam nodded slowly. 'Yeah, I guess that would have helped.'

Carlos hesitated and pulled Jordan close to him. 'This… is my boyfriend Jordan.'

Sam smiled and nodded at Jordan. 'I know. We've met. Several times, in fact!'

Jordan rubbed his forehead. 'That whole alleyway thing… we weren't doing any shady business. We were discussing the whole Jim scenario, but we were only meeting in private because… well…'

'I get it,' Sam said with a sigh. 'Carlos, I'm *so* sorry. That email… I shouldn't have thought-'

Carlos shook his head with a grin. 'What you thought was *fine.*

That thing at the park tricked you into believing it, I would've thought the same in your situation.' He sighed. 'Again, you're my partner, I should've been more open to you.'

Sam nodded and smiled. He extended his hand. 'Well. Here's to honesty in the future.'

Carlos took it and smiled. 'No more lies. No more secrets.'

'And no more mistrust,' Sam finished.

'Amen to that!'

Jim strolled over to Carlos and offered a hand. 'Detective Rodriguez. It's been a while…'

Carlos shook it. 'Indeed it has. Been in any more scrapes since we last met?'

Jim laughed. 'Hey… I wanted to thank you. For… well, for sticking up for me when the world thought I was a homicidal maniac.' He looked around to the others. 'You guys too.'

'Hey man, you saved my life, remember? I owe you one.'

'Hey guys,' Mary urged, 'I hate to be that girl, but we've got to get the hell out of here. If they see us all talking here, we'll be in a deep mess! Who knows, if we leave quick enough, they might think you ditched the car and tried to swim!'

Sam nodded. 'Mary's right, we should go.'

'Where?' Carlos asked. 'We haven't the faintest idea of what's going on, and I haven't even got a bulletproof vest on me right now.'

'We'll explain on the way,' Jim assured him. 'But right now, we're heading to find Murdock.'

'Murdock?' Mary exclaimed.

'I said we'd explain…'

They jumped in the car, squeezed so tightly in the back that they could hardly breathe. The *Rebirth* that Jim had mentioned had just begun, Sam knew that. But if he died today, he wouldn't die alone.

We're coming, Murdock. I hope for my conscience that you'll be gone by the time we get there.

***

SADIE
SEPTEMBER 11TH, 2025
REBIRTH

In a hopeless march, Sadie plodded on through the forest, tethered to the monster that had tormented her for days.

They'd chained her up at the wrists and clamped a collar around her neck as if she were a dog. Attached to this collar was a long chain which the creature, or Lazarus as some of the Circle now referred to it, enjoyed frequently yanking and tugging. Her feet were sore, since her shoes had been stripped from her, and she shivered frequently in the wind.

They were deep into the forest now. They had not told Sadie exactly why they were retreating into the woods, only that it was for some special meeting of sorts. She hadn't liked the sound of that. Already Sadie had counted eighteen men and women – a meeting would just mean more. How would her father fight back all of *them*?

The trees were nearly blotting out the sun, but the creature – or rather the man inside the machine – and the Children of the Reaper kept moving, determined to reach their destination. Sadie found herself croaking for air as she was repeatedly dragged forwards. Finally, Lazarus came to a halt, all the others following suit.

There was a humming in the distance.

Sadie peered through the trees to see several black vehicles – some vans, some motorbikes. They came at dangerously high speeds, weaving recklessly between the trunks and bobbing in the air over the rough terrain.

The vehicles slowed and pulled over before them. Dozens of men and women began to spill out of each side. They were all dressed differently. Some wore light blue gowns, others suits, and some even armour. All carried weapons, be it firearms, batons, or knives, and all wore malicious grins.

Lazarus stared out at its army in pride.

'Welcome. Welcome, all!' A hushed silence quickly overcame the armed individuals. Sadie walked forward to Lazarus as it violently tugged her chains. For hours she'd been restrained in these horrible, blood-restricting clamps.

'Today,' it continued, 'we start what has been long awaited for centuries.' It lifted his arms in exultation. 'The *Rebirth* is here!' It was met with a triumphant cheer.

'Now, I'll admit… back when you all knew me as Marcus Arwick and I first heard about all this – the stone, the group, your plans – I wasn't convinced. I thought it was some mad fairy tale designed to give this city a little excitement. But according to all our scanners, this house that my little brat has led us to, does indeed contain traces of the rare material arconium. Brigson was correct. The substance does indeed exist. Tonight, it will be ours! And soon to follow it: Nightdrop City!'

There was another roar of approval.

The machine began to pace back and forth, its glaring red eyes scanning the ones surrounding it. The only sounds were those of the harsh stomps on crunching orange leaves and the fierce breeze that blew through the forest, making Sadie shiver and tremble. 'I'd like to thank you all for coming, Circle members and Children of the Reaper alike. I know many of us have had discrepancies in the past, but I hope that there are no hard feelings.' It glanced at Nathan Blake for a moment with its cold, dead, robotic eyes. 'There is only… one issue. As eager as we all may be, only one of us can wield this item. If it truly does bring the bearer the right to morph the world to his will… well, I would hope we chose the right person to use it.'

The sound of rustling leaves hung in the air for a few moments.

'Murdock!' A woman burst to the front of the crowd and approached Lazarus in haste. 'It must be Murdock! He orchestrated this. He gave you the right commands, and he led us all down the right path.' She knelt on the floor and shut her eyes. 'A fine and noble leader. I choose Edward Murdock.'

Lazarus paused, seemingly taken aback, and finally moved its gaze. 'Any other ideas for candidates?'

'Me!' A large, bald man in a black tuxedo arose from the crowd and paced forwards. 'My name is Oliver Staine. I own a large range of hotels and businesses both in and out of the city. My influence, along with the power of our sacred rock, will help us spread our tendrils to the world and *seize glory!*' He clenched his left hand into a fist, and a few cheered. He knelt beside the woman. She seemed irked by this but said nothing.

The creature dropped the chain that attached to Sadie's collar and paced towards the two slowly. 'Well. If that's it, then I guess we'll have a vote…'

There was a pleased murmur in the crowd. Nathan Blake walked over and grabbed Sadie's chain, pulling her back a little. His face was twisted in concern.

Lazarus flexed its right hand, its only hand, and hovered it over the head of the woman. 'Who votes for… her?'

There were a few cheers, some mumbles, and the occasional nervous whisper.

Lazarus shrugged. 'Okay…' its hand hovered over the bald man. 'Him?'

There were a few more cheers; these louder and more confident. Some people were even clapping.

Lazarus stepped back, causing Blake to bring back his men a few metres. 'I think we have a winner, don't you?'

The crowd nodded slowly and mumbled a little. They seemed more relaxed now, since the vote, less intimidated by Lazarus's menacing presence.

The creature raised its hand in the air. 'The winner is… me.'

In an instant, it swung its hand through the air, and the lilac, translucent blade shot from its wrist. It sliced the blade straight through the necks of the kneeling Circle members, causing their heads to topple off with a spurt of blood.

The crowd gasped and screamed, running back several paces, as the monstrous being repeatedly hacked its blade through the decapitated mess of the former Circle members' bodies.

Finally, it calmed and slowly turned to Blake. Its head was stained with red droplets, and its weapon was still poised. Blake rushed to mop it off with a cloth, simultaneously giving the creature Sadie's leash.

It glanced down to its blade and retracted it in an instant.

'That, little girl, is what my high-concentration energy blade could do to your daddy if he doesn't obey me.' It stared inside of her, making her feel small and weak. 'One of Brigson's final updates. Shame he never got to tell me sooner.'

It turned to the crowd, viciously pulling Sadie forwards in the same movement. 'My companions, your saviour is here! For I am strong and have died once before. I promise you, you shall all see salvation before the setting sun tomorrow…'

They cheered, although not like before. Sadie knew the look in their eyes, the sounds of their voices. They were thinking, 'he's not one of us,' but dared not say it. She counted those who were still living; twenty-four Circle members, eighteen Children of the Reaper. What was it her father had said? *Even an army of a million men is only good as that of one, so long as they lose faith in the one leading the march.*

Lazarus began to stomp to the van, the crowds parting in a cowardly manner as it approached them. Sadie followed in its footsteps, wheezing from the repeated tugs at her throat. Finally, it stopped, right beside the back doors to the vehicle.

'When you see your father in a few hours, do tell him what I can do to people.' It opened the doors and hurled her inside, before slamming them shut, submerging her in total darkness.

Sadie lay there in total darkness, her knees sore, her throat dry. In an instant, she found herself hopelessly sobbing as she understood the situation that she'd been placed in.

A hand rubbed her shoulder, and suddenly she began to scream. There was the vague outline of somebody in the darkness, and now they were rushing to silence her.

The hand that clasped her mouth wasn't fierce, but instead soft and warm, and through the void, Sadie heard a faint shushing sound. It was soothing, the kind of thing her mother would do that would send her asleep a few years ago.

Finally, the hand dropped, and Sadie took some deep breaths. 'Who are you?' she asked the darkness.

The other figure was silent for a moment. 'A prisoner, like you.' She had a soft, hoarse voice. 'But I was taken a long time ago.'

Sadie stood up and took a few steps forward, squinting to try to see the mysterious woman's face. 'What does that thing want *you* for?'

The mysterious woman laughed. 'It's not me it wants. It's somebody close to me. Somebody who thinks I'm dead... I know why they want you though. You're Williams' child, aren't you?'

Sadie sat down cross-legged and slouched. 'They have something he wants.'

'I'll bet. The stone, right?' Sadie's head instinctively shot up. 'I know some stuff too. I've been in their captivity for the better part of two months. You hear things.'

Sadie hesitated. 'What... do you know?'

The silhouette of the woman sat at the other end of the area. 'Enough. I didn't believe it myself, to be honest. A magic stone? The Circle must have been crazy. But it isn't magic, not *really*. Just... some weird science. Like Lazarus. Just a wounded sociopath in a military machine, but he looks like any person's worst nightmare. If he wasn't a monster already, all that power and machinery have certainly made him one now.'

Sadie stayed silent. She knew anything that she could have said would be too risky in a stranger's hands. But this woman seemed nice. Reassuring. There was something about her. 'My dad was walking in the park at night with our old dog when he found it. The stone, that is...' Sadie recalled back to when he had first told her.

'There was this… mound, he said, next to a big hole, right in the middle of this field. So… Daddy went to check it, thinking it was some farming project or something. But when he got to the hole, he just saw a body lying inside, a revolver in its hands, and…' Sadie gulped. 'A bullet-hole in its head.'

The mysterious woman listened intently.

'My dad thought about calling the police. But Mom had just died, he'd lost his main job, and we were low on money. This man in the hole wasn't going to need it. So he jumped in to check the man's possessions. I suppose people will do anything if they're desperate enough.

'When he was down there, he noticed two other items. A small metal box, and some sort of the recording device. According to the recording, the man lying dead in the hole planned to destroy the "thing" that he'd been guarding for so long. Some eccentric scientific paper had been circulating in Nightdrop's underworld amongst the Circle of Saints and those trying to stop them, talking about the nature of the substance. Finally, he'd worked out how it could be done. The only issue was… the stone was too persuasive. Like the story, it could play tricks on people, make them do horrible things. Like shooting themselves. The man said in the recording that in case he did die, whoever found that message had to make sure the stone didn't fall into the wrong hands.'

The mysterious woman did not seem shocked. Sadie had expected her to say it wasn't possible, that it was ridiculous. Instead, she was met with absolute certainty.

'And your father believed it?' the woman asked.

'No…' Sadie responded quickly. 'He didn't. And in his curiosity opened the box just a fraction. The open side wasn't facing him… but it was facing my dog. In an instant Smeddles, my dad's

Rottweiler, began to attack him. Nearly bit off his leg. The gun… well, it was nearby.'

The woman sighed. 'Tough world, isn't it? I bet your dad didn't open that box again.'

Sadie sighed. 'I suppose not…' She hit the floor of the vehicle. 'I hope it kills these bastards. I hope it kills them like it killed my dog or the man before my dad. They all deserve to suffer.'

The woman grunted in amusement. 'Yeah… you aren't wrong there. But if the stone doesn't kill 'em? Well, they'll certainly kill us. Although… your story has got me thinking…'

'What about?'

The mysterious woman hummed. 'An idea. Something hopeful, maybe. I don't know if it'll work, but there may be a chance for us yet. What did your father tell you the dead man had again?'

Sadie thought back. 'Just a shovel, a recording device and a gun I think… Unless he didn't tell me something.'

'Perhaps he didn't tell you something else… but there's another more likely option. Why would the other man bring out a gun if he knew there was the risk of him shooting himself? Unless…'

'He needed it to destroy the stone!'

'Or, more specifically, he needed what was loaded in the gun to destroy the stone. You know what that might be?'

Sadie shrugged. 'Not a clue…'

The woman hummed and thought about this. 'Well… I suppose it doesn't make too much difference now. It's clear that stone's pretty damn dangerous so… I suggest we get the hell outta this city.'

Sadie leapt up in excitement. 'We *can?*'

'Don't get your hopes up. It's a maybe, but it's something I've been considering for several months. Arwick, or Lazarus, or whatever you want to call that thing, is completely blind. Figuratively that is. He's so focussed on himself that he lets his surroundings slip. We can use that.'

'And my dad? We can get him out too, right?'

The woman hesitated. 'Right…'

Suddenly the van began to rev, and Sadie found herself wobble from its momentum.

'I suppose we're moving then,' the woman remarked. 'I'll tell you everything on the way, but you must follow everything that I tell you to do if you want to survive. Understand?'

'Yes.'

The woman chuckled a little. 'You're Sadie, right?'

'Sadie Williams. You?'

'Lynda Griffen. I promise I'll get you out of here.'

***

EDWARD, LAZARUS, SAM
SEPTEMBER 11TH, 2025
THE BOX

This day was not going as planned.

Edward Murdock slammed his fists on the table in a frenzy and swept all items but the laptop off his desk. *Damn Marcus Arwick!* To think that that bastard had the nerve to upstage his rightful leader on the day of the *Rebirth*! *I was your superior once. I had control of you.*

Of course, no amount of blackmail would matter to Arwick now. As far as the rest of the world was concerned, that man was long dead. In fact, it would be fair to say he *was* dead. Since that night at the church, something had changed within him. Sure, he'd been a soul-stripped serial killer before, but now… he, or *it* as it would better be referred to, was something far more monstrous.

'Nearly there, Boss,' said the voice on the laptop screen.

While Murdock couldn't be at the *Rebirth*, having been persuaded that his services were "better off within the station," he still had eyes and ears all around. All high-ranking Circle officials were reporting to him through his communicator regularly, and now that he had Brigson's laptop, he could see through the eyes of the machine encasing Lazarus (as it so vainly referred to itself). Murdock had refrained from communicating negatively to Lazarus, however – despite his public denunciation and the murder of two of his Circle members. If Lazarus did get the stone, Murdock would need to be on the side with the most power, even if that meant a demotion.

'Good,' Arwick said on the screen. He was seated in the front seat of a large black van. 'Now remember, Williams will be armed, so bring out the girl first.'

Murdock jolted upward as there was a thud at his door. Quickly he shut the laptop and placed it in the hidden compartment under the desk. He jumped out of his seat, making sure to pick up some items off the floor and let them in.

In single file they arrived before him, their wrists cuffed, their faces forsworn.

Murdock gasped. He'd completely forgotten about the breakout earlier today. *I knew Griffen's supporters would be trouble*, he thought. *We should have hired Circle members only*. But here they were, the two detectives, the lawyer, and the Backstabber himself, all his captives. Except now, they were in Murdock's possession. This day was looking up.

'I trusted you, Mary!' Jim shouted. 'You were the only one left that I-'

She kicked him in the leg, causing him to collapse in agony. 'You trusted me!' she exclaimed. 'I knew you were troubled, Jim, but I never imagined that you were capable of becoming a monster.'

Murdock began to pace up and down the room. 'Well, well. It's the Backstabber and his supporters…' He turned his head to Mary, a pleasant smile across his face. 'Thank you, Mary. Looks like you're going to make an even better police chief than I thought.' He turned to the criminals in excitement, as he pondered on the many ways he would slowly torture them once the city belonged to the Circle. 'Sam? Carlos? I was so hopeful about you. As for you, Jim? Well, I think you should have learnt your lesson about putting trust in the wrong people, as well as messing with me.'

'So, you admit it then, *chief*,' Jim spat. 'You admit that I was falsely accused. That you lead the group behind the murders two months ago. That-'

'I would like to stop you there, Griffen. I did not and will not admit to such lunacies. I will, however, point out your denial of guilt, even after a video was found with you shooting Sebastian Brigson, and a recording found with you admitting to Tommy that you killed the officers in the hospital-'

'He was feeling guilty that he led them in there, asshole!' Sam shouted. 'Anybody would feel the same if they led a team to their deaths.'

'Yeah yeah…' Murdock replied with rolled eyes, 'and the gun was rigged...' He turned to Jim with a sarcastic smile. He was enjoying this. 'I mean come on… a rigged firearm? *That's* the best you can come up with?'

'Well, maybe we should look in the church's rubble and find out,' Jordan put forward. 'There, I'm guessing we'll find the firearm and may even be able to salvage Jim and Lynda's micro-recorders.'

Murdock shook his head in disgust. 'I've sent numerous crime scene investigators to that explosion site, and I *assure* you, they've not-'

'-found anything?' Carlos asked. 'Oh… that's rather odd. Not even, I don't know, Lynda's body? But that's probably because they're your guys, right? Tell me, where do you keep all the evidence against you?'

Murdock shook his head in frustration. 'Mr Rodriguez, why do you take it upon yourself to always scheme against me…'

Carlos laughed. 'Oh, I'm the schemer! *You're* the one who wanted *me* out of the picture! I assume that's why you asked that *monster* to frame me so Sam would arrest me?'

The chief fidgeted nervously. They'd figured it out, even so much as to convince Detective Turner. 'I've had enough of this. Mary, could you please put these criminals in temporary custody before I-'

'Confess?' Jim asked.

Murdock slammed his fist on the table. 'Lose, my, temper…'

Suddenly, all the cuffed men were smiling, as if they were sharing a joke Murdock wasn't part of. It was then that he realised they weren't properly cuffed at all. In an instant, five pistols, including Mary's, were aimed in his direction.

He sighed in exhaustion. 'You've got to be kidding me…'

'Arwick…' Jim said plainly. 'Where is he?'

Murdock laughed. 'It's "Lazarus," now, not Arwick, and what on this *earth* gives me any reason to tell you that?' He was met with silence. 'I mean, come on! Even if you had it in yourselves to shoot me, I wouldn't care!'

They glanced at each other nervously.

Murdock laughed. 'That's it? You plan to point a gun at me and threaten me when you know full well that I belong to a group whose core philosophy is overcoming death? And face it, the only one of you with any strength to shoot me is Jim, and even he knows you'll need me alive if you want to find Lazarus before he gets here.'

Mary looked furious. 'We don't need you alive for anything, you lying son of a bitch!' Suddenly the captain ran up to him, and in a flash, her foot came into contact with his jaw. There was a crack and a spurt of blood from his nose as he felt his body fall backwards.

'Wow,' he remarked. 'I'll be honest, Captain, I didn't know you had it in you.'

She began to run at him again, but this time Jim held her back by the wrist. 'Enough Mary… I think your first kick showed him just fine.'

'I could kick him all day and it wouldn't be enough!' she screamed. She turned to the escaped convict. 'I thought you were the monster, Jim! For two months I thought you'd betrayed me!' She burst into tears.

Jim brought her close and rubbed her shoulder comfortingly. Murdock found the whole ordeal amusing.

'Oh… you'd be doing more than kicking if you knew half the things I've done!'

'Enough Murdock!' Sam screamed. 'What's the point in not answering us? What could you possibly gain? Arwick doesn't care about you. Why would he? He only ever cared for himself! As soon as the Circle's use has been fulfilled, he'll throw you all in the dirt and you know it!'

Murdock hesitated before retorting. Turner was right. Lazarus didn't care. Well… then neither did Murdock. 'Perhaps you're right. But right now, we're on the stronger side… I'm not going to help you, what would that benefit me?'

There was silence. Suddenly the person Murdock least expected to talk stepped forwards. It was the lawyer, that Ellington guy. Was it Jacob? Jeremy?

'What if…' he proposed, 'we had something Arwick wanted?'

'Jordan, what are you doing!' Carlos urged.

Murdock grimaced. 'Arwick's about to get the world's rarest and most powerful weapon, what more would an anarchist like him need?'

'Not need, *want.* If you could give Arwick the thing he wants the most that isn't that stone, you'd suddenly be his best man. He'd let you follow him forever if you wanted to.'

Murdock shook his head. 'You think I can't tell a trick. How could you have something that Arwick wants…'

The lawyer smiled. 'Because we have-'

'Me.'

Jim stepped forward and spread out his arms. 'Straight out of prison. See, Murdock, if you don't send me to Arwick, then I can just run away,' he snapped his fingers 'like *that.* The Circle are miles away, I could be anywhere by the time he realises I'm gone! But… if you take him to me now, you'll have brought your leader his greatest adversary, the *only* man who's ever defied him. How's that for a deal?'

Murdock paused and frowned. It wasn't like the detectives had much hope, anyway. Lazarus wore a virtually indestructible shell and was about to hold a virtually indestructible weapon of mass force. The only person that this could benefit was Murdock. But then, why were they proposing the idea?

He saw the lawyer whispering something. Clearly, handing Jim over was far from what he'd had in mind when suggesting something that Arwick would have wanted. But perhaps… perhaps it could work.

Without speaking, Murdock made his way to his desk and

rummaged underneath for a groove. When he'd finally located it, he pulled out the base of the hidden compartment, revealing everything that he'd hidden there. There were files, frazzled devices, pictures, contact details, and newspaper articles. Most importantly, however, there was the laptop.

Murdock's enemies gathered around as he began to lift the lid, revealing once again the view from Lazarus's eyes. It seemed the vans that the monster's army was driving in had finally stopped, and that they were preparing to advance on the cottage. It didn't seem to be the best time to communicate with him.

'Is that…?' Carlos started before trailing off.'

'God, I always wondered what being a monster like him would be like,' Jim remarked. 'I never thought I'd actually see through his eyes.'

In haste, Murdock pressed a few keys, causing a black message box to emerge from the base of the screen. He typed: *I can bring you Griffen. He's with me right now.*

Through the video feed, they saw it freeze. 'I hope you're not lying to me, Murdock. If you're telling the truth, bring him to our headquarters. For now… well, I'm afraid I have some business to attend to.' It got out of the van and walked around, facing what looked to be a small cottage just a few miles off. 'Oh, and Jim? If you're watching this… Sam, too, Carlos, perhaps Mary… I just want you to know you've already lost. What hope could you possibly have against me?' More vans appeared and parked beside the monster. 'Well,' it raised its arms, 'enjoy the *Rebirth*.'

'It's too late,' Jim muttered in despair. 'They've already reached Williams…'

Murdock smiled. 'He's right Jim. You've got no chance…'

And so, they watched events unfold through the eyes of a monster.

***

Lazarus flexed its right hand, hoping to feel something, even if it was just a small ache. But once again, the effort was futile.

I'll lose this arm too if I'm not careful, it thought. *God, if only the bullet had stayed lodged in my neck instead of hitting the circuitry. The suit would have worked just fine instead of cutting off the circulation.*

Still, things were looking surprisingly bright. Just behind was an army, ready to follow its every command; just up that hill was the rock that would make all of its dreams come true; and just across the city was James Griffen, trapped in Edward Murdock's grasp. Considering Lazarus had been killed two months ago, things were going pretty smoothly.

Men and women poured out the vans by the dozens, each one armed with some form of firearm. Following close behind was Blake, pulling along the hostages like they were dogs on leashes. From within the suit, what remained of its face smiled.

'Well, if it isn't my two favourite people!'

Their faces were sullen, their bodies frail and bruised. Sadie's face was wet with tears, and Lynda didn't even try to make eye contact. *How rude,* it thought. It was tempted to punish her.

Lynda wasn't the same woman as she had been on that fateful day at the church. She remembered it all vividly; how Murdock had called her, telling her to stay inside or Jim would die; how Arwick had approached her, now a monster trapped in a metal shell; how it had pulled her away and dragged her through that tunnel just moments before the building's explosion.

For the first few days, she'd screamed. Oh, she screamed

from the moment he'd pulled her down that passageway. But a few jolts of pain were enough to shut anybody up.

Electric hands too! Oh Brigson, how you spoil me…

The former lieutenant hardly looked the same either. Months of confinement in a dirty cell, with rags, shaved hair and the occasional beating from a vicious Circle member had seen to that. Lazarus made sure little happened in the way of harming her, but sadly he hadn't always been around.

'Give the girl to me,' it commanded. 'Take Lynda to the house.'

Blake did so, the Children of the Reaper following closely behind. Lazarus gestured to the other Circle members to follow. All obeyed, leaving it and the little rat on their own.

She was looking at the floor, her eyes full of sadness and guilt. Something about the way she looked seemed so sweet, so innocent. Almost like…

Lazarus shook its head. That was another life. That life had died. As had the one after. *Thrice died, yet death defied.* He tugged the girl's chain so she would look up at him.

'Don't you dare misbehave in there. If I see you communicating in any way to Lynda or your father, or *anybody* for that matter, I will kill you all. Understand?'

She nodded slowly.

'Good. Let's go meet your father.'

***

Williams cried in agony as Blake hit him with the beater once more. He was coughing dollops of blood, clenching his wounds in a foetal position across the floor. Lazarus rolled its eyes.

'I'll ask again! Where's the stone?' It threw its arms up in the air. 'We're searching your place anyway Williams, you might as well tell me. Save yourself the pain.'

The man laughed. From the scars on his neck, it was clear to see that pain was something he was used to. 'I'll never tell you, you *monster!*' He turned his head to Sadie, who was seated by Lynda, sobbing. 'I'm so sorry, my angel.'

'*Answer me!*' Lazarus shot the purple blade out of his wrist and grabbed the girl. Sadie screamed as she was torn away from Lynda and began to jolt back ferociously as the blade approached her throat. 'You really think I care about killing children?' Sadie wriggled and screamed in terror.

Williams shook his head, his face full of tears. 'I know you had a kid once... I know you couldn't do it.'

Lazarus hesitated, and for a moment it could feel a man with a name underneath all that triontium metal. 'How do you...'

Williams smiled kindly. 'I figured it all out quickly enough. Some things I just know. I know who you are, Marcus Arwick! Your daughter was called Susie Arwick, am I right? Just ten years old? That's a year younger than you are now, right Sadie?'

Arwick hesitated. 'You...' Lazarus bowed its head. 'You can't trick me like that I'm afraid Mr Williams. Arwick's dead.' He brought Sadie's neck closer to the blade, ready for the head to come toppling off. She screamed and writhed, but it was no use. Williams shouted, but Lazarus didn't listen. It was just a few millimetres from the skin before-

'Master, stop!'

Arwick paused to see a Circle member by the doorway. It was

Tessa, the police's medical examiner. Oh, how she'd hated Marcus, but Lazarus? Lazarus was a God. In her hands was a medium-sized silver box that glimmered in the light. There seemed to be a faint whisper in the air… or perhaps that was just the breeze.

It beamed under its shell, before throwing the girl back to her father. He embraced her tightly, clasping her hand like he'd never let go. Lazarus didn't care. They could love each other for what little time they had left if they wanted.

Tessa approached her leader and bowed down in homage before it.

'Thank you, Tessa. Thank you so… much.'

Lazarus bent down to the ground and carefully closed his only hand around the box. No faster than a turtle, the monster weighed the box in its hands and listened to the whispers inside its mind.

'This box… it's triontium. Like my suit, correct?'

Michael smiled victoriously, clenching his daughter tightly in his arms. 'Yes, it is… The original box was presumably made from the metal of the meteorite it came in, but that wasn't protective enough, despite its uses.' He eyed Lynda, leading her to frown in confusion. 'An old friend of mine's a scientist down in Boston. I managed to persuade her to cover the first box in that stuff, make sure nobody could ever get it. I didn't even have to open it! And you know what's brilliant about triontium? Following its initial reaction, it's virtually indestructible in the shape you meld it to.'

Lazarus paused, moving the box in its hands, searching for some mechanism to open it. There was nothing. 'Oh… oh, you clever man… To think I'd be defeated by the metal of my own suit…'

Williams shrugged, moving Sadie aside so she'd be out of harm's way. 'I try my best.' He brought a hand across his mouth, wiping blood from his lips, and slowly pushed himself off the ground. There was an icy tension in the room. All eyes were fixed on Lazarus, waiting for an outburst of anger that would kill them one by one.

It sighed. 'You know… I had a similar predicament just a few months ago, following the incident that got me in…' it gestured to its body armour, '*this thing.* You see, a stupid bullet had passed right through my neck and into the wiring, causing the whole mechanism to malfunction. My bones were crushed horrendously, and every nerve in my body was fired with pain. Not to mention the many volts of electricity passing into my brain.'

It paced up and down the room, making sure not to look anybody in the eye.

'One side effect of this was that it managed to cut off the blood flow in my left arm. Gangrene ensued quickly, and I knew I would die if I didn't cut it off. The only issue was… well, as I said, my suit's made of the same metal as your clever little box. It's virtually indestructible as you say. Yet…' It lifted its left arm, the one severed from the elbow, decorated with numerous wires hanging down from its base. 'I managed to cut through.'

Williams' face dropped.

'As it happens, you can cut triontium with enough concentrated plasma energy. Or in more basic terms: the same way I'm going to cut through you.'

The creature lurched forwards, and the energy blade passed through Williams' chest in an instant. Williams silently gasped, his eyes wide. Sadie screamed and began to run for her father, but Lynda seized her quickly, yanking her back from the danger. Lazarus couldn't smell the sizzling flesh, but it could certainly hear it. Williams' eyes rolled back, and his legs gave way underneath him. He lay dead by the box he had sworn to protect.

'You should have destroyed that stone while you had the chance, Williams,' the creature chided. 'Or used it! But you were too afraid of what it could do.' It looked at the blade protruding from its wrist. 'It's a shame. I could have had two of these if I'd been able to keep the other arm. Imagine the bloodshed then!'

It plunged its blade into the metal, causing a horrendous hissing noise, followed by a blinding white light. Those surrounding it began to shield their eyes; some gasping, some weeping. Lazarus just smiled.

The white light died down, and the box collapsed with ease. The faint whispering in Lazarus' head built into a terrifying crescendo and green light began to spill out of the box. *This is it*, the monster thought. *The day has come.*

It engaged its surroundings. None dared challenge Lazarus, not even for the item they'd spent decades pursuing. To its right, Sadie was sobbing horrendously in Lynda's arms. Lynda's face was composed of dread, but that wasn't it. There was a look of determination in her eyes, a look that managed to bother Lazarus.

But then its attention was back on the broken box, and Lynda did not matter anymore. The light had died down a little, and Lazarus could vaguely see a shape amongst the glare. There on the floor lay a rough-edged, emerald coloured, glowing rock. It was just like the myth had said.

The monster's right arm lowered, its thoughts full of greed and malice. Everything it had dreamed to accomplish was right here. It smiled and ended the transmission to Murdock's laptop as it reached down for its prize.

Suddenly there was a commotion to the right, as the distracted Nathan Blake found himself being knocked to his feet in an instant. Lynda had pounced at his legs, pulling his weight from underneath him, and now she and Sadie were running for the exit, their chains dragging behind them.

Lazarus froze, inches from its dream. Barely anyone, Circle members and Children of the Reaper alike, had even bothered to stop them – they were so transfixed on what lay on the floor. The creature spoke softly. 'Let them run. They'll be easy to catch in due course.'

Its hand, or rather the machine's (though they had been made the same) clasped around the edges, and Lazarus soon felt a powerful surge pass through itself. In an instant, the world fell apart, all matter and energy drifting away into nowhere. Reality blurred all around, and Lazarus felt its body erupt into a state of *everything*.

There were screams. There was light. And then there was silence.

***

A tremor passed through the ground, and simultaneously every officer in the station felt a chill through their spines.

'That was…' Jim was lost for words. 'Lynda she's…'

The captain put a hand on his shoulder in a sympathetic manner.

'There was a tunnel,' Murdock said plainly. 'It was intended for Arwick before the explosion, so his body would never be found, and it would look like you killed him. But then… well, Lynda intervened and Arwick got shot. Ended up as Lazarus….'

Jim bowed his head sadly.

'Lazarus saw your wife's potential uses as a hostage… so it took her to us.'

Everyone remained still. 'For months…' Jim mused. 'I'd lost all hope… I nearly ended it for good.' A look of determination filled his eyes. 'I have to go get her.'

'Jim, you can't!' Carlos shouted. 'Not after we just got you out. Look, I know you love her, we all have people we love, but if you confront them, Lazarus will kill both of you in an instant. You think he's going to uphold a promise? You think he cares?'

Jim shook his head. 'No. But I have to try.'

'And what about when the stone gets here, huh?' Sam asked. 'Arwick's marching for this building, Jim! That's the Circle's end goal, right? To take the police department so they can take the city. And what are we going to do then?'

Jim shook his head. He couldn't think clearly. 'You're in safe hands. You've got Mary to look after you.'

Murdock coughed obnoxiously. 'I… don't think so.' They all gave him looks of surprise. 'What, you think I'm going to hand *my* station over to any of you?'

'Your station?' Jordan protested. 'We're the only ones who know enough about this to stop it, and you're one of the people trying to invade the place. I'm pretty sure police law ends when a mythical group led by a dead man have a rock that could destroy any of us in an instant.'

'Besides,' Sam added. 'This isn't *your* station, it's the commissioner's.'

Murdock grinned. 'And how often have you seen the commissioner detectives?'

There was a pause as it began to dawn on them. 'You haven't…' Mary exclaimed.

He shrugged. 'He was getting too involved with what I was up to. I don't like people who snoop around in other people's businesses.' He smiled and muttered, 'As your friend Alex no doubt understood.'

Mary's eyes grew irate. 'What did you say?' she whispered. '*What* did you say?'

She lifted her firearm and aimed it for his chest. The others screamed in protest.

'It's fine, it's fine,' Murdock said calmly. 'She's not actually going to kill me, even if I did kill her friend.' He watched her aiming hand shake. 'Poor man. He was just tidying my office like I'd asked him to. He shouldn't have seen all those emails I'd exchanged with my group.'

'You *bastard*,' Jim shouted. 'She spent months thinking the man had killed himself! Thinking it was her fault!'

'Well… he basically did kill himself.' Mary looked ready to snap. 'I suppose I've said too much. That's all right. You aim to take my station, and I'm outnumbered. I may as well put up a fight.'

Edward Murdock lifted his pistol and fired randomly. The weapon was pointed at Sam, and the blast was deafening. Mary responded with equal measures; her face full of rage.

As the bullet plunged into Murdock's chest, he smiled. At least he'd taken one of them. Sam should have considered himself lucky. Better to die from a bullet than from whatever Lazarus would have in mind later on.

His heart stopped. In his last few seconds of consciousness, he fell to the ground thinking, *so this is what death feels like.*

As he exhaled his last breath, he whispered, 'Perire finite non est,' and shut his eyes.

***

Sam felt his body thud as he hit the ground.

It had all happened so fast. The guns had fired, the others had moved frantically, and Sam had felt something hit his chest at tremendous force, launching him onto his back. A moment later, and the possibility dawned on him.

I've been shot.

He took deep breaths and attempted not to panic as he felt along his chest for anything, be it a wound, some blood, or just a little pain. He hadn't worn his vest today; he'd only expected to investigate the prison after all. There had been a lesson at the academy for just this kind of situation – though he doubted it would help if the bullet had passed through his heart.

But there was nothing there. Not even blood. Sam exhaled in relief and rubbed a hand over his chest. He sat up, smiling, grateful for the gift of life which he'd been allowed to keep today.

And then he saw what had happened.

At his feet Carlos lay almost motionless, his shirt soaked in blood. By his side was Jordan, holding his hand with teary eyes, while Jim called for an ambulance on Mary's cell. Presumably, Mary had run to get help; either that or she couldn't take it anymore.

Sam rolled up in an instant and ran to his partner's side. Carlos was just awake, but his face looked weak and pale. The wound in his chest was deep, and blood was spurting out at a rapid rate.

No… Sam thought. *No, no… you can't die now. Not here. Please…*

'Carlos,' Jordan was whispering through his tears. 'Carlos speak to me.'

Carlos looked at his boyfriend and smiled sadly. *'I'm here, Jordan. I'm right here.'*

Jordan smiled and nodded. 'That was stupid, wasn't it?'

'A little…' Carlos agreed with a grunt. 'Although perhaps it could have been excused if I'd chosen to wear my bulletproof vest today.' He slowly turned his head to Sam. 'Bet ya didn't see that one coming…'

Sam smiled and shook his head. 'I don't think anybody did…' He sniffed and suddenly felt a tear roll out his eye. 'You didn't have to do that… I barely got to know you. I didn't trust you, I *betrayed* you. And you took a bullet for me… I can't thank you enough.'

Carlos closed his eyes and rolled his head back to the ceiling, grinning. 'Well, you don't need to… Dead men need no thanks and all that. Especially this one.'

Jordan squeezed his hand. 'You're *not* going to die.'

Carlos laughed. 'I don't think that's up to me. But it's okay…' he cleared his throat. 'Every journey has its destination. Mine's…' He laughed. 'Murdock's office I suppose?'

Jim put the phone down and walked over to where they were crouched. 'The ambulance is on its way. You okay down there, Carlos?'

He smiled. 'I will be soon… Hey Jim, do me a favour. Don't waste your freedom, all right? They busted you out for a reason.'

Jim nodded sadly. 'Gotcha bud.'

'And… Sam.' He turned his head back to his partner. 'Make it out of this alive. Find a new partner. I know there won't be anybody as smart or good-looking as me, but… you can try to find someone close enough. Help them to start out, yeah? Teach them the ropes and all that.' He began to cough violently.

Sam shook his head and sobbed. 'I should have been better to you. I should've trusted you.'

'You did your job, Sam. You did what you felt to be the right thing, and I respect you for that. But listen. There are people who care about you. Not everyone's out to get you…'

Sam nodded.

Carlos turned his head to Jordan, his words raspy and quiet. 'Jordan…' Jordan brought his ear to the detective's mouth and smiled mournfully at what he heard, clenching his companion's hand tightly.

Carlos dropped his head back, exhausted. He shut his eyes and breathed no more.

A few minutes later, Mary burst into the room, followed by several worried-looking officers. But it was too late. Jordan was sobbing beside his lover's body, while Sam just shook his head solemnly. Jim just sat on the desk, staring emptily into the distance.

'Goodbye, old friend…' Jordan whispered.

Goodbye Carlos, Sam thought. *I'll be better. I promise.*

And as for Lazarus, he's going to wish he died in that church.

***

LYNDA, JIM
SEPTEMBER 11TH, 2025
THE FINAL GIFT

Through the twisted trees they sprinted, their chains rattling along the ground, the sun setting in a fiery blaze behind them.

Lynda looked back fearfully once more. Nobody was following them. Why? Was this a trap?

Sadie ran beside her, her face pale and weak. It was clear she'd been running for days, trying to escape from a wicked, relentless monster that cared for nothing but itself. Lynda feared the girl would collapse in an instant. This was no place for a child.

When she'd checked that they were alone once again, she slowed her pace; the girl following suit behind. They couldn't rest for long. If the Circle was coming, they'd need to get as far from the city as possible. But first, they'd need to warn the others.

Suddenly Sadie propped herself against a tree and burst into tears, gazing hopelessly to the ground.

'Hey…' Lynda said comfortingly, coming to the girl's side to comfort her (while still gazing behind her anxiously). 'Sh sh sh… It's all right.'

Sadie shook her head. 'No… it isn't, is it? When has anything ever been all right?'

Lynda nodded and crouched down, looking the girl in her teary eyes. 'Hey… I've been there. Trust me, I know how much it sucks. It's going to take a little time before things get better… but I promise you, this isn't the end of everything yet! Your daddy loved you so much, and you know he wouldn't want you to lose hope.' She squeezed the girl's hand in a caring manner, but her thoughts were still anxiously anticipating the arrival of Circle members behind them.

Sadie nodded slowly. 'Okay… Okay, I'll be strong.'

Lynda smiled. 'There's the fierce warrior I need!' She stood up slowly, taking a few moments to pause for thought. The forest was eerily silent. Perhaps they had lost the Circle. Or perhaps the Circle didn't care about catching them.

'If we're lucky, I reckon we'll reach the river by nightfall,' she remarked. 'From there we'll navigate along the edge until we find a bridge, and then we contact Captain Mary Parker as soon as possible. She'll be able to help us, I'm sure of it.'

Lynda was not the same woman that she'd been before that night at the church. Months under the frequent abuse and torture of the Circle of Saints would likely do such a thing to anyone. Every taunt, every smack, every evening she'd starved, she'd slowly felt her heart lose all the emotions she'd once had. That was not necessarily an awful thing. Yes, she'd lost the joy, and the hope; but she'd lost the bad stuff too. The fear. The pain. The rage - well, not quite. In fact, it felt as if the rage was the only thing left. For what they'd done to her. For what they'd done to Jim.

But through all that rage, Lynda was sensible enough to know not to stay. That stone… the things they'd said about it… it was easier to believe it was just a fairy tale.

'This captain…' Sadie asked. 'How exactly *is* she going to help us?' She seemed doubtful there was any possibility of help.

Lynda shrugged. 'She's got a car. We can be out of the city by tomorrow morning, maybe stop by the care home and warn some of your friends. I know I have some of my own to look out for…' She thought of Jim hopefully. Was what Lazarus said all true? Had her husband really escaped?

'We're not just going to run away!' Sadie exclaimed. 'Think of how many people live in this city. How many are you leaving to die?'

Lynda raised a hand. 'Listen, kid, how are we going to be *any* use against what's coming for this city? You heard what that rock can do, your father spent his entire life trying to protect it. The best chance this city has is if the military arrives, except none of them are going to believe any of this until some proper damage is done, and even then, it might not be enough. So, the way I see it, our best hope is to get the hell out of here.'

She began to walk in a hurry. The child was naïve. How the hell did she expect to stop the Circle now?'
'What if we don't need the military?' Sadie put forward.

Lynda stopped. 'Young Lady, you are *testing* my-'

'Nobody will believe in this mess until it hits us, fine, but just because we're on our own doesn't mean we're hopeless. There's only one way to defeat these guys, and that's destroying their strongest weapon.'

Lynda turned and threw her hands in the air. 'And how are we going to do that, huh? We know nothing about this stuff, how do you plan on destroying it?'

The girl put a hand in her pocket and rummaged around. She pulled out a small, glimmering piece of metal, curved at the end like-

'A bullet?' Lynda asked. 'What's a bullet going to do.'

'Everything has a weakness,' Sadie explained, 'and for whatever reason, the stone's is this.' She held it up into the light. 'Dad says it's from the meteorite the stone landed in, the same stuff the box was made from. Dad gave it to me in the barn. Clearly, he wants us to use it.'

'I don't understand…' Lynda said. 'A tiny piece of metal's all it takes to destroy that thing? Why hasn't it been done before?'

'I told you about our dog, remember? The stone messes with your brain, just like in the story. The man before my dad killed himself; maybe Daddy was scared the same would happen to him.' She looked at the bullet hopefully. 'But we've got to try. It's the only hope this city has. You know where we could find a weapon that this could fit in?'

Lynda looked at the metal curiously, unsure what the right thing to do was in this scenario. All sanity seemed to have been thrown out of the window.

And should Sadie be in the danger zone? She was just a little girl after all. *But what about the people who'll die if we don't do this?*

Lynda smiled, nodding. 'Yeah… I know a place.'

***

Jim stared hopelessly at Carlos' body. Just another person to fall from the Circle's actions. Sure, he'd survived the hospital, but the Circle had come back to bite him in the end. *Perhaps the same will happen to me.*

Despite this, there was one small consolation, one glimmer of hope. Lynda. Jim knew his wife, even in the awful state she'd been in that video. His wife was alive. *And I have to get her back.*

He rose from his chair, his eyes determined. All the others in the room turned their mournful gazes in his direction, their eyes hopelessly lost.

'Hey…' he began. 'Guys, I want to thank you all. For everything. All the help you've given me today, everything you've done for me. You've granted me freedom, even if only for a few hours, and, most importantly, you've believed in me. For that, I will always be grateful.'

He nodded to each of them and closed his eyes. 'But I can't stay here. Not when Lynda's in danger. I have find Arwick, even if it is just a trap. I need to see my wife again, and who knows, maybe it'll buy you some time.' He bowed his head.

There was silence. Finally, Mary arose from her place. 'Time to do what, huh? We don't know what to do! Nobody does. If you leave now, we'll just be sitting ducks waiting to be taken out!' She sighed. 'All right. Fine. Leave us for good, sacrifice yourself so you can see your dear wife again.' She paced up to him. 'But don't you dare leave this station without helping us first! We've lost far too many as it is, and I'm not ready to lose you unless I know that what you're about to do won't be for nothing.' She stood back and put her hands on her hips. 'So… before you go off to kill yourself… how are we going to stop these guys?'

Jim laughed. 'You think we can defeat them? Really? Sure, we had hope before, but now Lazarus has the stone and is headed for this building! What you need to do is evacuate this place immediately, get as many people away before the danger hits.'

Sam shot up to his feet. 'You're kidding, right? You're saying we should run away and cower in fear?'

Jim put a hand up in defence. 'All I'm saying is our odds of survival if we stay-'

'Carlos didn't die for this,' Sam responded adamantly. 'We didn't break you out for *this*. How many people will die if we leave now? How much more power are we laying into the Circle's hands if we let them take this place? We have to act. Even if it costs us our lives. Because even trying to do the right thing and failing is *better* than not trying at all, and you know that.' He walked closer to Jim, and Jordan rose behind him. 'Look, you can go try to find your wife if you want… but please… we need you right now.'

Jim paused and nodded respectfully. They were right. It would be selfish to leave them now. It would kill them as much as it would him. 'All right.' He looked around the room and shrugged. Mary looked weary, Jordan mournful, Sam determined. They were all he had.

No. Not all. This is a police station, one of the strongest, most armed buildings in the city. And we're right in the centre of it.

A thought resurfaced from the depths of his memories, and suddenly an idea sparked. 'Oh… that could work.'

'What?' Sam urged.

Jim sighed. 'Well, maybe… possibly, I'm not sure. Mary, how good are the tech guys here?'

'At what?'

Jim ran over to Murdock's desk, where the laptop, files and newspaper articles all lay. 'At building.'

Mary shrugged. 'I don't know, the best we have but that doesn't mean great.'

'It'll have to do.'

'*Jim*,' Sam demanded in an impatient tone. 'What are you planning?'

Jim pointed his finger in the detective's direction. 'What do we have that Arwick doesn't?'

Sam scrunched his eyebrows. 'Well, the answer isn't a robotic suit, a powerful weapon or an army.'

'Nope, you got it. We have an army,' Jim said plainly.

Sam laughed. 'Hardly!'

'We have the entire police department behind us and an armoury full of firearms, while Lazarus just has a bunch of fanatics and hired gunmen who are more interested in their own power and success than in helping him. But that's not all we have, no. What doesn't Arwick, or Lazarus, or whatever you want to call that thing, have?'

Sam threw his hands up in the air frustratedly. 'I don't know! Two arms?'

'Exactly,' Jim said with a smile.

Simultaneously, all three of his colleagues let out a surprised, 'what?'

'Think about it,' Jim inclined. 'Lazarus only has *one arm*. An indestructible shell, but only one arm.'

'Oh…' All heads turned as Jordan spoke for the first time in half an hour. The lawyer nodded with a satisfied expression.

'Sorry, could someone catch me up to speed please,' Mary asked. 'What's so special about Arwick cutting off his ar-' The penny dropped, and now the room understood. Mary smiled. 'The only thing that can cut through its armour is that energy blade…'

'Which,' Jim finished, 'as it confirmed earlier, is quite conveniently placed on both of his wrists. The very arm that Lazarus cut off will contain the mechanism necessary to destroy it. That's how we do this. That's how we win.' He paced up and down. 'But that's just the tip of the iceberg. Where is the arm, how do we activate it and how can we get close enough to Arwick – *Lazarus* sorry - that we slice it up with it? The *where* I may know but the *hows?'* He pointed to Mary. 'I need to leave up to you.'

'Me?' she exclaimed.

Jim shrugged. 'Murdock's dead, and so's the commissioner, apparently. No other captain, police officer or technician in this building is going to believe any of this unless you show them.' He grabbed the laptop and handed it to her. 'On here's all the proof you need. Hopefully, there are some schematics for the tech guys to work with, but if not, they'll have to make do with the arm once we find it. Find out Lazarus's other weaknesses, arm every willing man and woman in this building and prepare this station for a fight. If we fall, Nightdrop falls. Sam, you go with her. Once you're done, you can use the evidence to convince the rest of the station and rally those who are willing to help us.'

Sam nodded. 'On it. What are you two going to do?'

Jim shrugged. 'Jordan's going home, he's seen enough today, but I-'

'With all due respect Jim, I want to go with you,' Jordan demanded adamantly. 'Carlos worshipped you, you know that? You saved his life, and so he spent the rest of his life dedicated to saving you. I know I might not be able to keep you alive for the whole of today, but I'm not letting him down without a fight. And if I die, well I died doing the right thing. Not like I've got much left to live for, anyway.'

Jim nearly said some more, but the lawyer raised his hand in defiance. 'You're not debating with me on this one, there's not enough time. This is my choice.'

Jim nodded. 'Okay then…' He glanced around at the room at the four he could trust and gazed sadly at Carlos' body. 'Carlos won't have died in vain; I can promise you that. Let's go find that arm then.'

'And where might that be?' Mary queried.

Jim shrugged. 'It's just a hunch, but I expect the same place they want me to meet them for Lynda.' He picked up a file from Murdock's hidden compartment and skimmed through it. 'The Circle of Saints' headquarters… aha, the Bill Simpson apartments. According to Murdock's notes, just three yards from the rock's original crash site.'

***

SAM, SADIE, JIM
SEPTEMBER 11TH, 2025
HOPE AND DESPAIR

Sam glanced over at Mary's direction as the lift thudded to a halt. Her face was riddled with anxiety. 'You ready?' he asked.

She coughed. 'Nope.'

The doors opened, and Sam made a brisk walk through the corridor to the station's atrium. All heads turned as he pushed apart the blue double doors, and soon officers were on their feet; lifting their telephones and running around frantically.

'Ladies and gent…' Mary attempted. 'Excuse me… Ladies and…'

Armed officers were now running their way, their weapons aimed high. Sam had worried about this; he was a known fugitive after all.

Goodbyes had been swift but sad back at the office. As Jordan and Jim got ready to depart for the apartment buildings, Sam hadn't been able to help feeling a slight twinge of sadness. Despite only knowing Jim for a day, he'd suddenly grown rather fond of the man. Now it was a possibility he'd never see him again. *One moment you hate somebody, the next you're afraid for their life.*

Sam felt pity for the man. Jim had looked so exhausted, so low, so empty. Perhaps hope was the only thing capable of keeping that kind of man alive.

It was Jim who had reassured *them* not to lose hope, however. 'I've been in worse scrapes than this one,' he'd lied. 'I'll be back shortly. I promise.'

But now Sam wasn't sure that this plan was necessarily the best idea.

'Excuse…'

Sam turned his head to Mary and saw a face of utter hopelessness as she tried to gain the attention of the surrounding officers. The poor captain had lost so much and being acting commissioner was one hell of a pair of boots to fill. It was easy to see why she was having confidence issues. *Now really isn't a great time though Mary,* he thought, looking around at the many scared, angry faces, and weapons surrounding them. 'You may want to speak up a little…' he urged.

The captain closed her eyes and inhaled deeply, as the panic in the room grew greater, the volume increasing exponentially.

'Ladies and gentlemen, would you please shut up!'

A hush filled the room, and all were eager to hear what Mary had to say.

Sam nodded at her encouragingly as she looked to him for guidance. 'Just tell them what they need to know,' he hissed.

Mary exhaled deeply. 'Some of you will remember that two months ago, we had a very serious case regarding a group referring to themselves as the Circle of Saints. That case led to the deaths of numerous police officers in the department, and it was concluded by the evidence suggesting that there was no organisation, but that it was simply a well-co-ordinated attack from a terrorist group consisting of a scientist, named Sebastian Brigson, and one of our own…' she hesitated, 'James Griffen. Also known as the Nightdrop Backstabber.' She glanced over to Sam. 'Well today it is with great regret I am here to inform you that… we as a station have been so wrong.'

There was a confused, interested murmur amongst the crowd – many faces of anger dying down into faces of bewilderment.

Mary fiddled with her hands nervously, unsure how to put the next part into words. 'The so-called "Circle of Saints"… are real. And we have recently discovered that they've been amongst us for a long while now. Their whole objective in July was to lower our numbers and infiltrate our judicial system in preparation for a final attack on the station, known to them as the *Rebirth*, and we now believe that they are in possession of an extremely dangerous weapon and are headed for this station now. Proof of this is to be projected on your screens shortly.'

There were outcries of shock and fear as members of the station gathered around their monitors. *Thank God for our technical support team,* Sam thought with a smile. The evidence on the laptop was enough to convince that one team, and now it was being projected onto every monitor in the station. The only ones not convinced were those surrounding him and Mary, whose weapons remained ever poised and ready to fire.

Mary continued, undeterred by the stubborn, angry faces surrounding them. 'It is with greater regret that I tell you this, however… our own police chief, Captain Edward Murdock, as well as numerous other officers in this building, have been lying to us for years, and have been working for the Circle all this time. Members of this Circle have murdered dozens of their colleagues to gain control of this station, and it is likely that some are even amongst us now.'

She slowly reached into her pocket and pulled out a list of names. 'Edward Murdock. Thomas Knightley. Tessa Green. Bobby Sareen. Davita McConnell…' The list went on for a while, Mary listing out dozens of traitors to the station. There were nervous glances all around, followed by certain people proclaiming their innocence.

'Hey, hey, hey…' one man shouted with his arms raised as he found himself surrounded by many other officers, their weapons held high in his direction. 'Why do you believe her over me, huh? I mean, how do we know she's not just making it all up to protect her buddy, James Griffen?'

'Because James Griffen *is* innocent.' Sam proclaimed. 'Listen, everyone, you've seen the evidence, you've heard the names. The Circle is real and trust me, Jim isn't one of them. He's been framed!'

The officers just stayed in place, their faces slightly anxious, their weapons still raised. They weren't convinced.

'Listen, I was in your place once, all right? A few days ago, I wasn't capable of trusting anybody in this damn building, least of all Griffen. I mean, how could I? When the world had made it out that Griffen had murdered his own *partner* for crying out loud! But then… I met somebody who changed all of that. Somebody who blew me away because he was so determined in one man's innocence. And when I finally learnt the truth, I realised that I'd been living in a dark cave for so long that I'd forgotten what it was like to see the light. Of course, there are people in this world who we *can't* trust, sure there are, take it from me. We've been lied and betrayed to for so long, and most of them are marching to this station to kill us all as we speak. But if you trust us, if you just put a tiny bit of faith in the people who want to *protect* this city, then together we might be able to stop these sons of bitches…'

Nobody moved.

'Okay, you're not budging, I get that. You're not sure which side is the right one - which side you should blame for all the shit that's happened in the city - it's understandable. I'll help you. The bad people are the ones marching here with all sorts of powerful weapons, with the intent of destroying this building. They have two hostages, one being Lieutenant Lynda Griffen, the other a little girl. We, on the other hand, are two unarmed officers standing in front of you, begging you to help us save this city. I know you're terrified – we all are – but if you don't help us now, everything is at risk, including the lives of your families. It's just… it's a leap of faith…' He closed his eyes and reached his hand into his pocket to feel his father's silver bullet. *You need to show them.* 'And it goes two ways. So, to prove myself, I'll take the first leap for you.'

There was a slight commotion as all waited for what he was about to do.

'I'm going to take five steps forward. And I'm going to ask you not to arrest or shoot me. If you do… then so be it.'

Sam took one step. Then one more. Nobody budged. He took another. The officers with their weapons poised began to move back, their eyes afraid. Sam stepped again. And another time. And now Mary was following him. Everybody in the station looked afraid, but soon the men and women holding weapons began to lower them one by one, parting to form a sort of path for him and Mary, allowing them to reach to the centre of the room.

Sam jumped up onto a table so he could be seen by all. Mary followed suit, a proud smile on her face.

'Thank you,' said Sam in relief. 'Acting Commissioner Parker, anything to say?'

Mary shrugged. 'Well, I want every captain and lieutenant in this building to report to me immediately in the briefing room. Whatever's coming is going to be hard to beat… but we're going to try. If anybody wants to leave, go now, if not, we'll get you a weapon.'

She paused, waiting for movement. Nobody moved, except those she'd called out as members of the Circle who tried to shuffle away awkwardly before their path was blocked.

'Great. First thing's first. Officers! Arrest every man and woman who betrayed their city.'

The response was immediate.

***

'Got it!' Lynda proclaimed.

Sadie watched as the car sparked to life, the engine revving ferociously. Lynda turned around and grinned, her eyes bright with excitement.

Half an hour of searching had finally led them to the bridge that they so desired, taking the pair straight to a Nightdrop car park. They'd been lucky; a whole day had passed, the sun now setting in the sky, and *still,* the Circle hadn't reached them. What had they been doing? Had they taken a different bridge? Did they not care about her and Lynda anymore?'

'Never thought I'd be so happy to see somebody steal a car,' Sadie remarked.

'I wouldn't feel too bad anyway,' reasoned Lynda. 'Most people aren't stupid enough to leave a set of keys lying around!' Lynda exclaimed. 'And again, I'm sure they won't mind considering the circumstances. They'll be able to get out of the city should they need to, I'm sure the trains will be available.'

Suddenly she began to laugh.

'What is it?' Sadie asked.

She shook her head. 'Nothing. It's just… I used to be so harsh on my husband Jim for everything stupid thing he did. I never thought about why. I nevêr considered how he was feeling. I just judged him and got angry at him constantly. Same with all the petty criminals I'd end up finding as part of my job. I'd never been able to see past what they were. Now here I am, stealing a car.' She waved her arm. 'Anyway, we ought to get going. Come on, get in.'

Sadie crawled into the passenger's seat and yanked her belt across. Staring out to the skyline through the dusty wing mirror, she wondered how on earth she'd gone from her comfortable bed at the orphanage to a stolen car with a strange woman she'd never met. Life was just funny like that, she supposed.

'Hey kid,' said the woman, having opened the glove compartment, 'look what I found.' Reaching into the space, she pulled out a triangular-shaped cardboard box. It was a sandwich. *Finally*, some decent food. Sadie's mouth watered, and once again her stomach ached from hunger.

Lynda smiled and tossed it in the girl's direction. The girl ripped open the packaging like a savage animal and began to ravenously devour the food in her hands, not once pausing for air. When she had finished, she looked guiltily up at Lynda, who didn't look too well fed herself.

The woman smiled as she observed the girl's expression. 'Don't worry about me, honestly. You're a growing girl, you need it more than I-' Something in the wing mirror caught her eye, and suddenly the car was thrust into reverse.

'What is it? What's wrong?' the girl asked.

But her question was soon answered as she too glanced in the mirror.

Coming over the bridge were four black vans, each van in a

pair with another. Beside these were two lines of about three motorbikes, manned by men and women in helmets holding guns.

As their car began to move, Sadie could have sworn she saw something else. On top of one of the vans was a blurred white figure. Emitting from one of its arms was an eerie green glow.

Suddenly the car was shooting forwards, weaving between rows of parked vehicles to find the main road fast. By the time they'd reached the barriers at the edge, the vans were halfway across the bridge. Sadie screamed as Lynda pressed hard on the accelerator, smashing the van through the barriers with ease and sending them shooting up the main road.

Lynda glanced in the mirror again, but this time she screamed, 'Duck!'

Sadie followed her command and soon witnessed dozens of bullets flying through the windows from different directions, followed by a hot blast of what looked like a green beam of energy. Lynda too was forced to lower her head, impairing her vision of the roads and causing the car to swerve vigorously left and right.

Up ahead, Sadie spotted a four-way junction. Lynda ignored the red lights, instead speeding into the centre of the road, where she swerved to the left in an attempt to get out of sight from the Circle's line of fire. There were numerous honks and beeps as cars attempted to dart around her in the calamity she was causing.

Then there was the explosive sound of a revving motorcycle engine, and Sadie gasped as she spotted a bike rapidly approaching their vehicle.

'Hold on!' Lynda shouted, slamming her foot on the brakes. The bike swerved out of the way so as not to be hit and zoomed straight past, before slowing to turn back on them. While this was happening, Lynda revved the car into reverse, her head turned behind her to try to see what she was driving into as she sped back down the road.

Finally, she spotted a turnoff point, where she promptly spun the car around once more so that it would leave the main road in a forward direction. Sadie looked at where they'd just driven and saw the motorcyclist swerving between the many cars that had now stopped in the middle of the road.

Lynda accelerated far up the road until they were at least halfway up before turning the car into somebody's driveway. 'Get out! Now!' Lynda prompted. Sadie did so and saw that Lynda was running across the road.

'What are you doing? He'll see us!' she exclaimed.

'Trust me!' she responded.

Sadie sprinted across and followed Lynda to the other house, where they threw themselves over a gate to the back garden and hid behind the fence.

Soon Sadie heard the revving of engines and watched through a gap in the fence as the motorcyclist now advanced up the road. Seeing the parked car, the driver parked his bike next to the house across the road and began to investigate.

'Come on,' Lynda whispered. 'Let's get out of here.'

They climbed many more fences and trudged through numerous back gardens before they finally felt safe again. Sadie panted and fell to the ground. Lynda crouched down next to her.

'I think we should go on foot for the rest of the journey, don't you?' the girl remarked.

'Yeah,' Lynda replied. 'I'd say that's a good call.'

***

The alleyway was quiet. Too quiet. Jim shivered as the early evening air picked up a cold breeze and whistled through the walls of brick.

They had been led here by the arrows. Numerous white graffiti directional signs with skulls sprayed above them. While uncertain that this meant anything, it was certainly, as Jordan suggested, worth taking a look.

Jim looked back at his lawyer in pity as they crept into the darkness, Jordan's phone torch in his hand. The man showed no sign of expression, no sign of anything. Just a bleak emptiness that Jim knew all too well. That was the thing about losing somebody. Sometimes there wasn't even sadness, there was just… nothing.

Dad…

Jim slowed as the boy's voice came into his head once more. He'd been so dragged down by Lynda and prison life that he'd barely thought about Jake for the past two months. *I've been keeping occupied. Finding distractions. I can't forget, not after what Arwick did to him.*

'Jim, you all right?'

And what was worse was knowing that Arwick had still made it out alive. Or whatever was left, at least. Maybe there always would be something left, the scars that thing had left on Jim's life. Killing it would never be enough.

And what about the scars I left on his life?

'Jim?'

Jim shook his head as he returned to reality. 'Sorry… yeah… I'm fine. Is this the place?' He shone his torch around to try to get a good look at the area.

'I don't know... I guess they like abandoned areas.'

They kept walking; their steps slow. If anything else made a noise, they'd surely know about it.

'Hey...' Jim started. 'I just... I just wanted to thank you, you know. For everything. You and Carlos, you were the only people who saw through to me. And... well, I appreciate that. Without someone on my side, I don't know how I'd have the strength to keep going.'

Jordan laughed. 'Well as it turns out, you didn't need a court case to get you out anyway! But seriously, no thanks needed, Man. I saw the truth, and I did my job. Nothing more, nothing less. And... well you know I would have done anything for C...' His voice quietened and drifted off, leaving only a sad silence.

Jim smiled kindly. 'Hey... if it helps... I've been there. A lot. First my father, then my sister, then my... *son.* Sometimes it gets easier, and sometimes it doesn't. There are days, and especially nights, where everything will feel cold, and empty, and futile. You'll be there wondering why you were brought into such a universe as this, and you'll question how it is that maniacs and greedy bastards get to live while they, the only lights in this dark world, were lost forever. It sucks. And it hurts. And sometimes, you'll wish you could just change it all to be right for once...

'But... you've got to remember that life didn't stop with them, and that dwelling on what you've lost isn't going to bring it back. And sometimes, on rare occasions, you'll feel this warmth inside... and you'll remember the good times you had, the joy you felt when you were with them; you'll find that really... they're still there in a way. Because the people we lose will never come back. But the love that they gave you? That lasts forever. And when you remember that, on those brief occasions, you start to realise – that sure it sucks that they died; but wasn't it amazing that they lived in the first place?'

Jordan exhaled deeply. 'So... you do feel it then? Hope? Even after everything you've been through? Even back in that prison cell where you'd lost everything?'

'It was losing everything and ending up in that prison cell that taught me to be hopeful!' Jim exclaimed. 'I was ready to kill myself two months ago, but hope kept me going. Not much, mind you, but enough to survive on until today. And look at us now. Preparing to fight against all odds with an enemy we know we're not likely to beat. And Lynda... I thought she was dead for *months*. Sometimes Jordan, you've got to stick it out when life gets tough, you know. Don't do what I used to do, where I buried myself in a life of misery and regret. Find the good things, look for that hope, that warmth. And one day, you never know, you may find yourself winning for once.'

He froze as his torch passed over a reflective silver door, held shut by a golden padlock. In white graffiti on the front was their logo, the divided circle containing a shooting star and a skull, the words *PERIRE FINITE NON EST* sprayed crudely above. 'This is it...'

Jordan came up next to him and pulled out a firearm from the station, offering it to Jim. 'Would you do the honours?'

Jim lifted the pistol and aimed it at the lock. It flew apart with a loud blast, causing the door to swing open vigorously. 'I'm hoping that's the last locked door I'll ever have to try to open,' Jim muttered, before striding into the darkness.

After climbing a dark and creaky stairwell, they finally found a door one floor up, the Latin motto once again sprayed on the front. A firm shove brought them into what could be considered a living room if it wasn't so dead-looking. The floorboards were dusty, and the air so thick it felt solid in Jim's lungs. The only light available aside from his torch was that which poured through tiny cracks in the peeling wallpaper, revealing a room which had all the makings of a ghost house. Smashed glass tables, rotted wooden shelves, and broken vases decorated this "once-living" room and he could have sworn he'd heard the squeak of an animal.

They began to search in haste throughout all the rooms of the house - thoroughly checking under furniture, behind shelves and on counters. For a while, each room appeared to be as abandoned as the others. At last, Jordan called to Jim that he'd discovered something.

'What is it?' he asked, quickly running back into the room they'd first entered.

On the wall beside the lawyer was a large mirror, about as wide as a fireplace, its glass fresh and undamaged. Jordan was picking it up from the rim, sliding it off its hook to look behind it. There, directly behind the reflective glass, was a hollow alcove in the wall, filled with numerous peculiar items.

'Figured it was odd that this mirror was so pristine considering the state of everything else in the room,' Jordan remarked. He fished in and pulled out a long slender piece of white and black metal. 'Is this what you're looking for?' He chucked it to Jim.

Jim turned it over in his hands, his eyes wide with hope. 'Jordan this is… amazing.' He looked up in a wild, excitable frenzy. 'This could be it! This could be the key to defeating that monster! All we need to figure out now is how to-'

'Power it?' Jordan pulled out a small metal box and lifted the lid. Within it was multiple cylinders, each glowing a bright purple. 'These must be what powers Lazarus's suit. Some kind of fuel cylinders. If we could connect them in such a way then-'

He went silent and soon Jim too heard the revving of engines outside. In a hurry, Jim shoved the machine's arm back into Jordan's hands and led the man to an adjacent bathroom.

'What is it?' Jordan asked fearfully.

'Company,' Jim said, 'and they'll be using the front entrance.' He approached the bathroom window and pulled it up slowly so as not to attract too much attention to himself. Peering outside, he spotted a mass of armed men and women entering through the door. 'Listen to me Jordan, that thing in your hand is probably our best chance at stopping this guy. The moment these guys are clear you *need* to get out of here.'

'What, out the window!'

'If you land carefully, you shouldn't break anything. Aim for the dumpster!'

'And what about you?' Jordan queried.

Jim eyed the mob outside. He couldn't see Lynda yet. Then again, he couldn't see "Lazarus" either.

'If there's any chance Lynda and Sadie are still there, I need to get them out of here. Or… at least try.' He smiled at the look of concern on Jordan's face. 'Don't worry, I'm right behind you!'

Jordan hesitated and then nodded. 'All right. I'll watch through the keyhole and leave as soon as I know you're safe.'

Jim looked about to protest.

'Don't argue, Jim. They wouldn't forgive me if they thought I just left you.'

Jim shook his head. 'Fine. But if they capture me or torture me or… Well, all I'm saying is I'd rather face that knowing that this all wasn't for nothing.'

'If it comes to that, I'll leave with this as soon as possible,' Jordan reassured him. 'But don't do anything too stupid, yeah?'

'You know me Jordan, I'm stupid in a smart way. Odds are, Lazarus will want me alive to make a show out of me at the station, but if things look like they're going sour, I'll just run into the bathroom and jump out the window to make my escape,' he reassured. 'I'll be fine, I promise.'

Jordan nodded, and Jim shut the bathroom door, quietly waiting as footsteps pounded up the stairwell.

Thud, whirr, thud, whirr.

It's him, Jim thought. *No,* he corrected himself. *Not him, it. Him would mean human.*

The thudding grew louder and fiercer until it stopped. Few moments of silence hung in the air, until the door finally blasted open in a fiery blaze, the heatwave causing Jim to stumble back in pain, before falling to the ground.

Peering through the smoke, Jim spotted a pair of bright red eyes gazing back at him, followed by the silhouette of a slender, twisted monster. There was a second glow, that of faint green, emitting directly from its right arm. It was certainly true. The stone did exist, and it was being held by a maniac.

'Hello, Jim.'

Jim pushed himself off the ground, dusting himself off casually. The smoke had begun to clear, and already he could see the vague outlines of people standing behind Lazarus's cold outer shell. None of them, however, were Lynda or Sadie. 'Where's my wife you son of a bitch? Where's the girl?'

Lazarus groaned. 'I can't believe it. Two *months* we haven't seen each other, and not even a hello?' It shook its head. 'It pains me that you actually thought you were rid of me, Jim. How weak do you think I was?'

'Weak enough to fall into your own contraption! Weak enough to lose an ar-' Jim pointed at where its left arm would be and suddenly became lost for words. Instead of a tangle of wires, as he'd seen on the video, there was a grotesque, twisted, jet-black limb, its fingers tipped with long, thin talons. None of it was robotic either. The entirety of Lazarus's forearm was made of what looked to be some strange leathery organic material. The stone couldn't have done *this,* surely.

'And look at me now, Jimbo,' the creature taunted. 'I'm the most powerful man on earth, two arms and all. All thanks to you.'

'You're not a man. You're an abomination.'

It tilted its head. 'And proud.'

More Circle members were piling in now, as well as a number of men and women in black apparel. Jim recognised one face to be that of Tessa Green, Nightdrop's medical examiner, and another to be Nathan Blake. Clearly, the Children of the Reaper had joined too. It was Jim's penance for making enemies.

'So what now, then?' Jim asked. 'You take me hostage? Get Lynda and Sadie, bring us all to the police station and use us to manipulate the others into handing it over?' He shook his head. 'It'll never work.'

Lazarus began to step forward, its followers close behind. Jim shuffled back, but only as far as the bathroom door. There was a possibility that Jordan hadn't made it out yet. Jim couldn't risk them finding him too.

'You're right Jim, it wouldn't work. I don't have your wife or the girl, anyway.'

Jim smiled and prepared himself for his jump through the bathroom window. If that was true, he wouldn't need to stay here any longer.

'I don't have them… because they're dead.'

He froze. 'You're lying.'

Lazarus shrugged. 'It's true. They tried to escape. We let them run for a bit. There was a whole car chase, but eventually, we found them in somebody's backyard, exhausted.' It ejected a translucent purple blade from its right wrist and stared at it wistfully. 'It's so quick to kill people these days, Jim. But I wanted to take my time with your wife. She did defy me after all.'

Jim collapsed onto his knees, defeated. Lynda had been alive. He'd been so hopeful. And the girl… Perhaps there really was nothing left worth fighting for.

'And to think they would have been fine if they only hadn't escaped,' the tyrant continued, the stone clutched firmly in its grasp. 'They could have lived in comfort as my hostages. I was merciful to let them live in the first place.' It glared down at Jim. 'But don't worry. I won't make the same mistake with you.'

Jim cried out as the creature lunged towards him, its energy blade plunging right through his chest. The agony spread through his body like a poisonous weed, and soon he felt every organ within him shutting down, one by one.

Lazarus pulled the blade out with ease, sending Jim falling down onto his front. The gaping wound in his chest did not even bleed - for the blade was so hot, it had cauterized everything. *You killed my son, you killed my wife, and now you're killing me.* It was a fitting ending at least.

'Say hi to your family from me, Jim. If you end up with the angels that is.'

Jim smiled as he felt all his suffering lift away from him.

Perhaps he would see them, some way or another. Or perhaps there was more than this. Either way, Jim was ready for this pain to end.

He closed his eyes and exhaled one last time, his final thoughts of his family.

***

THOSE WHO REMAINED
SEPTEMBER 12TH, 2025
THE BATTLE OF NIGHTDROP CITY

A few minutes ago, it had been a police station. Now it was a battleground.

Sam looked out onto a mass of armed men and women, many of whom desk-workers who'd never fired a gun in their lives. Even with diminished numbers thanks to the Circle, there were many willing to fight, and the building was structured perfectly for adequate firing points and protection against attack. This was one of the best-armed, best-protected buildings in the city. No wonder the Circle wanted to destroy it.

Already, he'd organised the men and women into distinct groups, the few Tactical Response Team members situated outside, the rest crouched behind desks pulled over to act as barricades. While Sam had been managing the ground crew, the technicians were busy at work upstairs, attempting to use the data they'd been gifted to find anything useful; whether it was just for powering the arm - should Jordan and Jim return - or finding a new solution to defeat Lazarus and his army.

Nothing had been found regarding destroying the stone.

Even amongst Brigson's collected data on the substance "arconium," the writer had been unable to work out a method of its destruction; merely some of its bizarre side effects and known attributes, such as madness, mutation and some form of energy transfer that Sam couldn't quite understand.

He felt a tap on his shoulder and turned to find Acting-Chief Mary beside him.

'The military's out of the question,' she said plainly. 'They thought I was being ridiculous, that this was some petty crime thing they wouldn't be needed for. I mean, a gang of thirty-odd religious fanatics against an entire police station doesn't sound too threatening, does it? Even with a military machine…' She sighed. 'So, stupidly, I told them about Lazarus. And the stone. '

'They thought you were crazy?'

'Uh-huh. Either that or they must've thought I was some hacker. They patched me through to about six different people, but in the end, they told me the appropriate division for my situation are currently hunting vampires. Assholes.'

'So we're on our own?'

Mary nodded. 'Afraid so. For now, at least. I'm sure they'll change their mind when people start seeing the devastation, but by then it might be too late.'

'Sir. Ma'am.' An officer was running towards them. It was one of the technicians, the laptop under his arm. 'We have something.'

Sam was taken aback a little when he heard somebody refer to him as sir, but responded nonetheless. 'What is it?'

'We've taken a look at the schematics, and it turns out that there's a way we can interfere with the machine's circuitry. A lot of this is high-level stuff, not much we can work with, but…' he pushed his glasses up and paused as if trying to explain something complex to eight-year-olds. 'Lazarus' shell is fundamentally a machine, and as guessed, this machine was originally controlled by this laptop. Were somebody not inside it, things would be much easier. Given that the computer's unlocked we'd be able to shut it down in an instant. However, as it's occupied by… well the man you say I suppose, pretty much all remote functions are shut down and it's virtually impossible to control from the laptop. Even an experienced hacker wouldn't be able to de-encrypt the necessary procedures to do such a thing.'

'So, the laptop's useless?' Mary asked.

'Not quite,' the man responded. 'We can't forcibly stop his motion, nor can we terminate any of whatever systems are keeping him alive. However, there are other functions we can take advantage of. I believe I'm correct in saying that Murdock was using this device to communicate with the man inside the machine, yes?'

If he even is a man anymore, Sam thought. 'Yes, that's right.'

'Unfortunately for us, *that* and tracking the machine's location are the only things available to us. But we can still use that. Again, hacking the machine's motor functions or life support systems is not a possibility, but hacking its messaging system? I've looked at the software, and Brigson hardly bothered with that in terms of security. From his perspective, the laptop would only be in his and his partner's possession, and he was more concerned about the security of the primary functions. The messages appear in the user of the machine's line of sight, so, if we could send enough in one go.'

'We could temporarily blind it,' Sam finished.

'Or at least distract it, yes. Giving you the upper hand in doing whatever you need to do to destroy it. When's that arm coming by the way?'

'Soon I hope,' said Sam. 'It's kind of our best shot right now, otherwise we might as well surrender.'

'Well, even that's a bit of a long shot. Even when we get the arm, there's still figuring out how it works, as well as how to power such a thing. But we can only do our best. As for our little distraction, at the moment the laptop's set up so that it can only send so many messages at a time. However, for the last hour or so we've started work on developing a virus capable of interfering with the machine's messaging system, and I have some guys coming in from outside to help us. If we keep going at the rate we're going, we might be able to get it done in the next hour or so. Let's hope it won't be too late by then.'

'You could really do that?' Mary queried. 'I don't doubt your abilities for one moment, but Brigson was a smart guy, and this is a military-grade machine.'

'A military-grade *prototype* designed by one man in secret. Don't get me wrong, I don't doubt Brigson's intellect. This is his weakest area of software throughout the entire thing, and still, most people would be inefficient at getting past it. But even smart men have their blind spots. I have a team, I have resources, I have connections coming in to help us as we speak, smart programmers from across the city, some even members of Signision themselves. We can crack this in time, Captain. I'm confident. We just need to protect that laptop.'

She patted his shoulder. 'You're a good man. You all deserve more than a pay rise once all this is done.'

'Oh, I'm not doing it for that,' he said with a smile. 'I've got a daughter in the city; I can't risk her being in danger.' He straightened up. 'But about that laptop. Like the arm, a lot of what we do now rests on you keeping it out of harm's way, but… close enough for me to get the virus to you. Do you know where that could be?'

'Can't you do it on the laptop?' Mary asked.

He shook his head. 'If we want this to be ready in time, and if I'm going to have my whole team and more working on this, we'll need to do it in the computer rooms upstairs. They're the fastest in the building, they have the best resources and there are enough devices to go around. I've copied all the software that I can from the laptop already, enough to work with to make the virus, but obviously, we can't send it from the offices either, not without all the other necessary pieces of code on the laptop.'

'I see,' said Sam. 'That's quite the problem. So where can we keep the laptop safe until it's ready to be used? We could always hide it with someone in the chemical cupboards of the medical examiner's room, right?'

The technician sighed. 'That's the final bit of difficulty. The tracking works both ways, and I can't disable it. We can see where the machine is, but the machine will also know the geographical location of the laptop in seconds.'

'So how are we going to keep it hidden for long enough?' Sam queried.

'Hold on,' said Mary, 'when you say he can work out the geographical location of the laptop, you mean it's like when you see somebody's location on a map, right?'

'Yeah, that's right,' said the technician.

'So, he can't tell how high up it is?'

The penny dropped. 'You have a point,' said the technician. 'If you took it to the roof, it might take them a while to work out where you were. Then there's always the advantage of height. The only way up for them would be the ladder at the side of the building, you'd be safe for a fair amount of time.'

'Then we've got no time to lose,' Sam affirmed, patting the technician on the shoulder. 'Go finish that virus and when it's done, put it on a memory stick. Talk to Mary and me through channel seven but don't be obvious what you're doing in case any of the Circle happen to be listening. When it's done, let me know.' He took the laptop from the man. 'You're a good man. Your daughter will be proud.'

'Thank you, sir, I won't let you down.' He nodded to Mary. 'Ma'am.'

She nodded back and turned to Sam, who had now thrust the laptop in her direction.

'What are you doing?' she asked.

'Giving you this. To take to the rooftop.'

'Sam, I intend to fight this, not sit on my ass hiding a laptop.'

'You won't be sitting on your ass, Mary. He's right, this laptop and that arm could be the difference between us winning and us losing, and we need our best officer protecting this thing.'

'You don't understand, I can't let you all risk your life down here while I'm uselessly sitting up there!'

'It *won't* be useless!' Sam exclaimed. 'What if I sent an intern up there? Or a reception worker, or even another detective. They're not like you, Mary. They haven't seen what you've seen, and they wouldn't be near good enough to handle it if the situation went sour and Lazarus sent half his army up there. Besides, if we're all massacred down below here, we'll still need at least one of us alive, right? Nightdrop's relying on you, Mary. Let me handle things down below. We need you alive, and we need that laptop to be working.'

Just then something caught his eye at the doorway, a sight that went from hope to despair. Jordan was coming through the front doors, drained and seemingly lost in hopeless despair. The machine's arm and a small box in his hands. There was no Jim.

'No…' Mary whispered hopelessly.

Jordan shook his head mournfully as he approached. 'Lazarus. He… it… said it killed Lynda. And Sadie. Jim lost all hope. He didn't have it in him to try to escape. I saw it all through the keyhole… I should've tried to save him.'

Sam closed his eyes and nodded. Mary was in tears beside him.

'No, Jordan, you did the right thing,' Sam reasoned, despite feeling lost himself. 'If you'd tried, they would have killed you. Then we wouldn't have that in your hands.'

Jordan forced a sad smile. 'Let's hope it works, and that Jim didn't die in vain. We got the arm. And a pack of fuel cells, I believe, although I don't know if they'll be much use.'

'I'll get somebody to send them up to the technicians,' Sam said, walking over slowly and taking them. Now wasn't the time for mourning. They had work to do.

He put his hand to his communicator. 'To the man I was just talking to, sorry, remind me of your name.'

'Tim,' a voice replied. 'Receiving you loud and clear. What can I help with sir?'

'We've got the arm. And there's… a box of fuel cells, presumably made for the machine. Do you think… you don't suppose you'd be able to use these, would you?'

There was a slight pause. Finally, Tim responded. 'We've got the plans here, are they a sort of purple colour?'

'That's right, yes.'

Sam heard a laugh from the other end. 'My word, just one of those would be more than enough. And you have a whole box of them? We've got some parts from Signision brought by one of my colleagues as well as some basic mechanical components. If we use the blueprints downloaded from the laptop here… yes! Yes, it's possible!'

Jordan watering eyes suddenly began to glimmer with a vague trace of hope. Sam nodded to him with gratitude and re-assurance. 'Thank you, Tim. If you can do this, you'll be a lifesaver.'

'Yeah, well, let's hope we do it fast enough. Last time I checked they were well on their way. Over and out.'

Sam turned to Mary. 'Hey…' He put a reassuring hand on her shoulder. 'Jim would want you to be strong right now, you know that. As would Lynda and Sadie. I hate to be tough, chief, but the Circle are coming and… we need to be ready.'

She nodded and smiled. 'You're right…' She wiped her eyes and stood up tall. 'You're right. We can all grieve later. Now we need to act. I'm ready to go.'

Jordan raised a hand. 'Let me go with you. I don't even know what for yet, but you can explain on the way there. These bastards killed my partner and my client, I'm not going down without a fight.'

Sam sighed and finally nodded. 'You are relentless, aren't you? Well, if you survived them once, I think you'll manage. But you be safe, yeah? Both of you. And make sure to grab a gun on your way out, Jordan.' He smiled. It was a sad, uncertain smile, but one of gratitude and some hope, nonetheless. 'I wish we could leave each other on better circumstances.'

There was a shout from the other side of the room. Somebody had seen vehicles approaching down the road.

'That's our cue to leave,' Mary remarked. 'Knowing Lazarus, I'd say we'll likely be dead the moment we step out those doors.'

Sam nodded. 'I just wish we had more time. Well, if we do die, at least we die for something. And at least we won't be alone.' They made their way down to the front entrance. If everything went to plan, then perhaps there was a chance they'd make it through this.

'Into positions!' Mary shouted. Every man and woman in the room ran to their appropriate areas, taking cover where convenient. These people had families. Children. Far too many had died already, and far too many would die in what was to come.

He fished into his pocket, and once again found his father's bullet. *I'm going to give them hell, Dad*, he thought. *I'm going to be the man you never could be. And I'm going to help us win.*

***

There was a sinister feeling all around, drowning him like icy water. Everything was bright. Far too bright. Yet it was pitch black all the same.

You shouldn't be here.

He screamed, his whole mind a mess of confusion and mixed emotion. He couldn't be here. He couldn't be anywhere. He was… he was meant to be…

Don't be so shocked. You read the story, after all. I guess you never truly believed it until now.

***

One step after the other. That was how he was going to do

this. One step after the other.

Breathe Sam. Breathe!

Sam slowly pushed open the large revolving doors of the police station, his fingers twitching anxiously beside his weapon belt, loaded with a firearm, three grenades and a baton. What if he died today? Would anyone care if that happened? Sure, there was his mother, and there were Mary and Jordan. Perhaps there were one or two friends from the academy, but they'd forget about him soon enough… Who else would mourn for him? Who else cared whether he lived or died?

His colleagues crept close behind. Their survival was more essential than Sam's - he couldn't hinder Lazarus alone after all. If only the Circle could have been a little later, then perhaps the arm would have been ready before they arrived. *And I wouldn't have had to lead an army.*

Outside, the city was hung in deafening silence, disturbed only by the slight breeze that rustled the nearby bushes. Beside Sam were two low walls near the entrance, about three-quarters of a metre in height, and the same murky grey colour of the seven or so steps before them. Jordan and Mary quickly darted behind a wall to the right, keeping them out of the line of fire for as long as possible. About a dozen metres or so from the steps were numerous large black vans, two motorcycles and the familiar white exoskeleton of Lazarus – its eyes that same glowing blood red. Its right hand, the robotic one, was clenched tightly, but an eerie green glow managed to pass through the cracks of its fingers, indicating to Sam that the much-talked-about stone lay clutched in the creature's grasp. Even more disturbing, however, was that Lazarus was no longer missing a left arm. In place of what before was many dangling wires was now a long, crudely shaped, black mess of a limb, its nails sharp like talons. It was this arm that dragged Jim's body.

Sam sighed hopelessly at the sight of the man. His skin was pale, his eyes were shut. Frozen on his face was a look of content rest, but his chest suggested otherwise – a gaping red hole right through where his heart should have been. Jim had fought valiantly many times; he'd struggled through pain and loss and betrayal, and this was the death he got. Perhaps Lazarus would get the same. *That would be nice,* he thought.

Lazarus stood there for a while, motionless, as its army exited the vehicles and gathered behind it. Men and women of many backgrounds gathered behind, all armed, all masked in bandanas, all ready to kill. Many were eyeing the hand clutching the stone enviously as if hoping to snatch it for themselves, while others looked at their leader in awe as if the thing once known as Marcus Arwick was their Messiah. Sam was sure Lazarus did not requite their feelings. After all, if the Circle won, that thing would likely dispose of its army the minute it didn't need them. Then it would have everything it ever wanted. The stone, the city, and James Griffen – gone for good.

Lazarus tilted its head in confusion, pointing its hideous left arm at Sam. 'Really? That's who comes out to meet me? One single detective looking no older than a boy. You lot really have lost hope, haven't you?'

This was met with an uproar of laughter from the Circle. Sam stood his ground, smiling contently. If Lazarus thought he was the only one here, that meant it couldn't see the others.

As if reading his mind, the creature spoke. 'Of course, I do realise you're not alone. I think you're forgetting that this suit can read heat signatures. Look, detective, you don't want your friends to die, do you? Well, I don't want to spend a bunch of time and effort killing them. So, here's the deal, you hand me your little police station, as well as every firearm in that building, and I'll give all your colleagues a chance to start afresh – to join the new world as we progress our efforts further than Nightdrop. We could use the workers after all, and we do need some people to help us keep the city in check once it belongs to us. What do you say?'

Sam threw his arms up in the air. 'Why us?' he asked, enraged. 'Why this police department? Why the men and women in this building? You're more powerful than anybody could ever know, and you want to take a police station.'

The thing shook its head. 'You don't understand. It's not just the building we want, Sam. It's what it symbolises. Order. Order and structure and protection within the city. So long as there's still a police department to stand, the people of this city will always see me as a criminal, and they'll always bother me with their vain attempts at revolution.

'I've seen what I can do to this world, Sam Turner. Once I tear this building down brick by brick, then the real work will begin. I will start with this city; I will make it my… playground. Where, for once, nobody will ever have to resist the chaos within them, nobody will be forced to act a certain way, behave a certain way. This city will be free, freer than any city ever has been since the dawn of civilisation. It will be humanity's playground, a haven for giving into the destruction and chaos, and *I* will be the one ruling over it. I will be their God, and no doubt the rest of the world wouldn't dare interfere, not with a being as powerful as myself. Then, when the work here is done, we'll move on to the rest of the country, and the rest of the continent, and the rest of the world. This stone will keep me alive for a long time, after all. I'm here to stay.'

'I should've thought as much,' Sam provoked, desperately trying to bide his time. 'This isn't about some bigger picture with you. You just want the power, the glory. You'd bring the world to ashes if it meant you were the one holding the flames.'

'You don't know what you're talking about!' it shouted. 'You can't see what I see!'

'Here's what I think,' said Sam, glancing sideways to his colleagues, signalling with his eyes that they should be ready to run. 'The Arwick I heard of was better than this. He wouldn't have cared about things as petty as power, or some glorious new world.' He smiled provocatively. 'That machine and that stone have done something to you. You're not you anymore, Marcus Arwick. I'm not talking to the Phantom killer. He's dead.'

'Marcus Arwick is not- *I* am not dead!' it shouted. 'I am more alive than I have ever been, more powerful than I have ever been, and I have seen what needs to be done. If you had any sense, you would join me!'

Sam clenched his fist, enraged. 'Join you! You killed Jim. Jordan saw the whole thing happen. You stabbed him in the heart, after you murdered his son, framed him, and murdered his wife along with a *child.* You and your buddies led a whole squadron of innocent men and women to die in the explosion at St Luke's Hospital, while you shot and killed numerous police officers at the school of the same name. Three officers died at St John's Steelworks trying to save Jim's mother and wife, while many more innocent people have died just trying to stop you from getting that stone. And you think we'll just join you?'

Lazarus laughed. 'Jim isn't as innocent as you make him out to be. His mistakes cost the lives of Marcus'-' It paused. 'Of *my* family and have ruined the lives of many others. As for everyone else, you think I *wanted them to die?* They were the noble sacrifices necessary for a new, better world! When revolutions happen, or when protests are made, does history paint those people as the bad guys? No. Our current world needs a firm change from a firm leader, and this?' It held up the armoured hand clutching the stone. 'This is going to help us get it. Whilst I doubt it can bring people back from the dead, it can convert energy into any of its alternative forms in an *instant.* It could power cities, or it could burn them to ashes. Think of the endless possibilities that it could be used for!'

Sam shook his head. 'Not in your hands. I told you, Lazarus, you don't care about the world, you don't even care about your little army. You just want the power and the control with no regard for what happens to anyone else. And that's why you're going to lose. Because in the end, after all the atrocities you've committed, you are and always will be *alone!*'

This caused great murmuring within the Circle and many shaking heads. Lazarus looked around cautiously, slightly taken aback by the effect Sam's words had. 'Well,' it said, lifting its right arm ready to fire, 'looks like we'll both be alone then, after I kill everyone in that building!'

'Cover!' Sam shouted as he launched himself behind the wall to his right. He felt the immense heat from the green blast as it passed his feet, melting straight through the floor where he'd been standing one second prior.

'Firing Squad!' Sam shouted.

Suddenly dozens of police officers emerged from the behind the walls, each armed with a shotgun. What followed was a series of deafening shots from both sides, as the Circle had now pulled out their weapons too. In just a few moments there were numerous casualties on both sides, more so on the side of the Circle and Children of the Reaper following the surprise attack. Realising they had less cover, the maniacs of Lazarus' army quickly ran behind the black vans which had taken them here, leaving Lazarus out in the open.

A few bullets ricocheted off its impenetrable shell, but Lazarus stayed there, motionless, undeterred. Preparing to fry them all in a line, it lifted the rock towards them once more. Seeing a distraction was necessary, Sam pulled the pin out of one of his grenades and lobbed it over the wall.

This did better than he hoped. Not only did the grenade momentarily distract Lazarus, but it managed to roll along the ground, stopping just under the furthest left black van.

'Get away from the van!' Lazarus shouted moments before the explosion hit, consuming the van in a fiery blaze.

Some jumped away just in time, the explosion only just singeing their jackets, launching them to the ground. Others were not so lucky. One man who had been firing over the top had managed to get his foot caught in the door as it blew to bits, while others shooting at the back hadn't reacted quickly enough and were engulfed in its flames. Another, in a foolish attempt to escape the blaze, did not run for cover at one of the other vans, but instead sprinted out into the open, making her an easy target to be gunned down by the police department.

Lazarus was enraged. In an instant, he shot a long line of green flame towards the firing squad, starting with those on Sam's right. The flame crawled over the walls with ease, lighting officers in an instant. Sam heard the screams of agony as their bodies erupted in flames, their flesh emitting a foul, sickening smell. Mary and Jordan began to run, attempting to pull Sam with them as he was lost in a shocked trance, staring hopelessly at the burning bodies. Finally, he came to his senses, joining them in a frantic sprint to the left wall.

Suddenly the green beam of energy ceased. Sam peaked over the wall in curiosity as he saw the creature bent over in pain, shaking its right hand repeatedly and almost dropping the stone. *Perhaps it got hot,* Sam wondered, grateful for the opportunity. He wouldn't waste it.

'Everybody get inside!' he shouted, and a rush of officers

passed him to enter the station. Jordan and Mary went the other way, however, taking the advantage of the distraction to run around the building to get to the roof. A few bullets flew from the Circle, but most were focussed on their master, curious as to why their prized weapon of mass destruction was no longer working.

***

'Where am I? Why can't I… why can't I feel anything. Who… who am I?'

Your memories will return soon enough. I've got to hand it to you, sir, you're very good at staying alive. Almost as good as Arwick, or *Lazarus* as it so likes to call itself now. I wonder…

'I remember!' the other voice exclaimed. 'I was… how did I… the blade… how can I even be here?'

By mistake, really. Lazarus isn't to blame. He… *it* has no idea how I work! It thinks it's in control but… even now it's being hindered by such feeble properties as *heat*.

'You mean you're…' the confused voice paused. 'The stone?'

Suddenly the consciousness without form could see, but it could only see one thing. A man, with neatly swept black hair, wearing a pair of thick rectangular glasses, a black pinstripe suit and a crimson tie. The man's skin was pale white, like a corpse, or a snowy field. The man's eyes were strange and seemingly weren't fixed to one colour alone. At first, the observant part of the consciousness recorded them as a vine green, but at the same time, they seemed azure, hazel, maroon, turquoise, violet and so on. Around this man (if the disembodied mind was sure it was a man; the more he observed, the less he was certain) was an emerald haze, similar to heat waves on a tarmac road.

'That's better…' the "man" said with a sigh of relief. 'Do you like how I look? I tried mapping this image around those you hate the most. Arwick, Blake, Brigson, Murdock… yourself. You humans always seem to find it easier to communicate when I'm… visible in some way.'

Suddenly the consciousness without form felt a crushing, choking sensation in his mind, his spirit. He was overwhelmed with emotions, all negative, all exemplified – terror, hatred, grief, lust, lunacy and guilt to name a few. In a few seconds, seconds which felt like a few millennia, the torment ceased.

The image of a man smiled. 'I was only planning on working on Lazarus, but *two* minds? That's something else entirely. There's so much to farm from you…' It began to stroll about the blank white space that the disembodied consciousness found himself in, and eyed him like he was some kind of feast. 'You see, I am fundamentally broken. But you two… you will make me whole…'

'Why are you broken?' the consciousness without form asked. 'Where is your body?'

The Other paused for a moment and nodded. 'Yes, all right, I suppose I can explain. Human thoughts are always seem to be far more resistant when they have no idea what's going on. You've always been a stubborn lot. Perhaps explaining things will make you an easier meal.

'Arconium, as it has been named by a few humans, is not an element, as it is so wrongly described. Humans prefer this word because it makes sense to them. No. Arconium predates atoms. It predates your universe. It is neither matter nor energy, yet it acts like one and manipulates the other. It is itself. It is, I suppose, the catalyst of creation. When my two siblings and I were gifted with such a material, we became the most powerful beings known to the world. We infested everywhere there was, began to take control of the world around us. But something went wrong. An unexpected event brought us crashing to this planet, sending our resources like this rock scattering throughout your world's history. My prior form was incinerated in the crash, but *I* survived. Fragments of my consciousness, like yours, lived on through this rock - a sort of backup to use human terms – dormant in wait for somebody to find me. And one day… they did. But they have me long enough…'

'The Circle.'

'Yes. The Circle of Saints. Their minds were gullible, they were easy to fool. But they lost me fairly quickly. I attempted to penetrate the mind of the woman who stole me away from them, but she was resistant. She had a strength I had never encountered in any life form before, a mental flexibility as worthy as my own. Something was special about her. She buried me so that nobody would find me, and, despite the mental torment I put her through, refused to cease guarding me for the rest of her days, before passing it onto somebody she trusted so that they would do the same. So, I retreated away for years, waiting for a more opportune time. Before I did, however, I just managed to implant something in the mind of the woman guarding me, and in the minds of all those who came close within the city. The thought was small, unnoticeable and initially ineffective, but over generations, it would grow to consume their minds. Over decades it became an irresistible urge for those affected by it to find me again and to free me from my monstrous box.

'And now they have… Thanks to Lazarus, I finally have a body which I can take over piece by piece, as well as two delicious minds to feast on. Soon I will have a whole human city to work with. Then, I will be able to find my brother and sister - if they indeed survived - and awaken them from their slumber.'

Pain seared through the disembodied mind again, but that was the least of his concerns. Dying and pain did not terrify him anymore, for he had already experienced them both before. No, he feared for Sam. For Mary. For Jordan. For Elly and Nora and every living being on earth. If this thing succeeded, it would be more than Nightdrop affected by its devastation.

And even if it didn't. What had it said about its siblings?

Memories flooded through consciousness like an acid. He was hit, over and over by the pain. His father. His older sister. All the murder victims he had witnessed in his endless time as an officer. He saw his son, he saw Johnathan Mort, he saw Sebastian Brigson and all those people at the hospital that he had failed to save. He felt death and suffering and guilt. He was in hell, being punished for those he had failed. He was in hell and standing before the Devil.

The wicked entity smiled. 'You're not in hell, Jim. You're in my home. And if I were the Devil, I doubt you'd be as afraid.'

***

Lynda watched the chaos from behind a neighbouring garden fence, her hand clasped over her mouth in horror.

It was just as horrible as Lazarus said it would be. The stone… the way it incinerated those officers. How would a tiny piece of metal destroy a weapon like that?

Sadie eyed the army with a vicious glare, stretching her feet now that Lynda had finally managed to pick the locks on the clamps around their ankles with a discarded paperclip. 'We've got to destroy that stone.' She began to walk forwards. 'Come on.'

Lynda grabbed the girl's wrist forcefully. 'Are you crazy? You realise the men and women who imprisoned and tortured us are lined up outside that building. How do you plan to get in exactly?'

Sadie froze and sighed reluctantly.

'Look, we know the Circle are going to attack the inside of the building soon enough. It will be chaos. When *that* happens, we go in, find a pistol for this,' she unclasped her hand to reveal the bullet. 'And then destroy the stone'

Sadie nodded slowly. 'Easier said than done. We'll need to get it out of that thing's hands.' She pointed at Lazarus and turned back to look at the station. Then her face dropped, and she cursed quietly under her breath.

'What us it?' asked Lynda as she walked over. 'You're right, they're going into the building now. Right, let's go.'

'No, that's not what I meant!' Sadie exclaimed, distressed.

Lynda looked at her, puzzled, and looked back out to the Circle. 'Well, what else could you possibly mean, is it the-'

Then she saw him. He was being dragged across the road like a rag doll by the twisted, hideous talons of Lazarus. It could have been a mistake, somebody who looked similar but… no. It was him.

Lynda collapsed hopelessly and began to sob. Her one consolation through all those months of torture was the prospect of possibly seeing Jim again. And now… all that hope was gone. *I was so close…*

'Lynda?' Sadie queried. 'Are you… are you okay?'

Lynda sniffed and wiped her eyes. Rage consumed her. 'No. No more than that abomination over there's going to be. And as for his little army…' She stared at the girl piercingly, making sure her gaze was not lost on her. 'You know how many times that monster had made me suffer? The number of times he's hurt the people I love. I stayed strong, I kept to the law, and I kept sane while my husband went off the rails in a mad rush of vengeance. But I understand now!'

She pushed herself off the ground and tore her gaze away from the child's anxious expression, looking around enviously for something of use. On the pavement, just a few metres away from the glass back doors of this garden's house, was a large pebble, about the size of a child's fist. 'I'm going to finish this. And when I'm done, I will carve every one of them limb from limb until their screaming makes me deaf.' She advanced over to the house without hesitation, lifted the rock and smashed it through the windows, causing the glass to shatter everywhere.

'What are you doing?' Sadie shouted.

Lynda shrugged, not bothering to look back. She walked into the kitchen and pulled a long, sharp knife from its rack. 'I plan to finish this.'

She glanced at the girl, who was shaking her head in what was almost disappointment. *Does she think she has the right to judge me?* 'Go on. If you have something to say, say it, because the more time we waste, the more people will die.'

'Lynda… you need to calm down. Getting angry won't help us now!'

'What do you know?' she said, strolling past without hesitation. 'You're just a kid.'

'A kid who's seen people do things they'll later regret!' she shouted. 'I know you're angry, but if you go in there in a fit of rage, recklessly massacring them all, then not only will you accomplish nothing before you're shot down, but you'll lose a part of yourself. The part that makes you human. Please, Lynda, let's just focus on destroying the stone. The right thing. Not the thing that feels good.'

Lynda hesitated, her hand trembling slightly. She nearly dropped it, so nearly… But no. She couldn't just forget what had happened to her Jim. She couldn't let that monster off a second time after what it had done to Jake. 'You're stronger than me, Sadie. I can't let them go for what they've done. I can't. If they end up killing me because of it, then you can always get the bullet off my body and destroy that stone yourself.'

Sadie sighed, staring at the unflinching knife in Lynda's hand. 'All right, then. I guess I'll find my own way…'

'You do that, kid. I have the bullet; I'll try to destroy the stone and kill that bastard. You don't need to be here anymore. Run. Run as fast as you can and don't look back.'

The girl nodded quietly and walked away, before vaulting over the fence out of sight.

Lynda shook away the guilt. The girl would be fine, she'd made it this far. *But what have I become?*

She glanced at the knife, and then back to the station, smirking. *Exactly what you wanted Jim to be, I suppose. I'm full of surprises, aren't I Lazarus?*

***

Mary smiled, panting, as she lifted her foot off the final rung of the ladder. They had finally made it up, without a moment to lose.

'Let's do this,' said Jordan, who was now holding a pistol.

They sat by a wall, and Mary opened up the laptop. Instantly she regretted what she saw. Through the creature's eyes, she witnessed the chaos within the police station. While officers and Lazarus' army fired at each other from their respective covers, Lazarus was firing great beams of blazing light from the stone, incinerating desks and blowing up bits of machinery. Officers were darting from place to place as their cover was obliterated, a few flailing in excruciating pain as they were set alight, or limbs were incinerated straight off the bone. The creature aimed a beam at those firing from the balcony, and many tried to flee the blast. Those who failed were killed in the blaze that reached them, while some others who darted out of the way found the floor beneath them collapsing and fell from great heights to the floor below.

'How're you holding up Tim?' Jordan shouted into his communicator.

There was a brief pause, but Tim responded quickly enough. 'It's been a little manic, to say the least. Hard to stay focussed when the station's blowing to bits, but we're almost done with what you need. Sam's… uh… *item* is still being worked on. Hopefully, that shouldn't be too much longer.'

Mary nodded, understanding the meaning of his message. 'Well, make sure to send it up as soon as possible. It'll be hard for you to get that *item* across, I know, but I have every confidence that you can do it.'

'Thanks, boss, I won't let you down.'

From the computer screen, Lazarus froze momentarily, while bullets uselessly flicked off his impenetrable shell. 'Somebody's using the laptop!' he shouted to his army. 'It was activated a few minutes ago, they could be using it for something. They should be at the farthest right corner of the building; I want one of you searching each floor. Now!'

On the screen, over a dozen of the army flocked away from their master in an attempt to reach the stairwell. Mary smiled. Clearly, Lazarus hadn't caught onto them being on the roof. If they were lucky, much of the army would be shot before they even made it up the stairs.

'The technicians are on the other side of the building anyway, so the Circle shouldn't bump into them,' she reassured Jordan.

'Good,' he responded. 'I'm just hoping they'll be able to do it quickly. Close the lid for now, it's best we confuse him and don't keep alerting him to our location. We can see what's going on below from the-'

Suddenly a blast shot through the deep blue glass of the roof, shooting far into the sky, and instantly they could hear the screams and shouts of all those fighting below through the gaping hole.

Mary shut the lid and buried her head in her knees. 'This isn't right,' she said. 'I should be down there fighting with them. It makes me sick just hearing them.'

'Mary, we're doing the right thing. This could save lives. We just have to be patient.'

There was another bright blast, and the two could feel the heat from the flames. When would this end?

'It's all right,' Jordan re-affirmed. 'They'll finish the virus and the arm, and we can win this. All we have to do is-'

Suddenly a blast sounded, and the communicator shot out of Jordan's hand followed by a spurt of blood. He screamed in agony as he clenched his right wrist. He had been shot straight through his lower palm.

Mary turned furiously and found herself faced with a man in black poising a pistol in her direction. He did not have a mask like the rest of the Circle members but instead revealed his face to the officers, showing sleek silver hair, bony features, and a stitched scar on his right cheek that pulled up his lips into a forced, unnatural smile.

'Who the hell are you?' the acting-chief asked, reaching for her weapon.

The man moved his pistol so that it was aimed for Jordan's head. 'Ah ah ah. Lift your weapon and your friend here dies.' He gestured to Jordan. 'You too. Touch that laptop and you'll both die.'

The man seemed amused, as if this was the most excitement he'd had the pleasure of feeling for a while. 'I saw you run up here to the roof. What could you possibly be doing up here? Not cowering in fear, I hope? Or…' He pointed to the laptop. 'Could it be to do with that? My name's Nathan Blake by the way, but you can call me the Reaper.'

'The drug producer?' Jordan queried with a grunt.

The man shrugged. 'Used to be. Until your friend James Griffen ruined me, that is. With the help of my new leader, but that's besides the point. He made people afraid to buy our products, ruined our credibility. That's why I'm now with Arwick- Lazarus, I mean. Sure, Lazarus helped Griffen ruin me, but his partner was an old customer, and was willing to lend me a hand.'

'Until he no longer needs you,' Mary reminded him.

'Yeah. But I'll be powerful enough by then. You forget that a large portion of this army's mine, anyway! Lazarus wouldn't dare fight us all.'

'He wouldn't have to fight you; he'd obliterate you in seconds!' Mary shouted. 'He could destroy you and your followers with or without the stone. You think you're safe from him?'

'What I *know,* is that he'll be so pleased with me when he finds out I killed Nightdrop's acting chief of police *and* James Griffen's irritating lawyer.'

'Irritating indeed,' Jordan remarked. 'May the irritating lawyer point out that you can only kill one of us at a time? I'd say the time it takes for you to adjust from your pistol's recoil, and then to swing such a thing so that it makes a good shot on either one of us is just enough time for us to pull out our weapons and shoot you back, no? Even if you wound us in that time, miss a clear shot and we activate our weapon from this laptop.'

Blake smiled. 'How do I know you're not bluffing? You might not have anything on that laptop as far as I'm aware.'

'Are you willing to take that risk?' Mary queried. 'We're sure willing to risk our lives to set it off.'

The Reaper shrugged. 'And do what? Stun him for a few seconds or something? Shut down some of his systems? I doubt Brigson's engineering would even allow you to do such a thing, at least nothing ultimately damaging, eh?'

Mary smiled. 'Hit the right systems at the right time and it could make all the difference in the world. You have no idea what this device could do.'

The man sighed. 'I suppose it's a stalemate then… this should be interesting.'

***

Lazarus strolled through the station carefree, its dead enemy in one hand, the stone in its other, caring neither for the bullets that rang off its metal shell, nor the men and women of its army that were dropping like flies. Sure, they were outnumbered, and yes, they'd been caught off guard outside; but the former could easily be amended, and the latter… well, the police department had been lucky. They wouldn't have the same fortune a second time.

Without hesitation or announcement, it lifted the stone. Having played back through footage of a few minutes ago, it noted that it had been able to use the stone for a good fifteen seconds continuously before it had gotten too hot to hold. It was despicable that such a powerful being as itself could still be affected by such things as heat – but fifteen seconds would be long enough.

Lazarus clenched the stone and suddenly felt it coming into contact with its thoughts. *The light,* it commanded, *absorb it.* The stone did so. A cloud of darkness surrounded the Circle, making them blind to the police department, and the police department blind to them. The bullets began to slow, and Lazarus smiled under its shell. *Good. Now let's have some destruction.*

A green beam of energy shot directly into the desks at the centre of the room. The creature felt pleasure as it indulged in the sweet sounds of horrified screaming and sizzling of flesh before a thump as whatever part of the body that remained collapsed onto the ground. As the dark cloud disappeared around it, Lazarus saw the burning desks and charred bodies and began to move the beam around the room, incinerating officers by the dozens.

The stone became hot, and it ceased firing once more. 'Now!' shouted the irritating Detective Turner. Immediately officers jumped out of their hiding places and began to fire rapidly at the army, leading the Circle and Children of the Reaper to fire back in rapid response. They were dropping in numbers once more, something that Lazarus couldn't afford to happen if it wanted control of the city once the invasion was finished. *They forget,* it thought. *I don't need a stone to be powerful.*

It opened up its left hand, letting Jim's limp body drop to the floor. In an instant, it ejected its energy blade from its right wrist and began to advance on the firing officers. The clever ones ran, but some made an effort to be heroes and kept on firing in their place. *Such fools*, Lazarus thought. It grabbed one man's firearm and twisted the barrel, causing it to explode viciously when the trigger was pulled again. Lazarus plunged its blade into his chest with ease, before spinning around and slicing the head clean off another officer running towards it. More officers now approached it in its rage, but it had primed its arm blasters, and soon it was shooting deep holes in the chests of the many men and women that tried to attack it.

The creature turned to its army and smiled, beckoning them forwards with the first finger of its newly grown left arm. *This is easier than I imagined,* it thought. *Soon this station will be mine…*

Suddenly a woman of his army near the entrance stopped in her tracks, her face a mixture of shock and fear. There was a knife in her neck. A figure behind yanked the knife back out again. Tessa ran towards the individual with her pistol, but the figure with the knife dodged away from the gun and grabbed Tessa's shooting wrist, before plunging the knife into her shoulder. The former medical examiner collapsed to her knees.

The attacker had the silhouette of a tall, slender woman with short hair, and now went on to lift Tessa's firearm from the ground. 'Who the hell…' Lazarus began, and then he saw her face.

Lynda looked at Lazarus with enraged eyes as she pulled the knife from Tessa's shoulder, but suddenly several other members had turned their backs to the remainder of the police department to face her with their firearms. Without hesitation, Lynda sheathed her knife and covered herself with her newly acquired pistol, launching herself behind the receptionist's desk. The bullets fired in her direction, but she had made it behind cover, and now the rest of the police station were firing at the backs of Lazarus's army.

As if things couldn't get more irritating, Lazarus found himself receiving a call from Blake. 'What is it?' it snapped.

'Sir, we have an issue on the roof…' Blake replied. 'They have a device. I don't know what it'll do, perhaps nothing, they won't tell me, but they refuse to show me or shut it down. If I try to kill one of them, the other will kill me and then activate said device, if it isn't already on a timer to activate. How should I proceed?'

Lazarus sighed. Of course, the roof. It had been a long time since anybody had made it feel like such a fool. It hoped Blake made them feel pain.

'Just kill them, Blake,' it said, exasperated. 'I have full trust in your abilities, and I'm sure whatever they have against me can't do much given Brigson's capability as an engineer.'

The stone felt cool once more and Lazarus felt ready again to cull off some more officers. If only there weren't always so many complications.

***

Bodies dropped like flies on either side. Fires littered the atrium and bullets whizzed by like gnats. It was time for the weapon. But not yet. First Sam had to find that woman with the knife.

He had snuck to the front of the atrium near the entrance and was opposite the desk where she was situated. Most of the Circle had now turned back to their leader. The rest were firing at the woman at the desk, providing him with a small window of opportunity to get across. When Lazarus was turned Sam made a sprint across the room, hoping the bullets would miss him. Not quite. Some of the Circle spotted him and a bullet hit the vest on his torso sending a sharp pain up his side, temporarily winding him. He momentarily fell to the ground before crawling back to his feet and scarpering to cover behind the desk where she was situated.

She was firing her pistol rapidly, darting behind cover when necessary. Despite her many bruises and cuts, there wasn't a single bullet wound in her body, and it seemed she'd taken out many enemies already. Violent as it was, what she'd done at the entrance was bold, and it was shocking that she was still alive given the circumstances.

Sam ran over to the desk, just missing a bullet that whizzed over his head. The woman barely noticed him but kept on firing and reloading. 'Excuse me, ma'am!' he shouted over the bullet fire.

'Don't bother me, officer, it's been a tough day.' She jumped up and fired again, hitting a Circle member in the shoulder.

'My name's Sam Turner. I've been ordered to command the station in absence of the chief. Might I ask who you are?'

'Sam?' she said with raised eyebrows. 'Lazarus mentioned a Sam. Are you the one that saved Jim Griffen?'

'I wish he could have been safe for longer, but yes, I am. Who're you with? Decided to switch sides from his army?'

A bullet sprayed blasted through the wood of the desk, just inches from Sam's shoulder.

'No, I was their prisoner. Lynda Griffen. Jim's wife.'

Lynda? I guess she's not dead after all. 'You're alive? How did you escape from the Circle?' A more pressing question entered his brain. 'Where's Sadie?'

A look of guilt flickered in her eyes. 'Sadie's… strong. And alive, too. Listen, her father, Michael, he may have given us a way to destroy the stone.'

'What?'

She rummaged in her pocket and pulled out a small shiny object. 'This. Don't ask me how it works, but this bullet is our key to stopping them, all of them. Apparently, it's the same metal as the meteorite that the stone was in or something. Williams used this stuff to contain it. You think you could find a weapon that could shoot this?'

She dropped it in his hand, and he studied it closely. 'It's a .347 magnum round,' he remarked. *Same as Dad's,* he thought in mild amusement. 'Yeah, there'll be a Colt Python or two in the armoury. We didn't think we'd need them, but… you think this'll destroy it?'

She shrugged. 'It's worth a shot I suppose.'

'Boss!' shouted a Circle member. 'Our prisoner and that Sam guy are behind this desk.'

Lynda cursed. 'Better run then.'

'Good luck,' Sam encouraged. They both sprinted for their lives as the desk exploded in a green blaze behind them.

***

'Yep…' Blake nodded, a wicked grin on his face. 'If that's a risk you're willing to take, your wish is my command.'

He lowered the phone and tensed his hand on the base of the pistol. 'Sorry, but the boss wants you both dead. Anyone want to go first?'

Mary shook her head. 'You're bluffing. He'd never take that risk.'

'As far as he's concerned, you have no idea how to use a device like that. If there's anything to use. No doubt you're bluffing too, so it's a risk we're all willing to take. I'll ask again. Who's going to go for that laptop first?'

They both hesitated, unsure whether this was true or not. Finally, Jordan spoke up. 'Maybe not the laptop, but I can always slow you down.'

'Jordan, no! What are you doing!'

Jordan held a hand out to calm her down. 'It's all right, Mary. You've got people you love, I've… well, I've got nobody. Not anymore.'

Blake shrugged. 'Suit yourself. Anything you want to say.' He pointed the gun at Jordan's head.

Jordan closed his eyes and sighed. 'Only that… I hope you all fail spectacularly.' He looked ready to charge and began to do so, but suddenly Blake was smacked hard in the head, causing him to drop to the ground.

Behind was a little girl about ten years old, her face completely sullen, her clothes torn and her hair messy. In her hand was a large brick, decorated with tiny speckles of Blake's blood.

'Sadie?' Jordan asked. 'Sadie Williams? The missing girl returns! It *is* you, isn't it? You're alive!'

She nodded. 'So is Lynda, although I'm not sure she's quite the same as she used to be. I'm not sure I am…'

Mary felt a fierce hope within her at the mention of Lynda being alive. Perhaps there were still things worth fighting for. 'You saved our lives, Sadie!' she exclaimed, looking at Blake's collapsed body, the pool of blood around his head. 'I… can't thank you enough.'

Sadie shrugged. 'I saw him on the roof pointing a gun. Wasn't hard to put two and two together. It was nothing honestly, I'm just sorry it took me so long to find the ladder.' She glanced at the communicator. 'You may want to get that though…'

Lynda scrambled across and picked up the small device. 'Tim? Tim, are you there…?'

There was static for a while, before, finally, some noise. 'No. It's Sam. I'm sorry Mary, the Circle got in here just before I could. I shot the guy who killed them before he could get the arm but… all but one are dead.'

Mary stared out to the city skyline in lost silence. That one technician had helped them so much. Now he was gone like Jim. 'Did they finish it?' she asked. 'The arm? The virus?'

'Yeah… they did. One of them is okay – just about. He says

once you get it, you drag the file into the message box and click send. Lazarus will have no choice but to let it happen.'

Mary nodded. 'Well, get it to us quickly,' she said. 'In fact, one of us can collect it at the bottom.'

'All right,' said Sam. 'As soon as you receive it, you do what needs to be done. I'll probably be ready to attack Lazarus by then. Can't wait too long though, if the Circle gets this arm, or worse, if Lazarus gets it, then this'll all be over.'

'All right, let's do this,' Mary said affirmatively. 'Be careful, Sam. Good luck.'

'Thanks, Mary. I'll see you at the end. I hope.'

Suddenly Sadie screamed, and they bolted around to see Blake back on his feet, his left arm around her neck, his right holding a pistol. His face was consumed with rage. This time, however, both Mary and Jordan were ready, their firearms in position to shoot the drug-lord, but Sadie was blocking their shot.

'I wouldn't do that if I were you,' said Blake. 'Touch that laptop or refuse to lower your weapons, and I'll kill the girl.'

***

The sight was brutal. Dozens of good people - innocent, brave people – lay cold on the computer room floor, their bodies laced with bullets. *They weren't armed*, Sam thought in regret. None of them could have defended themselves. None of them had been given the chance to survive as they'd frantically tried to work out methods of stopping the wicked machine a few floors below. They would have merely stood there, as the shooter walked into the room and ended their lives. What would Sam tell their families? *I probably won't be alive to tell anyone.*

'Sam…' whispered the wounded man, the last surviving

technician. 'Listen to me… the virus… we…' The man beckoned him closer.

Sam held crouched lower and put his ear to the man's mouth. The last surviving technician whispered a few simple instructions, before peacefully exhaling his last breath and going limp.

Sam sighed and patted the man on the shoulder. Every one of them was a hero. He just hoped their work wouldn't be for nothing.

He reached down and picked up the arm. As promised, it was wired up to the fuel cell, which was taped to its side, and seemed to hum quietly as machinery inside worked hard. Sam slotted his left arm in as if it were a gauntlet. He took a few moments to understand the weapon in his possession, eventually finding a switch by his thumb. Following a simple flick of the switch and the clench of his fists, a translucent lilac energy blade shot out from his wrists.

He glanced down to the bodies and nodded respectfully. *Thanks, Tim. Thank you all. You were braver than the best of us.*

***

Sam plodded slowly down the stairs, finding the screams and gunshots to be quieter and less frequent now down below. He was lost within his dread and anxiety, and his heartbeat seemed to be all he could hear, the endless drumming within him that would potentially cease in the next few minutes.

He stumbled down the steps, his left arm behind his back with the blade retracted, and darted behind a pile of smouldering rocks as the few remaining members of Lazarus' army fired at him.

Only a few fighters remained, it seemed, with many others either dead, afraid or too injured to continue. Lazarus, however, was still at its prime, continuing to fire explosive blasts of energy from the mystical green stone that lay in its right hand.

Sam looked to his left as this round of green blasts ceased and saw a group of three officers huddled behind a set of desks. In a mad sprint, he darted over to them while they covered him with their gunfire.

'Listen,' he whispered. 'There's hope yet.' He peaked over the cover and saw with irritation that the few dozen remaining of the army were blocking the entrance. 'If I were to distract this lot, could you run around to the entrance and take this,' he gestured the USB drive towards them, 'to the roof.'

They nodded silently, although shaking in fear for their lives. 'All right,' Sam said. 'After that, you have my permission to get the hell out of here. This either ends now, or we lose. Either way, you might want to see your families first.'

They nodded.

Sam cleared his throat and nodded to them. *Be quick, Mary*, he thought.

'Lazarus!' he shouted. 'I wish to talk. I also wish to spare the lives of the men and women in this room. The police station is yours. Do I have your trust that we can discuss such matters before you obliterate me?'

'You have my word Turner, I assure you,' said the creature.

His word, Sam thought. *As if that ever meant anything.*

Sam rose slowly, his left arm behind his back for a moment. 'Now listen. You only have a dozen or so of your army left. My police officers will continue this fight if they see any of them firing at me. We're both smart enough to know that you could take this station at this point with or without them, but it would still inspire a little confidence if they were to lower their weapons. Drop them, maybe.'

The creature tilted its head, its cold dead robotic eyes in a constant unchanging glare. 'How do I know you won't just have your officers shoot them?'

Sam laughed. 'Like you care. But fine, I wouldn't do that because I know you'd kill whatever few of my people that remain. Besides, we're police officers. Proper police officers, not those Circle idiots you replaced us with. You think we'd be fighting you if we were monsters too?'

Lazarus paused but finally nodded. 'Okay, Turner. I'll stand them down if it means fewer funny tricks. You'll call off those officers upstairs too, yes? Those with the computer, whatever they're planning.'

'Of course,' said Sam with determination, almost believing the lie himself.

The creature shrugged. After all, what did it have to be afraid of? It raised a hand to its men, gesturing with its fingers for them to lower their weapons.

'But Boss!' said one of them.

Lazarus turned and shot a green beam straight through him. The man cried out momentarily, before crumbling to the floor.

'Now!' Lazarus ordered.

His armies slowly lowered their weapons, and finally, Sam knew it was time. When all the others were unarmed, he extended his left arm slowly until it was in full view of everybody watching and ejected the lilac energy blade.

There was a gasp from some Circle members and many of Lazarus's army went down to reach for their weapons.

'Ah ah,' said Sam. 'I wouldn't do that if I were you. Your boss doesn't want you to shoot me.'

'Don't I?' asked Lazarus.

Sam couldn't see the look on its face, but he hoped it was fear.

'No,' Sam said, desperately attempting to think of new lies. 'For many reasons. First of all, if they reach for their weapons, I'll just run for cover. At that point you could try incinerating me with the stone, but what if you missed? I could escape the police station if you're not careful, get the public to mass-produce this thing in my hand right here. The whole world would know how to get through your impenetrable shell. Including the military who no doubt will gain some sense sometime sooner or later and will come to this very location.' Sam smiled. 'In fact, now your entire army knows how to destroy you. They want that stone, and all they'd need to do to get it is pry this off my dead arm. That's why you can't let them kill me. Because then they'll try to kill you.'

'I could incinerate you right now,' the creature reasoned.

Sam chuckled. 'You could. Wouldn't that be lame? But even if you incinerated both me and this triontium arm, I'm still the only person who can unlock the laptop upstairs,' he made up. 'The laptop which, when a timer runs out, will overload your circuitry so that it sends enough currents of electricity through your brain to melt it into soup.'

'You're bluffing. The programming and technical skills needed to do either of those things go far beyond any police station.'

'No, you see, that's where you're wrong,' Sam lied, praying that Mary would just send over the virus soon. 'Brigson was smart, but our technicians managed to create a decryption algorithm, and downloaded a program onto the laptop not only able to decrypt the code but also able to change the programs necessary to turn your brain into jelly. The decrypting should only be a few minutes longer. That's why we haven't done it yet and I've been forced to resort to chopping you up with this. You see. You can't kill me. You're just going to have to convince me to turn it off. But first, you'll have to get this thing off my arm!'

Lazarus hesitated as if reading Sam's every expression, but finally loosened its grip on the stone by the smallest fraction of an amount, causing its eerie green glow to die down. It ejected the blade from its right wrist. 'Fine. Whether you're lying or not, I don't see what difference it makes. It just gives me an excuse to cut off your arm and put you through all the pain you deserve. I hope you think this was all worth it when your life's a living hell, Turner.'

Sam shrugged and lifted his blade in a ready stance. 'Yeah, I think I will. Let's get on with it then, shall we?'

Lazarus turned to its army. 'One of you, get to the roof now! Find that laptop or I'll chop you into small pieces.' One of the Circle members began to run, leading Sam to curse under his breath as he realised he'd just made the situation worse for Mary and Jordan.

Lazarus looked at the ten of its army remaining. 'As for the rest of you, I'm afraid Turner's right. I can't risk you getting a hold of that weapon.' In an instant it clenched the stone, and a green beam shot out again. The Circle tried to run, but the effort was futile. They all burnt to a crisp.

Well, that's one way to get rid of them, Sam thought with a sigh. Now it was just him and Lazarus, at least until the monster discovered his lie. His only hope was to kill the creature here and now before it was too late for the rest of the world.

He ran forwards screaming in fury and swung his energy blade down with great force in an attempt to gain the element of surprise. Lazarus blocked the blow with ease, causing the blades to collide and launch away from each other in a blazing white flash.

And then the fighting commenced.

***

Lynda rummaged through the boxes in panic, desperately searching for the revolver that could end this all. But nearly every box was empty and only two remained. Was this over before it had even started?

She opened the next box and sighed in relief. Inside were numerous revolvers, each with barrels of different shapes and sizes. She picked them up one by one, attempting to slot the bullet in the chambers, but none of them were working. Things were quieting down outside and she heard Sam shouting something to Lazarus. *I don't have time for this*, she thought, angered. Finally, about ten guns in, the bullet fell into the chamber with ease. Lynda grinned and snapped it shut, before turning to run to the door. She felt something hard smack across her face before she fell to the floor.

Everything went black for a few moments before she finally came to her senses. Her face felt sore and swollen, and she was struggling to pick herself off the ground. Suddenly she felt a hard boot on her back.

'Oh dear. You look hurt, Lynda! You sure you don't need an ice pack for that bruise on the side of your face?'

Lynda put all her effort into glaring up at her attacker. What she saw was blurry, but it seemed to be a woman with a rifle, a skull mask covering her face. Lynda's vision cleared, and her attacker removed the mask. It was Tessa Green.

'You backstabbing bitch! You betrayed your city...'

'I *saved* my city, Lynda! Don't you see? The world has been falling apart for quite some time now. Selfish leaders, changing climates, governments seizing control over everything! It's gone to chaos, and everybody's reverted to animals!'

'Says the person who follows a homicidal maniac,' Lynda retorted.

'I don't follow *that thing!* I *despise* it. Murdock and I only hired Marcus Arwick because he was necessary for the current task, not because we believed he'd lead us into the new age. It's that stone which I follow. That stone is our hope in this chaotic, distasteful world. It's our next stage in human evolution, and it's the only way we can survive as a species. You think *Homo sapiens* got so far because they lived in harmony with the Neanderthals? No. You wiped them all out, and now we have to do the same. You've destroyed this world long enough, and it's time for us to make it better?'

'By killing people? I'm not sure I'm following your train of logic.'

'Like you're any different Lynda! I saw you earlier, murdering my comrades like they were rats. You had vengeance in your eyes. Cold, bloodthirsty vengeance and you know it. What we do, we do for a cause. What you do, you do out of hate!'

'And what cause did killing my husband serve? Except for satisfying Lazarus's appetite. I know you also had a thing for Jim, you could have stopped it!'

'Nothing stops Lazarus. Nothing ever will. As much as I desired Jim, I knew that fact from the moment that thing got its hands on the stone. That's why the police department can't win this fight.'

'Oh yeah?' Lynda taunted. 'Well, maybe the Circle should talk less.' She pulled the knife from her pocket and slashed Tessa's foot, causing the medical examiner to recoil in pain. A look of fury was on her face, and she looked almost ready to shoot Lynda square in the face. Lynda picked herself up and sprinted forwards, pushing the weapon aside so that she wouldn't be caught in the line of fire. Tessa saw the knife in Lynda's hand and dropped her weapon, causing it to go off prematurely and shoot the wall, while she grabbed Lynda's wrist and yanked it away, causing the knife to fly across the room.

Lynda came back quickly with a punch, but it seemed to just enrage Tessa further, causing her to return with a flurry of hits and scratches. One hit the bruise on Lynda's face, and suddenly she found her head in burning agony. When the next hit came, Lynda caught Tessa's wrist and kicked her leg from underneath her, leading her to plummet to the floor. Lynda followed in an attempt to pin her down, but she was too quick and managed to roll away.

They both rose to their feet, but Tessa had done so slightly quicker, and now Lynda was receiving a flurry of kicks to the stomach. Clearly, the woman she was facing was trained at some form of martial art, as each kick managed to painfully wind Lynda to the point that she could hardly breathe.

As she was bent over, croaking for air, Tessa ran forwards and grabbed her neck, kneeing her in the face once before throwing her against the wall. Lynda slumped down in pain against several boxes, and soon she was being kicked again, numerous times in the stomach, helpless to defend herself.

She attempted to block the fists with her hands, but it was no use. Each kick was becoming exponentially more painful, and breathing was proving to be an impossible feat. As everything became dark and speckles of white filled Lynda's vision, she looked out the door to see the fight raging on outside.

***

Sam's blade was swatted to the left, catching him off balance and causing him to stumble. Lazarus attempted to thrust its blade into Sam's shoulder, but he leapt back and parried the blow. He ducked then, as his enemy's blade came back towards his side from the right, leading it to just singe the tip of his hair. Instantly he countered by swinging his blade to the right across the creature's chest, but Lazarus dodged back, the tip of Sam's blade only just leaving a singe-mark in the armour.

Swing after swing they seemed to alternate, attacking one moment, blocking attacks the next, constantly darting around the room as they faced each other in this torturous stand-off. Sam grunted as each blow came, his arms beginning to feel weaker by the second. Lazarus seemed to have the advantage, for his strength could have kept him going for hours. But then, in a moment of pure epiphany, Sam realised he might have had a chance after all, for he had something Lazarus did not. Speed.

Sam blocked another blow, but this time, while their blades were retracting, began to run around the creature. Lazarus tried desperately to keep up with Sam's swings around its body, moving vigorously either way to try to block the attacks. Suddenly it put its blade in Sam's path, forcing him to duck and slide under, during which he managed to slice a line across the being's metal leg.

Lazarus screamed in rage, and suddenly, as if it were some kind of last resort, ejected its arm cannon, shooting a bolt at Sam's leg. Sam collapsed as it shot into his thigh, sending a burning pain up his leg, but swung his blade as he fell and sliced the top off the cannon in seconds.

This led the creature to throw more and more vicious, angry blows at Sam's arm, which he valiantly attempted to block for what felt like an eternity, unable to get himself back up without the risk of being sliced into two parts. He was stuck at ground level, fighting for his life.

Come on, Mary, he thought. *What's going on up there?*

***

The Other had a look of concern on its face.

'What's going on?' asked Jim. 'What's happening?'

The being gave him a fake smile of superiority. 'Nothing. We're just winning, that's all. The police station's all but taken, Lazarus and I are about to kill your friends, and soon I will have that body *and* the city for good. By the time the military realise what's happened and get their act together, it'll be too late. Once I'm at full power, it will take the Devil himself to stop me. And even then, I'm not so certain he'd win.'

'They'll stop you,' said Jim. 'I know they will.'

'Oh Jim, you always were the fool.'

The pain began again, the excruciating pain.

'Yet you have so much emotion, so much thought, so many memories to feed upon. I won't be done with you for a long time, oh no. I'll make it a very slow, *painful* experience. Perhaps I'll even show you your friends' deaths on repeat, over and over. Wouldn't that be fun?'

***

Sadie took deep breaths. It would be all right, she reassured herself, it would have to be. Except… it was practically too late.

The gun against her temple was cold, and she could feel the Reaper's hands twitching around the trigger. It was as if he *wanted* to shoot her, was itching to do so, waiting for Mary or Jordan to fire or reach for the laptop so he'd get the opportunity. But neither of them did. They remained perfectly still; their eyes fixed on Sadie.

'Nobody dies…' Blake ushered, 'so long as you remain calm

until my boss is finished, understand?'

'You sick son of a bitch, you'd kill us anyway!' Jordan spat.

Blake shrugged. 'Perhaps. Perhaps you two. But not this little one. Perhaps we'll raise her like she's our own, let her join us in the new world. A good way to keep our numbers up, don't ya think?'

Sadie gasped. 'I'll… never… join you.' She caught Jordan's eye. At that moment, something passed between them, a knowledge, an acceptance of what needed to happen. Sadie was okay with the first part - she'd learnt not to be afraid the hard way. It was the second part that she'd have to live with later on.

Blake laughed. 'After enough pain, I'm sure you'll pull through, girl. After all, you know what they say, you can break anybody with just the right amount of-'

'Sadie, now!' Jordan screamed.

Sadie looked into his eyes, forlorn, but followed what he said, nonetheless. She reached her head forwards and sank her teeth into Blake's wrist, biting down so hard that his arm began to loosen its grip and she could taste blood in her mouth. He dropped her momentarily, but that was all the time she needed. She punched him between the legs with brutal force, causing him to stumble back closer to the ledge before he viciously smacked her aside.

Her face hit the floor with a crack, and she could see Blake pointing his pistol in her direction. 'You're going to pay for that, you little sh-'

But Jordan was running forward, a determined, almost satisfied look on his face. Mary screamed in protest, as did Sadie, but the lawyer didn't listen. His drive to do the right thing must have been too high. Or perhaps he was willing to go, to be reunited with his lost love. Whatever the case, he charged into Blake with full force, knocking them both over the edge like rag dolls. The last look Sadie saw on the Reaper's face was that of stunned surprise as he dropped his pistol and went plummeting over the edge with Jordan.

Sadie flinched away as she heard the crack on the ground, before running over to Mary, whose face was torn between anguish, anger and exhaustion.

'Damn it, Jordan!' Mary shouted, before closing her eyes. 'Not another…'

Suddenly they heard gunfire below. Sadie looked over and saw that three officers were in a shootout with a single member from the Circle of Saints. One of the three was shot, but the other two managed to finish off the Circle member.

'Hey,' shouted the surviving male police officer. 'We've got something for you.'

While the woman who'd survived checked on the officer who'd been shot, the man climbed the ladder in haste, handing Mary a small USB drive.

'Officer Turner said to hand you this,' he explained. 'Apparently, there isn't much time.'

Mary understood. Jordan was gone, but there was no time to mourn. They had a job to do.

She rushed over to the laptop and plugged it in. Instantly she went to the files section and dragged the small file from the USB drive to drag into the message box.

'Let's pray this works,' Mary said and dropped the file into the message box. A separate message box popped up, saying "loading, 1%."

'Come on, you stupid thing!' Mary shouted.

***

Lynda gasped as the kicking ceased and she began to regain consciousness. Where was Tessa? What had happened?

Across the room was the revolver, still lying there, primed for firing. One shot and - if Michael Williams was correct - the stone would perish. She needed to act now, despite the pain consuming her body. She began to rise, her eyes fixed on the gun.

'Where do you think you're going?'

Tessa advanced from the dark corner of the room, smiling. 'I was waiting for you to wake up. Think of all the fun we could have.' She was fiddling with Lynda's knife in her hands.

Lynda collapsed, reaching out for the revolver. It was just too far.

'Oh?' Tessa queried, amused. 'You want that silly old thing?' She picked up the revolver, checked the armed chamber was in the correct position and aimed it for Lynda's head, cocking the hammer as she did so. 'Well here. Have it.'

***

The Other smiled, rising, its body glowing bright green. 'At last, I'm nearly ready. It's almost been long enough. I'm afraid you'll be alone for a little while. But don't worry, I'll come back to visit whenever I'm… hungry…'

Jim felt afraid. Was this the end?

'Oh, I forgot to mention. Your wife. She's alive. I'll pay her a visit shall I, Jim?'

***

Sam continued to block the rapid blows, panting heavily as

his arm grew weaker and weaker. He had managed to crawl in a half Circle around the space while blocking Lazarus' attacks and had made it to near the entrance, where Jim's body now lay limp on the ground. *Perhaps I'll be with you buddy,* a minute fragment of his brain thought.

Lazarus threw down his blade again, countered by a fatigued Sam, and held it. The white glow between the blades was blinding.

'Give up, Turner! This is a losing battle and you know it! Turn off that device, hand it over to me and show me the laptop. Then perhaps I'll be lenient with your friends.'

Its voice was beginning to sound distorted. Different. As if something else was taking its place. His arm was shaking in agony, and he could feel the heat coming off the two blades. He was getting exhausted now, and part of him wanted nothing better than to tell Lazarus that he had been bluffing.

'Hold on…' the creature said with a pause. 'I can… *hear* you now.' It laughed, a horrific, shrill laugh. 'My power is only growing stronger. The stone is letting me enter your mind and you're too weak to stop it!'

Sam felt as if something was crawling into his brain and vainly tried to resist it. He saw flashes of green, and images of a man in a suit and tie smirking at him. This wasn't possible. How could anything allow somebody to read his thoughts like they were words on a page?

'This isn't impossible, Sam,' it responded to his thoughts. 'Just beyond your understanding. I can see everything! Every dark day you ever had! Your poor father! Grandmother! Carlos! They're all there, in the forefront of your mind!'

Sam groaned, the pain was too much, and his blade was slowly being pushed closer to his chest.

'And what's this?' the creature mocked as flashes of the battle he'd just had flashed through Sam's brain. 'Let's have a look at the few minutes just passed?'

Sam could now see his conversation with Lazarus as he'd ejected his just moments before. The more he tried to hide his lie, the clearer it was to the creature that had so horrifically infiltrated his brain.

'So it was a lie then,' Lazarus remarked. 'I don't need you alive to stop anything. There is no automatic program to fry my brain! The only plan you have against me is a foolish, manually-operated virus that will make me blind. And you think that's going to stop me? If Nathan Blake didn't kill those fools on the roof, then my other man certainly did! You've lost, Sam Turner!'

This was it. The creature had called his bluff. It would not hesitate to kill him now. Sam closed his eyes and awaited his end, his final thoughts of Carlos and Jim and his father. Perhaps they were waiting for him somewhere.

'Yes, quite right, accept your death,' Lazarus beckoned. 'Savour the agony that you've brought upon yourself as your only life ends in a flash of pain and anguish. As you die, I want you to remember the pain to come for the world you've left behind. The world you've left for me. I want you to think of the screams of all those who you failed!'

In fury Sam used all of his strength to push Lazarus' blade away from him, and swung his energy blade to the side, opening his chest hopelessly to embrace the final blow.

If Lazarus could have smiled, it would have done. It lifted its blade above Sam's chest.

***

Uploading complete. Are you sure you'd like to send this item?

'Yes please,' said Mary, determined, as she hit the okay button and prayed for the best.

***

A message box appeared in its field of view. It was large, taking up a fair proportion of the screen, but was comprised of completely random letters and characters.

The creature hesitated to bring the blade down for half a second, but that was all the time it took for three similar messages to appear, this time not in the bottom right corner of his vision, but around the centre and the left. Lazarus desperately tried closing the messages that appeared, but more were popping up now at an incredible rate, and it found its vision almost completely clouded by long messages of arbitrary nonsense.

It screamed in rage, but – not allowing itself to be distracted - remembered the task at hand. It couldn't see for the time being, but he knew where Turner was. It brought down the blade to kill the detective.

But Turner wasn't there.

Lazarus turned, confused, looking around to try to find his adversary as it desperately closed the messages clouding his line of sight. At moments it would be able to see areas of the police station around him, empty it seemed, save for James Griffen's limp body on the floor beside him. But where was Turner?

Suddenly it saw movement from an unobstructed area of his sight to his right. It fired a beam from the stone in an instant, but the blast seemed to have missed his target. In fury, Lazarus span around, blasting its entire surroundings in a hope to catch Turner.

But there was no sound anywhere. Turner had hidden away, and Lazarus was blind.

***

Sam ducked undercover as the beams flew over-head. He'd been lucky to roll out of the way as Lazarus had gone blind, but he knew it was now or never if he wanted to finish this.

Lazarus stopped firing for a moment, desperately looking around the area in a search for Sam.

Sam was ready. He just had to get the timing right.

***

'Come on, Turner!' the creature shouted, knowing it'd regain its sight shortly. It had simultaneously been fishing through the settings, searching for the option that would disable its messaging system.

It fired two blasts into the air. 'Come and face me like a man!' it shouted.

Finally, Lazarus found the appropriate setting and toggled it off. The messages disappeared, clearing its vision entirely. 'What is it, Turner? Don't trust me to play nice? That would certainly make sense.' It began to turn, searching for the detective's heat signal. 'I believe I'm correct in saying that trust hasn't been your strength since dear old Daddy popped off?'

It saw the heat signature of the detective behind a smouldering pile of desks and began to lift up the stone to finish its enemy.

'Well, I tend to agree with you, Turner. Minutes ago, I missed an opportunity to kill you because I believed you were telling the truth. It just goes to show you can't trust anybody in this world. Least of all your enemies.'

The stone began to glow as the creature primed it to fire.

'And so, I know you'll understand what I mean when I say you can trust me not to kill you.'

It fired the bolt of energy at its target.

And then felt a harsh slice through its right arm.

***

Lazarus' energy blade powered off in seconds. The stone and arm dropped simultaneously and landed silently on Jim's resting body.

Lazarus turned hopelessly to Sam as it gazed at its stump of a right arm.

'Liking the one-armed look again, Lazarus?' Sam jeered and jabbed the blade in its direction. The creature stumbled back, the blade just missing its body. 'Looks like you shouldn't have trusted your heat signature readings either. While that wasn't part of the original plan, one of our technicians told me with his dying breath how'd they'd changed the virus.' Sam swiped his blade again and Lazarus dodged it again, darting backwards once more. It was eyeing the stone desperately, but Sam and his energy blade were in its way.

'Just before I came down,' Sam continued, repeatedly sending the creature back with his blade 'he told me that they'd managed to find one more weakness in that machine's software to exploit. The thermal imaging. All they had to do was alter it so that anything above sixty-eight degrees Fahrenheit was shown to you as exactly room temperature, making me invisible to your thermal scan, while creating a false heat image elsewhere in the room, which you so confidently blasted over there. And now, I think we both know what's going to happen.'

He stabbed the blade through the creature's abdomen, causing it to cry out in pain. From the mark of the blade, he could see abnormally dark, thick blood pouring out, as well as smoke from the smouldering metal.

'You see Lazarus, I did trust somebody. I trusted an entire team of people.'

He slashed at its leg, causing it to stumble onto one knee.

'They had my back, and they died working to stop you.'

He brought the blade into its upper shoulder and heard it hiss and curse.

'And now, because of them, and because you were too afraid to trust your own army, you're going to die right here. Alone.'

Sam swung the blade for its neck, but the creature, in a flash of rage, snapped forwards and grasped Sam's blade arm with the sharp talons of its unnaturally-grown oily black limb. Sam screamed as the creature fiercely tugged the blade arm, finally yanking off the weapon with such force that it tumbled across the room. Sam was now unarmed against the wicked being, and it wasn't long before it grabbed his throat and rose to its feet, choking the air from his body.

'You thought you could stop me?' Lazarus questioned. 'No, Sam Turner. You can't kill the Devil.'

Sam clawed away at it in agony and collapsed to his knees. Lazarus squeezed harder, suffocating him to the point where everything was beginning to turn grey. He'd been foolish, and now Lazarus had the upper hand once more. Was it over?

***

Tessa froze as she stared at her leader in terror and bewilderment through the door, giving Lynda just long enough to react.

She hopped onto her feet, fighting the pain inside her, and charged into the medical examiner with full force. Tessa lost her balance and fell to the ground, causing the pistol to fly out of her hands. Lynda punched her square in the face twice, before grabbing her head and slamming it into the floor. She then grabbed her hair and stood up, before dragging the horrid woman across the armoury against the wall.

Lynda released her at the far end of the room, and Tessa was howling from the pain. She soon went quiet, however, when she saw the barrel of the shotgun Lynda had now picked up aiming for her head.

'You let my husband die,' Lynda remarked. 'I suppose your boss is going to let the same happen to you.'

Tessa smiled. 'Go on then. Finish it off and dear Jim will be avenged. I've done my bit.' She closed her eyes. 'Perire finite non est.'

Lynda hesitated, remembering what Sadie had said, remembering every day she'd lost Jim to the darkness inside of him. All that time she'd hated him for it. Not once had it occurred to her that she might go through the same thing. Yet here she was, ready to end somebody's life out of pure vengeance.

There was a loud blast.

Tessa had opened her eyes and had seen the mark on the ceiling that Lynda had made.

'You shot the ceiling?' she queried. 'I don't understand.'

'And you never will,' Lynda finished, dropping the rifle. 'Because you're a cold-hearted monster who lies to people before killing them. But who's to say you didn't have some good in you once? And who am I to punish you for something I know nothing about?' She dropped the shotgun and walked to retrieve the Colt Python revolver. 'You can kill me if you like,' she said as she picked it up. 'As if that would make a difference. But I don't think you will. If I were you, I'd leave while you still can. Whether your boss wins or we do, it's not going to go well for you.'

Lynda walked away, not looking back once.

Tessa only looked at her in bewilderment, yet she did not consider lifting a weapon against her adversary, not after what had just happened.

But Lynda was right. She'd need to get away pretty fast.

***

'You have the nerve to stand against me, you pathetic excuse of a human?' Lazarus shouted viciously. 'My arm will grow back in seconds once I pick that stone up once more. It answers to nobody but me, for I earned its glory. I am a *god!*' Its taloned hand clenched harder, and Sam's eyes now felt as if they would soon burst. Something had changed about Lazarus. Its voice. It was so much deeper, far more sinister if that were even possible. 'So… I'll give you a quick death. So long as you call me *master…*'

Sam began to splutter, and tiny pockets of dry air just managed to escape his throat. '*You… are nothing more than a hopeless sociopath!*'

The creature paused. 'Not anymore! Marcus Arwick is gone, and soon Lazarus will be gone too. I don't expect you to understand what I am, Mr Turner, but I will be relentless in my full form. Safe to say, you won't live long enough to witness that!'

A searing pain shot through Sam's body like nothing he'd

ever experienced before. It was as if something had crawled into his brain and stuck a sharp needle right through its centre. Not only was there physical pain, but a sense of emotional anguish too, millions of poisonous, toxic, torturous memories resurfacing. His father's face showed up multiple times.

But then Sam saw something; not a memory, but something in real life; inducing far more terror than Lazarus or any tragic memory could possibly fathom. Yet it brought a glimmer of hope, too. Behind Lazarus' shoulder, a figure began to rise, the green stone glowing brightly in his hand. The man was reasonably tall, of a thick muscular build and with messy brown hair. His skin was pale, his eyes were saggy and tired looking, and his lips seemed almost blue.

Despite everything that Sam had come to reason within his life, every piece of logic and rationality that he had ever acquired, nothing could explain why Jim Griffen was standing up, alive, the hole in his chest no more than a large scar behind his torn shirt.

Lazarus turned, seeing the surprised look on Sam's face and dropped him to the ground instantly, freezing in bafflement as its once dead enemy now wielded the most powerful material in the known world.

The few remaining officers rose from their feet to witness the sight, not sure if their brains could comprehend it. At this moment Lynda exited the armoury and gasped at the sight before her. Mary and Sadie entered the building next, immediately dropping everything they were holding as they faced this unfathomable sight.

Lazarus could not speak. And it didn't have to. Everybody could tell that the only thing it felt under that cold metal shell and cold flesh was pure terror.

***

Jim looked around, dazed and confused, like a newborn who'd just entered the world for the first time. In his hand was the stone, shaking and whirring as if trying to resist his grasp. But there wasn't much left of whatever was inside it to resist against him now. Most of whatever had greeted him in that other world, that Other, was currently inside Lazarus, motionless, confused, waiting for something to happen. He clenched the rock tightly and aimed it at the creature, a solemn, regretful look on his face. This had to be done. For the sake of the world. For the sake of the people he loved. Lazarus nodded and was suddenly chuckling. What was so amusing? Jim had to wonder. Everything, he supposed.

Jim pointed the weapon at Tommy, Marcus, Lazarus, the Phantom – so many names for one lost mess of a living being. Jim looked deep within himself but found no feelings of vengeance or anger. Only regret. Perhaps Marcus Arwick had been a good man once. Perhaps he would have had a future if not for Jim's mistake all those years ago. Perhaps they all would. *Or perhaps this was always going to happen. Like destiny. Perhaps this was all part of that Other's plan.*

There was a little hesitation, but then whatever piece of consciousness that remained inside the stone gave in, for Jim's willpower was stronger. A green beam of energy was released from the stone, shooting directly towards Jim's enemy. It hit Lazarus' shell with great force and held there for a few moments before finally, the suit cracked under the tremendous power of the stone. Soon pieces of the outer machine began to melt or fly off, as the stone wore away at the tough metal which made it. Finally, all the parts inside flew apart, and Lazarus, or whatever remained underneath, shot backwards from the force of the energy, crashing unseen behind one of the barricaded desks. Jim could have continued, could have incinerated that thing's body further, but then he too would lose himself in all that power. No, this had to end now.

The beam ceased. Jim apathetically dropped the rock onto the ground.

'How do we destroy it?' he said plainly, unsure whether he meant the stone or Lazarus.

Lynda stepped forwards, an awestruck, baffled look in her eye. Jim too gaped in bewilderment, but soon his confusion turned to joy, and he embraced his wife fiercely, a few tears running down his cheeks as he held her.

'I thought you were dead,' he whispered. 'Lazarus… Lazarus said…'

'Someone's gullible,' she whispered. 'I only jumped to conclusions when I saw your corpse.'

This sent an icy shiver down Jim's spine, and slowly the two pulled away from each other as they exchanged an unsettled glance. Almost instinctively the pair looked back to the stone, now suddenly aware of its horrid, supernatural power. Then Lynda rummaged into her pocket.

She pulled out a silver revolver and a single metal bullet, and handed them to her husband slowly, her hands shaking a little. He took the gun, loaded it with the bullet and placed his hand on hers. He nodded confidently, almost knowingly. 'This needs to be done.'

'I know it does,' she said. 'You feel it too?'

He sighed. 'Yes. I do. Some barriers were never meant to be crossed both ways. Death is one of them.

Jim walked over to Lazarus' body, or whatever remained of it at least, which lay helpless and weak at the other end of the room. What lay there was far from human, yet not too dissimilar from the man Jim had once known. It was covered in torn rags of clothing, its skin thin, a dark shade of grey, riddled with areas of oily black bumps not too dissimilar and texture from its grotesque left arm. Its face was vaguely similar to Arwick's, except its eyes were much larger, the pupils taking up almost the entire area of its eye socket. As for its hair, only a few strands remained on the top of its head, each a wispy, dying white.

'You going to kill me, Jim?' it croaked. Its body was physically smoking, for the stone had burnt it well. 'Shoot that bullet through my brain?'

Jim crouched down, analysing the body with mild intrigue. 'You didn't know, did you? You had no idea about what that thing could do. That it would… bring me back. Recover me.'

'The Other did, Lazarus didn't,' the thing on the ground replied. 'Right now, I'm not sure where one ends and the other begins. You were the first death in proximity to the stone for a long time. Your consciousness jumped straight in. You were lucky.'

'You kidding?' Jim asked. 'I think I'd rather the alternative after all that's happened. I expect you'd want the same, right? In fact, it would be crueller for me not to end you right now.' Jim stood up and sighed. 'Sadly, this bullet's unique. And it's not for you.' Jim turned and aimed his weapon at the stone.'

'No! Please!' the creature on the floor shouted.

Jim turned his head and listened to its words.

'Jim… if you destroy that stone, you're stopping all the wonderful things it could do for this world. You're ending all that, here and now. You realise that, right?'

Jim shook his head. 'That thing would only cause pain and misery, not joy. This has to be done.'

'In that case… please. You have to kill me some other way. Please, Jim. The Other doesn't want me saying this, but… I don't want to go on. I can't. Not like this. Besides, as long as I'm alive I'm a threat. The stone's touched me now, as it has you. The Other resides within me. If you must destroy that stone, at least destroy me with it.'

Jim sighed. 'Anybody got a different gun I could use?'

'I'll go find one,' Lynda volunteered.

'Don't bother,' said Sam with a laugh. He reached into his pocket and grabbed something out of it into his fist. He strolled over to Jim and placed it in his palm.

Jim looked down. It was a silver bullet, the exact size for the weapon. Engraved on the side was a lion's head on a shield.

'It was my father's,' Sam explained. 'It's the right size. It should fit if you want to use it.'

Jim shook his head, amused at the chances of such an event. 'Sam, I can't use this. It's amazing that you even have this, but I don't see why we can't just get another gun.'

Sam smiled. 'Listen. That man's long gone. And memories of him aren't exactly much use to me anymore. He earned that bullet the wrong way, through deceit and doing the wrong thing for what he thought were the right reasons, and I've never been able to let it go. It'd be nice to get rid of it doing the right thing, you know?'

Jim nodded and opened up the chambers of the gun, slotting the bullet in gently and carefully. 'Thank you, Sam. You're… a good man.'

He closed the chambers and walked back over to the creature on the floor. Both their faces were filled with pain and regret. They both knew, however, that there was no other way.

'Is Marcus in there?' Jim asked. 'Is there any of him left?'

The creature hesitated. Then it shrugged. 'Who's to say? Maybe.'

'Tell him I'm sorry.'

The creature nodded.

Jim aimed the revolver for Lazarus's head and closed his eyes. The blast resonated across the entire building.

Jim then turned around, unwilling to look at the mess that remained on the floor. There was one more thing to do. The stone lay ahead of him, weak and defenceless. But beside it was a little boy.

'Don't do it, Daddy,' said Jake.

Jim's heart suddenly ached at the sight of his son. For the past two years Jake had appeared only in Jim's sleep – never before had he appeared his waking moments.

Jim looked at Lynda, and from the look of her face, he could tell that she saw their boy too. Deep down a part of him mourned, however, knowing what this sight truly was.

'If you destroy the stone, how are you going to get me back?' Jake asked him innocently. 'You could use it for good, Dad. You could undo all the pain that Arwick's caused you and we could be a family again!'

Jim squinted, confused, slightly queasy. He felt dazed, perhaps drunk. This was not real. It couldn't be.

'You've killed him, Dad,' Jake said with an encouraging grin. '*You* now own the stone. You know what it could do. You could use it to save me! You could bring me back! Then we can stop them all, every criminal that's ever plagued this planet. You'd have the stone; nobody would be able to stop you!'

The temptation drowned Jim. It poisoned him, burned him right through to his heart. Perhaps there was a way… Perhaps…

No.

Jim looked up and smiled at his son. 'I love you, Jakey. I love you and I failed you. For that, I am eternally sorry. But whatever I do - whether that's using that damned rock, seeking revenge or grieving for the rest of my life – I can *never* bring you back.'

The image of Jake began to wail, a high-pitched, hideous scream, causing all officers to shield their ears. Jim gritted his teeth and lifted the revolver, aiming it for the stone. He pressed the trigger.

And the explosion was bright.

***

January 2026

EPILOGUE
JANUARY 24TH, 2026
THE VISITOR

'Looks like you have a visitor, Mr Griffen!' the nurse exclaimed.

His eyes flickered open, and the light flooded in, making his head sore for a few moments. Jim was awake. He was safe. He was alive. It was a feeling he wasn't quite used to.

He rubbed his eyes wearily, rising from his hospital bed with achy bones. 'Please tell me it's not another member of the press.'

'No, but I can be just as annoying from time to time,' said a voice with an unusual accent, placing him somewhere midway from being an American or being a Brit.

Jim smiled. 'Well, you recovered fast. How's it going, Sam?'

Sam limped into Jim's claustrophobic hospital room, bruised and pale. His hair was a mess, and dirt still stained his cheeks. In addition to being shot by Lazarus in his thigh, a piece of rubble had landed on Sam's lower right leg following the explosion, very much like the accident Carlos had all those months before, but nowhere near as severe. Yet still, despite all odds, he too was alive.

'Well the leg's on the mend,' he remarked with a smile. 'Although let's hope I won't have to do any more frantic sprints anytime soon. And it's my birthday, so that's a positive, apparently.'

'Ah, happy birthday!' Jim remarked

'Eh, I'm not going to lie, being 28 could have waited a bit longer.'

'Wait till you're in your late thirties, then you really start dreading each birthday!'

Sam laughed, and they both went quiet for a few moments. 'More importantly, how're you holding up Jim?' he asked, his tone gentle.

Jim hooked his legs over the side of the bed and Sam sat next to him. He wheezed a little as the dull ache returned in his stomach, but it was soon gone. 'I'll be honest, I'm pretty used to this pain stuff. Happens quite a bit.' He laughed. 'But yeah, I'm good. *Great,* even. I mean… we did it. We stopped Lazarus, we stopped them all despite all the odds against us! And we're all alive, so I suppose that's a bonus…' He caught the hurt look in Sam's eye. 'Oh… Carlos. Jordan. Look I'm sorry Sam, I didn't mean-'

'It's fine,' Sam replied. 'It's more guilt than remorse, you know. He gave his life for me…' He gazed out the window sadly. 'He saved me when all I ever did was try to attack him.'

Jim nodded. 'Yeah. I know the whole guilt thing all too well.' He looked Sam in the eye. 'Guilt and grief are a nasty combination, Sam. Grief, at least, is natural. Guilt and anger… they're the ones that change us. They're destructive. They separate a Marcus Arwick from a Carlos Rodriguez. Don't give in to it, because it isn't your fault, and it's not what Carlos would have wanted.'

Sam nodded understandingly and smiled weakly at Jim. 'He

saved my life. I guess I owe it to him that I live it to the full.'

Jim patted him on the back. 'There ya go!' he remarked. 'You're way better at that than I've ever been, kid.'

There was a silence between them for a few moments until Sam finally spoke. 'Jim, I have a few questions.'

Jim tilted his head. 'I was wondering when you were going to ask. Go ahead but… don't blame me if I don't have all the answers.'

Sam nodded and frowned. 'Your son appeared, didn't he? At least… I saw him. How could he be-'

'What you saw was the stone. That thing… whatever it was… it wasn't just some rock. I saw things in there, Sam. When I was… you know… not breathing.' Jim shuddered, 'I saw…' He tried thinking back to his encounter with the Other, but he was struggling to remember. It was as if the conversations taking place in whatever realm of reality they'd been in what just some distant dream. Some memory that had suppressed itself within the recesses of his subconscious. He told Sam all he could just manage to remember. 'That stone wasn't just an object. That's all I know. Something was there, something trying to find a pathway into our world. That's what you saw. It didn't want me to kill it, so it used Jake to try to break me. A fairly smart strategy, I suppose.'

Sam looked to his hands, bewildered. Clearly this wasn't any consolation. 'I mean, it's just mad, isn't it? How the hell is anybody going to believe this.'

Jim shrugged. 'They won't. I've already had some strange men in dark suits greet me earlier today; asked me to keep my mouth shut. You had the same?'

Sam nodded. 'Yeah, there were some strange people at the police station. What did they call themselves? Some weird name.

Apcase? Epcos? Said they'd help fund us to renovate it so long as we said nothing of what had happened. Even had this whole cover story for us. They took… they took *its* body, I believe.'

Jim nodded. 'Well, I suppose whatever remains of that thing's better in their hands than ours. I expect the government will just make up some story about a gas leak or something, find ways to keep people's mouths shut. Good luck to them, I say. The fewer people that know, the better.'

'And the stone?' Sam urged. 'And *you?* Jim, you came back to life for goodness sake!'

Jim shrugged. 'People believe what they want to believe, but in the end, it's the opinions of those in power that become the "facts." I'm not even sure *I* know what happened that day, and I was there. I expect the only thing they'll remember of the battle is the devastation it caused, not the minor details.'

Sam paused and nodded. It was true that people had already started mixing up details of what had happened. 'Jim?' Sam asked.

'Yeah, sorry,' Jim replied as he turned back to Sam.

'What about Lazarus?'

'It's dead,' Jim said bluntly and plainly. He was certain of that fact. 'Your silver bullet worked a treat it seemed. There was a part of me that worried…'

'Worried about.'

'Well, the stone grew his arm back. If he could heal that fast, would a shot through the head be enough? But it was.'

Sam raised an eyebrow anxiously. 'You're sure?'

'Completely,' Jim said affirmatively. 'Before I shot him, I saw

Arwick's wound trying to heal around the chunk of metal that had pierced his body. The healing had stopped pretty soon after the bullet entered his brain. Whatever monster that stone created out of that already unstable man, it's dead. For whatever reason, your dad's bullet did the trick.'

Despite saying this with such certainty, Jim frowned a little. What was it that thing had said?

The stone's touched me now, as it has you. The Other resides within me.

Sam nodded in relief. 'Probably the best thing Dad *ever* did. Perhaps I was always a bit harsh on him though. Until this week, I couldn't imagine trusting anybody who'd break the law like he did. And then I broke you out of a prison!'

Jim laughed. 'So you did. How skilled were we, right?'

Sam smiled. 'Well, I guess that's it then. All questions answered, no stone unturned. I'll check in on Mary before I leave, of course. That woman saved all of our arses.'

'And don't forget Jordan,' Jim added. 'Or the technicians. In fact, let's not forget the entire police department. It was every one of them who saved our asses! They all deserve the best funeral they can get, those guys.'

Sam nodded. 'I completely agree, although I can't imagine any of their families doing it at the new St John's Church that they're building.'

'A new one?' Jim queried. 'Seriously?'

'Something to do with rectifying the mistakes of the past. Like arresting you, I suppose. By the way, have they sorted out your whole situation yet?'

Jim sighed. 'They're working on it,' he said. 'I'm pretty sure they don't need to gather *every* scrap of available evidence to prove my innocence, but I don't care. Those government people said they'd help out too. Once again, only if I kept my mouth shut.' He shook his head and sighed. 'I'm just glad it's nearly over.'

Sam arose and patted his shoulder. 'Aren't we all Jim? I've got to rush, got a lot of work to do now with the whole station scenario. And then there's all the charity work, paperwork, news interviews, paperwork, officers to visit, paperwork! What a mess.' He smiled. 'I'll see you later, Jim Griffen.'

'You too Sam! Make it a police station worth working at.'

Sam laughed. 'You bet.'

Jim waved Sam goodbye as he left and lay back down. On his way to the pillow, he hit his head against the headboard. It didn't hurt too much, but Jim cursed and hit the headboard in frustration.

His fist ploughed straight through the wood, and right through the plaster walls behind it. Jim studied the hole he'd just made and slowly retracted his fist, before carefully studying his knuckles in bafflement. There was no pain, nor was there a single scratch or drop of blood.

***

Sam gazed at the station in awe, a smile across his face. All windows had been replaced; all walls patched up. Not a single mark of the atrocious battle remained, aside from singe marks on the road from the single explosion of the van. Officers were filing in and out at a rapid rate, and, for the first time in months, this pinnacle building was starting to see some life once more. The business of the area was refreshing as if a new morning had dawned on Nightdrop City, or a tide had washed all the previous chaos away for good.

Mary walked up behind him, a smile on her face too. 'Here

we are. You ready?'

Sam laughed. 'It's practically like it was before. Newer, in fact!' He turned to her. 'Stronger. Yeah, I'm ready. The city's crime may have had that huge drop, but I expect there'll be a lot of work to do. Haven't been at our full strength these past few months.'

'Oh, you bet! But I wouldn't worry, you're not alone, detective.' She pointed to the front entrance, where a woman with long brown hair seemed to be pacing back and forth, confused.

'A partner?' Sam queried. 'So soon.'

Mary shrugged. 'She's a Sam as well. We need our numbers high more than ever now, after all! Besides… it's what Carlos would have wanted.'

Sam smiled. 'All right. Let's give this a go.' He approached the station, determined, before stopping in his tracks and turning. 'Hey, chief!'

Mary smiled. 'Yes, Turner?'

'I just want you to know… I think you're going to make this place amazing.'

She nodded appreciatively. 'I hope so, Sam. I hope so…'

***

Sadie arose in the comfort of her bed and yawned. No nightmares tonight. That was a first. Her sheets were dry, her bed laid out almost as perfect as it was set. It would seem she'd slept like a log. Lazarus could not keep her awake any longer.

Suddenly a boy of her age burst through the door. He was short, round, and had messy black hair with oval spectacles. 'Oliver?' she muttered. 'What is it?'

He panted for a second before finally responding. 'You're on the TV! Come down, quick!'

She crawled out of bed slowly, feeling the warmth of the morning sun glow against her back. She couldn't recall doing interviews of any sort, but it seemed unlikely that a boy like Oli would lie.

When she had made it downstairs, she saw the whole orphanage gathered around the musty living room's television screen, the old mistress Miss Pennyweather sitting in her regular armchair. 'Sadie, dear,' the old lady said with a sad smile. 'You just missed your debut appearance!' Something seemed amiss, for tears were streaming down the old woman's face.

The television reporter spoke clearly. 'Numerous claims from officers and witnesses near the site of this tragic conflict have claimed this strange figure to be none other than the Phantom himself, back from the grave to seek vengeance. NDC News understands that this killer, now better known to be city resident Marcus Arwick, had already faked his death once before, sending Daniel Crockett to the house of detectives James and Lynda Griffen to murder their five-year-old son. Recently, Arwick was discovered to be posing as Nightdrop Detective Thomas Knightley, in an elaborate plan tailored to frame former detective James Griffen for numerous homicides around the city.

'Although it does not seem completely implausible that Arwick survived his "second death" numerous months ago, government and police officials alike are reassuring the public that Arwick has been dead for months and that whoever this strange figure was, they were no more than a pretender.

'Rumours are even stranger, however, surrounding the aforementioned former detective and ex-convict James Griffen, who some claim to have died in the ensuing battle. Others remain hushed about the entire affair, saying they barely saw any of the ensuing action that occurred in the last minutes of the conflict. Griffen, once known as the "Backstabber," who has recently been declared pardoned for his falsely accused crimes, has denied these claims and-'

The TV faded to black. Sadie turned to see Miss Pennyweather, teary-eyed, her hand on the remote. 'Well,' she remarked, her face bent with a sad smile. 'That's enough of that, I think. We'll be going on a walk today, so make sure you're all ready for ten o'clock.'

A few orphans moaned, but none dared disobey her. Only Sadie stayed.

'Are you all right Sadie?' the governess queried.

'I was going to ask the same thing. If you don't mind my asking… are you crying, miss?'

She laughed, pulling out a handkerchief and dabbing her face quickly. 'Me? Oh… oh.' She laughed. 'I may seem stern sometimes, but even I can feel sad too. Just seeing all those hurt people on the television. Well, it upsets me, you see. Reminds me of things from the past.'

Sadie crossed her arms. She knew it was not the whole truth.

The orphan-mistress sighed. 'But I appreciate that you care, Sadie. You were always a thoughtful one. I can see why she wants to have you.'

Sadie dropped her arms in shock. 'Who?'

The mistress laughed. 'Have I not said? There was a tall woman, with short black hair. Famous police lady from the TV. She said she'd met you before, somewhere amidst all that chaos. Said you'd changed her in a way nobody could ever know. She wanted to adopt you'

Sadie beamed, and now she too felt tears come to her eyes. *Adopt me. Finally? After all this time.* But who was the woman? There could only be one person that Sadie knew of.

'Lynda,' the orphan-mistress recalled. 'Yes, yes, that's right. Lynda Griffen, that woman they mentioned on the television. The police station has created the title "Cloak of the Night" for her or something.'

'After all this time…' Sadie remarked. She beamed at the orphan-mistress. 'Thank you! Thank you so much!'

'Hey, don't you thank me. Thank yourself! Clearly, you're as lovely a young lady as I've always thought you were. Now go on, you don't want to be late for the walk, do you?'

Sadie nodded and ran up the stairs, her body fuelled with excitement. This was the start of something new, something exciting. After years of waiting, she'd finally have parents she could trust.

And although she missed her father greatly, Sadie couldn't help but feel excited about her future. There was much waiting for her ahead, and the next stage of her life had just begun.

***

A few days later and Jim was free to go. There was still a lot to do. He needed to pay his respects to various people, go to a few court cases, do some charity events for the police station and head to the orphanage with Lynda. Firstly, however, he needed to make an important visit.

On leaving his room, he spotted his wonderful wife further down the corridor. He ran up to her and kissed her passionately. After a moment, they broke apart, but still lovingly gazed in each other's eyes, grateful to have what they had both so nearly lost.

They descended the stairwell slowly; Jim limping on his

sprained ankle while Lynda held an arm around his neck. Once they had made it downstairs, Lynda paused and took a deep breath. 'Jim, I need to ask you something. Are you still sure you want to give this care home thing a try?'

Jim looked at her and paused. Suddenly he beamed from ear to ear. 'Well, it depends what *she* wants, and what you want, and whatever's best and legal of course. But… yeah. I'd be happy to try again.'

Lynda hugged him gently, careful not to cause his ribs any pain. 'A family again?'

'A family again,' Jim agreed.

Finally, they made it to the second floor and limped gently to the third door along. Jim peered through the open door and felt nauseous in the pit of his stomach as he spotted two familiar faces.

'You ready?' Lynda asked him.

He nodded. 'Yeah. So ready.'

And so, on that day, in the entering of that room, Jim Griffen threw his years of history behind him. All that had happened to him no longer mattered, except for how it had made him in the present day. Of course, much was to come in the future. There would be appraisals, death-threats, funerals, court trials, meetings and interviews. He would eventually have to find himself a new job. His mother would eventually die. He would have to come to face with whatever that stone had given him and would have to cope with his paranoia and bad dreams, as the notion that Arwick or the Other had survived would surely re-surface at night-time.

But for now, in that single moment, the past and future did not matter. Because right now, Jim Griffen was a new man. Jim Griffen was in every sense re-born. And he was happy.

And so, he entered the ward, and warmly greeted his mother and sister.

***

ABOUT THE AUTHOR

Harry Threapleton is a sixteen-year-old author from Surrey, England. He has been fiction-writing and inventing stories for as long as he remembers but has been writing books since the age of thirteen and has finally published this one after three and a half years. Despite having two years of A-Level work remaining at his school, he intends to keep writing, and has already finished the first draft of the first book in a science fiction/fantasy trilogy which he plans to publish in 2021. He believes anything is possible with enough perseverance, and that age should never prohibit somebody from aiming high for what they want. "A page of A5 a day is a book in a year, and there is always time to write a page." Harry has no website yet but does have a YouTube Channel (A Page a Day with Harry Threapleton) for writing tips, discussion and analysis of writing and stories, an insight on what it's like to be a sixteen-year-old writer and book updates. He also has an Instagram, harry_threapleton, where he posts similar notes and updates.

PRINTED EXCERPT

4c3a2048656c6c6f3f2057686f20697320746869733f2057686572652061 6d20
493f20546869732e2e2e20746869732069736e277420726967687421 0a543a2
0497420776f726b65642120497420616374756 16c6c7920776f726b6564210a
4c3a2057686174206469643f2057687920697320697420736f206461726b3f2
05768792063616e2049206f6e6c792073656520796f7572207772697374696e67
3f205768792e2e2e2077687920636 16e277420492066656c3f0a543a20536f
206d616e79207175657374696f6e732e2e2e2042757420616c6c2072696768
742e204920686176652074686 96e677320746f20646f20736f2049276c6c20626
520627269656 62e2042726967736f6e2773206d656d6f7279207265747269 65
76616c2073797374656d2e20497420776173206f6e65206f6620746865206c6
17374206269747320686520616464656420626566 6f726520746865206f7468
657220796f752e2e2e2077656c6c2049276d20737572652 0796f752072656d6
56d6265722e0a4c3a204e6f2c2061637475616c6c792e204d79206d656d6f726
96573206172652072617468657220667 57a7a792e20537472616e67652d6c6f
6f6b696e672e2057686174206 46f20796f75206d65616e20746865206f746865
72206d653f0a543a204e6f7420746f20776f7272792e20546865206d656d6f72
7920726574726965766 16c2072656c6f636174656420746f2061206261726e2
0696e20746865206d6964646c65206f66204d6973736f7572692e2055736564
20746f20626520427269677 36f6e277320666174686572 7320756e74696c206
8652064696564206 96e2061206472696e6b2d64726976696e6720616363696 4
656e742c20627574207468617 427732062657369646573207468652070 6f696
e742e20455043415320666f756e64206974207768696c6520696e76657374 69
6761746 96e67207768617420686170 70656e656420696e2053657074656d626
5722e205468657920666f756e6420796f75210a4c3a2057686f206172652045 5
04341533f0a543a20446f6e277420776f727279206 1626f7574207468617 42e2

05468657920666f756e6420746865207061697220 6f662075732c20616e6420
6e6f77207765206861766520612063686616e636520746f2061636869657665 2
0776861742077652061 6c776179732077616e7465642e2057652074686f7567
6874207468652073746f6e65207761732061732073747261 6e6765206173207
4686973207768 6f6c65207468696e6720676f742e20427574207468617420 77
6173206f6e6c7920746865207469 70206f66207468652069636562657267 2e0
a4c3a2054686572652773 2e2e2e206d6f7265206f662074686174207468696e6
73f0a543a2050657268617073 2e204f72207065726861707320 6e6f742e20546
86520706f696e742069732c20776520776572652 06e65766572207468652 06f
6e6c79206f6e6573206c6f6f6b696e672e2054686520 6f74686572732077686f
207765726520686176652066617220 6d6f7265207265736f757263657320616
e6420696e666c75656e636520617420746865697220646973706f73616c2e20
416e64207468657920 6e65656420757320746f2068656c70207468656d21205
4686973206973206f7572207365636f6e64206368616e6365210a4c3a2049206
46f6e277420756e6465727374616e642e20486f772063616e20492068656c702
07468656d207768656e20492063616e20626172656c792072656d656d62657
22077686f204920616d3f0a543a204d656d6f726965732074616b6520757020
61206c6f74206f6620646174612e205468657927726520636f6d696e67207468
726f75676820736c6f776c792c206275742077652772652077 6f726b696e6720
6f6e20746861742e205468652072657472696576616c2073797374656d20626
1636b656420757020657665727974 68696e6720746f2074686520706f696e74
206f66204772696666656e20636f6d696e67206261636b2e20596f7520726 56
d656d62657220746861742070617274207269676874 3f0a4c3a20426172656c
792e2049206f6e6c792072656d656d62657220736861706573 2e20696e64697
374696e677569736861626c652073686170657 32e20416e642e2e2e20686f77
20492066656c742e20486f72726f722e20466561722e20416e6765722e204465
666561742e2057687920 63616e277420492073 74696c6c206665656c2074686
f7365207468696e67733f0a543a2057652063616e20646f206f7572206265737
420746f207265637265617465207468656d2e2042757420657665 6e20696620
796f7520636f756c642c20776f756c6420796f752077616e7420746f3f2057687
9206665656c20616c6c207468617420737566666572696e673f20416c6c2074
686174207061696e3f0a4c3a20426563617573652069742 76c6c2072656d696
e64206d65206f662077686f204920776173 2e2057686174204920 73746f6f642
0666f722e2057687920492064696420776861742049206469642e204974276c
6c206d616b6520746865206d656d6f72696573 20636c65617265722c20616e6
4206974276c6c2072656d696e64206d65206f66206d7920637572736564206 5
78697374656e63652e0a543a204e6f7420796f7572206d656d6f726965732e20

4869732e20596f75277265206a7573742061207368656c6c206f6620796f7572
20666f726d65722073656c662e2041207573656675c207368656c6c2c20627
574206a75737420612063f64656420636f70792e2054686572652773206120
68756d616e20656c656d656e7420746f20616c6c2074686973207468617420 6
e6f626f6479206861732071756974652077 6f726b6564206f757420796574202
d20612070617274206f66206f7572206d696e647320796f752063616e277420
6d6170206f6e746f206120636f6d70757465722e2048697320697320 6c6f6e67
20676f6e652e204e6f77206f6e6c7920796f752072656d61696e2e0a4c3a20492
0756e6465727374616e642e0a543a2042757420766572792077656c6c2c2049
276c6c20676976652079 6f7520656d6f74696f6e732c20696620746861742773
2077686174 20796f75206465736972652e0a4c3a2049206465736972652 0746
f2062652064656164 2c2062757420492 76d20736d61727420656e6f75676820
746f206b6e6f7720746861742077696c6c206e6f742068617070656e2e0a543a
204e6f2e0a4c3a2054686973206973207 7726f6e672054657373612e20536f20
766572792077726f6e672e2049206f6e636520746 86f756768742072657665 72
73696e67206465617468207761732 06d7920676f616c20696e206c6966652c2
0627574206e6f77207468617420492065787065726965 6e6365642069742e2e
2e204920726561 6c6973652069742773206120 6f6e652077617920676174652
074686174207368 6f756c64206e657665722068617665206265656e2063726f
737365642e0a543a20596f7572206f70696e696f6e73206172652079 6f757220
6f776e2c206275742049 207374616e64206279207468617420492 7766520616
c77617973207361 69642e2049276d20746865206f6e6c7920536169 6e74206c
6566743b204920696e74656e6420746f206b656570206f75722070687261 736
520616c6976652e0a4c3a2041682079 65732e2022506572697265204669 6e69
7465206e6f6e20657374 2e2220546f20646965206973206e6f7420746865 20
656e642e220a543a20496e646565642e20446561746820697320 6f6e6c792074
686520626567696e6e696e672e204d79206d617374657220646964206f6e6
3652c2068697320776f726b20696e636f6d706c6574652c2068697320746173
6b2064656665617465642e20596f752077696c6c206e6f74206d616b6520746
8652073616d65206d697374616b65732e0a4c3a20596f7520646172652073 70
65616b20746f206d65206c696b6520746861743f20596f75206c6f6f6b656420
757020746f206d65206f6e63652e20596f7520666f6c6c6f776564206d652074
6f2067726561746e6573732e0a543a2049206c6f6f6b6564207570 20746f2068
696d2c206e6f7420796f752e2057686174657665722079 6f75206d617920626
56c696576652c20796f752077696c6c20646f2061732049207361792c206173
2045504341532073617973 2e205472757374206d652c20796f7520646f6e2774
2077616e7420746f207269736b2075707365747469 6e67207468656d2e0a4c3

a204f682054657373612c20796f7527766520676f7420697420616c6c2077726
f6e672e20446561746820697365277420746865206375727365652e2044656174
682069736e27742074686520746869726720776520656564420746f2072656
d6f76652e204f6e6365207468657265207761732006f6e6c792064656174682c2
0616e64207468656e2063616d652074686520636861 6f732c20746865207375
66666572696e672c2074686520666561722c2074686520746f726d656e742e2
044657374726f79696e672064656174682069732061206666f6f6c6973682c206
d69736775696465642061696d2e0a543a2054686174277320 6e6f7420796f75
722063686f69636520746f206d616b652e20596f7520646f6e277420657861 63
746c79206861766520 6d756368207361792069 6e2074686573652074686 96e6
77320616e796d6f72652e0a4c3a204f722207065726861707320 6e6f742079657
42e2049276c6c20626520636f6d706c69616e7420666f72206e6f772c2062757
420796f75276420626574746572 20686f7065204920646f6e27742067657420
6f7574206f662077686572657665722 0796f75277265206b656570696e67206
d652e0a543a20596f7520776f6e27742e200a4c3a2042656361757365206465 6
17468206973206e6f7420746865206375727365205465737361 2e2044656174
68206973206e6f742074686520706c61677565206f662074686520756e69766 6
57273652e200a543a2049276c6c2074616c6b20746f20796f7520746f6d6f727
26f772e0a4c3a20492068617665207468652 06d656d6f72696573206f6620612
06265696e6720746861742068617320 6c69766564206 16e642064696564 2c20
616e642061732074686520666972737420696e6f7267616e69632062656 96e6
720746f20626520637572736564207769746820746 86f756768742c2049206e
6f7720756e646572737461 6e6420746865207472757468 2e204c6966652 0697
320746865206469736561736 52e20416e6420492 0696e74656e6420746f2063
75726520692d0a0a2a50726f6772616d205465726d696e617465642a0a